Farewell
to the Liar

TALES OF FENEST

Widow's Welcome
The Stitcher and the Mute

FAREWELL
TO THE LIAR

Book Three of the Tales of Fenest

D.K. FIELDS

An Ad Astra Book

First published in the UK in 2021 by Head of Zeus Ltd
An Ad Astra Book

9 7 5 3 1 2 4 6 8

A catalogue record for this book is available from
the British Library.

ISBN (HB): 9781789542561
ISBN (XTPB): 9781789542578
ISBN (E): 9781789542554

Typeset by Divaddict Publishing Solutions Ltd

Printed and bound in Great Britain
by CPI Group (UK) Ltd, Croydon, CR0 4YY

Head of Zeus Ltd
5–8 Hardwick Street
London EC1R 4RG

WWW.HEADOFZEUS.COM

For our mums, Sheila and Veronica

The Swaying Audience

Abject Reveller, god of: loneliness, old age, fish
Affable Old Hand, god of: order, nostalgia, punctuality
Beguiled Picknicker, god of: festivals, incense, insect bites
Blind Devotee, god of: mothers, love, the sun
Bloated Professional, god of: wealth, debt, shined shoes
Calm Luminary, god of: peace, light, the forest
Courageous Rogue, god of: hunting, charity, thin swords
Curious Stowaway, god of: rites of passage, secrets, summer
   and the longest day
Deaf Relative, god of: hospitality
Delicate Tout, god of: herbs, prudence, drought
Engaged Matron, god of: childbirth
Exiled Washerwoman, god of: sanitation, rivers, obstacles
Faithful Companion, god of: marriage, loyalty, dancing
Filthy Builder, god of: clay, walls, buckets
Frail Beholder, god of: beauty, spectacles, masks
Generous Neighbour, god of: harvest, fertility, the first day
   of the month
Gilded Keeper, god of: justice, fairness, cages

Grateful Latecomer, god of: good fortune, spontaneity, autumn

Heckling Drunkard, god of: jokes, drink, fools

Honoured Bailiff, god of: thieves, the dark, bruises

Insolent Bore, god of: wind, bindleleaf, borders

Inspired Whisperer, god of: truth, wisdom, silk

Jittery Wit, god of: madness, lamps, volcanoes

Keen Musician, god of: destiny, wine and oil

Lazy Painter, god of: rain, noon, hair

Missing Lover, god of: forbidden love, youth, thunder

Moral Student, god of: the horizon, knowledge, mountains

Needled Critic , god of: criticism, bad weather, insincerity

Nodding Child, god of: sleep and dreams, innocence

Overdressed Liar, god of: butlers, beards, mischief

Overlooked Amateur, god of: jilted lovers, the wronged, apprentices

Pale Widow, god of: death and renewal, winter, burrowing animals, the moon

Penniless Poet, god of: song, poetry, money by nefarious means

Prized Dandy, god of: clothes, virility, bouquets

Querulous Weaver, god of: revenge, plots, pipes

Reformed Trumpeter, god of: earthquakes, the spoken word

Restless Patron, god of: employment, contracts and bonds, spring

Scandalous Dissenter, god of: protest, petition, dangerous animals

Senseless Brawler, god of: war, chequers, fire

Stalled Commoner, god of: home and hearth, decisions, crowds

The Mute, god of: Silence

Travelling Partner, god of: journeys, danger and misfortune, knives

Ugly Messenger, god of: pennysheets, handicrafts, dogs

Valiant Glutton, god of: cooking, trade, cattle

Vicious Beginner, god of: milk and nursing, midnight, ignorance

Weary Governess, god of: schooling, cats

Wide-eyed Inker, god of: tattoos, colour, sunsets

Withering Fishwife, god of: dusk, chastity, flooding

Yawning Hawker, god of: dawn, comfort, grain

Zealous Stitcher, god of: healing and mending

One

The man's story took him through the woods. Cora followed.

There was no path, but he walked in a straight line, as much as was possible between the densely packed trees. He looked as if he knew where he was going. The shadows cast by the canopy dappled his back and gave his certainty a kind of calming quality – Cora hadn't felt anything close to calm in a long time. The man stopped in front of the largest tree in the wood. Cora had been following him for ten, maybe fifteen minutes, keeping her distance but keeping him in sight. This was looking like a story for the Liar, thick with mischief.

Now that the man had stopped, Cora could see that he was heavy-set, and his hair was a curly brown. He looked young, twenty-five if she had to guess, and he seemed to be wearing Seeder clothes. Cora corrected herself: *Lowlander*, not Seeder. Though did that matter, now, getting the name of that southern realm right and avoiding what the Lowlanders said was a slur? Death was death, and the Widow heard that story, whatever you were called. Constable Jenkins would say it mattered. But Jenkins wasn't here. Cora had left the police. She was on her own now. That was the way it had to be.

The cloth of this *Lowlander's* shirt was so tattered, what remained of it so filthy, she assumed he was from the camp that lay between the wood and the southern wall of Fenest. As she watched him, wondering what he might do, Cora became aware of a new smell cutting through the damp earthiness of the wood. Something sharp, but sweet too. Something bad. The wood was silent. Silence that felt thick, somehow, like a fog that Cora couldn't see. But that couldn't be right. Shouldn't a place of trees be full of birds and their song? But there were no birds here. Nothing but trees, and a Seeder man staring at one like this was the first he'd seen in his life.

He'd been purposeful the whole time she'd been following him, and it was this sense of a purpose that had drawn Cora to him in the first place, while she waited for Ruth to finish her meeting – the meeting Cora wasn't allowed to attend, despite the fact she was trying to keep Ruth safe. The woods had seemed empty when they first arrived, but then Cora had caught sight of this man. A man walking like he had somewhere to be.

As she watched him now, he started fishing in the grass and leaves beneath the tree, then expressed no surprise when he found some metal spikes. Weapons? Maybe he *was* here to harm Ruth after all. Cora glanced over her shoulder. She had no idea where Ruth was at this moment, who she was meeting, or why. And all of that was Ruth's fault: she'd said it was better that Cora didn't have all the details of the meeting, that *Cora* would be safer not knowing... All of it foolish talk, but Ruth was hard to argue with. Always had been. That was older sisters for you.

The Seeder was fitting two of the metal spikes to his boots. Then he took two more spikes, one in each hand. To Cora's amazement, he began to climb the tree, using the metal spikes like claws.

A sound drifted to her. Sobs. The Seeder was sobbing as he climbed.

She edged closer. The strange smell was even worse here, and she had to fight not to purge the contents of her stomach over her boots. In no time at all the Seeder had reached the first branch. He threw the spikes to the ground where they settled in the same place that he had found them, and the loop of actions chilled her. He was leaving the climbing spikes ready for the next visitor to this place.

She looked up. There was something on the branch. The Seeder was uncoiling it. A rope. Left ready, like the spikes. It was tied around the branch, and at its end… She knew then what it would be. And there it was, in his hands.

A noose.

Cora broke cover and raced to the tree. 'No, what are you— Stop!'

He looked down at her, and she saw that he was younger than she'd thought, more like eighteen. His face was round, his mouth full. Tears coursed down his cheeks. He was surprised that she should be there – she could see that. Could see, too, that he wasn't going to stop. She shouted anyway, all the time he was putting the noose over his head, getting to his feet, and right up to the second he closed his eyes and stepped into the air.

The Seeder jerked in the air above Cora. She could see the

holes in his boot soles, was grateful for them to focus on as the boots themselves bucked and kicked. Then stopped.

That was the moment she started moving herself, as if she'd woken from a dream. Cut the rope. For Audience sake, cut the rope. This didn't have to be a story for the Widow. Cora dropped to her knees in the grass and searched frantically for the metal spikes the man had used to climb the tree and then thrown to the ground. Her hands seemed to have stopped working, her fingers useless. Without looking up, she was aware of the body hanging in the air above her. Was he even still alive? She couldn't see his face from down here. Couldn't hear any wet, tortured breaths. Where were the blasted spikes?

Her hand grazed something cool and sharp. She ransacked the grass nearby to find the others. Somehow, she attached two to her boots and then gripped one in each hand. She took a deep breath of air that was sharp and sweet and terrible, then sank one of the spikes into the trunk above her head, ready to haul herself up.

'It's too late.'

Cora spun round. A short, slight woman stood a little way off. Her face was all but hidden beneath a cowl, but Cora knew it anyway. Knew the woman's arms and chest beneath her woollen sleeves were richly inked too, tattooed like all Caskers. This woman might lack the Caskers' usual brawn, but she made up for it with ink and piercings. Nullan, the Casker storyteller and Ruth's most trusted companion.

Cora couldn't meet her eye. 'I should have stopped him, Nullan. I should have tried to—'

'And would he have thanked you?' Nullan came towards Cora. She pushed back her cowl to reveal her tanned face.

8

Since telling her election story, Nullan had gained some new piercings. The rings and ball-bearings in her brows and the left side of her mouth had no gleam in the poor light of the wood, and the tattoos creeping up her neck looked blacker than Cora knew them to be. Nullan was half Cora's age, but the events of the last few weeks had aged her. In the short time that Cora had known Nullan, Cora had associated her with death: her election tale had been one of plague, and she had been the lover of Nicholas Ento, Ruth's murdered son. And now here she was at the site of suicide.

'He wanted to do this, Cora,' Nullan said softly. 'Needed to. They all do.'

'All? You mean there are others here?'

'Follow me. You need to see this.' Nullan headed deeper into the trees.

'We should cut him down,' Cora called to her. 'Take him back to the camp, to his people.'

Nullan turned, held out her palms. 'And what will his *people* do with him there? They have no land to bury their dead.'

Nullan was right. The Seeders who'd come north to the camp had given up so much to survive. The cost was high, but not as high as staying in the far south. Not if Lowlander Chambers Morton built her walls and kept her own people on the southern side. The burning side.

Cora followed Nullan, and at once the sharp–sweet smell was worse. She understood what it was now: the smell of decay. She took a handkerchief from her coat and pressed it to her face, but that didn't seem to help. The smell was in every blade of grass, every leaf. Even the gloomy light seemed cut with it.

Nullan stopped and pointed ahead. Cora looked, and wished she hadn't.

'Widow welcome them,' she tried to say, but no words came out.

In the trees before her, bodies hung. Two, three, four. She stopped counting. They were in sight of one another but not what could be called close. Men and women. No children, thank the Audience, but who knew what horrors lay deeper in the trees? From the state of the skin, the flashes of bone, the hangings had been at different times. And there would be more to come, of that Cora had no doubt.

'The bodies last longer than they should,' Nullan said. 'The animals, the birds – they won't come in here. Nothing eats them.'

'But that's…'

'Unnatural? Of course it is.' Nullan pulled up her cowl. 'There's nothing natural about this place. Don't tell me you can't feel it, Cora. I know most police have as much feeling in them as a wooden barge, but I thought you were different.'

'I'm not with the police anymore, remember? But I can't imagine many people wouldn't feel the strangeness of this place.' She gestured towards the bodies hanging in the air. 'Do you know who they are?'

'Only that they're likely to be the ones who've spent the longest in the camp,' Nullan said. 'After a few weeks the despair becomes too much. From what I've heard, a look comes over them. A glassiness in the eyes. They stop talking, and then within an hour or two, they get up and walk into the trees. As if they're drawn here by some call they can't fight.'

'Doesn't anyone try to stop them?' Cora said, and as

she spoke the smell crept inside her mouth. She spat, but it wouldn't go.

Nullan shook her head. 'Think about it, Cora. If your purpose in life is to be a good custodian of the land, and everything on that land dries to a husk, dies, and then the very fields themselves get eaten by Wit's Blood—'

'—then you've got nothing left to live for,' Cora said. 'If Chambers Morton stops people moving about the Union, it will only get worse. She's condemning her own people to this.' Cora gestured towards the trees and their terrible burden.

'Morton's a pragmatist,' Nullan said, closing her eyes as if she couldn't bear to look at the bodies any longer, but couldn't turn away either. 'She knows much of the southern Lowlands have already been destroyed by the Tear widening, and that more still will be lost as it opens further. She wants to save the parts of the Union she can, and keep the people she favours safe inside it. If that means condemning some Lowlanders to take their own lives in despair, so be it.'

'You almost sound like you agree with her.' Cora reached into her coat for her bindle tin but found her hands were shaking too much.

Now it was Nullan's turn to spit. 'This is a disaster for the whole Union. If the Wayward can win the election, help the Union understand what's happening and make the right choice for the future then we might stand a chance.'

'The Wayward storyteller needs to stay alive to tell that story,' Cora said. 'That's the first step.'

'And we've already failed at that once.' Nullan looked at Cora, and her face was set with grim determination. 'Nicholas's sacrifice can't be for nothing, Cora.'

'We're doing our best to make sure it isn't. Not that my sister makes it easy.'

'You're more alike than you think,' Nullan said.

'Now, Storyteller Nullan, why did you have to say that? I was just beginning to like you.'

Nullan gave a grim laugh. 'We should get back.'

'Has Ruth done what she needs to?'

'For now. The message she's been waiting for – it's come.'

'What a place to meet someone,' Cora said.

'You're the one who keeps saying Fenest isn't safe,' Nullan said.

'Nowhere's safe for Ruth until she's told the Wayward story.' She glanced at the trees around them, ready to hear the crunch of leaves, hurried breaths – signs of Morton's people hunting Ruth. But there was nothing. The wood was silent as the Mute. 'And we've got to make it back through the camp,' Cora muttered.

They turned away from the men and women who had decided it was better to join the Audience than face what the future held, and retraced their steps. When they came to the curly-haired Seeder who had taken his life in front of Cora, she made a point of looking at him. She didn't turn away from his darkening face, from the blood on his chin, on his shirt front, caused by him biting his tongue in his final moments. She would not turn away from this, as Chambers Morton wanted to.

'Where were you anyway?' Cora asked Nullan, once the dead Seeder was well behind them.

'Hm?'

'You were meant to be with me and Ruth while she waited for her contact. We agreed, Nullan.'

The Casker shrugged. 'I had something I needed to do.'

Was she avoiding Cora's eye?

'Something more important than protecting the new Wayward storyteller?' Cora said, louder than she meant to.

'There's many ways to do that, Cora.'

'Too many to tell me, it seems.'

Another shrug from Nullan, and that was the end of it. Another mystery Cora would have to solve herself.

They walked in silence until the clearing came in sight. Then Cora spoke the thought that had been taking shape ever since the curly-haired man had dropped from the tree in front of her.

'People must come for the bodies eventually,' Cora said.

Nullan glanced at her. 'What makes you say that?'

'Because the ropes are left ready for the next who need them.'

Ruth was waiting for them in the clearing where Cora had last seen her, before she'd disappeared into the gloom of the trees to meet her contact. Whoever that was, there was no sign of them, but Ruth was pacing, her gaze darting around.

She was shorter than Cora – like most women – and wiry where Cora was broad. To look at them, Cora knew few people would guess they were related. Her sister looked tired; her thin face seemed to have gained new lines in the last few days. More grey peppered her temples and reached back into her dark hair, which had been long until that morning but was now cut close to her crown – Nullan's work, after Cora's insistence. There were only a few years between them, but Ruth looked so much older than forty-three, as if the years away from Fenest had counted double what they would inside the capital.

Cora was going to call out but then stopped herself. It didn't feel right to shout in such a place. Hardly felt right to speak at all.

Ruth saw them and threw up her hands. 'I told you not to leave the clearing, Cora! From the look on your face, I can see you now understand why.'

'All too well,' Cora said, and lit a bindleleaf. There was still a shake in her hands, but it wasn't as bad as before. Steady enough to light the rolled leaf rather than burn herself, which was something.

'Well this makes a change,' Nullan said.

Cora and Ruth glared at her.

'It's usually the detective here telling you what to do, Ruth, or telling you what you *can't* do.'

Detective. Cora winced at the word.

'Don't call her that,' Ruth told Nullan. 'That's from the past. We've got to look forwards.'

'You got what you needed then?' Nullan said.

'Our friend told me the place. It's not far from where we thought.'

Cora had no idea what they were talking about, and she got the distinct feeling that wasn't an accident. There had been plenty of these cryptic conversations since she'd joined Ruth's web. She drew deep on the bindle and tried to control her frustration.

'How long?' Nullan said.

'Four days and it'll be ready.' Ruth took the bindle from Cora and took a short drag. 'Can *your* friend get us there that soon?' she asked Nullan.

'She'll say she can...'

'And can we trust her?'

Nullan stood taller, squarer, somehow. 'Definitely. I'll send a note to ask—'

'Even the Stowaway would be sent mad by you two,' Cora said, grabbing the bindle back from Ruth and scorching herself in the process. 'And the Stowaway *likes* secrets! If I'm going to help you, Ruth, you need to tell me what's going on.'

'Soon, Cora. But for now, it's best you don't know.'

'Best for who?'

Ruth gave her a long look. 'Best for the Union.' Then Ruth strode past her. 'We should get back. There's a lot to do before we leave.'

'Leave? Where are we going?'

'I hope you don't get barge-sick, Cora.'

Two

They reached the treeline without seeing anyone else in the woods, dead or alive, and then the camp was before them. The structures here looked even more temporary, if that was possible, than those close to the city walls. People sheltered under roofs made of crates, or blankets spread between carts. This was the back of the camp, where the new arrivals set down their burdens. By the looks of things, there were plenty of newcomers. Cora, Nullan and Ruth made their way through those who stood around looking dazed, grubby and worn out from the journey north, and into the densely-packed tents of those who'd been here too long already. Cora wondered which of these poor folk would be the next to enter the trees, to find the ropes left ready for them?

What had been a sad huddle of canvas lean-tos outside Fenest's southern wall just a few days before had by now become a sea of awnings and poles, grubby scraps strung on lines between them that *might* be clothing, if the wearer was desperate. The number of people coming up from the south was growing. Having seen the changes in the Tear for herself, Cora now knew why.

She'd left the smell of death behind her in the woods, but the smell of life in the camp was just as hard to bear. There was a latrine dug somewhere near the south gate but, judging by the poor air, it wasn't enough for all the wretches scratching an existence on this scrubland between the city limits and the start of the Lowlands' good earth. The road leading south, away from Fenest, capital of the Union of Realms, had been left clear of tents, but on either side of it, every inch of ground was being used by someone. The camp seemed weighed low with the sense of waiting.

On the journey from the trees back to the south gate of Fenest, they didn't speak – not of the barge trip Ruth had hinted at, nor of the people swinging from the trees. They each kept their own counsel as they stayed in single file, which Cora insisted on: Nullan in front, then Ruth, and Cora bringing up the rear. And they had to go at Cora's pace too. A pace set by many years of smoking bindleleaf.

It took a while for Cora's vision to readjust to the sunlight after the gloom of the wood, but she felt easier about being in the open with Nullan there: another pair of eyes to see danger coming, and Nullan was pretty handy with the short cutlass she carried. But still Cora was nervous. This kind of terrain, the sheer number of people – it was almost impossible to know if it was safe for Ruth. Smoke curled into the air from the scattered fires. From some hidden place, reedy singing drifted. A song about a land rich with sinta fruits. A sad song from the Seeders – *Lowlanders*, Cora corrected herself again.

She couldn't quite believe how *much* the camp had grown. It had only been, what, a few days since Detective Cora Gorderheim – as she had been then – had returned from the Tear. Not so long as a week, Cora was almost sure, but time *had* been getting away from her. That was what happened when you stopped working. She'd admit freely, if anyone asked, that since losing her job she'd become like a Casker barge drifting in a current, no hand on the tiller.

But no one *had* asked her. There were other, more important things to think about. The Tear was widening. The southern Lowlands had been consumed in lakes of boiling Wit's Blood. The election wasn't over – there were two stories still to tell, those of the Rustans and the Wayward. And there was a storyteller who needed protecting: her sister, Ruth.

Lowlander Chambers Morton wanted to change the Wayward story, and that meant stopping Ruth, now the Wayward storyteller. Cora had to keep her sister safe, keep her alive to tell her story. But the Audience knew, there were some days that Cora felt like pushing Ruth into a pit of boiling Wit's Blood herself. Thirty years without Ruth in her life, and now that she was back everything had changed. Cora felt as if her own life had fallen into the Tear since Ruth had reappeared.

As they picked their way between the tents, Cora heard Chief Inspector Sillian's parting words in her head again. That had been happening far more often than she'd like, couldn't seem to get rid of them: *On this day and from this day forwards, you, Detective Cora Gorderheim, no longer bear this rank. You are henceforth stripped of all titles and duties, barred from entering all police premises in Fenest and the wider Union, forbidden to speak to, or fraternize with, any serving officers. . .* There'd been more to it, of course: like all Commission activity, removing someone from their post was long, dull, and involved too much paperwork. But it was Sillian's words which wouldn't go away: *you, Detective Cora Gorderheim, no longer bear this rank.*

The camp. That was what she had to focus on. Protecting Ruth was her job now, and it was all that mattered. Make sure Ruth could get safely back inside the city. Make sure Ruth told the Wayward story.

They passed two girls drawing in the mud with sticks, passed an old Rustan man, old as the Rusting Mountains he'd left behind, mumbling into the sleeve of his slipdog hide coat – *The bats, where are the bats.* In front of Cora, Ruth slowed, her gaze drawn to a sinta crate piled with cups and saucers, red flowers the pattern – the things people saved when the world was falling apart around their ears. Cora caught the smell of horses that seemed always to cling to Ruth: sweet and sour at the same time. Once you'd lived as a Wayward, travelling the Union by horseback, as Ruth had been doing since she'd left Fenest all those years ago, there was probably no way of washing it out.

Ruth's fingers trailed the lip of a cup and then a woman dragged the crate away. The back of her white shirt bore a web of vines, stitched in bright green thread. But there was mud all over the cloth. Like the soil for the stitched vines, Cora found herself thinking. All these people, their lives uprooted, their futures uncertain. How would the Union protect them?

Ruth. Ruth was the answer.

'Keep moving,' she muttered to her sister. The high arch of the south gate wasn't far now. Just a little further, and they'd be back in the safety of the streets Cora knew so well.

A cart clattered out of the archway towards them. It was

travelling fast. The density of the tents had forced Cora, Ruth and Nullan closer to the road than Cora liked. They had to cluster together to let the cart pass. When it was all but past them, Cora caught sight of the man hanging on to the tailboard. A Fenestiran by the look of him. Young, well built, and staring right at Cora. As if he'd been expecting to see her there, outside the city's south gate, at this time in the afternoon. With Ruth, a storyteller who a Chambers was looking to kill. Cora pulled out the weapon that had replaced her police-issued baton: knuckledusters. Easier to hide in her coat, quick to make use of. She was liking them more and more.

'You see him?' Cora said, without looking at Ruth. 'Get behind me.'

There was no response.

'Ruth, for Audience sake!'

She turned. Ruth wasn't there. Neither was Nullan. The air drained from Cora's lungs. She looked desperately across the tents. Finally, she caught sight of her sister's newly shorn head making for the arch. Cora spun back to face the man on the cart, gripping her 'dusters, but the cart was heading down the road, the man on the tailboard picking his nails, no care for Cora, or for Ruth. It was getting to her, this fear for Ruth's safety. And if she were honest with herself, she was feeling the lack of her badge. *You, Detective Cora Gorderheim, no longer bear this rank.*

Cora hurried to catch Ruth and Nullan, feeling the burn of many years' bindle-smoke tearing at her chest. Her sister was certainly fitter than her, after a life in the saddle and building other people's fences, and Ruth wasn't about to wait for her rasping, breathless younger sister.

'Beginner hear me, Ruth, do you *want* to get yourself killed like Ento?'

The name of her son brought Ruth to an abrupt halt, her boots deep in a puddle. Nullan kept walking, her pace quickening, as if she could outrun her own loss. Somewhere nearby, a dog was whining. Ruth's thin shoulders seemed to quake. She didn't turn around.

'I'm sorry,' Cora said. 'I shouldn't have said that, about Ento. Nicholas, I mean.'

Nicholas Ento – the Wayward storyteller murdered on Chambers Morton's command. And now his mother was putting herself in the same danger.

Cora reached out to touch Ruth's arm, but her sister slipped away and started walking again.

'You're so keen to be back in the city, Cora, we'd better keep going, hadn't we?'

'Ruth...'

This time, Ruth did turn round, and her pale, worn face looked at once like Ento's. Cora hadn't noticed the likeness before, but then, when she'd found his body in the alley between Hatch Street and Green Row all those weeks ago, it was hard to get a sense of what the man had looked like before his death. Him being strangled, his lips sewn shut.

'What?' Ruth said quietly.

Cora inclined her head to the right. 'This way. It'll be safer, further from the road.'

They let Nullan go on ahead. Cora suspected the Casker needed that.

'Got any more bindleleaf on you?' Ruth said.

Cora passed her sister the tin. 'Since when have you been smoking?'

'Since you made me put these clothes on.' Ruth tugged at the lapel of her green felt jacket as if just to have it anywhere near her was unpleasant.

'Morton's people are looking for a middle-aged Wayward woman with long dark hair,' Cora said. 'That woman had to disappear.'

'Fine,' Ruth said. 'But did I have to end up looking like… like…'

'Like?' Cora asked, feeling a laugh coming on for the first time in she didn't know how long. Now wasn't the time, though the Drunkard knew it felt good.

'Like a jumped-up Seminary brat!' Ruth shuddered.

It had been Beulah, the old chequers who ran the Dancing Oak, who had found Cora the clothes. No questions asked, but it was another favour that would have to be repaid at some point. Given what she now knew about the Tear widening, Cora had stopped caring so much about paying off debts. Things like that, they didn't seem important anymore.

Ruth was rolling her shoulders and stretching her neck with discomfort. Beneath the jacket she had on a shirt of dark cloth with bits of lace around the collar, and her trousers were as Fenestiran as they came: close-fitting, soft wool. With her thin frame, her hair cut short, and finally out of the Wayward riding habit, Ruth could almost pass as a man. The fashions, Beulah had told Cora, were those of today's well-to-do Commission staff – those from the better families, those on the rise through the ranks. Those like the Gorderheims, in fact, before Ruth fled Fenest and ruined the whole family's life thirty years earlier.

'You might ride with the Wayward now, Ruth, but you *are* a Fenestiran.'

'I haven't been that for a long time. Too long. Some things you can't go back to.'

'And yet here we are,' Cora said.

The arch of the south gate was before them, and with it, the noise of Fenest. Cora made Ruth wait while she checked the way ahead, then they slipped back into the bustling city.

On the steps of a coaching inn just inside the arch, pennysheet sellers shouted their competing headlines. Carts clattered over cobbles. A dog howled and a woman cursed. The bread man told stories of his rivals' less than savoury habits in the flour room. A line of chattering Seminary children, their studies over for the day, were herded by an aged teacher whose stick tripped a chequers, his eye on his slips. Here, inside the city was life, in all its noisy glory. Outside, there was only despair.

Cora let out a sigh of relief. The story of today wasn't one for the Drunkard after all. Instead it was a story for the Calm Luminary, who heard tales of forests and of peace. Cora hoped those in the trees had found peace at last.

'Rustan Hook opens tomorrow!' cried a pennysheet boy. 'Queues expected overnight for the *Wonder of the Rusting Mountains*.'

A Hook – a glimpse of an election story, displayed three days before the story itself was told. Designed to whip Fenest into a frenzy for the tale. From the sound of the queues, the Rustan Hook was working before it had even opened to the public. An older woman stopped the headline-shouting boy and bought a 'sheet. Several more eager customers were unwisely drawing out their coin-purses – Perlish, by the look of their oiled hair and feathered jackets: visitors to the capital for the election. They'd be wise to keep their wits about them. There were always light fingers in this part of the city, so close to the gateway to the south. Cora turned away. That wasn't her problem anymore. Nullan was waiting for them at the entrance to an alley, and Cora and Ruth headed over.

The Rustan story would be the fifth tale of this election – the two hundred and ninth election of the Union of Realms. Each realm sent storytellers to the capital to win votes, votes that won that realm control of the Assembly, which in turn meant power over the Union for that term. Every five years this happened. It wasn't a perfect system, but it had lasted.

But what would happen after Ruth told the Wayward story and the news of the Tear widening was known? Would the six realms of the Union break apart, separated by the wall Lowlander Chambers Morton wanted to build? That was a story for the whole Union to learn, and a story for another day. For now, Cora could only think about keeping Ruth safe. And that meant getting back to the distillers where they'd been hiding out since yesterday; the last in a long line of safe houses that Nullan had arranged for Ruth and her allies.

They turned into an alley where the noise wasn't so bad and there were only rotting vegetables to deal with, rather than skittering crowds.

'Send word to your friend,' Ruth told Nullan. 'Once the Rustans have told their tale, we'll need her.'

'I will. I'll meet you back at the distillers.'

'And bring some hot food!' Ruth said.

Nullan grinned, the piercing in her lip flashing. She turned to go, back to the main thoroughfare, but Cora stopped her.

'We might have a problem first.'

From the shadows at the other end of the alley, a man had appeared. A heartbeat passed, nothing more, and then he was running at them.

Cora drew her knuckledusters and told Ruth and Nullan to find the knives each carried, but they seemed slow about it. Too slow, the speed this man was coming for them.

'Nullan, watch the other entrance!' Cora barked. 'Get yourself against the wall, Ruth.' *Try to close down the space. Protect your back. Keep all entrance points in sight.* These were the words from her constable training, as loud in her head now as if the sergeant in charge was standing beside her, shouting in her ear.

But Ruth wasn't against the alley wall. She was running to meet the man, head on. Except Cora couldn't see Ruth's knife, and couldn't move. Then there was a hand on Cora's arm.

'He's one of us,' Nullan said.

'Are you sure?'

By now the man was close enough for Cora to see the stiff cape he wore, and the bandiness of his gait. A Wayward. A Wayward out of breath and with marks on his face. Soot, Cora realised, as the smell of smoke reached her.

He all but collapsed into Ruth's arms. Cora and Nullan rushed to them. Cora recognised him, just. There were so many faces in Ruth's web: people came and went, and few shared their names with Cora. It was better not to know.

'Thank the Audience I found you,' he said, and sucked a deep lungful of air. 'You can't go back. It's too dangerous. They found us.'

'What happened?' Ruth said.

'The distillers – it's gone.' He let Ruth ease him to the ground. His cloak was marked with scorches and one knee of his trousers had been burnt away. On the flesh beneath, blood. 'The flames tore through the place, and when they reached the upper floors. . .'

'How did it start?' Cora said grimly.

'I don't know. I was in the attic. Sinnla and Jeyn were there.' His voice was hoarse, cracked with smoke, Cora guessed. Whatever he was about to tell them, it wasn't going to be good. As she listened, she kept checking both ends of the alley. 'We were looking at the maps and then smoke was coming up through the floorboards,' the Wayward said. 'By the time we got to the stairs, they were burnt away. I had to climb out a window, onto the next roof. I made it down to the street. Thought Sinnla and Jeyn were just behind me. I waited. I waited for them to follow me.' He covered his face with his hands.

'How many of our people are dead?' Ruth asked, her voice hard.

He drew himself from his sobbing and said, 'They were still pulling them out when I came to find you.'

Ruth grasped his shoulder and held it for a long moment, then she stepped away, turning her back on him. It was a cold thing to do, no doubt about it, but that was what these times called for. There were many more people living in squalor beyond the city walls, walking the long roads up from the south, who needed Ruth to keep her head. To keep her life.

'Looks like we're moving again,' Cora said. She thought about lighting a bindleleaf then decided against it. The smell of smoke in the alley was thick enough already.

'Seems so,' Ruth said.

'That's, what, the fifth time in as many days?'

'I gave up counting safe houses when Nicholas was killed. I'd suggest you do the same, Cora. It's not a good use of your time.'

Cora turned to look at the Wayward slumped against the alley wall and thought of the dead man she had been called to find, back at the start of the election. Only a few weeks ago, but it felt like so much longer.

'We both know the odds on that fire being an accident,' Cora said. 'These attacks are getting worse, Ruth. You have to be careful. Going to the woods today—'

'And if I'd stayed at the distillers, Cora, I'd have been one of the bodies dragged from the burning ruins. We have to keep moving.'

'I won't argue with you about that. But this talk of Nullan's friend, the barge. That sounds like travelling to me, and *that* sounds pretty risky. Unless your next safe house is on the city's docks.'

'Not quite...'

Nullan was helping the Wayward man to stand. 'We wish you well in the days and weeks to come, friend.' From somewhere amid the baggy trousers she wore – Casker fashions seemed always to involve folds of dyed cloth – Nullan drew out a small purse. 'This should help.'

'Thank you for your service,' Ruth said.

'I'm not going with you?' the Wayward man said, the disappointment in his voice loud.

Nullan met his eye, which Cora had to admire. There was no flinching with this former storyteller.

'We can't risk you being followed,' Nullan said. 'Take the

others, those who got out of the distillers, and get out of the city.'

'That's it?' he said.

'That's it.' Nullan held his gaze. 'Good riding, friend.'

He bent his head and made his slow way back up the alley.

Cora decided to light that bindleleaf after all. 'Where's next on the list?' she said.

She offered Ruth her smoke, but her sister's eyes looked glassy. She was staring at the spot where the Wayward man had lain.

'The Bird House,' Nullan said. 'It's in Murbick. The head herders will know to meet us there.'

Murbick: the poorest part of Fenest, and the place where the recent outbreak of Black Jefferey was thought to have started.

'You take me to all the best places, Ruth.' Cora dropped the end of her bindle into a puddle. 'Well, if we're going, we'd best be on our way. Ready?'

Ruth gave no answer. Didn't lift her gaze. Cora and Nullan exchanged a glance. It was Nullan who reached out to Ruth, taking her elbow. It was Nullan who held Ruth all the way down the alley, and Cora who followed and kept watch.

Three

From the outside, everything about the Bird House was small. It was wide enough just for the door and a narrow window next to it, and the second floor looked to only be a half-storey – surely no one would be able to stand upright once they'd risked the stairs. If there *were* stairs. The building was squashed between two much taller places: on the one side a cooper's with two floors of whores above, and what looked to be a tailor's shop on the other. Everything about the Bird House was dirty too, from the glass in the window to the sign that was just about still attached to the wall, proclaiming the place 'Wingéd Wonders'. As she headed for the front door, Cora stepped over what looked like the remains of a pigeon smeared across the cobbles. It was too grim an irony, even for the Drunkard.

'Round the back,' Nullan said, and led the way down a narrow cut-through between the Bird House and the tailor's.

Ruth hadn't spoken since they'd set off, so Cora had little hope of any answers about all this talk of barges. But she could be patient when she had to be.

Cora caught the faint sound of cheeping, and then came

the smell: birds' mess, ripe and sour. She counted four rats in the cut-through, none of them bothered by the presence of people. Waiting to get their claws into the birds, she guessed, and tried not to think about Lowlander Chambers Morton wanting to do the same to Ruth.

They reached a door in the back of the building. The remains of red paint were being overtaken by mould, and the wood itself was almost gleaming with damp. Nullan used the handle of her cutlass to knock: twice slow, three times quick. That was today's agreed signal. Tomorrow there would be another, and another after that. Across the city there was a web of people from the southern realms, loyal to Ruth and to the Wayward cause, passing messages, sending word, readying new safe houses. And now, dragging charred bodies from burnt-out ruins.

The door opened wide enough to show an eye which flashed its gaze across the three of them before they were quickly ushered inside, into darkness and the stink of the birds. The only light came from a lantern held by a tall woman. Cora caught a glimpse of unclothed arms and the dark patterns swirling up them: a Casker. Some friend of Nullan's, no doubt. The woman had a band of cloth across her mouth and nose – to protect her from the smell of the birds, or to hide her identity? Both seemed likely. Without a word, she turned and led them down a passage. Something shifted behind her; in the poor light, Cora made out a shadow moving to stand across the door they'd just come through. Another part of Ruth's protection.

The lantern revealed glimpses of cages and the scruffy scraps of things inside them. Gleaming eyes and scratching, and the calls – it was enough to make Cora's ears bleed.

'You're not selling them for their songs,' she said to the Casker's broad back.

'Not their meat, neither,' came the muffled reply.

That didn't leave much, but Cora suspected this place wasn't really about trade. Murbick had more fronts than it did legitimate businesses. As a detective, that had been of some interest when she'd been after thieves. Now it was someone else's problem; having lost her badge, Murbick's problems had become its charms.

Those charms didn't excuse the smell of bird's mess, though. It was so bad, Cora had to tuck her nose in her elbow. The air was thick with dust as well as the stench. Feathers drifted from the cages and lay in a soft layer on the floor. As she and the others made their way along the passage, the feathers swirled around their feet like a strange kind of snow. A storyteller could make that sound beautiful, but for Cora there were too many stories already featuring feathers: Morton's hired hands had left them as warnings. The fact Cora was here in the Bird House, tramping after her sister, the new Wayward storyteller who Morton wanted to kill, showed just what Cora had made of those warnings.

The passage sloped suddenly, and then they came to another door. The tall, masked Casker opened it, and it was as if they stepped into someone else's story entirely.

They were in a wide, high-ceilinged room. No windows, but there were candles and lamps everywhere. A vent somewhere too, because the air wasn't smoky. The bare wooden boards of the passage had given way to a rich blue carpet. Padded chairs were dotted around, and tall leafy plants in shining silver pots. On the far side stood a table piled with bread and cheese, platters of meat, towers of fruit.

The room was full: Wayward, of course, as well as some Caskers and a pair of Rustans, even a Torn sitting quietly by himself, his mouthpiece flaring as he read a pennysheet. Everyone seemed busy at something, or they had been until Ruth arrived. There was a brief pause as people registered her, then it was back to murmured talk, sorting papers, oiling saddles. But the atmosphere felt brittle. No one's gaze seemed to rest easily. A dropped stirrup glancing against a table leg made a number of folks jump.

The edges of the room, now Cora had time to take it all in, were full of Wayward horse gear. It was a strange sight, all that leather and rope alongside the good furnishings. It was as if they thought they'd have to leap onto their horses and gallop away at a moment's notice. And maybe they did.

Cora recognised some of the faces from the other safe houses: people who supported the plan to tell the Union about the Tear widening, tell the news calmly, openly, and then work together to safeguard everyone in the fiery future which awaited. The supporters didn't include all in the southern realms though. There were rumours of a faction within the Torn who favoured Chambers Morton's ideas of walls. Cora let her gaze pass over the room.

'This a council?' she asked Nullan, her voice low.

'Something like that. Losing the distillers, the fire... the head herders will be worried.'

'Them and me both.'

She and Nullan stayed near the doorway, but Ruth had gone straight to a Rustan woman. Cora recognised her, but was sure the woman had had more hair last time she'd seen her. The soot marks across her forehead told a story of burning. This was one of the survivors.

'Your sister will need your support,' Nullan said.

'More than she does already?' Cora said.

'Not the kind that involves a knife.'

What else was there, when all was said and done?

Nullan's eyes never left a pair of Wayward across the room: two men, one much older than the other. The older was a head herder – the small group of senior Wayward, those who rode at the front of the herd, so Ruth had explained. Cora recognised the younger one from previous places Ruth had stayed. Tannir, his name was. He was perhaps twenty, twenty-five, though it was always hard to judge a Wayward's age, given how their time in the sun lined their faces more quickly than the other realms. Oddly, his hair was clipped almost to nothing – more like the hairless Torn than the usual Wayward fashion of wearing their hair long and braided.

Tannir hadn't been around all the time, but Cora had noticed him coming and going. Partly, it was his unusual hair, partly his fancy for fine gloves – which wasn't much of a Wayward thing either. But mostly, Cora had noticed Tannir because of the way he watched Ruth while he whispered with the head herders.

'Tannir won't be able to stop himself,' Nullan muttered. 'As if today hasn't been bad enough already.'

'He looks like he's got a tale for the Dandy though,' Cora said.

'What?'

Cora nodded in the direction of Tannir. 'His gloves are

gone. Those green leather ones with the red stitching. I've never seen Tannir without them.'

'So?'

Cora shrugged. 'I just noticed, that's all. Nullan, look at his hands – they're so much paler than the rest of him. Hidden from the sun for so long and yet now he takes them off. Why might that be, do you—'

'You need to get a grip on what's important, Cora. You're not after cutpurses now.' And with that, Nullan stalked away to where Ruth was now sitting with a group of Caskers.

But that was what Cora did. What *detectives* did. They noticed things that other people didn't, and they asked questions. Anything could be important. Hard to turn off that part of herself after all these years. *On this day and from this day forwards, you, Detective Cora Gorderheim, no longer bear this rank.*

Cora took the chance to head for the table, hunting for a coffee pot. The Wayward seemed to only drink tea, and strange flowery tea at that. Cora had tried it once and once only. The Torn man was seated nearby – all but hairless, and scarred. He looked up from his pennysheet as Cora approached.

'It say here,' the Torn said, 'that the people of the south, they come for Fenest's money.'

'Let me guess – that would be the *Daily Tales* you're reading.'

The Torn gave a low laugh and his mouthpiece emitted a gentle puff of smoke. At once, the air around Cora smelt of sulphur. A pair of Caskers nearby stepped away. Not many wanted to get too close to the lump of burning tornstone that sat inside the glass mouthpiece strapped to the Torn's face. It kept him alive, kept his lungs working in Fenest's air, which was so different to that of the Tear. The reason so few Torn left their homeland. But now, Cora found herself thinking, that homeland was coming closer to Fenest.

'Is ridiculous,' the Torn said. 'What is said in pennysheets. Ridiculous!'

Cora grunted her agreement then crowed as she spotted a coffee pot among the plates and cups. She positioned herself so she could keep Ruth in sight: a reflex action these days.

'The *Daily Tales* is the *most* ridiculous of the pennysheets,' she said to the Torn, 'which is saying something. It's a crowded field.'

'No – is *ridiculous* people not question why southerners come to their doorstep. Why they live on ground outside city walls. To believe that people would suffer like that only for Fenest's coins. Why no one ask, is there something else at root, something all should fear?'

Cora took a swig of coffee. It wasn't hot, but it wasn't Wayward tea, which was something. 'People would rather believe southerners want to rob them than face the truth.'

The Torn shook his head, and his scars seemed to jump in the lamplight. 'Weak people, Fenest people. Yourself excluded, Detective.'

Her old life had preceded her. She thought about asking the Torn how he knew who she was but then decided there wasn't any point finding the start of *that* story.

'I'm not a detective any—'

'Ruth Gorderheim,' came a loud, male voice from the other side of the room. 'I would speak with you.'

All other conversation fell away. The room was suddenly so quiet, Cora thought she could hear the sputtering of the candles, and then a squawk – just for a second, a sound from the Bird House beyond made it into the hidden room.

'*Him,*' said the Torn under his breath. 'All talk, this one. Before you come, Tannir talk much against your sister.'

Ruth stood to face the young man, and stood tall. Her back was straight, her chin out. The shakiness Cora had seen in the alley when news of the fire had reached them – that was gone.

'And what, Tannir, would you say to me?' Ruth's voice carried across the room.

'That as storyteller you must give way to someone else. With the loss of life today – surely, even you must now admit that the risks of you continuing as the storyteller for the Wayward realm are too great.'

'So for once you're prepared to speak openly,' Ruth said, 'rather than just whispering behind my back.' She glared at the man flanking Tannir's side, the head herder. 'I know what's been said, the talk against me and against my son's story.'

'You make this too personal, Ruth.' Tannir fussed at his wrists. As if he were pulling down his missing gloves. As if he hadn't wanted to be without them. 'The whole realm was devastated by the loss of Nicholas Ento.'

'You aren't fit to say my son's name, you who seek to take away his story!'

'We must do what's right for the Wayward realm,' said the head herder.

'Telling Nicholas's story *is* the right thing for the realm,' Ruth shouted, 'for the whole Union. This was agreed by the

Council of Riders on the Steppes. You were there, Herder Hyam. I heard you support the story myself.'

Hyam turned away, couldn't meet Ruth's eye. 'That was before the violence, before poor Nicholas…'

'Save your tears,' Ruth snapped. 'This is about giving way to Morton. What has she offered you? Any of you?' She spun on her heel, turning to face each part of the room, her eyes wild. 'Did she tell you she'd save a place for you behind her wall, that she would keep you safe from the horrors to come? How could you believe such—'

'Morton will stop at nothing to kill you,' Hyam said. 'She will do anything to keep you from telling Nicholas's story.'

'And attempts on *your* life mean that others will die,' Tannir added, sounding exasperated. 'The fire at the distillers, we lost—'

'We can't stop now,' Ruth said, gripping the back of a chair so hard Cora thought she'd pull it over. Better that than throw it at Tannir, which it looked like Ruth wanted to do. 'I have to tell Nicholas's story, I have to tell the Union the truth about the Tear. I will tell no other tale.'

'That itself is an abomination!' Herder Hyam spluttered. 'That you should tell someone else's story! But why should I expect a Fenestiran to understand the ways of the Wayward realm?'

'Isn't that why you asked her to help you?' Cora called. 'Because she's an outsider?'

All eyes turned to Cora. Soft chuckling came from the Torn beside her, along with small puffs of sulphuric smoke from the Torn's mouthpiece. Ruth's expression was hard to read, but Herder Hyam and Tannir – they looked murderous.

Cora took a swig of her cold coffee. 'You wanted my sister to help you Wayward win your first election in... How many years has it been?'

'Too many!' said the Torn.

'This year you need to win – the whole Union needs you to win. And so *you* need my sister to tell her son's story.' As Herder Hyam made to speak, Cora pressed on. 'I know, I know, you've got that rule that you can't tell someone else's story, but look at the facts. That's my business, facts, and counting them, because I work for the Commission.'

'Not anymore you don't,' Tannir said, but she ignored him.

'Fact one. Your original storyteller, Nicholas Ento, was killed. The first storyteller in the history of the Union to be murdered. Anyone can see that makes for a special case. And then there's fact number two. Your new storyteller is the murdered man's mother. That's pretty special too. You can't ask Ruth not to tell her son's story. It's the only story she *can* tell.'

Ruth caught her eye and gave the slightest of nods – they'd talked about this. Ruth had explained.

'Then the storyteller must step down,' Herder Hyam said.

'That'd be no help to anyone,' Cora said. 'You know as well as I do that if any realm fails to tell a story, the whole election is void. The Commission would assume control of the Assembly until a new election could be held.' At the mention of the civil service of Fenest being in charge, all in the room seemed to be appalled, and Cora agreed: no one wanted those ink-scratchers making decisions.

Ruth slammed her hand down on the table. 'We must ensure the Wayward win.'

'And to do that you must make way, Ruth!' Tannir's cheeks flamed red and spit shone at the corners of his twisted mouth. 'You must let a new storyteller take over!'

'Got anyone in mind?' Cora said dryly.

Once again, Tannir made to secure his missing green gloves. 'As it happens, I have a story ready to tell.'

'What a surprise!' Cora said.

Tannir ignored her, gesturing instead to Herder Hyam. 'My tale has the backing of a majority of the head herders. It only remains for Chambers Arrani to—'

'Over my dead body,' Ruth said.

'That is what Chambers Morton desires over all else,' Tannir said, 'and you would let her kill innocent people in the process.'

'The blood of those who died today is on Morton's hands,' Ruth said, 'not mine.'

'Enough!' said a low voice that reached around the room.

Cora almost dropped her coffee cup. It was Wayward Chambers Arrani.

For one of the most powerful people in the Union, with a presence that was unnerving and compelling in equal measure, Chambers Arrani had arrived without a sound. He stood in the doorway, the dark of the passage behind him making his brown Chambers robe seem almost to glow. His grey eyes were as cold as ever.

'The Wayward realm has already suffered for this election,' Arrani said, his voice booming as it must also do in the Assembly Building when he debated with the other Chambers of the Union. 'We will not shed one drop of blood in our work to do what is right.'

Tannir was squirming so much, he looked like he was about to throw himself at his Chambers' feet.

'Your honour,' Tannir said, 'it is the safety of the Wayward people I fear for.'

'And there you are mistaken,' Arrani said. 'It should be *all* in the Union for whom you are concerned, Tannir. Our storyteller knows this, and this is why she has my support, as did her son before her.'

'But Morton—'

'Forgive him, your honour.' Herder Hyam grasped Tannir's arm, firmly, from the looks of it. 'The impetuousness of youth. But this is not the end of this matter, Chambers. There is too much at stake.'

'That at least,' Arrani said, 'we are agreed on.'

Hyam led Tannir and a retinue of Wayward from the room. The door slammed behind them, and for a moment, Cora could hear frantic squawking from the cages in the passage in response.

Arrani strode over to Ruth and, to Cora's surprise, took her sister's hands in his. Perhaps there was more to Arrani's support than just the needs of the election.

'First time I've seen him with Ruth's people,' Cora said to the Torn man.

'The Perlish, they keep him busy in the Assembly,' he said, scrunching his pennysheet into a ball. 'They rush through their last business before their control of the Assembly ends. And with two Chambers, there is always a brown robe ready to speak.'

'You seem to know a lot about the Wayward Chambers,' Cora said, looking at the Torn with fresh eyes. 'You work for him?'

'I have the pleasure,' he said. 'I am Galdensuttir. The Chambers' messages that come to your sister, wherever she stays, I organise. To keep her on my map makes me work, your Ruth Gorderheim with her always moving.'

'She has his support.' Cora's words were a statement rather than a question, but the Torn still felt the need to answer.

'Until his dying day.'

'All this talk of death... even the Widow will be ready to see the back of this election.'

'She has not long to wait now,' the Torn said, then hurried to his feet. Arrani was headed for the door, and the Torn followed. They left without a backward glance. In the Torn's wake, the air bore the faintest taint of tornstone's sulphur. As if the Chambers leaving was a signal to the rest of the room, everyone else dispersed. The web had their tasks, and Ruth had hers.

So did Cora. Keeping Ruth safe had just got a lot more difficult.

Four

R uth sank into a chair and covered her face with her hands.

'He's wrong, that Tannir,' Cora said. 'It's not your fault about the fire.'

'I'm starting to wonder,' Ruth said, without looking up from the floor. 'But that's the price that must be paid.'

Nullan came over to the table and poured a glass of something red that smelt of spices. She handed it to Ruth. 'Lowlander wine. Good for shock. Not for enjoying.'

Looking at Ruth slumped in her chair, Nullan propping herself up against the unlit fireplace, lost in their own thoughts, Cora suspected both were still mulling Tannir's words. But if the Wayward story were to be changed, that would be giving Morton what she wanted. They'd come too far for that. Cora hadn't left her badge on Chief Inspector Sillian's desk only to give up and hide in some fancy cage.

'We need to keep an eye on Tannir,' Cora said, 'but we need to keep him at arm's length too.'

Nullan stirred, as if woken by Cora's words. 'Should I change the safe house lists, make sure he's not with us from now on?'

'Yes, but make sure there's a way we can stay on his trail.'

'The Torn Galdensuttir says he's seen Tannir near the Assembly building.'

'Well,' Cora said, 'from what just happened here, it doesn't seem likely Tannir's there to talk to Chambers Arrani.'

'Morton?' Nullan said.

'Galdensuttir isn't sure,' Ruth said, and sipped the wine.

'Can we trust that Torn?' Cora asked. 'There's been so much talk of factions within the Torn. He could be siding with Morton.'

'We can trust him. Galdensuttir's been with Arrani as long as I've known the Chambers,' Ruth said.

And how long might that be? Cora wondered. Ruth had been gone for thirty years. Her life as a Wayward was still a mystery to Cora.

Ruth refilled her wine glass. 'It can't be good, Tannir being near the Chambers – any of them.' She gestured to Cora with the wine bottle.

'I don't drink, remember?' Cora said.

'Ah yes, it's bindle that's your vice.'

'Don't forget the betting,' Nullan added.

'Haven't had much chance of that lately.' Cora pulled a stool over and sat down heavily. She gestured towards the now empty seats. 'They've all made their way to the next few safe houses, I'm guessing.'

'Those still loyal to Ruth have.' Nullan kicked the fireguard.

'So now we have to worry about threats from your own people as well as from Chambers Morton,' Cora said. 'I'd better look into some extra protection.'

Ruth's fingertips grazed Cora's arm, just for a second.

'You're all I need, Cora. The way you stuck up for me with Herder Hyam!'

Cora shrugged. 'He seemed to forget that asking you to be involved was the Wayward's idea in the first place. You're sure about this, going ahead with Nicholas's story?'

Ruth looked her hard in the eye. 'I'm sure.'

'Then we carry on.'

Cora went over to the table. It had borne plenty of food when they'd arrived but now was a mess of upturned bowls, crumbs and smeared fruit. Cora managed to pick out a sinta and some hard cheese. She leaned against the table, facing Ruth and Nullan.

'I know I'm not going to like what I hear, but now that we're alone, I think you'd better tell me about this plan to leave Fenest on a barge.'

Ruth gave a sad smile. 'A trip out of the city, away from Morton's hired hands and Tannir's raging ambition – what's not to like, Cora?'

'Much, I expect.' She tried the cheese. It was good. Perlish. But still.

'I need to go inland,' Ruth said. 'Up the River Tun.'

'How far up the Tun?'

'Should be about four days sailing, there and back,' Nullan said, 'with a fair wind.'

'Sailing?' Cora said, her heart sinking. 'Why not ride? It'd be much quicker.'

'True,' Ruth said. 'But Arrani thinks a barge will throw people off the scent.'

Cora mulled this over. 'He's probably right. Four days sailing... We'd better have some stories for the Bore then,

44

hadn't we?' The sinta wasn't quite ripe, but Cora ate it anyway. She couldn't remember when she'd last eaten. Time with Ruth, it was hard to track. 'And the reason for this trip, when your life is in danger and you're about to tell an election story?'

'I need to collect the Wayward Hook,' Ruth said.

The sinta seemed to sour in Cora's mouth, turning from unripe to well past its best. She tried to control her anger, but it wasn't easy. 'You need to do *what*?'

Ruth stood and held out her hands. 'Cora, I have to. The person making the Hook – they won't release it to anyone but me.'

'But you're the storyteller, Ruth! You've got other things to think about, not least the target on your head.'

'She wasn't meant to be a 'teller,' Nullan said quietly.

Ruth put her hand on Nullan's shoulder. Nullan who had been the lover of Ruth's murdered son. Then she turned back to Cora. 'What Nullan means is: I wasn't meant to be in Fenest right now. That wasn't the plan. Nicholas was going to tell the Wayward story, and I was meant to bring the Hook to him when it was ready. But when word came of his death…'

Cora let the two of them have a moment together, then said, 'Send someone else to get the Hook. Nullan will go, won't you, Nullan?'

'She can't,' Ruth said. 'I'm the only one the Hook maker will release the Hook to. It has to be me, Cora.'

'Why?'

'It's… complicated.'

'At least tell me what the Wayward Hook is.'

Ruth smiled. 'You deserve some surprises, Cora.'

'Since you came back, I've had enough to last me until I join the Audience.'

'This one will be worth waiting for, I promise. And there's no other way.'

Cora let out all the air in her bindle-rattled lungs. 'Fine. I don't understand, but fine. At least let's go by horseback. It'd be much quicker.'

'It has to be by barge,' Nullan said, spinning round. The lamplight made her piercings flash.

'Look, I don't like riding either, Nullan, but it makes no sense to go by barge. Ruth will be that much more vulnerable. You must see—'

'We go by barge,' Ruth said, and in her voice, the way she held herself, the look in her eye, Cora knew there was no arguing with her. 'We'll stay for the Rustan story, then we set sail. My contact in the wood this morning, he told me where the Hook will be, and said it'll be ready for us. But if you don't want to come, Cora, I understand. I know it's not without risk.'

'Not without risk? That's a good one for the Drunkard. Keep telling yourself that, Ruth, all the way up the River Tun, while Morton's hired hands are finding new ways to kill you. I'll be right by your side to see them try.'

Ruth smiled. 'See that you are.' She turned to Nullan. 'I want a list of those who died today, their families.'

Cora headed for the door.

'Where are you going?' Ruth called.

'Somewhere people are honest about bad odds.'

The Dancing Oak wasn't too far from Murbick, the part

of Fenest where the Bird House stood. Close enough to walk rather than take a coach, which was something. The Dancing Oak – betting ring, whorehouse and carousing barroom – prided itself on being rough and ready, but not *that* rough, not Murbick rough. The ringmaster, Beulah, liked to say she had some standards.

It was early evening when Cora set off. The walk was good for her still-healing leg – the injury she'd picked up when the Hook barge had caught fire. The flares of pain were growing cooler and didn't wake her so often in the night. That story was becoming less interesting for the Stitcher, and that was fine by Cora.

There was enough light left in the day that she could see who else was about. There was a good chance she was being followed by Morton's people. Though, glancing behind her as she dodged a cart, there were no obvious suspects in sight today. When she'd joined Ruth's web, Cora had debated with herself whether to keep going to the Oak. On the one hand it made her predictable: at the Oak she'd be easy to find. But on the other, there was some value in keeping old habits. It would show anyone watching that her life was continuing as normal, nothing 'electoral' to see here. Some nights, she slept at the lodging house that had been her home for the last however many years. But since she'd walked out of Bernswick police station for the last time, she'd developed some new habits that weren't so obvious to anyone watching.

Beulah kept the keys to many doors that led below ground. And behind those doors were passages that criss-crossed the city. Cora had been getting to know them well in the last week. Walk into a pastry shop near the Wheelhouse, where the Commission's bean counters noted all the grains of wheat grown in the Union, and come out of a candle maker's in Uppercroft, half a mile away. For those tasked with following her, they'd lose her trail as often as they'd pick it up.

As the entrance to the Oak came in sight, she stepped clear of two pennysheet girls fighting over a fruit crate to stand on and shout their headline. The truth of it was, Cora thought, a person *could* be safer in Fenest than anywhere else in the Union. It was easier to hide in the twists and turns of the city than out in open country, or on a river… Whichever way she turned Ruth's plan to sail up the River Tun to retrieve the Wayward Hook, it was madness.

But then, if someone – one of Beulah's customers, say, too long propping up the front bar – had told Cora a few weeks ago that she'd be kicked off the police force, reunited with her long-lost sister after more than thirty years and pursued by a Chambers, not to mention that the Tear was widening, pulling the southern Lowlands into its fiery mouth? Well. She'd have said, go home, you've had enough. That was a story not even the Audience would believe, and there were many in that swaying mob who loved a tale rich with intrigue and unexpected turns. After all that had happened, maybe Ruth's trip upriver wasn't so foolish after all. At least Cora would be by her side. She'd do her best to keep her sister, and the Wayward storyteller, safe.

That was what she told the Latecomer whose niche was at the top of the stairs that led down to the front bar. As the Audience member for good fortune, it was no surprise that it was his roughly carved form at the entrance to the Dancing Oak. Tucked around his feet were offerings: a few pennies, a twist of string, even a ready-rolled, unsmoked bindle which Cora resisted the urge to pocket. Instead, she set beside the Latecomer a feather that had somehow attached itself to her coat collar in the Bird House.

'Been a few of these since this story started, Latecomer. At least this one wasn't left behind on a body. Unless I'm the corpse, still walking...' She shook that thought away – this was meant to be a story for the Audience member who favoured tales of luck, not the Widow and her stories of death. 'I hope my tale tonight will be one of fortune. Not my usual kind. No bets, Latecomer, my fortune will be a friend. Together, we'll come up with something worth listening to.'

Stories: the Swaying Audience loved them. Spend your life telling the Audience your tales, keeping them entertained, and then, when you took your last breath you'd be sure to join them. If the Audience didn't think you'd shared enough tales with them during your life then your only companion would be the Mute who'd keep you in Silence. No stories. No sounds at all. It didn't bear thinking about, so tales were told, yarns spun, and the Audience listened. They'd be all ears now, Cora knew, as she reached for the door to the Dancing Oak.

But the door was wrenched away from her hand. A tall man lunged at her. Cora took a step back, steadied herself, and reached for her knuckledusters. Then she noticed the man swaying on his feet, pitching as if on a barge himself. But this was no Casker. The man was wearing Seeder clothes that stuck to him with sweat. His pinched face was slick with it, and the smell of spirits leached from him. Cora steered him towards the stairs that led back to street level.

But before he made them, he dropped to his knees and brought up all he'd eaten and drunk in the last few hours.

'Best you get yourself home, friend,' Cora said. 'And lay off the hard stuff for a while.'

He was likely just another visitor to Fenest for the election, having too good a time between stories. The Oak was no safe house, but it was filled with such distracted folk it was safe enough to meet a friend here. A friend who should be waiting for her, if the note had found her – tucked into a pennysheet as it was, and delivered by a certain bawling girl named on Drunkard's Day. Cora hoped Marcus had done what was needed.

The front bar was full, the benches and stools packed with people from across the Union, most of them looking as worse for wear as the sweating man heaving his guts up outside. Cora pushed her way through, nodding to the barman as she passed. He was an old hand. Half as wide as he was tall and with a large chunk missing from one ear. Sidney? Simmons? Quick with troublemakers, that was what mattered, and a sharp eye for people who came to the Oak for more than just bets and whores.

'Evening,' she called over.

'Detective.'

She had a feeling she'd never lose that title here. Once with the police, always with them, far as the games houses were concerned. Didn't matter she wasn't on the payroll anymore. The way people treated her – the way she treated *herself* – she might as well still be in the police.

'All well out the back?' she said.

'As well as it can be, after plague. Numbers still down.'

At the mention of Black Jefferey, which had only recently

been contained, several of the drinkers near the bar spluttered into their glasses. Cora even caught one lad glancing at his friend's wrists, as if looking for the telltale black marks. She hurried on towards the back room. It wouldn't pay to stick around if drunks started accusing each other of being infected.

She thumped on the door that led to the betting ring and the whores. It opened wide enough for an eye to appear and take her in, and then she was inside. Tonight, the door was watched by a youngish woman whose all-but-bare chest, highly glossed cheeks and feathers in her hair spoke of a second job.

'No ash beetles tonight, Detective. We're back to rats.'

'I'll live.' On another occasion that would be disappointing news, but tonight, she needed to concentrate, and rat fights were easy to ignore. Only fools bet on rats.

She gave her coat to another whore to keep safe, but not before she'd retrieved her bindle tin. This whore was a lad, one she didn't know, but she liked the look of him as he walked away, his tight backside moving through the knots of people.

'I'd stick to just looking, Detective, unless you've got a new job. A paying one.'

Cora turned to see the tiny figure of Dancing Beulah: chequers, ringmaster and owner of most of the games houses in Fenest. She was old as the Oak herself, and just as gnarly.

'I'm not here to spend,' Cora said.

'Going to settle your debts instead?' Beulah put her hands in the deep pockets of her red velvet housecoat, which trailed to the floor, and made a point of scrunching the many chequer slips she carried at all times. Cora didn't want to think about how many had her name on.

'I'm meeting someone.'

Beulah chuckled. 'And I think I can guess who. Not seen her in here before. Looks startled as a gresta bird about to go in a Seeder pie.'

'That sounds about right,' Cora said, trying not to look in the direction of the ring where fresh sand was being raked, new boxes of rats standing ready. The warm air was already stale with old blood mingled with the spice and flowers of the whores' perfume.

'That one with her though – Brawler take me, she'll empty my coin chest before the night's out.'

'What? I don't—'

But Beulah was walking away, clearing a path through the whores and their customers, the chequers and theirs, despite her small size. Cora could only follow.

'They're over here,' Beulah said. 'You could take some lessons from the older one, though not in any of *my* houses, Detective.'

On the other side of the ring were the tiered booths where spectators spent their nights – those who didn't need to grip the side of the ring and shout at the creatures carrying their fortunes. As they reached the first row of seats, Beulah took her leave. 'And just in case you'd forgotten, your line of credit is—'

'I know, I know.'

Cora climbed the tiers, heading for a familiar figure: tall, lean, and with more enthusiasm for her work than Cora had thought possible in a Fenestiran. The young woman was deep in conversation with an older companion who was clutching a sheaf of chequer slips and staring intently down at the ring. Neither seemed to notice Cora approaching.

'You got my message then,' she said.

The young woman turned and Cora was greeted with the huge grin of Constable Jenkins.

Five

'**D**etective!' Jenkins rushed to her feet and then stopped awkwardly.

For an uncertain moment, Cora feared the constable was going to throw her arms around her. That would be a new development, and not one she was keen on.

'It's just "Cora" now. Or plain old Gorderheim.'

'I'm not sure I'll ever get used to that,' Jenkins said.

'You'll have to try, won't you?' said the woman next to her. She reached across Jenkins to thrust her hand at Cora. 'Donnata Jenkins, Willa's mother.'

Willa? Cora realised she'd never known Jenkins's first name. Never bothered to ask.

'It's good to meet you at last, Detec—Cora.' Donnata smiled at her own slip, and Cora could see where the constable got her large teeth from. But there wasn't much more of a family resemblance. Donnata's hair was silvery white, long and tied in what looked to be a severe knot at the back of her head. She was one of those women who'd gone grey early, because she wasn't the age of Cora's parents' generation – her skin was unlined and tight across her high cheekbones.

Cora sat down. 'Jenkins here has told me about your old job as Director of Electoral Affairs. Senior role in the Commission. That must have kept you busy.'

'It was just as awful as you can imagine. The election... Managing all those purple tunics, the story sites, the garbing pavilions, not to mention keeping the voting chests secure.' Donnata spoke at a clip, her hands seeming to gallop in the air as fast as her words came tumbling. 'And just when you think you've finished the business of one election and can have a rest, it's time to start all...'

Donnata's eye was straying to the large numbers board that hung over the ring. As soon as one chequers, clad in their signature black-and-white coats, rubbed out a line of numbers, another chequers chalked up the new odds in its place.

'Jenkins never mentioned you were one for the chequers,' Cora said. 'First time in the Oak?'

Donnata's mouth opened as if to answer, but no sound came out. Her gaze was now firmly on the numbers board and Cora could almost *see* the woman making her choices.

Jenkins gave Cora an embarrassed glance. 'My mother tends to bet in the rings closer to home. She doesn't come to this part of the city much.'

'Glad you've made an exception.'

'Delighted!' Donnata said, all at once focused on the conversation again. 'Once Willa said you'd asked to meet her here, well – I thought I'd come along, see what the Dancing Oak offered. One can be daring in retirement, and we don't see many rat bouts in Derringate. But you'll have to excuse me. I just need to...' And she was away to bend the ear of a chequers.

'Not a habit that runs in the family then,' Cora said, 'unless you were keeping that quiet when we were at Bernswick?'

Jenkins gave a low laugh. 'No. My mother says she got a taste for the chequers when she started at Electoral Affairs.'

Cora opened her bindletin.

'I thought you were trying to give up,' Jenkins said.

'Decided it wasn't the best time for that. Glad to see you remembered to leave your uniform at home. The Oak can spot a constable's uniform at fifty paces.'

Jenkins looked down at her dark purple shirt and black wool trousers. 'I know you're trying to keep a low profile, now that...'

'Now that I've been sacked? It's all right, Jenkins. You can say it.' Cora got a light from a passing whore and dragged deeply on her bindle. 'So, Marcus delivered you my note.'

'She did.'

'And was she loud enough to let the whole of Bernswick station know your old boss wanted to see you?'

Jenkins laughed. 'She managed to keep quiet about that. It was all in the pointing, like a story told without words.'

'I'd have liked to see that,' Cora said. In the ring below them, the boxes were opened and the rats came streaming out.

'Marcus saved her noise for news of the Rustan Hook opening tomorrow,' Jenkins said. ''Sheets say it's going to be a spectacle. *The Fenestiran Times* claims there might be actual flying!' The constable was beaming, her levels of excitement about the election as high as ever.

'Not sure how the Rustans will find so much as a breeze inside the Seat of the Commoner,' Cora said drily.

Jenkins's shoulders dipped. 'Oh, that's true...'

Cora was surprised to find that she felt a brief stab of guilt at disappointing Jenkins. 'But if it's in the pennysheets…'

'It must be true!' Jenkins said and grinned again. 'But I'm guessing you won't be able to go to the Hook, whatever it might be.'

'I'll be there.'

'Will that be safe?'

'I'm still a free citizen of the Union, Constable. Yes, I investigated a Chambers and accused her of two murders, but that's not a crime. Not yet, anyway. So what's to stop me joining a queue to see a Hook like anyone else?'

'Nothing, I suppose. But you won't be able to use your badge to jump that queue.'

Cora groaned. 'You're right. But it's not the Hook I'm interested in, flying or otherwise. There's someone there I need to see. Anyway – enough of the Rustans. Tell me, how are things at the station?'

Jenkins leaned back in her seat and sighed. 'In some ways it's the same. Sergeant Hearst is still on the roof feeding the birds more than he's in the briefing room, trying to keep out of the chief inspector's way.'

'Bet that works for Sillian too.'

'Us constables are doing double shifts,' Jenkins continued, 'what with the election.'

'Surely things are a bit quieter with Black Jefferey gone?'

Jenkins nodded. 'Thank the Stitcher for that.'

'And how *is* the Bernswick stitcher?'

'Oh, you know Pruett – still bemoaning the fact people die and end up in his cold room. The cells are leaking worse than ever, he says, the water getting into his boxes and salves.'

'Sounds like the place is surviving without me.' Cora tapped her bindle's ash onto the floor. It glowed for a second, then it was just dirt. She ground it into the boards with her boot.

'And yet it isn't,' Jenkins said. 'It feels all wrong. The chief inspector hasn't replaced you. There's no detective at Bernswick now, and Sergeant Hearst can't do that job.'

'What with the birds.'

'Sillian doesn't want him to.' Jenkins gave a *huff* of frustration – the closest the constable came to outright rage. But she kept her voice low, and Cora was confident that no one nearby would be able to hear their conversation – not with the cheering directed at the ring where the new rats were scrapping. Jenkins's mother was the loudest of them all, waving her slips and hollering.

'That's why I asked to meet,' Cora said. 'I need to know if anything is being done about Morton's involvement in the deaths of either Nicholas Ento or Finnuc Dawson.'

'Well, *that's* an easy answer,' Jenkins said. 'Nothing is being done. Nothing at all. Chief Inspector Sillian says the cases are closed, all the right paperwork filed in all the right places, and so I'm to stop asking questions. She even called me in to her office on the top floor to tell me that. I'm back to chasing cutpurses and checking Perlish cheese permits.'

'Two jobs you're very good at, Constable.'

'But I don't want to do them anymore! Not since working on the murder case, finding the scale of corruption.' Jenkins turned to face Cora, and her expression was one of such frustration, Cora felt bad for plucking Jenkins from the ranks of constables to help her investigations. 'I can't go back to pretending everything is fine, that the Assembly is doing what it should. That it's not the end of the world.'

Cora's bindle was smoked out, but at the mention of the Tear, she felt like lighting another straight away. 'I know. But you don't have to go back to that.'

Jenkins's eyes lit up. 'Really?'

'But you do have to keep pretending. I need you to pretend that you're just a normal constable doing normal constable things.'

'But?'

'*But*, you're going to watch someone for me. Tell Hearst. You'll need his help for this.'

Jenkins's breath seemed to be coming faster and colour had crept into her cheeks. 'Who?'

'A Wayward named Tannir.'

'Why?' Jenkins said.

'It's better if you don't know. I want reports about where he goes and who he meets. If you can get close enough to hear what's said in those meetings, I want that too. You should be able to pick up his trail at the Assembly building. Tannir spends a fair bit of time there.'

At the mention of the Assembly, the colour left Jenkins's face and her large teeth disappeared from view – there were no smiles now.

'You want me to go into the *Assembly* building? Where the Chambers are – the most powerful people in Fenest, one of whom has been ordering murders?'

'Keep your voice down, Jenkins.'

'Sorry. It's just—'

'I know. It's dangerous. It's what got me sacked.' Cora drummed her fingers on her bindle tin. 'But I'm not asking you to risk your job. It would be no help to me if Sillian cast you out, would it?'

'I suppose not,' Jenkins said.

'And besides, I wouldn't want to risk the wrath of your mother if you got sacked.' Cora glanced to the top of the tiered seating where Donnata Jenkins was haranguing a chequers. The poor man was quailing beneath her jabbing finger and cries of shoddy accounting. Below them, ringside, several whores stood watching, some laughing, but within the knot of feathers and glossy cheeks was Beulah, watching grimly. It was time Cora was away.

'How will I know this Tannir you want me to watch?' Jenkins asked.

'He's a young man. Wears his hair short, almost as short as the Torn do, no braid. Likely wearing gloves too. Just keep an eye on him when he leaves the Assembly. Let me worry about the rest.'

'And how will I get word to you?'

Cora stood up. 'Seems like our arrangement for tonight worked well.'

Jenkins slumped in her seat. 'Oh no, not her. Detect—I mean, Cora, there has to be another way. She's so loud, and so *angry*.'

'That she is. But Marcus likes you, Jenkins. All that time you spent in the archives together, looking for Tennworth.'

'Don't remind me.'

'I'd say you've got a friend for life. Now, Sergeant Hearst is paying Marcus to keep the Bernswick briefing room supplied with pennysheets. If you've got anything for me, hand it to Marcus when she does her delivery.' Jenkins looked like she was about to argue, and really, Cora couldn't blame her. 'It's safer this way, Jenkins. The less you know, the better. If Sillian questions you, you won't know anything, will you?'

'I suppose not. It was good to see you… *Cora*.'

'You see – anything's possible, Jenkins.' She waved to Donnata, still hectoring the chequers, and made sure to avoid Beulah's eye as she left the Oak.

Six

Cora spent the night at her lodging house rather than join Ruth at the next safe house on the list. She tried to tell herself it was because she needed to change her clothes – her shirt had the stink of birds in its weave, as well as coffee, bindle-smoke, pastry grease, the grime of gig journeys, pennysheet ink… When Cora thought about it, she couldn't remember *when* she'd last changed her clothes. But if she were honest, she stayed at her lodging house because the thought of the distiller's going up in smoke didn't make for the most relaxing night's sleep, and the Child knew, Cora needed a rest. Being on high alert to keep Ruth safe, it was exhausting.

It was exhausting too, dodging her landlord. Cora was always late with the rent – being a regular at the Dancing Oak meant her coin purse was light soon after pay day – but even by her standards, this month's rent was very late. She couldn't blame her landlord for lingering in the stairwell to catch her on the days she came back to her room.

But she was broke – there was no getting past that. Running a protection service for the Wayward hadn't paid anything to date. They didn't seem too interested in things like pennies and marks, or paying rent. All their minds were fixed on the election story, on keeping the Union together. 'The bigger picture', that was something Ruth said all the time. But being able to buy a decent breakfast was part of that picture, surely? Maybe it came from being Wayward. They slept under the stars and seemed happy to eat dried roots they found by the wayside. Cora had seen as much when she and Ruth had travelled south.

Truth be told, she hadn't worried too much about rent and breakfast herself for a while after that, not when she'd first got back from seeing the Tear. But in the last few days, back in Fenest and focused on Ruth, keeping her safe, it was easy to forget the threat that was slowly coming for the north and the hardship it would bring.

Though she'd seen it herself, with her own heat-scorched eyes, now she was back in the alleys and the cut-throughs of the city, with the cries of the pennysheet sellers sounding at all hours of the day, she could almost tell herself it wasn't real. That the Tear was where it had always been. Still where it was since it came into being and drove the first peoples north, with only the people who became known as the Torn staying in that fiery place, their bodies changing to keep them alive.

And when the news of the Tear widening seemed fanciful – a story – that was when Cora could see what Ruth and her allies couldn't: that the people of the north failed to make sense of the half-truths in the pennysheets, of the camps outside Fenest's walls, because they didn't *want* to make sense of it.

Was it any wonder that Morton's plan to build walls, to keep some people safe and let others suffer to maintain the version of the Union she preferred, was an attractive one?

Part of Cora wanted to be on the safe side of any wall that went up. Part of her wanted what Morton was offering.

These thoughts were with her as she went down the stairs of her lodging house. They were with her as she opened the front door to the street. When she shut that door behind her, they lingered in the little lobby along with the coats, umbrellas, walking sticks and boots no one claimed to own. But the thoughts would be with her again before too long. There seemed no escaping them.

No escaping the people watching her either: Morton's people, trying to find Ruth.

Across the street from the lodging house, a young woman was trying to quieten a mewling baby. Nothing out of the ordinary in that. But the woman, the way her gaze darted to Cora as soon as she stepped into the street then quickly back to the blanketed baby she was rocking, Cora knew this woman had been waiting for her.

Cora took out her bindle tin and lit up a ready-rolled smoke. The woman didn't look at her again, but she didn't move either, just stayed in the middle of the pavement. She wasn't waiting at a gig post or buying from a 'sheet seller. There were no stalls or shops on this street. No one had stopped this woman to talk. She was just standing there. And she had made the mistake of looking at Cora.

To be sure, Cora headed down the street, but in the opposite direction to the safe house where she was due to meet Ruth and Nullan. The woman with the baby followed. She kept her distance, but she was there, and whichever turn Cora took, the woman took too. Cora had one last drag of her bindle and threw the still-burning end into the street.

The safe house wasn't far, but it looked like Cora's route

would be longer this morning. She'd memorised the map of below-ground passageways that Beulah had given her, for a price Cora had yet to fully determine, and knew that there was a door nearby. A pennysheet boy hove into view, and Cora stopped to buy from him. Behind her, the woman's step faltered, then quickened as she made the choice to walk past Cora rather than linger in the middle of the street.

The pennysheet boy was talking. 'There's none dead.'

'What?'

'The fire at the distiller's. It's a miracle, they're saying.'

The woman was a little way past Cora now. Cora let the boy chatter on, only half listening as she handed over a penny for the 'sheet.

'What are they saying caused the fire?' she asked him.

The boy shrugged. 'Something to do with the windows.'

The woman wore a coat of light blue wool that dropped low across her backside. The baby's pale blanket hung over her arms.

'Windows?' Cora said to the boy, keeping the woman at the edge of her gaze. 'How do windows start a fire?'

The boy was sloping off. 'You'll have to read the 'sheet, won't you.'

The woman's pace had slowed. Watching her, Cora could almost feel her need to turn back to see her mark. But that would give the game away, wouldn't it? A few steps more, and the woman was forced to turn a corner.

Cora took her chance and ran in the other direction, trying to ignore the tightness in her chest that came from all her years smoking. She wondered at what the 'sheet seller had said – none dead at the distiller's? That wasn't what Ruth's people were saying. But there was no time to think about that now. She ducked into a tool-sharpener's shop. The man at the workbench looked up from his knives.

'Can I help—'

Cora flashed him Beulah's key – the sign all the door guardians knew, so Beulah had told her – and he nodded. 'Down the back. There's a rug, trapdoor beneath it.'

Why did it have to be a trapdoor? There were easier ways to leave a place.

'A woman will come in,' Cora said, 'with a baby. Keep her talking.'

He was grumbling about needing more from Beulah for his pains, but Cora had seen the rug. She caught the higher pitch of the woman's voice – just the sound – as she shoved the rug aside. The key fitted the lock, as it did all the doors Beulah controlled, and Cora lowered herself into the darkness. The trapdoor had some kind of spring mechanism which allowed it to fall back, the rug attached so if the woman should find some reason to check the back of the tool-sharpener shop, there'd be no sign of a way out.

This was the moment Cora tended to panic, when the darkness was absolute. But she knew there'd be the makings of a light nearby. That was a condition of having guardianship of Beulah's doors, and being paid for it. She took a deep breath to calm her chest then fumbled on the floor. The surface of this passageway was sandy, gritty. Sometimes there were boards, once even carpet. Her fingers closed on the cool glass of a lamp, and beneath it were flints. She struck a light and felt her heart ease almost at once. Time to get going.

She was heading for a baker's that was near the safe house. Not a long journey underground today, or at least it shouldn't be if she went the right way. Since joining Ruth and needing to throw Morton's people off her sister's scent, Cora had had some trips that went on and on, time becoming meaningless. That was when doubt crept in: Had she taken the right turn? Was there meant to be a bend here? Shouldn't she be out by now? There were risks in using Beulah's underground routes, risks the old chequers had been keen to point out.

'A few have joined the Audience down there, Detective, I can't lie. They get lost and then expire before anyone else comes across them. I'd hate for *you* to join the Audience that way.'

'It'd make for a good story to tell them when I arrived.'

But not today. She kept the route in her head and kept going. The important thing, Beulah had said, was to avoid turning round. That was how people got lost, no sense of direction. On she went, passing under who knew what shops, houses, story venues? Beulah might have routes that ran beneath the Wheelhouse, home of the Commission. Even now, above Cora's head, there might be hundreds upon hundreds of Commission staff, all wearing their various shades of purple, noting every detail of life in the Union. Once in a while, faint noises reached her from above – what sounded like furniture moving, a bell ringing, and even the sharp high note of a woman's laugh.

Her lamp revealed a fork in the passage, and a picture crudely chalked on the wall. Cora held the lamp closer. Was that white square meant to be a bag of flour? She squinted. Or a tooth? Was she heading for a stitcher who pulled teeth?

'You need some better picture-makers, Beulah,' Cora murmured, and was surprised how loud her voice was. Not that there was anyone to hear her. Or was there? Cora had no idea how many people Beulah had given keys to. There could be anyone down here. That thought spurred her on, and she tried to focus on something that had been circling in her head since she'd left the Bird House the day before: the Wayward Tannir and his missing gloves. She mulled on that as she trudged the hidden ways beneath Fenest, and at last, there was a change in the stale air. Wafting along the tunnel was the warm, stomach-tightening smell of freshly baked bread.

She found Ruth and Nullan looking at a map of the River Tun. They were in the small back room of the hat-maker's that was the current safe house. There was cloth everywhere: rolls stacked floor to ceiling, drapes of it hanging from precariously tilting rails. And scattered about were wooden blocks crudely carved into head shapes. It made Cora think of the carved and hewn representations of the Audience found throughout the capital and the Union, in Seats and outside betting rings, as if the Audience had all had their heads chopped off, and they'd somehow ended up in this stuffy room.

'Got any coffee?' she asked Ruth.

'Yes, but it's not hot.'

'I don't care.'

Ruth looked her over then poured a cup from a reassuringly huge pot. The cup felt too fragile in Cora's large, calloused hand. She worried she'd crush it and the coffee would stain the piles of cloth that were impossible to escape.

'You all right here?' Cora asked her. 'Any problems overnight?'

'No fires, if that's what you mean,' Ruth said.

From the floors above came enough noise to suggest at least some of the Wayward election contingent, Ruth's allies, were crammed into the same building.

'Nice of you to finally join us,' Nullan said. The Casker was perched on a bolt of deep black cloth.

'I was waylaid.' At the sight of her sister's worried face, Cora added, 'Nothing to fret about. Here.' Cora handed over the pastries she'd bought from the baker's. The smell had been too much to resist. She cleared a stool of a tray of pins and sat down. Her leg, still healing from the Hook barge fire, was feeling the effects of the walk. 'Before I go to see the Rustan Hook, tell me something. Who knew you'd be away from the distillers yesterday?'

Ruth took a bite of a pastry. 'Only you and Nullan.'

'What about the lad who found us near the south gate, when we came back from your meeting in the wood?' Cora asked.

'Him too. But that's it.'

'So Tannir wouldn't have known you'd left the distillers?'

'He *shouldn't* have known,' Nullan said, 'let's put it that way. But with the head herders backing his case to replace Ruth as the storyteller, who knows who might be tempted to say more than they should.'

'No,' Ruth said, and swept the crumbs from her lap with force. 'Tannir did *not* know I would be leaving the distillers yesterday. Cora, why are you even asking about this?'

'Old habits die hard,' Cora said, and stretched out her legs as much as she was able in the tightly-packed room. On her injured leg, the flesh was still tight and hot to the touch. And the person who had rescued her from the Hook fire was on her mind now. 'I think it's worth investigating what happened at the distillers.'

'Why?' Ruth said. 'We know it was Morton. She's been after me ever since I arrived back in Fenest. You've been telling me that every hour of the day.'

'It wouldn't hurt to be sure.'

'You think Tannir was involved?' Nullan said. 'I can't see the sense in that.'

'Not been much sense in anything since this election started,' Cora muttered.

Nullan turned to Ruth, 'But if we can find something on Tannir's involvement, something we can prove, then you'd have some leverage with Hyam and the other head herders. That would go a long way right now.'

Ruth appeared to mull this over, then said to Cora, 'If you do investigate the fire, it needs to be done quietly. If the head herders thought we were accusing a Wayward of killing our own people...'

'Trust me. I know someone who can help.'

'Can we trust *them*?' Nullan said.

'I'd trust him with my life.'

'Let's hope it doesn't come to that,' Ruth murmured.

Seven

Since the Hook barge had ended up at the bottom of the River Stave, thanks to the fire which had nearly killed Cora, the election Hooks had been displayed at the Seat of the Commoner. Cora arrived at the Seat in plenty of time for the official opening of the Rustan Hook, but the queue was already snaking down the street. From the blankets draped across shoulders, the baskets now empty, and the yawns that broke into excited chatter, many had slept outside the Seat to make sure they were the first inside. Cora joined the end of the line. Constable Jenkins had been right about Cora's inability to jump the queue without her badge.

If Jenkins herself were here, she'd be just as bad as those around Cora – loud and grinning. She'd say it was no wonder people came to see the Hook in such numbers. It was the closest most of them would get to the election story due to be told in three days' time, after the Hook had had its Commission-authorised time on display. The idea of the Hook was to hint, to keep people talking, to keep them speculating about the Rustan story to come. And to keep them betting, of course: chequers in black-and-white jackets worked their way along the queue, taking advantage of people with time on their hands and excitement in their bellies. There were a few constables among them, keeping the crowd safe and orderly, but none she recognised. The Seat of the Commoner was in a part of the city not usually covered by the Bernswick division, and Cora was grateful for that. She didn't want to see any familiar faces from the station.

As the queue shuffled forwards, the man behind Cora – a fat Perlish as oily as one of their cheeses – bumped into her. She gritted her teeth and inched ahead, getting uncomfortably close to the person in front of her: a Seeder, from the looks of her. Great, Cora was stuck between people from the two northern realms of the Union. The north that not only looked down on the south, but also cheated it too, over-charged it, robbed it blind in some cases, always aided in doing so by the capital, Fenest. That was what Ruth had told her, and after all that had happened, Cora could believe it. Could believe, too, that their parents had been part of it with their work in the trading halls.

The Perlish man behind her shuffled forwards.

'Keep your distance, friend,' she said, without a hint of anything approaching friendly.

He folded his arms and eyed her over his spectacles, the glass of which was small as pennies. Surely he couldn't *see* out of them? More Perlish fashion nonsense.

'I've got every right to stand here,' he said. 'You don't own this bit of street, do you? Fenestirans.' He looked like he would spit, if he wasn't so fancy. 'You think this election is all about you.'

'Fenestirans are the ones who vote, no one else,' said the Seeder woman in front. 'That's the Commission rule. It's laid down in article fifteen, point three, where it also says that the voting pool should be drawn from as wide a range of Fenest's population as possible. Now, the way I see it is: the districts must be equally...'

This had the makings of a long morning. Cora considered slouching away, but there was someone she needed to meet and a good chance he'd be here for the opening of the Rustan Hook. So she gritted her teeth and gazed out at the street.

The queue made slow progress. Cora was close enough now to the doors of the Seat to see the carvings on the wood. With each step closer, the faces and bodies carved into the wooden panels grew more distinct, more like the bodies queuing to get inside. As unthinkable as it was to have Hooks displayed in a Seat, the choice of the Stalled Commoner, Audience member for stories of decisions, and of crowds, was in many ways appropriate.

Just a few feet from the door, she spotted who she'd been looking for: Serus.

She saw his hair first. As usual, the auburn length of it was pulled into a topknot that flashed in the late spring sun. It was a good match for the warm colour of his slipdog hide coat that he wore all year round, whatever the temperature. The worn hide was like nothing else, and had a kind of give to it like butter. She grabbed Serus's arm as he passed and felt the softness of the coat. And the firmness of his muscled arm beneath.

He pulled back, ready to curse whoever it was that had got hold of him, but then he saw Cora. A smile set his metal cheekbones sliding over one another. A Rustan body modification was still a sight she had to get used to, even at her age.

'I was beginning to think you'd left Fenest,' he said, moving close to her, his voice low and just for her ears. 'I went to the station,' Serus said. 'The sergeant there, the one who likes the birds...'

'Hearst.'

'He told me what happened, with Sillian.'

'Not here,' she murmured, and gave the tiniest nod to those either side of her in the queue.

Serus understood at once. 'Come with me. I was heading inside anyway. The first display is about to start.'

The Seeder woman beside her gasped then whispered excitedly to the child clinging to her knees.

'Display?' Cora said to Serus.

He grinned. 'Don't you read the pennysheets? It's been all over them, though not the timings. That side of things has been kept quiet. For the surprise.'

'Serus, I have no idea what you're talking about.'

'Time to find out.'

Together they entered the Seat. Cora felt the closeness of Serus beside her and had to admit it felt good. Commission purple tunics flanked the doors, controlling the numbers to stop a stampede.

'Fire Investigator Serus,' Cora said loudly, 'I hope your realm has something to show these good people?'

On hearing Serus's official title, the young purple tunic nearest them stood a bit taller and tried to puff out his scrawny chest. Cora did her best to hide her smile.

'That was almost cruel,' Serus said, once they were past the tunics.

Cora laughed, and she'd be damned to Silence if that didn't feel good too.

They inched down the aisle, along with half of Fenest, it felt like. The benches on either side were full too but with a nod to a Rustan woman with a metal shoulder, Serus found them seats in the middle. As they sat down, he glanced up to the eaves.

'I think this should be a good spot,' he said. 'Of course, it's the first display, so you'll have to forgive them if they're a bit... well, rusty.'

Others in the Seat were looking up, craning their heads, twisting around as if they didn't know where to look exactly, but they knew there was *something* in the roof that deserved attention. Cora couldn't see anything but the old, dark wood of the Seat's eaves. But then she caught a flash of movement in the shadows there.

'Serus, is that... Did I just see a *face* up there?'

He grinned, and his cheekbones slid over one another in an alarming way. 'They should be in place by now, and not too nervous, I hope. They've been practising for months.'

'I still have no idea what you're—'

His finger was on her lips. 'You should have some surprises, Cora.'

She could taste spice on his skin.

The noise and chatter of those crammed into the Seat began to drop away. A Rustan woman made her way down the aisle towards the carved figure of the Commoner at the far end of the Seat, away from the doors.

'Thank you, one and all!' the woman called from beside the Commoner.

There was the sound of the great wooden doors being shut. The Seat was at capacity, and here Cora was inside it, next to Serus, about to be surprised. Or so he said.

'We thank you for your patience,' said the woman. She was tall, but broad with it. She looked like she could handle herself. 'I promise, what you're about to see will be worth the wait.' Her voice carried across the open expanse of the Seat, reaching all those on the benches, and reaching up to the roof too – her words bounced off the wooden beams that stretched from each of the four corners of the Seat up to its apex. All eyes were on the eaves and the shelf set just below them that ran around the stone walls. There was definitely something, or someone, up there.

'As many of you will know from the pennysheets,' the woman continued, 'the Rustan Hook will feature displays. The performance you're about to witness has been specially timed to open the Hook, but subsequent performances will be random. When members of the troupe decide to appear.'

'Troupe?' Cora whispered. Serus gave her a knowing smile.

'All who step foot inside this Seat,' said the Rustan woman, 'will have the *chance* to see something rarely glimpsed outside the Rusting Mountains. And that is what we bring you – the possibility of wonder.

'First, however, a word of warning. I must ask you all to stay seated during the performance. No one will—'

There was a giggle. It came from overhead. Everyone craned their necks to see. Cora couldn't make out anything.

The Rustan woman coughed and attempted to regain the attention of her audience. 'No one will be in any real danger, though at times it may seem—'

Something fell from the ceiling. It was a blur of colour – red? And then there were cries from somewhere in front of Cora. Purple tunics rushed to the spot. People were squirming and pushing one another out of the way. A hand shot up from the bench where the thing had landed, and in it looked to be a holen, the fruit squashed and seeping its juice onto one unlucky person. The crowd broke into frenzied noise, no small part of which was laughter.

Beside her, Serus groaned. 'They can't behave themselves for one minute. Even here, for such an occasion!'

There was more giggling from above, this time from all four corners of the roof. The sound echoed across the Seat so that Cora had no idea how many were up there. It sent the crowd back into an expectant silence.

The Rustan woman at the front shrugged with some resignation. 'Ladies and gentlemen, boys and girls, I give you... the Rustan Hook!'

Eight

Music began – some tootling and a pattering drum. A small figure crawled out from under the eaves of the Seat. As Cora watched, her mouth dropped open: the figure was a child of perhaps five or six. He or she was dressed head to toe in blue, and they were climbing onto the nearest beam. Gasps and cries rippled through the crowd as more and more noticed the Rustan child.

'How's it possible they don't fall?' Cora whispered.

'Watch first,' Serus said, 'then I'll tell you.'

The drum's rhythm became faster, and the child in blue scaled the roof beam on all fours, and at speed too. It wasn't a scramble. It was more graceful than that. The child moved quickly, as if they were climbing a tree rather than the ceiling of a Seat, some two hundred feet from the ground.

As the child reached the very top, the music stopped. It felt as if the whole Seat was holding its breath. Then, the child fell backwards.

Everyone gasped.

But the child wasn't tumbling onto the benches far below. They were hanging from the apex of the roof by their feet. By their *feet*?

The child's arms were dangling, and Cora now saw that the blue one-piece suit they wore had a small sail of cloth. It hung from their back, and was now unravelling as they were upside down. A sail unravelling to reveal the Rustan realm's symbol: a pair of peaks. Whichever instrument was doing the tootling now gave something of a flourish, and the crowd cheered and clapped.

The drum began again and the tune continued, this time with more instruments. More children appeared from the corners of the roof, each one dressed in a suit of a different colour: red, green, yellow, purple. They raced along their respective beams, bouncing and bounding – one even did a flip as they went.

Cora couldn't look away. In time with the music, two children jumped from their beam, right into the air. Many in the crowd shrieked or squealed – surely this time one would fall!

But instead, the children caught each other. The two wearing red and green clasped hands with the blue, and all three hung there.

A moment later, the child in yellow grasped the foot of the red, the purple child the foot of the green. All of them together in a strange kind of star. No – it was something else. The colours.

'Like a rainbow,' Cora said.

A rainbow under the eaves of the Seat, made up of children in brightly coloured clothes. A rainbow that curved up and over the symbol of the Rustans.

'They're doing very well,' Serus said.

As the applause continued, the children bounced back onto their beams and took a bow. Then sharing glances and cackling, they all reached into their suits. Holens and other fruit were dropped with childish abandon. Those below who were hit began to curse and shout at the adult Rustans at the front, who were looking on in dismay. The rest of the crowd hooted with laughter.

'Serus, are you blushing?' Cora asked.

He wouldn't meet her eye. 'Just when you think they're going to behave, they go and ruin it.'

'I think they're fantastic!'

And they weren't finished.

The drum beat changed, slowing down but booming out across the Seat. The child in blue once more took up their position, hanging upside down from the beam. Then, the red child leapt into the air only to be caught by their feet. With each beat from the drum another child took flight, was caught, and added their momentum to the swing of the pendulum.

When the last child joined the display, the applause was thunderous. Cora let out a breath she didn't realise she'd been holding.

A line of Rustan children, arcing through the air and reaching from the roof beams.

Then, one by one, starting from the bottom, the children scrambled up each other, then ran along the beams. Their speed was incredible, and within a few beats of the drum, the column of children had dispersed. From the ledge that ran around the roof of the Seat, five small faces peered down. The crowd waited. And waited. The children stayed where they were.

From the way the music trailed off, as if the instruments had been abandoned, one after the other, Cora had the sense the show had ended earlier than the adult Rustans had planned.

'Do you think they've finished?' she asked Serus. From the babble in the Seat, it sounded as if everyone was asking the same question.

'Who knows? Our children are a law unto themselves.'

The Rustans at the front had a huddled discussion with much pointing and handwringing, then the tall woman who'd opened the Hook thanked everyone for coming.

People stood, and the central aisle was at once jammed, the purple tunics unable to do anything except bemoan the lack of organisation from the Rustans. For Cora, to see representatives from the Commission in a flap was an extra highlight.

As they waited to join the lumbering procession out of the Seat, she wondered what this Hook meant for the Rustan election story. Would their tale be one of flight, and so escape? Or childish innocence, perhaps. There was also the rainbow. That was a beautiful thing made of different parts. But *five* parts in the Hook. Was that significant? There were six realms in the Union.

'The Hook has certainly set you thinking,' Serus said.

'Is it that obvious?' Cora smiled. 'They were amazing, the way they just flung themselves into the air.' The courage. The trust they had in each other. The trust they had in themselves.

'I wouldn't be surprised if the rascals decide to do their best work when the Seat's empty.'

'You mean that *wasn't* their best work?'

'Honestly, Cora, what you've just seen, they could do that in their sleep.'

'But *how*? You said you'd tell me.'

'Hair,' he said.

She glanced at his topknot.

'Not there. On their hands and feet. That's what lets them climb. That and a complete lack of fear.'

'Rustans have hairy hands and feet?'

'When we turn twelve, thirteen, those tiny hairs fall out, and our climbing days are over. The end of childhood is a painful thing in the Mountains.'

'Sounds sad.'

'It is... unimaginable,' Serus said, and there was such misery in his voice, she had to change the subject. Which was no bad thing. She needed his help.

'The fire yesterday,' she said quickly, 'at the distiller's.'

'What about it?'

Cora looked around, but the others queueing to leave the Seat were wrapped up in their own chatter. 'Do you know who's investigating that fire?' Cora asked.

Serus's metal cheekbones began to vibrate. Was he... was he grinding his teeth?

'Funny thing about that fire,' he muttered. '*No one's* investigating.'

'How is that possible?'

'A message came from the Wheelhouse,' Serus said. 'Commission said that the recent hot weather, combined with some poor ventilation practices, was to blame. Too much heat and the making of spirits... No mystery there.'

'I've read as much in the pennysheets.'

'That's just it, Cora – that story was in *The Spoke* before I'd heard from the Wheelhouse.' He paused, letting that sink in. 'In short, no one has properly checked the distiller's, and I'm telling you that as the Chief Fire Investigator for Fenest.'

'But *why* isn't there an investigation?'

Serus shrugged. 'I was told it isn't a priority. It's an old building in a less important part of the city. No one can trace the owner. No one died in the fire.'

'That's not true!' But even as she said that, she realised she hadn't seen any bodies. Who had spoken of them? The lad who met them at south gate. The head herder, Hyam. And then Tannir, who would tell another Wayward story if he had his way. 'I need to see it for myself,' she said, as they reached the door of the Seat. Emerging from the gloom, she and those around her squinted against the early morning light.

Serus rubbed his chin. 'What's your interest in this fire, Cora?'

'I'll tell you that when you've told *me* what caused it.'

He gave her a long look, then agreed.

Nine

Cora and Serus caught a gig. When the driver dropped them off – two streets from the distiller's to cover their trail – Cora reached for her coin purse and found it worryingly light. Serus stepped in, waving away her half-hearted effort at protest.

'I'll fill in a few Commission forms to claim it as a work expense,' he said.

The gig clattered off, the driver seeming to think her coins might be at risk if she hung around any longer. What more could you expect from a Clotham's gig? At least they'd managed to take that cheaper option. Cora would have felt worse about Serus paying if it had been a more expensive Garnuck's coach.

She started walking in the direction of the distiller's. There was smoke on the air.

'So, here we are,' Serus said. 'A once-detective and a city fire investigator, at a fire the Commission decided *doesn't* need investigating.'

'Serus, I don't want you to risk—'

'It's fine, Cora. I should have been asking questions about this before now.'

'Then why didn't you?' The words were out of her mouth before she'd thought them through.

The look he gave her – she couldn't work it out. Was he hurt? Or guarded? Either way, it wasn't good. But she'd had to ask him. It came from spending all this time with Ruth: her sister wasn't afraid of difficult questions. In fact, she seemed to love them and the uncomfortable truths they often brought to light.

'The Commission's message was unequivocal,' Serus said, his voice cool. 'This fire was not a cause for concern.'

Cora checked her bindle tin, just to have something to look at. 'And you wouldn't go against that, no matter how much you thought it was wrong?'

'There are risks to breaking the rules, Cora. You of all people should know that.' He swept past her.

'Wait, Serus – you don't know where you're going!'

'The amount of smoke still hanging about, it'll be hard to miss the source.'

She caught up with him, and they made their way down a narrow, cobbled street, side by side, but Cora felt far away from him. So much for starting something new with Serus.

They were on the edge of Derringate, where that part of the city slid into Easterton. Fewer well-to-do houses here than in Derringate proper, but the distiller's was on a decent enough street. Easterton Coach Station was in sight, but its noise couldn't be heard from here, and there were none of the cutpurse hideaways that dogged the streets nearer the coach station. Cora kept half an eye on those passing by, and each time she and Serus turned a corner, she glanced back to see if they were being followed.

'Expecting company?' Serus said.

'There's a cutpurse for every corner.'

She could tell he didn't believe her.

The ashy smell grew stronger and stronger, until in front of them were the still-smoking remains of the distiller's – Ruth's previous safe house, now not safe for anyone. Cora had spent a night here before the trip to the woods with Ruth and Nullan. She hadn't slept much, but that was hardly a surprise, given the narrow bench she'd been lying on. She and Ruth had been sleeping on the second floor. There wasn't much of that left now by the looks of things. The roof had collapsed, taking the third floor and most of the second down with it. All that remained to see from the street was the front wall of the ground level rooms, the glass in the windows blown out.

'I think they were blue, the exterior walls,' Cora said, looking at the now blackened stonework. 'And the door was impressive – this big glass pane made of the bottom of bottles. All different colours.'

Serus stepped towards the gaping entranceway then squatted amid splintered wood, broken glass and the few pennysheets that had drifted into the mess. 'Not much of the door left now. This kind of blaze would melt something like that. You said the place was packed with spirits?'

'It looked like a going concern to me.'

'Which makes it hard to believe no one has claimed the building,' Serus said, 'or that the Wheelhouse can't trace an owner in its records.'

A thin purple rope was strung across the doorway, and on it was pinned a neat square of white paper. *Do not enter. This building is scheduled for demolition and is unsafe.* Then a long file number that would mean something to only a handful of people deep inside the Wheelhouse. At the bottom of the page was the spoked wheel: the sign of the Commission. Serus yanked the rope away and tossed it among the old pennysheets drifting around the doorway.

'What were you saying about rules?' she said.

He went inside.

'Wait – is it safe?' she called after him, then remembered she was with the Chief Fire Investigator of Fenest. With care, she picked her way through the doorway.

She found him standing at the end of what had been the hallway. Ash flakes danced in a breeze she couldn't feel. The walls remained, but there was nothing above them save the grubby clouds. She hoped the Audience were enjoying this story. Was it one for the Pale Widow, Audience member for death? The Wayward claimed that people had died here, but the Commission and the pennysheets said everyone had made it out. They couldn't both be right.

A cool sweat crept across her neck as she caught a smell. It was the same sweet-sickness that had been in the woods beyond the camp. If there were bodies buried in this rubble, it wouldn't take long for them to declare themselves. A few hot days and the stench would be wicked.

'Cora?' Serus was frowning at her.

Stray ash flakes had settled in his knot of auburn hair. She wanted to brush them away. But she didn't.

'Stairs were ahead,' she managed to say, 'some leading down to the cellar, and another staircase going up.'

'And these rooms either side of us?'

She glanced through the blackened door spaces into burnt chaos beyond. 'This was an office. Lots of papers. The other was a kitchen. I can't remember the rest. It was dark when I arrived, and dark when I left early the next morning.' The place had been lit with few lamps, but enough to catch all the different coloured glass bottles. It had been pretty.

'How many windows in the back walls?' he said.

'Ten on each floor? Maybe more? Except the third storey. None there.'

Serus walked carefully around the space, stopping every so often to look at a pile of wood – fallen beams? He carefully poked scatterings of plaster and broken glass. The way was blocked more than it was clear, and to Cora, the ruins of the distiller's was a mysterious mess of smoking rubbish. How could there be answers here?

But he was looking for things she wouldn't see.

'The line from the Commission, and the pennysheets, is heat and poor ventilation caused this fire,' she said. 'Could a few sunny days really do that?'

'The making of alcohol is a dangerous thing,' Serus said quietly. He picked up a blackened rag and sniffed it. 'From what I know of the process, the air is the enemy. Alcohol vapours can ignite if not carefully and properly managed. Did you see anything broken when you were here, Cora? Anything being repaired?'

'No. Like I said, it was late when I arrived, and dark. But the whole place was tidy, well organised. That's the kind of place Ruth—'

She stopped herself, but too late.

Serus folded his arms across his chest. 'You still haven't told me why you were here, Cora. What's your interest in this place?'

She had a choice: tell him that her sister was the new

Wayward storyteller, whose life was under threat from the hired hands of a murderous Chambers. That Cora was trying to keep Ruth alive. That it was hard – one of the hardest things she'd ever done.

Or tell Serus nothing.

'I don't want to put you in any danger, Serus.'

He shook his head. 'It's a bit late for that, given where we are. Is it that you *can't* tell me what's going on, or that you *won't?*'

'They're the same thing.' A fine rain of ash settled on her hand.

'No, Cora. They're not.'

'Serus—'

'Then tell me something else. Was it hot the night you spent here?'

She thought for a moment. 'Not especially.'

'You're sure?'

'I don't sleep well in the heat. I didn't sleep well that night, but that was something else. But I do remember going to the window to smoke. It was already open.'

'Were they all open?'

'I couldn't say.'

He beckoned her over to the end of the corridor, where there'd been a window before the fire. 'See this?' he said. There wasn't much left of the frame, but he pointed towards the brass fittings for the window. The arms were fully extended, hanging mid-air like leafless branches.

'Open,' she said.

He turned away and headed down the stairs to the cellar. 'As I thought,' he called back. 'The cellar's in better shape.' With every step down, the damage lessened, so by the time she reached the cellar's floor, there were no smoke marks on the walls. The sweetly sick smell lessened too, but something replaced it. Something sharp: spirits. For the first time, she could smell the stuff that had been made here.

Serus lit a lamp, and in its bright beam, she could make out row upon row of glass. There were bottles and vials and large domed vats, all empty. Dotted among them were strange twisting pipes, corks and sacks of grain. All neatly arranged, just as she'd remembered the upstairs rooms had been when she'd come to spend the night, but she hadn't come down here then. Beyond the light cast by Serus, the cellar was shadowy, but she guessed it ran the length of the ground floor.

'What saved this part from the fire?' Cora asked.

'The door must have been shut. It's thick enough by the looks of it, and tightly fits the jamb. The floor above is solid too. A well-made place.'

He was standing next to a table and examining its contents. She went to join him, her boots making a *tap tap* on the tiled floor.

The table was covered in what Cora guessed must be more distilling stuff, but this was a wreck compared to the shelves. In the lamp's beam, broken glass and puddles flashed everywhere.

Serus stuck his finger in one puddle then sucked it. He winced. 'Strong. Not the finished product.'

'Should I be worried?' she said, and righted a pair of flasks that were too close to rolling off the table and smashing to the floor.

'Yes and no.'

'What's that supposed to mean?'

'Best not be down here too long, and not with a lamp.' He turned for the stairs.

'Wait!'

She'd seen something under the table and now pushed aside boxes, yet more flasks and some kind of long spoon. Her fingers brushed against something soft, almost as soft as a slipdog hide coat. It was tucked away, kept away from all the spirits sloshing about. Not it. *Them.*

Cora pulled out a pair of green gloves with red stitching. Just the kind she'd seen Tannir wear. He was always wearing them. Until the distiller's burnt down, that was.

She straightened with a groan. 'I'm getting too old for this.'

'You and me both. What have you got there?' he asked.

Cora held up the gloves. 'Not so long ago I would have called these a lead.'

'Let's go back upstairs. You can tell me about those gloves, and I'll tell you my best guess for what happened here.'

'Sounds like a good trade.'

When they were both standing in front of the building, Serus began. 'My best guess, and that's all this can be, Cora – a guess. Without time, without resources—'

'I understand, Serus. Just tell me – was this a deliberate fire?'

'Yes, that I'm sure of. And I'm fairly confident it started inside.' He tapped the wall, next to where the front door had been. 'The damage is worse around the front door and those rooms that looked out onto the street. There are fibres there that suggest piles of cloth were set alight to spread the fire. Whoever did this, they wanted to make it harder for people to get out.'

Nausea washed over Cora, and she swallowed hard.

'It burnt hot and quick,' Serus said, 'and that's down to the spirits. From what I can see upstairs, the patterns of the burn marks – someone doused the place. Not with much of a system, mind you.'

'They were in a rush?' she asked.

He nodded. 'And hesitant, perhaps.'

'You can tell that from a burnt building?'

'Sometimes. There's a feeling in what a fire-starter leaves behind, their traces. You must know that from crime scenes, Cora. The way bodies are left.'

She looked at the broken husk of the building, the life of it now gone. Maybe it wasn't so different from a body. 'Them being hesitant, does that explain the mess down in the cellar?'

'I think so. My view is, they got their materials together down there. Grabbed some bottles – I saw gaps on those shelves – and broke some of them. That would explain the smashed glass, but little fire damage. The spirits went everywhere. They were probably covered in it themselves.

'They went to the front door and the windows looking on to the street, then emptied the bottles as quick as they could.'

'Ignition?'

Serus shrugged. 'People never believe me when I say that's the least interesting part of investigating fires. In a building like this, where people worked, ate, slept, there's no end of ways to make a flame. I lit this lamp without any trouble.'

'And no problems with ventilation?'

'Not that I could find evidence for. There's more to it than opening a few windows, of course, but I'd still say this was a deliberate fire. The question of who started it, that I'll have to leave to you. Unless the Commission changes its mind.'

'I think I've worked that out.'

'Now, why doesn't that surprise me?' he said. 'The gloves?'

'If the Commission ever opens an investigation, I'll let you have him.'

'Hey! We had a deal.'

'Maybe when I get back,' she said.

'Back? From where?'

Cora cursed her loose tongue – that had never been a problem back when she was on the force. This time, she decided to be honest with him. She owed him that much, and much more.

'I'm going up the River Tun.'

'The Tun? Why?'

'Because it's a pretty river,' she said. But he didn't laugh. 'Don't worry, it'll only be a few days. I need to be back for the Wayward story. It's the Wayward I'm going with... and my sister.'

He looked disappointed. A grown man, sad not to see her for a short time.

'Come with me,' she said, surprising them both. 'Spend a bit of time on the river. They say the country out that way is good to look at. Even for Perlanse.'

Serus laughed. 'Well, when you put it like that. But then again...' His gaze slid to the gaping doorway of the burnt distiller's and the horrors of that smouldering rubble.

'Something tells me it might not be so relaxing. In fact, I'm guessing it might be outright dangerous.'

'I can't promise it won't be.'

'Can you tell me why you're going, Cora?'

'Not yet. But I'll send a note with the dock information, the time. If you're on that barge when it leaves, I'll tell you everything.'

Ten

Cora returned to the hat-maker's after investigating the fire, to find Ruth standing in a corner of the small, cluttered room. She was facing the wall and didn't turn around when Cora came in, or when Cora said her name. It was only when Cora took hold of Ruth's thin shoulders and shook her that her sister woke from what looked to be a kind of half sleep.

'What's wrong?' she asked, guiding Ruth to a stool. 'What's happened?'

'Hmm? Nothing. I was tanketting.' Her eyes looked huge, glassy.

'You were *what*?'

'It's a Wayward word. Each realm has their own version of it. Not widely used, of course, they refer to something only done by storytellers.'

'You were practising the election story?'

'It's deeper than that. Tanketting, it means to strengthen memory, and push it forwards, push into the story to keep it live. But also to restrain the story, hold it, *because* it's a live thing. It doesn't want to stay the same. It's hard to explain.'

Cora checked the coffee pot. It was cold – too cold, even for her. 'I'd often wondered how storytellers remembered their tales, them being so long. But then, you were always better at Seminary papers than I was.'

Ruth smiled. 'And I've finally found a use for that talent. Only took, what – thirty years?'

'Father would be proud.'

'Yes,' Ruth said quietly. She reached for her long hair and then evidently remembered that Nullan had cut it.

Silence came between them, as if Cora's mention of Victor Gorderheim had somehow brought the swaggering, soiree-loving man into the room. Their father's stories had been for the Liar and the Latecomer, always told with a glass of something expensive in one hand, a cigar rolled from hard-to-come-by leaves in the other. Until that night he'd decided to join the Audience early by drinking something darker, harsher.

'I wish you could have heard Nicholas tell a story,' Ruth said, dispelling the memory of their father. 'The way my boy drew you in, his voice – it was like he was clasping you close with his words. Hearing him, you could believe he was telling the story just for you, even if there were hundreds listening. That's a rare gift.'

'But if you're telling his story, it'll be the same, won't it?'

'It'll be the same words, but it won't be the same story.'

'I'm sure riddles are the kind of thing you do for fun on the Northern Steppes, Ruth, but we've got other problems. Is it safe to talk here?'

'Depends what you want to talk about. Given the thick smell of smoke about you, I think I can guess.' She went to the door and locked it.

'Where's Nullan?' Cora asked.

'Said she had some things to sort out for the trip upriver.'

'I'm beginning to think that you leaving Fenest isn't such a bad idea after all, Ruth, given what people here are prepared to do.' She told Ruth what Serus had made of the fire at the distiller's, and then she produced the gloves.

'The Weaver take Tannir!' Ruth shouted. She hurled his green gloves at the wall. 'He'll pay for this.' Ruth was on her feet, doing her best to pace in the small room and muttering ways to have Tannir join the Audience earlier than he might like.

'Tannir might be acting alone, independent of the head herders,' Cora said, 'working on the orders of Chambers Morton, or—'

'Or I've got a new problem.' Ruth slumped against the bolts of cloth piled by the wall, which swayed alarmingly. 'The head herders want me dead too.'

'No good options there. But I've decided to play him at his own game.'

'You've got someone watching him?'

'One of my best,' Cora said.

'It's three days until the Rustan story, and then we'll be on our way.'

'There are no guarantees you'll be any safer on the river, Ruth.'

'True. But the change of scene will be something, won't it?' She laughed, but it was brittle.

'The Brawler knows, boats still catch fire,' Cora muttered. She thought of the Hook barge, and of Serus. Would he join her on the trip upriver? 'But then there'll be the coming back, and the story itself.'

'It's not so many days to keep someone alive, is it, Cora? You can do it?'

'And after the story, Ruth? What then?'

She threw up her hands and laughed. 'Oh, Morton can do what she likes with me! Hang me from her new walls if she wants.'

'Ruth, that's not funny.'

Her sister sighed, a deep, loud sigh that seemed more than her scrawny body should be able to make, somehow. 'Once I've told the Wayward story, my part will be done. So will yours, Cora. The news of the Tear's widening will be impossible to ignore. It'll be up to the voters to choose who will lead them through the crisis that follows.'

'You make it sound like you'll just give up,' Cora said, when what she really wanted to say was, *Ruth – you're only just back, after more than thirty years away. You can't leave me yet.*

'Maybe I will give up,' Ruth said. 'I'm tired enough. And losing Nicholas…' She wiped her eyes. 'I have one job to do, and I'm going to do it. No one is going to stop me, not Morton, not the head herders, and certainly not that bald upstart Tannir.' She retrieved the gloves from the floor then grabbed the scissors lying nearby. Within seconds the fine green leather had been sliced to ribbons. Ruth turned to Cora with a triumphant look on her face.

'Take it you weren't planning on confronting him with those?' Cora said dryly.

'What would be the point? He'd deny everything, and he has the support of Hyam. Besides, the fire is out. The dead are dead. I just need to keep going for a little longer, and we'll be out of the city soon.'

'With Tannir on our trail?'

'There's a chance of that,' Ruth said. 'He knows I'm the one going to get the Wayward Hook. But what I *have* tried to keep quiet are the details of the trip – that we're going by river, when we're leaving. That information is known only to me, Nullan, the crew she's hired and you, Cora.'

'We'd better hope this barge Nullan's organised is a fast one.'

Ruth reached for something on the floor, beside the bolts of cloth. When she turned back, she had an armful of clothes.

'Fancied a change from that Fenestiran get-up, did you?' Cora said.

'If we're going to hear the Rustan story, we'll need to keep a low profile. Here. Nullan said this one should fit you, so it's her fault if it doesn't.' Ruth handed Cora a pale blue shirt richly stitched with a design of leaves and fruit. 'There are hats being made for us as we speak. Our host appreciated the business.'

'You want us to dress as *Seeders*?' Cora said.

'Well we can't go to the Rustan story looking Wayward, can we? Or Torn, unless you want to strap some burning tornstone to your face. Perhaps you'd like Nullan to ink your arms?'

'At least the look of a soil-scratcher is easier to be rid of afterwards,' Cora grumbled. 'And before you ask, I do *not* want to cover myself in feathers like the Perlish.'

'I told Nullan you'd say that.'

The shirt Ruth had given her was made of good cloth. Cora didn't know much about these things, but she could feel the softness under her calloused fingers, and the colour was the same blue as the sky she and Ruth had travelled under when they'd journeyed to the far south. When Cora had seen the damage already caused by the Tear widening. The fruits stitched onto this shirt were nothing like the dried husks abandoned in the yellowed fields there.

'What about getting inside the story venue?' she asked Ruth. 'My badge would get me a seat in the public gallery, but now…'

'Our friend Galdensuttir has helped there. He's seen Electoral Affairs records that suggest there's more than a few blind spots in the security.'

'Hard to police an open venue like the Water Gardens,' Cora said.

'We've identified a particularly vulnerable point, where you and I will go in. It'll be much easier to slip into the Water Gardens than somewhere like First Wall, for instance.'

At the mention of that place, where the Torn storyteller had died after taking off his mouthpiece, Cora could almost feel the strange breeze that drifted through the enclosed space of First Wall. Much better that the next story would be told in the open, and not just because it meant being there to hear it would be easier. But it was one thing to get a seat in the public gallery. It was another to get out safely after.

'You're sure it's a good idea, you going to hear the Rustan story?' she asked Ruth.

'It's not about it being a good idea, Cora. It's essential. I'm a storyteller. I need to hear the other realms' tales. We're all part of the same spoked wheel.'

'Then why do some realms want to smash that wheel?'

'Because that's the easier response to what's happening

with the Tear.' Ruth spoke as if this was the most simple truth in the Union, as if she were giving a lesson to Seminary children not yet able to tie their own shoes. 'To hurt instead of help. That's what Morton wants. And I'm not going to let that happen.'

Eleven

Though Cora was nervous about Ruth going to hear the Rustan story, it was a relief to have the day arrive, and to know they'd be leaving the city as soon as the Rustan 'teller spoke their final words – as long as she and Ruth could get in and out of the Water Gardens in one piece.

Cora was on her way there now, due to meet Ruth at the spot on the perimeter where security was thought to be weakest. She hoped her sister was right about that. Getting stopped by purple tunics or constables would be a quick way to alert Lowlander Chambers Morton's people to Ruth's presence.

It was a warm morning and looked to be a dry one, which was something. Hearing a story at the Water Gardens in the rain would be a grim prospect. There was little shelter there ordinarily, bar the bandstand at the centre where she guessed the storyteller would stand. Rain would likely put extra pressure on the 'teller, who would have to work harder to keep the voters' attention.

So it was a risk then, to be given the Water Gardens as a story venue. Was that some doing of Morton, leaning on Electoral Affairs? These days, Cora found it hard not to imagine Morton's fingerprints on every part of the Commission. She could only guess how deep the corruption went, and those guesses were grim. But lucky for the Rustans, it was turning out nice.

'Don't you have a hole to be digging?' someone grumbled nearby. Grumbled at *her*, because here she was in this ridiculous Seeder get-up, stitched vines climbing up her arms and a broad hat pulled so low over her eyes she could barely see. And that included getting a clear view of the lumpen Fenestiran now uncomfortably close to her, the smell of beer on the man's breath – this early? That was elections for you.

'I *said*—'

Cora rammed her 'dusters into his gut. The arc of her fist was small, given the press of people in the street, but she put some strength into it, and he went down gasping, which felt good. The people immediately around her moved back, like a river parting around a rock. Cora kept walking.

From her lodging house she'd caught a Clotham's coach – the fare paid by Ruth's coins – then walked for a stretch, doubling back on herself by a few streets. She'd stepped into a whorehouse wearing her own worn wool trousers and grubby shirt, and left by the back entrance clad in the Seeder clothes. Then she'd caught a second coach and told the driver to take the long way round to the north side of the Water Gardens. She hadn't seen the woman with the baby again, the one who'd followed her into the tool-sharpener's shop, but the old man studying the pavement outside her lodging house this morning had looked a little *too* interested in the kerb stones, so she'd spent time throwing him off her scent.

Now she was safely among the people making their way to the official gates into the Gardens, hoping to get seats in the public gallery. If they couldn't get in, they'd stand outside, blocking the way of coaches and gigs, harassed by pennysheet sellers and those hawking pies, chequers shouting the changing numbers. People often talked about the atmosphere outside story sites – how the air seemed to hum with the power of the story being told nearby, the guesswork about its contents, the odds on a win. Cora had heard plenty of that talk in the front bar of the Dancing Oak, and from Constable Jenkins, but she'd never understood it.

In the three days since the Rustan Hook had opened and she'd watched the children hurl themselves across the Seat of the Commoner, Serus at her side, Cora had felt she'd been twiddling her thumbs. She'd been to the Oak but with no money to spend it was a noisy, sweaty form of torture just to be there. And there were only so many times she wanted to go down into the passageways accessed by Beulah's keys to confuse those following her. So she'd stayed in her lodging house and read the pennysheets.

The 'sheets' opinion of the Rustan Hook was mixed. Those who'd been lucky enough to see the children's display thought it was the best Hook of the election – better, even, than the Seeders' mostins. But there was a problem: the children only performed when they wanted to.

According to the hack writer of *The Daily Tales*, many – himself included – had queued for hours to see the Hook, only to find that, once inside the Seat of the Commoner, nothing happened apart from odd giggles from the eaves, before a purple tunic told them their ten dull minutes were up, and they had to make room for the next group. And even worse, it had rained constantly since the Hook opened, so the crowds were damp as well as disappointed.

The effect of all this was that the odds on the Rustans winning the election had halved. In that morning's edition of *The Fenestiran Times*, the head of the Rustan election delegation had expressed her regret, but Cora suspected this would be half-hearted. The Rustans wanted the Wayward to win, and Cora strongly suspected that their story would help prepare the way for it, just as the Caskers had done, right at the start of the election.

The people ahead of her were slowing, the way becoming blocked. This appeared to be the queue to get inside the north gate. There were four entrance points to the Water Gardens: one on each side of the square that was the site. From here, the sunken Gardens were hidden by the buildings that flanked them on this side, but she could hear the slow tumble of water beyond. Her way in lay elsewhere. Cora elbowed her way past the north gate, past the purple tunics counting people in, checking wrists and ankles for the marks of Black Jeffrey but with less care than they had at the previous stories. The plague seemed to have well and truly passed, but there was worse to come for the Union. Much worse.

She came to one of the many bridges that crossed the River Stave. The buildings fell away and the Gardens came into view on her left: an unlikely patch of countryside in the middle of the capital. The Gardens were a little way below street level, the waterways fed by the Stave, which was partly diverted at this point in its journey to the open sea by a series of complicated sluices. The pennysheets had been reporting problems at the sluices for as long as Cora had been reading: clogged, crumbling, too easy for a body to fall into them after a night in a whorehouse. The repair costs kept the entry price to the Gardens high – one reason Cora hadn't visited in years. That and the forced nature of the place. There was something unnatural about it.

Visitors to Fenest often fell into the trap of believing the Gardens were built by the Caskers, and there was a kind of sense in that: the small canals that snaked through the lush grass and the rockeries, the floral displays and the viewing platforms – such things spoke of the people who lived on the waterways of the Union. But in fact, it was a Perlish merchant who'd built the Water Gardens, two generations back, winning the land from an old Fenestiran family in a game of cards. As she thought about it now, Cora realised it was a reverse of one of the 'tales within tales' of the Perlish election story.

When her mother was a child, she'd known the last surviving member of the family that originally owned the land: an old woman with grey hair down to her knees who was so bitter about her family's losses that all her teeth had fallen out. That was what bile did to you. Or so Ruth had told Cora, even though the old woman had been dead long before Ruth and Cora were born. When their mother had spoken of 'Dear Alexa' it had been to bemoan the sad end of a 'great' Fenestiran family at the ignoble hands of 'new money' from Perlanse. According to their mother, the Perlish merchant had no right to even presume to join the card game, let alone make such a vulgar bet and then go on to *win*. But that was Madeleine Gorderheim's story. Another was the story held by common consensus in the memory of

Fenest, that 'Dear Alexa' was not only hopeless at cards, but also arrogant and lacking any kind of vision for the land in question – aside from refusing to let anyone build on it and so drive up the value.

Cora stopped on the bridge to look down at the work of the Perlish merchant. To her eye, the hand of Perlanse was all too clear in the tightly controlled borders of flower beds, the painful neatness of colour and the ridiculous wrought iron that curled and flourished everywhere on the paths: benches, lamp posts, even bird houses. If the Water Gardens really had been made by Caskers then the narrow, humped bridges over the little canals would be replaced by uneven boardwalks with smoky lamps, with beer stops every few metres. That would be more to Cora's taste, but even she had to admit that the Water Gardens were looking good today in the late spring sunshine.

The bell rang out from the Seat of the Poet across the city, marking the hour. It was time to meet Ruth.

On the other side of the bridge from where Cora had stopped, there was an alley – narrow and uninviting, even by Fenest's standards, and easy to miss. Cora glanced up and down the street. No sign of the man who'd been outside her lodging house that morning. No sign of anyone else paying a bit too much attention to her either, though there were still plenty of people about, making their way to the north gate and enjoying that much-talked-about 'atmosphere'. Without checking her stride, she ducked into the alley then round its many dark turns as it wound between houses and took a course it had no business having. This was the kind of thing Galdensuttir had been talking about. Though the Water Gardens appeared tightly walled in and with limited gates, in reality there were many ways to slip inside: old cracks in the walls that were conveniently left unpatched.

As Cora made her way along cobbles that were slippery from the last few days of rain, she saw a figure ahead. Too shadowy to see if they were wearing purple. She gripped her knuckledusters, flexed her arm, ready to strike, but then the figure turned, and she saw a hat like the one she was wearing.

'Thought maybe you weren't coming,' Ruth said.

'And miss an election story?'

Ruth shook her head at Cora's sarcasm. 'You know, there are many people who are desperate to hear this story.'

'I know – I just had to fight my way through a load of them. You have any trouble getting here?'

'No, but we're not inside yet.'

'After you.' Cora gestured for Ruth to go first down the narrow, twisting staircase that lay at the end of the alley.

'How kind,' Ruth said flatly.

The short flight of stairs brought them to the level of the Gardens, but they still had some cover: a long-closed pie stall flanked the stairs, hiding them from view. Ruth adjusted Cora's hat, Cora lit a bindleleaf, and they stepped out, into a riot of colour and noise.

Twelve

At ground level, it was impossible to map the space of the Water Gardens as Cora had done from the bridge. Now that she was on one of the many twisting paths that wound between the flower beds and shrubs and fountains, and had crossed the canals to where all the food seller stalls were set up, she had no idea which way to go. The place was packed with people from all corners of the Union laughing, pointing, shouting, and among them, purple tunics and blue-jacketed constables attempted to keep order.

'This place is a maze!' she said to Ruth.

Ruth pointed. 'There – the garbing pavilion. See it?'

Cora stopped, narrowly avoiding tripping over a weeping child sat in the middle of the path, and saw the large, white tent that was part of every election story – the voters would be inside getting into their robes and masks, being handed their voting stones.

'We'll head for the pavilion,' Ruth said. 'The public gallery will be nearby.'

'Let's hope so. We don't have—'

'Oi – where did you two spring from?'

It was a purple tunic barrelling their way towards them. The wearer of said tunic, uniform of those working for Electoral Affairs, was a lad of around eighteen. First posting, Cora guessed. From the way he was throwing his arms around and shouting about illegal entry, she guessed he'd go far. People were starting to look.

Ruth's face greyed. 'Cora – what are we going to do?' she whispered.

'Don't worry. I have a feeling this young man is about to regret stopping us.'

'What do you—'

'Argh! He kicked me! He kicked me!'

All eyes turned then to the source of the bawling voice that had drowned out that of the purple tunic. At the lad's feet, sprawled on the path and shouting as if her young life depended on it, was Marcus: pennysheet seller, informant, loudest child in the Union. Cora was almost glad to see her, though hearing her was a different matter. She wasn't sure how old Marcus was, because Marcus herself didn't know, but she had the lungs of a burly adult Casker captain.

'Get me a constable!' Marcus boomed. 'I want this villain done for assault.' The tunic made the mistake of trying to help Marcus to her feet, which only made her shout louder, which Cora hadn't thought was possible. 'Don't try to shut me up! All these people saw. Didn't you? Didn't you see him kick me?'

'I take it this is your handiwork?' Ruth said.

'Marcus is a blunt yet powerful instrument, and she's always on time.'

'She's called *Marcus*?'

'Named on Drunkard's Day, but more reliable than that member of the Audience. See – problem solved.' The purple tunic was scurrying away in the opposite direction. Marcus hopped smartly to her feet, and the crowd closed over the moment.

'Effective, if painful,' Ruth said. 'Messenger take me, she's coming over to shout at you now, Cora.'

'Not if she wants the marks I've promised her. Morning, Marcus.'

The girl spat, rubbed her grubby sleeve across her mouth and looked Cora up and down. 'You moving south, Detective?'

'What? Oh, the clothes... It's only temporary. And I'm not a detective anymore.'

'Once you've had one of them badges and been allowed to hit people, you're always one of them, I say.' Marcus sniffed. 'I told Jenkins that when I seen her. I said, Jenkins, Detective Cora don't need no badge to go hitting people. She'll hit 'em if they needs hitting.'

Cora took hold of the girl's hood, aware of Ruth's raised eyebrows, and pulled Marcus behind a flowering shrub in an effort to avoid everyone in the Water Garden staring at them. Ruth hovered nearby.

'Any news from Jenkins?' Cora asked Marcus.

The girl pulled herself free of Cora's grip. 'See – you are the same as always! Jenkins says to tell you... Now what was it?' She made a show of biting her lip, lifting her eyes to the few thin clouds above. 'Um...'

'I know how this tale goes,' Cora said, and took out her worryingly light coin purse. 'Information first, and quickly. I've got a story to hear. A new one.'

Marcus grinned. 'I seen Jenkins this morning, and she said to tell you, the Wayward bloke you wanted her to watch, she seen *him* in a pastry shop.'

'There had better be more to this than a Wayward buying pastries.'

'There is! The pastry shop was near the Assembly building, the one where the window keeps getting broken. You know, it's got the—'

'The point, Marcus.'

The pennysheet girl rolled her eyes. 'All right, all right. Your Wayward was in there, and then another bloke come in and sit with him, and Jenkins says this second man is someone important. She says to tell you he works in the office of the Seeder Chambers, that one you don't like.'

That was one way to describe Lowlander Chambers Morton.

'Cora – we need to go.' Ruth was glancing anxiously up and down the paths, and Cora could see for herself that the crowds had thinned: people must be taking their seats.

'What else did Jenkins say?' Cora asked Marcus.

'She sat near them and heard a bit of them talking. The man from the Assembly asked your Wayward if he'd done the job right, and your Wayward went all shifty and said partly, and the man from the Assembly got all shouty and said, "She won't be pleased," or something like that.'

She? Morton. And the job was likely the fire at the distiller's, with the aim to kill Ruth.

Marcus was rushing now. 'Then, *your* Wayward' – Marcus jabbed a finger at Cora – 'he promises the Assembly bloke that he won't fail again. That'll he'll do it right next time, whatever it is he's meant to be doing. And the Assembly bloke says, see that you do, or you'll be joining her at the bottom of a river.'

Ruth grumbled behind her. Cora had heard enough. She dropped a few coins into Marcus's outstretched, grimy hand and turned away. But Marcus stopped her.

'Detective, there's more. Jenkins says your Wayward told the Assembly bloke there are many rivers. She said I had to make sure I told you that – "many rivers" – and that you have to keep away from them.'

'Keep delivering the 'sheets to Bernswick station,' Cora said, 'and you know where to find me if Jenkins sends more information.'

It was only after Marcus had disappeared into the maze of paths that Cora remembered she wouldn't be around for the next few days. The girl would figure something out. She was resourceful enough.

'So,' Cora said, turning to Ruth, 'now we know Tannir *is* in Morton's pay, and that he's planning something else.'

Cora glanced up and down the paths, which were now empty: not a good thing. Quiet had settled around them. The only noise was that of water: the fountains, the sluices. The back of her neck prickled.

Ruth set off down one of the paths, heading for the centre of the Water Gardens. 'Come on, Cora – we don't have much time.'

'Didn't you hear what I said?' Cora called after her, all the while looking about her, trying to check the many paths and bridges around them. 'Marcus thinks there'll be more to come.'

'But not here,' Ruth said. 'Not now.'

Cora gestured to the small canals that snaked through

the Water Gardens. 'Take a look around you. We're in a place of *many rivers*.'

'No, Cora, we're not. These are fancy puddles. If I was at the bottom of one of these, I'd still be standing.'

That Cora couldn't argue with. But if Tannir hadn't been talking about striking at Ruth in the Water Gardens then that meant they had another problem.

Cora jogged to catch Ruth then spoke with bindle-shortened breath. 'Sounds like Tannir knows about the trip to get the Wayward Hook – Morton's man telling Tannir he'd be joining you at the bottom of a river.'

'*A* river, Cora. There are plenty in the Union.'

'You're saying it's coincidence? You're about to sail up the River Tun, and the man who's already made one attempt on your life just happens to mention waterways to an agent of the *other* person who wants you dead? Those are poor odds, Ruth.'

The quiet was lifting. Voices drifted towards them. Ahead was the garbing pavilion, its white canvas glaring in the sun.

'Not everything in life can be boiled down to bets, Cora. Winning this election, what it will mean, that's beyond the world of chequers.'

Cora was about to tell Ruth that she was wrong about that – elections were the biggest bet in the Union. On the tip of her tongue was the phrase people were endlessly saying to her: *Don't you read the pennysheets?* But there was no time.

They'd reached the back of the public gallery – rows and rows of seats all facing the covered bandstand that stood at the exact centre point of the Water Gardens. The bandstand was made from the same curling wrought iron that was found across the Water Gardens – the benches, the bird cages. But unlike those things, the bandstand was painted red and blue: the colours of the twin duchies of Perlanse. In the summer there were concerts here. If you happened to be passing in the streets above, you could hear the faint tunes and be reminded of the lack of pennies in your pocket to go through the gates and hear the music properly.

No sign of the masked voters yet, but the way the crowd was quietening, they were likely getting ready to leave the garbing pavilion and take their seats: fifty of them, set apart from those of the public gallery, and those of the Commission box too. She caught sight of the banners fluttering high above the box: one bearing the spoked wheel, symbol of the Commission, and six others, each with the symbol of a different realm. A sign of unity to have them all lined up like that, when the Union was anything *but* unified. The division between north and south felt as wide as the Tear itself. And just as dangerous.

The canopied Commission box was full – she could see the press of finely-clad people, if not the faces of the great and the good of the Union who'd be sitting there on padded chairs, flanked by side tables of drinks and tiny bits of food on sticks. All the Chambers would be in the Commission box, apart from Rustan Chambers Latinum who would be with her storyteller, out of sight, sharing some last words of encouragement. Senior Commission staff would be in the box too, Chief Inspector Sillian among them. At the thought of her former commanding officer, Cora was glad of the rows of people seated between her and the Commission box. Glad, too, of the Seeder clothes Nullan had found for her, though she wasn't about to start admitting that.

'Looks like we're too late for a seat in the public gallery,' she said to Ruth.

'We'll have to make do with this.'

Ruth sat on the wide stone lip of a fountain, the centrepiece of which was a bronze statue of two intertwined kenna birds – the ridiculously long-necked creatures that, twisted together like this, were the symbol of Perlanse. One for each of the Perlish duchies, east and west, because the Perlish could never do anything singly. Not even build a fountain. From the mouths of the kenna birds, water arced into the air. The spray cooled the air at Cora's back, which wasn't unpleasant, given the heat. The Commission box might be protected from the sun, but everyone else had to put up with it. How many election stories were remembered for the sunburn they came with?

The fountain's spray reaching her back meant a blow could do the same. They were unprotected here, the whole of the Water Gardens open behind them. Ruth was so confident nothing would happen here, but maybe...

A bell rang, sending such thoughts out of Cora's head. It was time.

Everyone got to their feet, and once the noise of the chairs catching on gravel had eased, there was silence. Someone had even thought to turn off the fountains: the cool spray at Cora's back vanished. The side of the garbing pavilion was raised by an unseen hand. From the darkness within, the Audience came.

They were themselves like the darkness they'd come from: fifty Fenestirans, drawn from a pool of three hundred to hear the Rustan story and cast their vote, all dressed in black robes. All black, except for the masks of the Audience which gave each voter their own flash of colour. As the voters made their way to their seats, Cora could make out the pale green of the Vicious Beginner, his mouth pursed, then the Dandy in brazen red, then came the Trumpeter in gold, her mouth an O to bellow. The whole Swaying mob came out of the garbing pavilion, each with a stone in either pocket: black for yes, white for no, to be cast into the huge voting chests at the end of the story. The Rustan tale was the fifth to be told. The Wayward would be the last.

A figure appeared in the bandstand – the Master of Ceremonies.

'Not a bad view,' Ruth said, 'all things considered.' The edge of the fountain she and Cora were sitting on was higher than the public gallery in front of them. Ruth patted it, as if it were a horse.

But the stone was hard beneath Cora, and with nothing to support her back, it was going to be a long afternoon. She'd taken off her coat and folded it on the stone ledge beside her. She kept her hand resting on the top of it, feeling the shape of her 'dusters tucked inside the cloth.

She stretched her back, and already there was the start of an ache. 'I might not be able to get up again,' she said to Ruth.

'Me neither. You'll have to fetch back that pennysheet girl to help us.'

'And have our ears assaulted for the second time today?'

The Master of Ceremonies opened his arms wide. 'Audience, welcome. In this, the two hundred and ninth election of our realms, we give you a 'teller who gives you a tale.'

'The Audience is listening,' came the response from the

masked voters. Had Constable Jenkins been beside Cora, she would have mouthed the words along with them. The Master of Ceremonies bowed to the Audience, then turned to bow to the second figure who was making their way into the bandstand.

The Rustan storyteller had arrived.

From this distance, Cora couldn't tell if it was a man or a woman. They were slim, their reddish hair clipped short as Ruth's now was. The storyteller looked to be her sister's age too. If the 'teller had any metal additions to their body – beyond the lockport in her spine that Serus said all adult Rustans had – Cora couldn't see it from here. She'd have to wait to read the pennysheets for a full description, though the hack writers would likely invent a few extra metal limbs.

'You saw the Hook,' Ruth whispered to Cora. 'What do you think the story will be about?'

'You mean you don't know? I thought that, given the southern alliance—'

'Storytellers would share tales in advance?' Ruth shook her head. 'That would be a break with tradition too far. All I know is that the message of the Rustan story will support that of the Wayward, and the Caskers too. Broadly speaking.'

'The Hook suggested the story might involve flying.'

'No surprises there,' Ruth said.

'And maybe jokes.' Cora was thinking of the dropped holens and the giggling Rustan children.

'A funny might not play well, given the exit polls after the Perlish story.'

'But Rustan humour wouldn't be the same as the Perlish,' Cora said. 'It would have more metal in it for a start.'

'Speaking of which…'

The Master of Ceremonies had stepped away, and the Rustan storyteller now stood at the centre of the bandstand, their head bowed, hands clasped before them. It was then Cora caught sight of a wink of silver: metal fingers. The storyteller slowly lifted their head, turned to look out at all those waiting in the Water Gardens – the Audience, those in the Commission box, in the public gallery, and at two Seeder women seated on the edge of a fountain. Cora felt the storyteller's gaze on her, and her pulse quickened. This was what made a great 'teller: the power to connect with a stranger before you'd even said a word. Would Ruth be up to this challenge? Her sister was looking down into the now still pool of the fountain, not watching the Rustan storyteller at all.

Cora looked back to the bandstand. The storyteller rocked on their heels, once, twice. Then they began.

'All things are new once.'

The Rustan Story

All things are new once. All things have a first sighting, a first use, a first telling.

But you people forget.

We tell the stories again and again until nobody can imagine a time without the riding of a horse. A time without fires in the night. A time without Rustans in the sky.

Old Man Berklum is a bonesmith, and a bonesmith is what Old Man Berklum is. From the top of his crown down to the nubs at the end of his toes: bonesmith.

Look to him now, hunching over his forge. Hunching from concentration, sure, but hunching because that's his way of holding himself in these, his latter years. But wait, I hear you thinking: How's a bonesmith not seen to his own problems? How's a bonesmith not righted his own crooked back, and a man of such purported talent at that? Ask him. Go on, ask him.

'Too invasive,' Berklum mutters. 'Spine work's dangerous.'

'What's that, Palla?'

Berklum looks up from the fire and metal in his lap. He has to squint across his own workshop to where his daughter, Unun, stands. She is fuzzy at the edges like only the young can be – still too much to be decided, they are incapable of being still. Or so Berklum thinks.

'I don't trust no one to work on me myself,' Berklum says.

'Is that what you're working on?'

It isn't, not by some long way, but Berklum can only shrug. 'Spine work's dangerous,' he says, and so he settles back to his hunching, the fire snapping and barking like a pricked dog.

A bonesmith's workshop bears some describing. But not as much as it bears some tidying. It is a dizzying place, even to those who've grown up there, like Berklum and Unun both. Tools hang from all four walls, only making grudging way for the low workshop door. The many tarnished and blackened iron tabletops are buried under sketches, half-formed hinges, sticks of charcoal and a graveyard's worth of bones cast in metal. Everything from knuckles and jaws to thighs and ribs. A charnel house. That's what you're picturing, isn't it? But that means death, the destruction of the body, bones pulled apart and out of their rightful living place. And there can be no denying the workshop is a dark, iron-tasting place, with more shadows than—

'Tallow costs too much,' Berklum says.

'I know, I know.' Unun comes to stand behind her beloved palla.

'Wayward trying to sell me candles like they brought the sun itself.' Berklum gestures with his pliers to the ceiling and to nowhere. 'Tell them forge-light is all a workshop needs. Tell them that.'

'Palla, the Wayward have gone.'

'Shh, girl, I'm working.'

'Tell them that,' he says. Forge-light is all a bonesmith and his workshop needs, but you can better picture Old Man Berklum, hunching, working, amid his many made bones if you can picture shadows.

Unun, a middling beauty, too generous with her time, melts back into those shadows.

The room snuffs to black. More so than even Berklum and Unun are accustomed to. He grunts. She makes a lighter noise. And then, from Berklum's fiddling at the forge comes a dazzling flare. It singes the strays of his bushy eyebrows and tightens the skin of his wrinkled face. When the forge settles, he holds the fingers in his pliers. Behold his work, as he does: the smooth thin lengths; the machinations of the knuckles; the tapering as natural as any unbroken bone. They look like a terrible claw, which is about the right of it.

'Finished?' Unun says, unable to keep the hope from her voice.

Berklum stares hard at the fingers. 'What do you think?'

How could we know? We did not take this order. Who are these fingers for? What were the measurements, what was asked for, how will they be affixed?

He waves away such questions. 'Listen to the girl.'

Unun leans close to the fingers, taking the pliers herself to better examine the work. 'Palla, they're finished!'

'Easy. No need to wake the whole spire.'

But there is a need. Unun glances about the workshop and its scattering of unfinished business. Orders unfulfilled, forgotten, discarded. How many days, months, years has it been?

'Not so long as all that,' Berklum says.

Unun's expression is schooled flat, which tells its own story.

Old Man Berklum stands and stretches that crooked spine, too dangerous to work on. He picks up a shinbone from among the detritus. 'Nothing to this,' he says. 'Where's the pride in such work?'

'Right next to the coin,' Unun says, but she can't meet his eye as she does so.

'Any bonesmith can make coin. You'll see that when the workshop's yours.'

'Palla, don't talk like that.'

His laughter grates along his three metal ribs. 'It's how Nibalt talks. I've heard him telling his stories to the Audience.'

'No...'

Yes. Nibalt, her husband, wheedles and whines, wishing today away for a tomorrow of his making.

'You see, they hear him,' Berklum says. His toothy grin does nothing to settle his daughter. Instead, she grasps the fingers as if they were opportunity made manifest. All this talk of her husband, Nibalt, has made her keen to be away from the workshop. To be away before his return from his work as a wincher. She can stand no more arguing between the two men of her home.

'We could take the fingers to the buyer,' she says.

'We'll take these to the buyer,' Berklum says, as if it were his own idea.

'But...' Unun hesitates. Doubts herself. 'They're all the way on the ridge.'

'That's not so far. Only one ropebox.'

'And who will pay for only one?' she says.

He wraps the fingers in the cleanest cloth he can find. 'I'm sure our buyer would find gratitude for us in saving them the trouble.'

'Gratitude.'

But he will not be dissuaded. When he claims the walk would be to an old man's benefit, Unun accepts defeat. He covers the forge, which kills the flames to embers, and gathers his stick. He uses this to walk and menace in equal measure. His thumb and little finger click into place at the head of the stick, the rest sitting neatly in his still fleshy palm. With a precise wiggle of his thumb he can extend the stick upwards of ten feet, the finger retracting the cane to a length of mere inches. Very useful for the busy walkways and ropeways of the spire.

'Don't forget the ridge,' Berklum says. 'No respect for no one, on the ridge.'

Said like a true spire-man.

'Palla, please, you know I don't go much for that kind of talk.'

'No one goes much for the truth.'

The workshop locks like a vault. Its door is thicker than Berklum or his daughter, far heavier, and worth more than any of their other possessions. Iron only on the surface, a far more complicated blend of metals hides beneath. Deeper still are the twelve locking mechanisms that Berklum laboriously sets to engaging – some with simple keys, some with ornate keys that look more like latticework or filigree, and some by pressed patterns that no one would recognise as a key.

Unun waits with practised patience, more interested in the narrow street that winds its way up and down from their home. Not cobbled, but the effect is not dissimilar. The street is a corridor – floor, building frontages, and vaulted ceiling all hewn directly from the rock of the spire. The floor's rock has worn smooth from generations of angled feet; rare are the times in the Rusting Mountains that you are neither going up nor down. It is hard to stand still. Unun wanders, not far, to the windows of the other shops and businesses that crowd the street.

Berklum joins her. He has to turn slightly to avoid colliding with two youngsters coming down at pace – the street not wide enough for three.

'You're welcome!' he calls once they are safely round the bend and away.

He stands beside his daughter, and together, they browse the window of a tailor.

The cuts are unusual. Daring, one might say. The materials he recognises, or at least he tells himself he does. Slipdog hide, tatterwing bat skin, feathers and furs from the Mountains. But looking deeper into the window reveals the Union in panels, linings, collars and cuffs. Colours made from the grinding of Torn beetles. Patterns that could be as easily inked on a Casker's arm as stitched onto a jacket. Hats that only the Perlish would find occasion for. He stares as if it is a travelling exhibit.

They are quiet for a while, thinking.

'Not just thinking, *looking*. Properly looking. Why else do we have eyes, as well as ears?'

Unun takes his arm in hers. 'I don't know, Palla, why?'

'Because we're too foolish to just listen. So we stare, and we talk, and somehow we learn. You can learn from seeing such things.' He presses a finger against the imperfect glass. 'See there? Who cuts a cloak so slim? What would that do to someone standing alone on the mesa?'

'Do?'

'Exactly. Without the wearing of it, we cannot know.'

She smiles the smile of the indulgent. Because that is easier, and Unun's time is hard enough. Arm-in-arm they make their way up the street, stopping to note new arrivals from the more adventurous traders. That trade is a benefit of being on the spire, the closest of the Rusting Mountains to the northern edge of the Tear. That the spire is the end of the mountain chain is the price they pay – getting to the cone is arduous, the mesa near impossible. That the fingers now nestling in Berklum's pocket were ordered by an individual on the ridge was no coincidence. Commerce can only travel so far, only so fast, along the mountains.

'You're quiet this evening, Palla. Are you tired?'

'I was just listening about the mountains.'

'What? I thought we were too foolish to just listen.'

'Sometimes it's in the lessons meant for others that we learn the most.'

Unun arches an eyebrow. 'Where did you hear that?'

'I didn't hear it. I just said it.'

She is unused to such wisdom from her palla. It worries her. Aphorisms are the harbingers of the dying mind. Fortunately, he keeps any more to himself.

The street ends in a series of steep steps. Normally Unun would tackle them without thinking. But her palla prefers to take the vertical ropebox, which they have to wait for. The woven box is its own kind of deliberately ponderous. Reassuring. Predictable. Safe. Berklum cranes his neck to watch it. The pulley system is as simple and old as the Rusting Mountains themselves. There was no living without the ropeboxes, from the very beginning. That was, except for the children.

'Do you miss your hairs?' Berklum asks.

Unun follows his logic easily enough – were she still a young child, she could have quickly climbed where the ropebox inched. 'Not always,' she says, a little surprised by her own honesty. 'But most days.'

'I've forgotten,' he says. 'I suppose you'll forget too, in your time.'

'I don't think so. That feeling... the freedom. It's still missing from me.'

'You cried. That first day and every day after for a whole year.'

'No—'

'You did. I cried too, for you,' Berklum says. 'To see you paw uselessly at a wall was the hardest thing. Worse than your meiter's death.'

Unun clears her throat. 'Meiter was ready. I wasn't.'

The ropebox settles drily on the ground. A lone woman nods her way past, and Berklum struggles to remember her name. Was she the tailor who knows her Perlish from her Wayward? No, no that is a taller woman. A baker? Did he see the ghost of flour in her hair?

It isn't until the ropebox lurches upwards that he realises he doesn't know the woman at all.

Three curling streets and two boxes later, they reach the top of the spire. There is a short queue for the ropeway over to the ridge. Unun knows the man ahead of them, and they enter into an easy, empty conversation. Berklum looks out, past the edge, to where the ropes run into the billowing cloud and smoke. The darkest patches are from the Tear below, ash-flecked and soot-heavy. The lighter, cleaner clouds descend from above but are soon stained. Everything that begins above is ruined, eventually.

'Not ruined, just different,' Berklum says.

Perhaps it is a matter of perspective.

'Look at that. Who could say ruined?'

Unun and her friend look too. Among the dark clouds, sparks flare into life and then die. So many, they flash like a shoal of fish.

'A what of fish?'

'You're right, Palla, it does look like a fish.'

'No, it doesn't,' her friend says. 'Besides, only tatterwings can fly in those clouds.'

Berklum squints at him. 'How is your shoulder?'

Without thinking, the man rolls his arm. 'Much better, much stronger. And no pain.'

'Good. Good.'

They resume their prattle, and Berklum resumes his vigil. He did not see fish scales in the clouds, he saw the Tear. He saw heat and violence – or the echoes of those things. Eventually, he sees the ropebox.

Winched along on metal-reinforced ropes, the box between the mountains is three times the size of the vertical kind. There is a wide, cleared area, which houses the large wheels of the mechanism as well as room for embarking and disembarking. The box thuds into place against its restraints. A door swings open, and a stream of people come out, including a couple of Seeders. They look paler than usual and not so steady on their feet. More than one person offers to help them along.

A man with brushes instead of hands begins working on the box's woven sides. Those in the queue turn away and cover their mouths as dust and ash fill the air. But the man's work makes sure there are no stray sparks or embers. Satisfied, the man gives a nod, and the queue begins to board. When their turn comes, Unun hands over the two pennies as if she might not see the like again.

'You worry too much,' Berklum says.

'You don't worry enough.'

'Then together we should satisfy the Keeper.'

'There's no satisfying any of them,' Unun says.

'Would a ropebox plummeting out of the sky do?'

More than one other passenger glares at Berklum. He waves them out of existence. He gazes out at the brutal, unrelenting beauty below. The black hills and red rivers of the Tear can only be seen in snatches between the clouds of smoke. From a thousand or so feet above, the land becomes an unreal thing: small when it is actually vast, quaint when it is deadly, barren when there is life. Perhaps it is because the view is never uninterrupted for long, but Berklum has not tired of it in all his years. It alone is worth the penny fare.

Unun is not so taken with heights. She stares resolutely at her hands. Hands she is trying to still.

'Tell me a story,' Berklum says, hoping to distract her.

'Palla, please.' Unun blushes, glancing at those nearby. Her friend is no longer with them, but on the other side of the basket.

'You don't visit any Seats,' Berklum says. 'You don't leave offerings, not at the workshop or anywhere I've seen. If you're so keen to please the Mute, you could stop nagging me so much.'

'Fine. A story.' The box lurches, and everyone tenses, many grabbing hold of the sides. Berklum takes his daughter's shaking hand and smiles.

'Our neighbour, four doors down,' she says, 'you know her but can never remember her n—'

'I do remember Iri!'

'Well, *Hassi*, she has two children. Two boys. She is up day and night with those boys. Her husband travels to the northern realms so often she's starting to wonder if she imagined the whole marriage. Except the boys are a regular cure for such wishful thinking.

'One of the boys, the younger, has recently found the joy of dropping things on his meiter. She endured the same with the elder. It's just a stage.'

'You did the same,' Berklum says. 'From the top shelves of the workshop.'

'Do you want to hear a story or not?'

Berklum nods. So do a number of other listeners.

'Hassi's youngest, he is nimble. When he can be made to concentrate, he's as fine a nester as any on the spire. Says he enjoys sneaking about the rockface and telling the Bailiff all about it after. All this is to say, he's not just good for climbing, but good for holding too. He drops nothing by accident.

'So when a metal foot hits Hassi top of the crown in her own home, she knows it's no accident. Least, she knows an hour or two later when she comes round on the floor, her blood sticky and tacky on one of their best rugs. When the room stops spinning, she looks up to find two pairs of eyes belonging to the most frightened two boys in the Tear. They've cried themselves silent, fearing she was dead.

'And Hassi, instead of raging or shouting, she starts laughing. This scares the boys all the more. They start crying again, and Hassi only laughs the harder.

'The foot belonged to her dead palla-in-law. When he was alive, she always said he'd be the death of her. "Almost," she said, hefting the foot.

'Now, any time her youngest son looks ready to drop something on her, she starts laughing. He soon thinks better of it.'

Those listening nearby smirk or find their own way of showing their appreciation for Hassi's struggles. Berklum is more pensive, and this is not lost on his daughter.

'Did you not like the story, Palla?'

'As good as any I've heard of late.' He spits over the side and rubs at his teeth. 'I made that foot,' he says.

'Made to last,' Unun says.

'Unlike the rest of him.'

There isn't much to say to that, so Unun goes back to staring at her hands, the other passengers at their feet, Berklum at the clouds. The story may not have been election-worthy, but it did what any story – good or poor – should: it passed the time. They are not so far from the ridge now. It is into this after-story quiet, when each man and woman is alone in that small crowd, that Berklum cries out: 'Rainbow!'

No one else hears him, not properly, just that the noise is enough to startle them. An unexpected noise from an old man, the kind most prefer to ignore. His daughter humours him.

'What's that, Palla?'

'Did you see it?' He turns to her, years younger. 'Did you?'

'See what? A tatterwing bat?'

'The rainbow.' He leans out, far as he can, and eyes the black ever-moving air below.

'But Palla, you need rain for a rainbow. We've had no rain in—'

'There!'

A flash of colour. A flash of all the colours. Not just the red of molten rock, or the orange of the embers. But blues and purples and greens and everything in-betweens. He sees them all in a parting of clouds.

She sees nothing. It is writ large and clear on her face. Where there should have been wonder, there is worry.

All the way to the ridge, he watches for more. He will not be dissuaded nor distracted, no matter how hard Unun tries. Eventually she gives up and leaves him to it, unable to join his hunt for the rainbow. She can't look out of the ropebox, not for long, the urge to throw herself out grows too readily, too strong.

Berklum doesn't see the colours again in the clouds between the spire and the ridge. But patience, bonesmith, they will come to you once more.

'So you say.'

There's little under the Audience that happens by accident. And even those rarities find their way into someone's story.

★ ★ ★

The ridge is wide and thin at its peak, and short as a mountain can be. We Rustans aren't too imaginative in our naming of things. We name it as we see it. A ropebox is a box threaded through with ropes. The Rusting Mountains are mountains the colour of rust. And each one of those mountains dresses a fair way different from the rest – like the flat, stunted ridge. That the other mountains look down on the ridge is just part of Rustan life.

Even so, Berklum should be too old for such nonsense. He's seen the good and the bad of all the Rusting Mountains and knows there's little between the two, little but perspective. But old habits have a habit of outliving their welcome.

He accepts a stranger's help down from the ropebox, Unun following behind him. They hurry from the hewn, sheltered landing; a woman is already brushing down the woven sides of the box, creating her own clouds. The steps that lead deeper into the ridge are steep but fortunately few in number. Berklum takes care with them, not concerned by the younger bodies streaming past him. Their haste is just their affirmation of what Berklum has known for a good while now: we all have somewhere to be, and no time to be there.

Unlike the winding, spiral streets of the spire, the ridge's main thoroughfare is a single, wide, flat affair. It's possible to go lower in the ridge, someway lower still, but the air is not so good down there. Unun takes her palla's arm as they make their way along the street. Many trades and shops have closed for the evening, while others are just getting started. At the entrance of a drinking establishment, Berklum slows, feeling a sudden thirst as if his throat is shaken down with sawdust. But Unun is having none of it. She doesn't drink, remember? Still blames the Seeders' spirits and hops for her meiter's passing. When she's not blaming you.

'That was a long time ago,' Berklum says, stopping at the swinging doors of the barroom.

Unun looks too. She's remembering another time, isn't she? Maybe you were there, Berklum, or maybe you were in the workshop. Maybe her meiter took her here, too young for such a place. What did she see? What did she hear? Was this a formative time for the little girl Unun, perched high on the wall of a barroom, her meiter drunk below?

Berklum glances at his daughter, frightened of what he might see on her face if he stares too long. He pulls her away despite his thirst.

At his age, when you've lived such a life, even a thirst is complicated.

Their destination is not so far now, and Berklum can see the forge-light warming the street as it darkens. Lanthan's workshop, so different from his own, but she's a bonesmith he respects nonetheless.

He clangs his metal knuckles against the workshop door and waits – the traditional Rustan way to announce oneself, metal-to-metal.

Lanthan is busy fixing a new hip. The smell of iron, old and new, is everywhere. The recipient is lying face down on a polished table, suitably senseless on a concoction of herbs and spirits. Lanthan's gloved arms are streaked red, and the woman is humming.

Berklum and Unun wait and watch, and they mostly watch while they wait. It is good to see another bonesmith at work – and not just at the forge. The affixing of a modification is just as much part of the craft as the crafting itself.

'You see how she parts the rear muscle and clamps it?' Berklum says. 'Good access for the joint.'

Unun nods. 'Though it can make for a longer recovery.'

'Some things take time.'

A face appears above them, over the door. A boy, maybe seven or eight years old, looks down at them impassively.

'Hello,' he says, his voice high-pitched but oddly flat. 'Meiter is busy.'

'We can see that...' Berklum struggles to remember the boy's name, until Unun rescues him.

'Thank you, Acti. We have a delivery of fingers.'

'Meiter hates fingers,' Acti says, as if this explains everything: their being there, Lanthan's current business, the whims of the wind.

'Tricky things, fingers,' Berklum says. He wiggles his own three metallic fingers on his right hand as if to demonstrate. 'Full replacement is impossible if you want this sort of movement. But grafting – there's where we can make some *real* wonders.'

Acti stares first at this strange old man's fingers, then at his own, which are covered in fine hairs. They may as well be different species. The boy is sitting on a narrow shelf that runs at two feet below the ceiling. Most Rustan rooms have such a shelf, unless a conscious decision is made not to have children. Or to never invite any inside. We've learnt the hard way that not providing such succour and comfort for our children increases the kind of bad behaviour that Unun's friend, Hassi, has endured.

This boy's shelf is bare of ornamentation, bare of potential projectiles, with only a pile of soft blankets in one corner. This is a very well-behaved little boy, even Berklum can see that. Unun can see it too – she herself had hoarded all manner of workshop tools and paraphernalia up on her shelf. She wasn't a dropper;

she simply enjoyed the having of things. Enjoyed the feel and shape and variety, and hiding them in a place for Unun and Unun alone.

For her, the hardest part of her friend Hassi's story is the idea of having a sibling. How horrible that must be.

'Come in, if you're coming,' Lanthan says finally, as she straightens. The recipient lies open still, their new hip joint settling into its pocket of bone and muscle. Lanthan rolls her neck, and there's an audible click and crank. Yes, Berklum, we know: spine work's dangerous, fingers are tricky, and no one appreciates a good bonesmith in their own time. We are listening.

'About time someone did,' Berklum says, satisfying everyone and ambling into the workshop. He is getting better at this, starting to understand how this might work – the telling of his story. What a relief, you think, he is starting to test your patience. It would be a long afternoon with Old Man Berklum otherwise.

They are all looking at him: Unun, Acti and Lanthan.

'Your fingers,' Berklum says, unwrapping them from the close-to-clean cloth. One index and one middle. Not complete, not inert blocks of metal in that way, but grafts made to measure. Flexible, useful.

Lanthan inspects the work, turning each graft over using a pair of delicate tongs. The middle finger is a series of connected partial tubes, shaped and filed to an exact depth and following a demanding set of contours. Berklum inspected the client's crushed hand not long after the accident, at Lanthan's request. She quickly recognised the need for Berklum.

It feels good to be needed, doesn't it, old man?

Berklum *harrumphs*, and Lanthan finishes her inspection.

'Fine work,' she says, 'as expected.'

'I appreciated the challenge.'

'Are you really that short of work?'

Unun almost chokes on her own tongue as a means of holding it.

'Work worth doing,' Berklum says. 'Ever since that second-rate butcher opened up on the cone... no one will travel for quality. I've been stuck making shins.'

Lanthan can only grimace. 'Save me the trip, and I'll send more work your way.'

'Good work,' he says.

'Good work,' she agrees. 'Care to watch me finish up?' It is an open invitation, but they all know it's first and foremost for Unun's benefit. She's eager, as a bonesmith's apprentice should be. You have to love the craft, love the work; that much, at least, Berklum has given her. She hurries to the table, bobbing like a bird to best see the other woman work.

Berklum watches long enough to satisfy himself of Lanthan's method of stitching, and then his attention wanders. The boy, Acti, is back on the shelf. But he is watching too. Everyone except Berklum looking at the prone body on the table, at the gradually disappearing wound, at the polished surfaces spattered in blood. Not at the blankets that fall from the shelf.

No one else sees it happen, do they, Berklum?

Acti is on the other side of the room. It's nothing to do with him.

The blankets fall, and inside them is a rainbow.

Another rainbow. The perfect ordering of colour. Nothing accidental or coincidental about it. The bleeding spectrum of all we can see, all we can know, how we understand the world around us. There, wrapped in the dirty blankets of a small Rustan boy.

As they hit the floor, everyone looks up at the noise. The

mystery dawns on them slowly – Lanthan turns to Acti, Acti shrugs, as surprised by his own innocence as anyone. But even his very presence is enough for the two women to relieve themselves of this small burden of the unknowable – the boy, the shelf, the blankets falling from a height. Simple cause and effect, even if they can't quite discern every connection.

But not you, Berklum, you don't dismiss it. For you, it's the second small wonder of the day.

He stands before the pile of blankets as if it is a shrine to the Stowaway. He's ready to offer up his secret, his story of a secret, in return for... what, Berklum? What would you like to know?

'Who is she?'

She, Berklum? *She*? What is this 'she'? A rainbow beneath you in clouds, a rainbow beneath you in blankets – where is the woman in this?

'A girl,' he mumbles.

Oh. Oh, I see. That is how you've decided to shape this idea, this happening: a girl. Is she in the rainbow, or of the rainbow?

'She *is* the rainbow.'

Ever the romantic, ever the sentimentalist. This is what comes of cutting people open and replacing parts of them with metal. There is nothing left for a man or woman who does such a thing daily; they must at some stage find beauty somewhere. So this is yours, Berklum: the rainbow girl.

He kneels at the blankets but doesn't offer the Stowaway a story. Instead, he wants to find one. He reaches out, tender and tentative, and picks up a blanket. Rough – even to his calloused hand – he wants it gone, away from her, so he tosses it aside. Nothing. Another blanket, this time too threadbare to even register. Still nothing. More and more blankets are cast from the heap, but no girl.

There! You see it, don't you? A flash of blue running to purple? Hurry, Berklum, hurry before she's gone again.

He is frantic; he isn't thinking, not breathing properly. So when he sees it on the bare rock floor, he doesn't recognise it. He searches for a girl, perhaps curled in on herself, perhaps lying on her back, perhaps crouched and ready to run.

He stares at the feather.

'A feather.'

That's right. That's what it is. He knows this because of the hollow shaft at the bottom. But if it weren't for that, he would struggle. It is large, too large for any of the birds in the Tear; wings that size would be a liability with all the embers and hot ash in the air. Mark that, Berklum: a liability.

But look at those colours! The vane is a long, almost square bar of unrepentant colour. The base of red, shifting through shades that are only too familiar, but then comes the shock of it. Blue and green, Berklum. They are enough to part the clouds that swirl between the Rusting Mountains. They are what catches your eye among a Rustan boy's rags. It is hard for anyone who lives outside the Tear to understand the rarity of real blue and green. So easy are they to take for granted when one is always above, another always below.

Tell them, Berklum. Tell them when you have seen such a thing.

'Never.'

Quick, you must hide it. Quickly now, old man.

'Palla? Are you all right?'

Good, good, into your heavy robe with it. Make sure no hint or flash of incriminating colour can be seen. They will take it from you. How could they not?

Unun kneels beside her palla. She doesn't understand why he

is down there, the pile of fallen rags off to one side, the bare floor in front of him.

'I... I thought I saw a stray spark,' he says. 'In the blankets.'

Masterful. Bravo. We will shape this story, together, into a legacy. One that won't be forgotten again.

She helps him back to his feet. His explanation hasn't quite satisfied, but she isn't sure why. She feels it, doesn't she, Berklum? The tug and pull of events beyond our control. Impossible to discern in the moment, but they crystallise with the hindsight of generations. Now, Unun feels her palla lying to her, and she doesn't know why.

'I'm not lying,' Berklum says, as any good, dishonest man would. 'I saw something.'

'I know, Palla, I know.' She holds his hands for a touch too long. Then she leads him back to Lanthan's table. They watch the woman stitch the livid flesh of a hip, careful but assured, as if closing the door of another's home behind her. Unun asks questions unobtrusively. Lanthan applies a salve to ease the anger and memory of her incision, and to avoid infection.

For a long minute, they stare down at the prone body. Two bonesmiths and their apprentices. That tug and pull again, Berklum. You feel it, don't you? The symmetry of the four of you, attending this table, here in this workshop. How could it be anything *but* the beginning of a story worthy of the Audience?

No, don't touch the feather. Not yet. Not yet.

Old Man Berklum, the bonesmith, returns home with his daughter and with his secret. They don't stop – not for a drink, not to look in windows, not to talk to strangers. Berklum has eyes only for his feet. He doesn't want to see the rainbow again.

Why not, Berklum? What has you so scared? Are the colours too much for a Rustan of your years? And look how Unun worries.

That's right, you've both been furtive since leaving Lanthan's workshop. In the quiet streets of the ridge and in the ropebox back to the spire. She wonders why you don't look out at the clouds, or down at the Tear, or ahead to home. She isn't used to you mirroring her, both turned inwards, shoulders hunched against the catastrophes that are all too easy to imagine. Just how strong are those ropes, do you think? How old are they? How many journeys have they felt the strain of, how many times have they gone slack then tight then slack? You don't want to answer such questions. That's understandable. Perhaps you're tired of questions, just as you're tired of talking.

That's one story of the Audience. You've surely heard it, though perhaps you don't believe. This story says the Audience is so old, so ancient that they stopped wanting to talk altogether. They have nothing left to say. They have seen too much, heard too much, and so little changed. It explains their silence, doesn't it? Not the Silence, but their silence. But perhaps there's not so much difference between the two. Both are total, seemingly unending, and it's frightening to dwell on either for long.

The point of this story, Berklum, is that we may want an audience's attention, we may demand it even, but their silence? Their total, unending, damning silence? Nothing could be worse for a storyteller.

And yet, people tell their stories to the Swaying Audience every day.

Where's the applause?

'You were keen to be away from our workshop today,' Berklum says, eager himself to think on something, anything, else. 'Why?'

Unun sighs. She had just been pondering the same. She

considers her own lie, or perhaps the simpler approach of silence. 'Because of Nibalt.'

Is that your doing, Berklum? Raising a daughter who can't lie? At least, not with you looking right at her.

'Why because of Nibalt?' he says.

'He would have been... difficult. If we'd seen him before the sale, there would have been an argument, I just know it. He says you haven't sold anything in months.'

'He's right, I haven't.'

Unun turns to face her palla. 'He thinks it's time I take over the workshop.'

'He's probably right again.'

'Palla, no!'

She's scared, Berklum, but you don't need to be told that. You see it for yourself, and you were the same at her age. Such a thing is too much responsibility. What good does responsibility do for the young?

'But I was always going to sell those fingers,' he says. 'Why would Nibalt have been a problem?'

'It's not that simple, is it? One sale in months – he would see that his way.'

'One sale in months.' Nibalt says this, these exact words, as his wife foretold. He stands, huge, in their small kitchen. One eyebrow arches, thicker than most men's fingers, and he blows on his tea. Nibalt drinks tea when he returns from work. It helps his aching muscles, and he's not too proud to admit it. He is one of the unseen winchers of the spire. His toil keeps Rustans moving. So he drinks tea, like an ox cradling a white tulip.

'Fingers,' Berklum says, wiggling his own. 'Good work.'

'All work is good work,' Nibalt says.

'Not so, not to someone who creates. There's a difference.'

'If you say so.'

'I do!'

Unun puts a hand on her husband's arm. 'Please,' she whispers, just for him. Look at them, Berklum. Look how they tolerate you, your outbursts, your whims. See the restraint from a man who handles taut ropes all day long. Which will snap first, do you think?

Nibalt sips his tea. He embraces Unun – they kiss, they are young again with each other. Her worries lift like the bad clouds they were.

Because the man is no ogre. He may hulk like one, and wouldn't that be simpler for those listening? If he threw that bulk of his around, broke the already chipped crockery, raised his hand to his wife. Drank, whored, smoked bindleleaf. An easy figure to hate – isn't that what we'd prefer Nibalt to be? You shake your head, Berklum, because you know. You *know* it doesn't work like that. Life isn't so simple. But our stories are. So, what is this, Berklum? Your life or your story? Maybe we'll decide later, when we're near the end.

'He's no ogre,' Berklum mutters.

Not an ogre, no. He wants to replace their winter throw with something thicker, something with Seeder wool or Perlish down. He wants to buy cuts of meat without wincing as he hands over the marks. He wants his wife to be happy in her work, not fretting about her palla. Does an ogre want such things?

'I said he wasn't.'

That you did, Berklum, that you did. But away with you now, old man. Shoo, shoo, down to your workshop and leave us with the two lovers. We deserve a little lightness. We deserve the warmth of another. There must be more to our stories than the shadows we cast, or the disappointments we swallow, or the hurt we turn our back on. We're not done with you yet, Berklum, and we know where to find you. Everyone knows.

'He looks worse today,' Nibalt says, once they're alone. 'Pale.'

'He insisted we both go to the ridge. I should've known it would be too much.'

Unun pours herself tea, as her husband readies a meagre meal. It is he who chops the vegetables, picks the single spice and rations the salt, stirs the broth. She has no aptitude for such simple tasks – she's a bonesmith, albeit an apprentice. Whatever she turns her hand to, turns to metal. At least, that's what Nibalt says. A broth such as the one he prepares now would somehow, under her influence, become molten. Filings would settle on the bottom, rust would redden where pan meets broth, and every mouthful would make him suck his own cheeks. She can't taste such things, and he says that's the problem: she has no taste. You can imagine the jests that follow well enough.

So, instead she watches him. He chops vegetables as if guided by an equation. Their asymmetrical nature is a challenge to be overcome, a form of chaos to be set to order. Occasionally he is bested and must resign himself to uneven chunks of potato, though tonight he is satisfied. The rhythmic thud of knife on board is a soft way to fill their silence. But it doesn't last long.

'Did he really sell something today?' Nibalt asks.

She wonders how deep his distrust goes – a disbelief that her palla might actually make a sale or, worse still, that they might lie about it.

'Fingers, just like he said.' She puts down her cup as if to say, this is serious, I'm telling the truth, you can believe if you try. 'And there was promise of more.'

'More?'

'The bonesmith on the ridge,' Unun says. 'She's so busy, she has more work than she can manage.'

'Wouldn't that be something.'

'She said she'll pass on work like fingers. The kind of work Palla likes.'

Nibalt clears the chopping board straight into the pot. 'That's good,' he says, but Unun can't be sure if he means the broth or the news of work. He measures, to the grain, the salt he adds. 'The food is almost ready,' he says. And without needing to be reminded, he sets out three bowls.

Meanwhile, Berklum descends to his workshop, away from his family. He locks the door behind him, and this is the door from the house to the workshop. An internal door, for the use of those that work and live there, not one to be used by customers. He locks it now because he doesn't want Unun to follow him. Why is that? We might wonder.

But Berklum doesn't know why either, he just did it. He crosses to the forge and stokes the embers. Why? He doesn't know that either, not really. There's a want in him somewhere. It's strong but old, and its roots are as deep as anything that grows on the spire. He just calls it 'good work'. Those are only words – weak things to describe something much greater.

So, he stares at the hot colours of the forge and finds some comfort there. Red, orange, yellow. Colours he knows better than any other. Better than the blue of a sky the Union takes for granted. Better than the green the Seeders work so hard for. He sits with those familiar colours like friends who don't need to talk. He sits, then falls asleep. But not for long.

★ ★ ★

'Hello?'

Wake up, Berklum. You heard right: someone is calling for you. You aren't dreaming, but it will feel that way. It will feel that way for some time.

'Hello?'

Berklum comes to in his worn, tough slipdog-hide chair. It has as many scars and burn marks as he does. His mouth is tacky with sleep, and he can smell his own stale breath. Not the most glorious way to wake up, and not an unfamiliar one – a marriage bed is a sharp kind of loneliness to a widower. A day of aches and pains is preferable to that. But Berklum, we're losing our focus. There was a voice, remember?

He grumbles by way of a response.

Look who's here, Berklum. You have to look, up there. See?

A small, round face, framed with blonde hair. A girl.

That's your first thought, and it's not so wrong as to be worth telling the Drunkard. A little girl up on the high workshop shelf. Such a thing has happened before: Unun loved to watch you from up there. And she wasn't a dropper, remember? She respected the workshop. A dream, that's your second thought. A palla's dream of simpler times that were, at the time, anything but.

Only, Unun isn't – wasn't – blonde.

Unun didn't look so old when she was so young. This girl, she looks old. Even with her round, pink cheeks that are so smooth you doubt they have ever seen the sun. But age shows in many ways.

'Hello, Berklum.'

You flinch at your own name – your name said in a girl's voice, but with the weight of all the Audience behind it. Your hands are shaking, Berklum.

'H—' He clears his throat. 'How?'

How, indeed. But how... what?

The girl smiles, and he's ready to weep in relief. Both the internal door and the workshop door are still locked. He locked the latter in leaving, the former in coming – locked from the inside. These are the details he remembers, details that he clings to, even as their clarity tells him – as we keep telling him – this is not a dream.

'There's no need to be afraid,' the girl says.

He didn't realise he was scared until she said so.

'How did your parents? Where did you get in here?' He muddles his questions, but she understands. She understands that, and so much more.

'I'm coming down now. Don't be scared.'

Why, why would you be sca—?

She unfurls her wings and glides down from the shelf.

She has wings, this girl, as long as her arms and sprouting from her shoulders. Her feathers are all the colours of the rainbow.

From inside his robes, Berklum pulls the feather he found earlier. It's hers, as if there could be any doubt. He holds it out to her, but she shakes her head.

'That was a gift,' she says. She stands before him, no more than four feet tall, and entirely at ease. Her arms hang by her side, and her wings at rest. She is wearing a pale blue dress, cinched with string around the middle. Her hair is bound by a wreath of ivy. All of which is to say, she could not possibly look *less* Rustan.

'I saw you,' Berklum says, 'in the clouds.'

'You did.'

She had been flying in the Tear, as easily as she flew down from the shelf.

This eclipses all other thoughts for Berklum. His earlier questions – how she came to be in his workshop, where her parents were, sensible questions, both – are forgotten. Were he to follow either too far, he would not like the answers, because they speak of even less tangible impossibilities than a girl with wings.

'May I see your hands?' he asks softly.

She rocks back on her heels, then forwards, before giving a little nod. It's a precocious gesture, more innocent than she has seemed so far. We are growing to like this girl, aren't we, Berklum?

She shows him her palms, because she knows what he is asking. They are as bald as his own, but smooth where his are lined and calloused.

'Would you like to see my feet?'

She has one half-raised before he says no.

'I've never had the hairs,' she says. 'Not in all my years.'

Listen to her, talking like she has more stories for the Audience than you do. Perhaps she does. One of those stories could tell of a Rustan aberration. A girl with wings, hiding between the ridge and the spire, cast out by a family unable to understand their own daughter. No friends her own age; those hair-handed children who climbed like spiders would look jealously at her flight. It is just as plausible a story as any other. But it's not true.

'Why me?' he says.

She leans closer, so close her button nose almost touches his own. 'Because we're going to do great things together, Old Man Berklum who is a bonesmith, and a bonesmith is what he is.'

There is a knock at the internal door.

He is distracted, the shock of being caught – caught doing

what exactly is not so clear as the feeling – and when he turns back, the girl is gone.

'Palla?' Unun calls through the door. 'I have dinner.'

He isn't hungry, but she doesn't like it when he doesn't eat. She doesn't like it when he locks the door either. What if something happened? That's what her look says now, as he stands back to let her in. Well, it did happen, didn't it? A girl with rainbow wings.

Unun clears space for a bowl of broth on one of the tabletops. She moves a few paces away, and waits. She is waiting for him to eat – she won't believe unless she sees it for herself. Berklum obliges his daughter mechanically, spoon to bowl, to mouth, to bowl, all the while thinking of what the rainbow girl said: great things. And she said it with our words, the impish little thing.

'Palla, what's this?'

Berklum blinks. The spoon wavers halfway to his mouth. Unun is holding a rainbow in her arms, and for a moment he sees a body in its folds – small, mostly skin and unmodified bones. Then she shakes the blanket open, and by the way she looks at the air in surprise, she expected dust and soot but finds it clean. A clean rainbow blanket. Berklum stifles a cry, pretending to have choked on the broth. He steadies himself at the tabletop, but Unun is not so easily fooled.

'Is this new, Palla? I've never seen it before.'

Careful, Berklum, such a colourful extravagance. 'A gift,' he says. 'From a neighbour.'

'Which one?' she says.

'I don't remember. They're all too nosey to leave me alone.'

'That's nice of them,' Unun says, unable to keep the doubt from her voice. Generous, guileless Unun.

'Tomorrow, I want you out of the workshop,' he says. 'I need peace, and you need some time with your husband.'

'Palla, I don't—'

'No!' he says with enough force to shock them both. 'No.'

In the ensuing silence, she folds the rainbow blanket and puts it next to his leather chair, where he sleeps. 'Don't get cold,' she says quietly before she leaves.

Does she have a name? This is what he wonders as he watches the rainbow girl from beneath the blanket. She is tidying the workshop. In those first waking moments, he was gripped by a familiar concoction of irritation, irrationality and possessiveness – his workshop is his place of business, his livelihood, where he practises his craft, of which he is a master. Who is this little girl to tidy it, wings or no? Had he been fully awake, some kind of eruption would have been inevitable. Instead, he watches her and that volatile concoction changes to something tempered by a grudging admiration. The girl seems to know exactly how to carry his tools: with an amount of respect that doesn't tip into reverence. She knows where they all belong in the chaos. Once cleared, she wipes and polishes the tabletops. She clears the ashes from the hearth and banks it with fresh coal. But she does not light it.

Instead, she busies herself among Berklum's rolls of paper. They are in the far corner of the workshop, as far from the hearth as possible, and he has to push himself up to see her properly.

'What are you looking for?' he says.

By way of answering, she makes a triumphant noise and pulls out a large roll of paper. Perhaps the largest of them all. Her prize in hand, she hops onto the big tabletop with a flutter of her wings.

A small, unconscious thing for her, but somehow, it has such beauty to send a crack along the hardened shell of an old man.

'First we must draw them,' she says.

'Draw what?'

'That's how this works, isn't it? When someone wants you to make something, you draw it first?'

He shuffles over to the tabletop, doing his best to ignore the aches of yet another night sleeping in a chair. 'When someone engages my services as a bonesmith, they first tell me their name.'

'Why?'

'So I know whose order is whose for a start.'

'Do you have many customers with these?' she says, stretching her wings and rolling her shoulders.

'It also helps when talking to them. I can't keep calling you "the girl with rainbow wings".'

Quite right, Berklum, that won't do at all. We're already tiring of that phrase, no matter how vote-winning it was to begin with.

'What would you like to call me?'

'So far, nothing but a nuisance.'

A nuisance that has tidied your workshop. Oh, Berklum, if only you drank even a drop, you'd be a favourite of the Drunkard.

'Newsands,' the girl says, cleaning the sound somehow to make the 'new' and the 'sands' ring clear as crystal. 'I like that.'

We like that too, seeing how it irks Berklum.

'Well then, *Newsands*, what would you like me to make you?'

'Draw first,' she says.

'Yes, yes, draw first then I make it. That is, if you can afford it.'

The girl smiles, which changes her from a girl to something much different. 'Don't worry, this isn't for me. It's for you. All of you.'

Did you feel that? A chill?

No, you don't believe in that sort of thing, do you, Berklum?

But we do. We felt it.

'All of us?'

'That's right,' she says. 'It's time you found your wings.'

Perhaps this is a development the Audience anticipated? Perhaps having listened to so many stories – thousands of stories over thousands of years – members such as the Musician or the Weaver spotted the symbolism earlier in our tale? Was Newsands' gift of a feather too much, they may ask? Surely not for the Drunkard or the Dandy, not for those easily distracted or those who seek a simple escape in their stories? Those Audience members will be wondering just how Berklum, an old bonesmith who only wants to do good work, could ever turn his hand to something so ambitious, so audacious as sending the Rustans to the sky.

And the Critic? Well, there is no pleasing them, is there?

But Berklum, he was not expecting such a twist.

He stares hard at this little girl, this Newsands who appears and disappears on a whim, who comes bearing promises of great things without a coin purse about her person. One day it will shame him to recall his first thought at this moment, but we understand when he says, 'Unun won't like it.'

That aging smile from the girl again. 'Oh, she will. She will.'

So mollified – and it didn't take much – he turns to the blank roll of paper. He weighs it down at the corners with a hammer, some tongs and two metal toes, and then smooths the surface with his hand. A simple, unconscious gesture that became habit long before he became the master of this workshop.

'Wings,' he says.

Not so hard to imagine, are they, especially with a bright pair right in front of you.

'May I?' he asks.

She opens them, stretching them as wide as they'll go, by way of invitation. The violet band at the bottom of her wings separates, each feather becoming a spear tip, fading to shafts of blue and green until they are bands once more. He runs a finger delicately up the rachis. Is that a new word to you, Berklum? No. Of course not. A bonesmith knows such words, words that describe the parts of things. Not so different from a spine, really. And what do we know about spine work?

'It's dangerous,' Berklum mumbles, good sport that he is.

But this is a wing, a feather, and this is the hollow shaft where it meets the colourful barbs – the rachis. The Audience know this word, but it never hurts to remind them of their knowledge.

Further up he touches the deep red of the downy top covering. Here, he presses the issue and feels solid bone. But light, so light he worries his touch has hurt her, and he glances to her face. She is staring just as he had, as if the wing is a new wonder to her too. She looks terribly serious, Berklum.

'Impossible,' he says, letting the wing go. He briefly considers the blank paper, then flees from it. 'Impossible,' he tells the furthest wall. 'Impossible.' He rubs his hands on an oiled rag, just to rid himself of the feel of feathers.

'And yet...' She pirouettes.

And yet.

'You're too heavy,' he says.

She pouts. Then proves him wrong by flapping her way up to the high shelf. There she settles, kicking her heels against the wall.

'We're too heavy. Our bones, our muscles, our organs. None of it purposed for such a thing as wings.'

'Are we purposed to run as swiftly as a horse?' she says.

'No.'

'Can you see as far as the eagle, Berklum?'

'No.'

'But you *can*, by arranging curved pieces of glass. You arrange for the horse to do the running for you. And you even root through fire as the ash beetle does, thanks to those metal tools of yours.'

'That is different,' he says, obstinate. But despite himself, he is gnawing at the edges of the problem. He drifts back to the paper, and begins to draw.

What of dear Unun? You may ask. Banished from the workshop – banished from what is now her palla's, but will one day be her own. Is she enjoying a day with her husband? Don't laugh, hold your cynical sniggers, such a thing is possible. But, sadly not for Unun. Her dear husband has already washed, dressed and departed. He looked tired. He did not sleep well.

In fact, neither of them did, with Unun tossing and turning. She does the same now, awake, lying among twisted, threadbare sheets. She is wrestling with more than just the peculiarities of her palla; she is wrestling with her future. Something she is caught between wishing for, and wishing away. At least the Audience understand such mortal complexities.

Eventually, when she can turn over the soil of her problems no more, a seed of an idea falls – from where, who could say – onto that most ready of places: the restless. She only glimpses it, a flash of a thought, dismissed for being too bold but alluring all the same. She could ask... but no, no, that would not do. They might... no, no, why would they?

It wouldn't be the first...

'No!' she says, wringing the sheets with both her hands. Though she knows this seed will grow regardless, she still finds solace in fighting it.

At the basin, she splashes cold water on her face, washes under her arms and dresses in a simple, thin robe. She does this because it is what she does in the morning. She eats because she is hungry, and chews mint because she likes the taste. None of this is because she intends to visit someone. And that someone couldn't be an old friend.

And that old friend couldn't be, by chance, a moneylender.

Ah, the games we play with ourselves.

Unun makes ready to visit Hassi, the moneylender who nearly died by the metal foot of her palla-in-law. By the time she closes the door behind her – not the workshop door, with all its locks and heaviness, but the house door, which is plain and locks just once – by the time she is on the street, the game of that morning is gone. In its stead is resolution.

She will borrow money today, enough to clear their old debts and enough so Unun may take over the workshop. Somehow she convinces herself such a thing is a clean start. She decides it is time for her palla to retire.

Do you hear that, Berklum?

He can't, not through that heavy workshop door, not through the years of quiet servitude that Unun has given him. Besides, he is too busy drawing the impossible.

Unun doesn't have to go far, just four doors down. Hassi's home is large, but not ostentatiously so – it just isn't burdened by a bonesmith's workshop. Unun knocks, metal to metal, and waits.

She is kept waiting just long enough for a seed of doubt to fall – from where, who could say – beside the sapling that has become her conviction. Until this moment, she hadn't realised how closely she'd been clinging to that conviction, how important the feeling of doing *something* was. She doesn't want to feel lost again.

The door opens. Purpose returns.

The core of an apple flies past her shoulder and is swallowed by the street.

'Osum, that's enough!' Hassi says. She is wielding a broom like a spear, jabbing at the monster of her own making, the monster that stalks the high shelves of her home. Her youngest. 'Back. Back I said. Meiter has a visitor.'

A pudgy face appears in the top corner of the doorway. 'She's not wearing shoes.'

Both women look at Unun's bare feet with equal surprise.

'I... Sorry,' Unun says. 'I'll come back.'

'No!' Hassi says with a vehemence that surprises them both. 'No, please, come in.' She applies the broom liberally, and a flurry of boyish limbs retreats from the doorway.

Hassi's home smells of old, dust-laden rugs. It's not unpleasant, just different. Bonesmiths have no love for rugs – they catch fire too readily. But Hassi has decked her home in them; so many patterns that Unun finds it difficult to look in any one place for long, but they are soft beneath her feet. She is led into a comfortable reception room – another luxury lost to a bonesmith – and offered a seat. There's a small hearth, laid but not lit, and a table between the two settees. The table is conspicuously clear.

As Unun sits, she keeps her gaze firmly set on Osum, the little boy perching high above them. More specifically, his hands, in case he finds something more substantial than an apple core to throw. Like a metal foot. When Unun told her palla the story of the foot, she embellished as any good storyteller does. There was no end to Osum's dropping; his meiter's laughter did nothing to stop him – though it made for a better story, didn't it?

But it is a wail, not laughter, that begins *this* turn in the story.

Such a sound of pain, low and guttural, that everyone glances back to the doorway. What wounded animal is this, that stalks the halls of a moneylender?

'My eldest boy,' Hassi says, no more than a whisper. 'He's lost his hairs.'

Unun gasps, raising her bald hand to her mouth, her own pain remembered afresh then.

'He just wanders the house, making that sound, always running a hand along the wall. He screams worse if I try to pull him away.'

'Oh, Hassi…'

'He won't go outside. Scared he'll see his friends.'

'Why?' Unun says.

'He's early. This shouldn't have happened for another year yet.'

An extra year, a year of wailing isolation; the enormity of such a thing is not lost on Unun.

'I'm so sorry.'

'Osum, take your brother upstairs,' Hassi says.

But the boy doesn't move from the high shelf. He stares at the open doorway. From the twist of his lips and the sweat lining his hair, he knows exactly what horrors lie beyond. The horrors of adulthood.

'My boys will have plenty to tell the Amateur, and others besides.' Hassi pours Unun a glass of water. 'Plenty of stories for those leeches.'

Unun forgives the woman's mild blasphemy, knowing the

Audience hear much worse every day; insults they can abide, it's Silence they abhor. Even the Mute, the self-loathing fool. Caught between the wanting of a thing, and the shame of that wanting; who would be so at war with themselves? Whether it's stories, or a bonesmith's workshop... Who would spend their life that way, Unun?

She doesn't answer. That's a privilege of her palla's. Instead, she tries to express her sympathy once more, but Hassi has had her fill.

'So, what brings you four doors down?' Hassi says.

'Without shoes,' Osum adds.

Unun blushes, can't help it, but at least her feet are fairly clean. 'Business,' she says. 'I want to borrow some money.'

'"Want",' Hassi echoed. 'That's not a word I hear so often. *Need* – that's what I hear more.'

'It's not like that.'

'What is it like?'

Unun can't look the woman, or her youngest son, in the eye. But she at least has the strength to say it out loud. 'When I take on the workshop, I don't want to take on my palla's debts too.'

'Why?'

The simple questions are the hardest to answer.

'Because I'm not buying the workshop from him now,' Unun says, firmly. 'The loan is to secure the future of it. So I *control* the future of it. That's mine, and I want it on my own terms.'

'And what terms are those?'

'The kind that are mine, not my palla's. The kind I decide on.'

'I see. That we can accommodate.'

Old Man Berklum, a bonesmith for more years than he's been a father, is also wrestling with numbers. These numbers won't sit still on the paper. If he so much as glances away, they skitter and shift, arranging themselves as they see fit into no kind of order. Wilful numbers that defy his attempts to tame them, and to tame the forces they represent.

He hunches over his table, a lone candle close enough to warm the side of his temple. If he had hair left, singeing would be a real risk. In the shadows of that candle, roll after roll of discarded papers are scattered about the floor. All kinds of sketches, some detailed and intricate, others no more than impressions in fat lines of charcoal. But for their differences they have a singular thing in common: the sweep of a wing.

This, of course, is the easy aspect of the impossible. The difficulty comes in making such a sweep translate to flight.

That he can't do it is quickly apparent. There is just no amount of molten, shaped metal that can turn Rustan into bird. But he tries, and tries again. His fingers are blackened to the second knuckle from the charcoal and his eyes dry from staring.

When he finally does put down the charcoal and stretch his grumbling back, he realises he is alone. The high shelves are empty of little girls with rainbow wings. He feels the sudden, irresistible urge to touch those wings again, to feel the varying softness of the different feathers. He wants to hold that which he's been hunting among rolling dunes of paper; he wants to see those colours after so much black and white.

But she is not there.

Was she ever there, Berklum?

'Yes, yes,' he mumbles. He has proof, doesn't he? Something more reliable than his own memory: a feather.

He lifts sheets on the table, sending their numbers tumbling again, but the feather isn't there. Was it ever there, Berklum?

'Yes, yes.'

He kicks the rolls on the floor, then wonders if the feather might be inside them. He picks up each one and peers at it with a single, fat eye searching for colour. The jumbled, tumbling, rolling black lines mock him: his failure to bring a simple impossibility into the world. We can all imagine wings, can't we? The biggest wings we've ever seen – we can picture those. And we can imagine them sprouting from the back of a person. It's not so hard, once we try. It almost feels natural, as if we *should* have wings. Perhaps they were taken from us? That's a comforting thought, Berklum; you aren't trying to create, but reclaim.

He lifts everything in the workshop that isn't bolted down. Some things he lifts twice. He shakes out his blankets, searches the gaps in his old slipdog hide chair, runs a hand along the high shelves.

In defeat, he looks about his workshop, taking in the disarray.

But there's one place you didn't look, Berklum.

'No, not there.'

Yes, there.

'It can't be...'

Burnt up in the hearth? It can, it might, it probably is. Though knowing will be the challenge – those brilliant colours won't bleed into the feather's own ashes, surely? Like so much in the Rusting Mountains, the hearth's colours are fixed. Who can tell one set of ashes from another? But first you have to look.

That's right, slowly, Berklum. That way the feeling can grow. It spreads from the pit of your stomach, going deep into your bones and turning them to lead – those not already turned by your own hand, of course. Leaden steps for a leaden heart.

'No one touches the heart,' Berklum says.

Oh, Berklum, if only you could hear yourself. How sad you sound, and how right you are.

Unable to stop himself, he peers into the hearth's embers, looking for what he doesn't want to see. He can accept the shades of grey, the cores of black, and the colour that fidgets from deepest red to sharpest yellow. He tells as much to the Beholder. Tells a story of the beauty found in low flames. Beauty enough for anyone. It doesn't need anything more. Let that be a separate story.

'Look up,' Newsands says, her small voice unmistakable despite her being nowhere to be seen.

He doesn't want to, fearing his feather will just be ash scattered about the chimney of his hearth.

'Look up,' she says again, but more encouraging this time.

There! See? All the colours of the rainbow on a single feather, bobbing and weaving in the black chimney flue. Is it stuck? That is our first thought, but not yours, Berklum. Yours is joy. Something pure, unburdened by reason or rationale. You are so happy to see it. Your eyes, Berklum, they're no longer dry. So happy.

You don't want to hear it now, but you'll know this later: you're happy because you believe this is proof.

Of what? Well, that's still to be decided, isn't it?

'Do you see it, Berklum?' Newsands says. 'Do you see my gift?'

'I do.'

'What's it doing, do you think?'

'Floating,' he says.

Floating.

'That's right,' she says, still hidden. 'And you know how it's floating. Berklum, you know.'

He is too distracted for such serious thoughts. The effect of colour on him is a kind of enchantment, a state of blissful befuddlement that causes children to get into trouble. But there's nobody to call Berklum a daydreamer, to call him idle, or to roughly pull him away from distraction. There's no parenting an old man. But the little girl tries.

'You know how, Berklum. Say you know.'

'Hot air,' he says. He feels it on his face, and on his hand as he reaches up for the feather: the heat of the hearth. It doesn't come as a constant, instead it buffets him, one moment soft the next strong. He imagines the fire breathing, in-out, in-out, soft-strong. He changes his breathing to match it.

Now holding the feather over the fire, holding it by the thin shaft, he watches the rainbow vanes ripple in the hot air. He has to hold it tight; it wants to be away, up and up, away through the chimney.

'It wants to find the sky,' Newsands says, appearing at his side. She leans in over the hearth. 'You can feel it.'

'Yes, *yes*.'

'To know such a freedom once, to then have it plucked from you, is to know a life of wanting. Rustans know this.'

'Yes, yes,' he says again. Is he listening? Perhaps on a deeper level than we can appreciate.

'Show them you understand, Berklum. Show them all.'

The girl looks up at him, and disappointment pinches her perfect cheeks. He hesitates. He still doesn't believe – maybe he understands, but he doesn't *believe*. And that's what a girl with rainbow wings needs from him.

'Come see, Berklum,' she says. 'See for yourself.'

With a few dainty hops, she is at the workshop door. She can reach the handle, just about, but not all the locks. She pulls at them with a child's simple determination. And it opens an old wound, doesn't it, Berklum? To see a girl paw uselessly upwards – such a sight splits that scar tissue.

Without tears, but an undeniably deep aching, he clicks and clatters open each lock. The tears, they come when she smiles up at him. That's too much. Looking away, he wipes his eyes, and just in time.

'Palla?'

Unun is at the house door. Picture it with us now: one street, one house, two doors side-by-side. So, the street has one door for the workshop, for the use of all, and one for the house to be used only by family. She is coming, you're going. And yet, and yet, look to her now, Berklum. How does she seem to you?

'Stealing,' he mumbles.

'What's that, Palla?'

What's that *indeed*. She *does* look like she's stealing into her own home. She was hunched over the keys in the lock, as if they weren't hers even as they turned. And now she's flushed – not just her cheeks, but her neck. Poor Unun, she's burning up with her guilt.

'I-I've just been to see a friend,' she says. That's the lie of a much younger girl, a lie that relies on a seed of truth. You remember that one, Berklum, and back then the 'friend' was a boy. Could it be a different boy? No, her love for Nibalt is too big; there's no room in her for another.

She's been four doors down.

'Four doors down?' Berklum says.

She flinches, as if stung. 'My friend. She... Where are *you* going, Palla?'

Clever girl. That cleverness is your fault, Berklum.

'I-I just...'

Oh, this is a merry jig, isn't it? Two dancers caught in their own special guilt.

He feels something nudge his hand. His field glasses; Newsands is giving them to him. Their heft, their weight, steadies him. 'I wanted to watch the tatterwings.'

Until he says it, he didn't know it. But Newsands nods – that's right, that's where they were going all along, to watch the tatterwing bats.

'You haven't done that for years,' Unun says.

'Tell her you know that,' Newsands says. 'Tell her you wish you hadn't worked so much. That you've missed too much.'

He glances at the girl, then at his daughter.

'She can't hear me, Berklum. She can't see me.' Newsands flaps her wings. 'That much should be obvious.'

Oh dear, Berklum. This is all getting rather crowded, isn't it? How will you cope?

'I've missed watching the tatterwings,' he says carefully. 'Too much working.'

This, at least, is the right thing to say. Unun brightens. 'That's good, Palla. You should be enjoying yourself at your age.'

You let that comment pass, just to be away. It's hard to say who's more relieved as you part.

Walking up the street towards the rope boxes, Newsands takes your hand. It's nice, holding someone's hand. When was the last time you did that, Berklum? No, not a steadying hand, that doesn't count.

'She didn't want to come with us,' Newsands says.

'No. She's never liked watching the bats. Doesn't like the heights.'

'A Rustan who's scared of heights.' She shakes her head. 'That's one for the Drunkard.'

'There's more of them than you might think.'

'Not for long,' she says.

He doesn't understand what she means, but he's given up trying to understand everything she says. Some riddles just aren't worth the effort; the answers are so often disappointing.

Unun closes the house door behind her, not too quick, not too hard. And then she collapses against it. She rarely has stories for the Liar; lies aren't easy for Unun, and they weren't even as a younger woman. But this isn't an outright lie. This is more of a scheme, a longer form of deception. For some reason, she takes no solace in that.

She wishes there was another way.

Unun tries to distract herself until someone comes home, but she's no good at this. She eats without tasting. Drinks something hot, just for the heat, and lets it grow cold. She stares at nothing. Eventually, because she doesn't know where else to go or what else to do, she drifts into the workshop. Berklum didn't lock it in his haste. His haste to be away from her, away from her lies – her schemes.

It's warm in the workshop, with the fire more than embers. But she can't see anything in the forge, or in the hearth itself, to suggest what her palla had been working on. Instead, she sees the rolls of paper scattered about the floor and the tables. He doesn't usually draw so much, unless he has a particularly demanding client. He must have made every bone and every modification ten times over by now. So why so much drawing, she wonders?

She wonders a lot more when she finds the papers blank.

Even those scrunched up into balls and tossed aside, blank. She presses the papers flat, holds them up to the candlelight, turns them this way and that. There's a riddle here, in her palla's workshop, and we've said all we need to about *riddles*, haven't we?

'Unun?'

She drops a piece of paper, as if caught in the act.

'Yes,' she admits, but too softly. 'Yes?'

'Ah, here you are.' Nibalt stops at the doorway from the house to the workshop: a threshold he knows not to cross. She goes to him, hugs him fiercely.

'I'm glad you're home,' she says.

'So am I.' He kisses the top of her head. 'So many using the boxes, you'd think Fenest had come *here* for the election.'

Careful, Nibalt, careful with such heresies.

'I have something to tell you,' she says, her face buried in his chest.

'Should I be sitting down to hear it? Better yet, with a drink at the ready?'

'If you pour me a glass too.'

That surprises him. His wife doesn't drink, everyone knows that.

She follows him back down the corridor to the kitchen. For the first time, perhaps in all her years, she feels glad to be away from the workshop. And that doesn't bode well now, does it?

He finds a bottle of something at the back of a cupboard. A Seeder blend, and expensive by the look of it.

'How long have you been hiding that?' Unun says.

He raises the bottle to the light. It's half full... or half empty, depending on where you're sitting. 'Not long enough,' he says. 'But then I've only myself to blame, isn't that so?'

He's only half asking, but Unun nods regardless. Neither she nor her palla have touched a drop, not since her meiter joined the Audience. That she had a seat beside the Drunkard was a given, but who else would her meiter have stories for?

'Only a little for me,' she says.

'Only a little, for a little problem.' He pours himself considerably more.

'Problem? Is it so obvious?'

'From the moment I walked in.'

'Oh, Nibalt.' She sips from her cloudy glass, surprised but pleased with the heat. 'Why does doing right sometimes feel all kinds of wrong?'

'Usually because *that* sort of right is hard. No one doubts themselves when the right is easy.'

'I started something today that can't be stopped,' she says. 'I've been avoiding it for so long now, I feel... I don't know what I feel. Scared? Relieved? Or just confused.'

'It had to happen eventually. Your palla can only keep working for so long.'

She smiles weakly at him. Of course he knows what this is about, likely knew well before she was ready to admit it – likely as soon as he found her alone in the workshop. For better or worse, he's a husband who really knows his wife.

'I hoped,' she says, taking a deep breath, 'I hoped he'd be the one to start it. That he'd give me the workshop, rather than me taking it. Does that make me a coward?'

'What do you think?'

'I think it does.'

'Hoping for an easy path away from your troubles doesn't make you a coward. *Taking* it does. Now, do you want to tell me what you actually did today?'

'No.'

He doesn't say anything, doesn't push the matter, and a silence settles comfortably over them. But remember, silence is the one thing the Audience abhors. So, to their satisfaction, we turn again to an old bonesmith and his young friend with rainbow wings.

When Berklum reaches the end of the street, intending to take the vertical ropebox higher up the spire, he finds himself joining a queue. It's as Nibalt said – a lot of people out today. At least Berklum doesn't recognise anyone about him; another moment of peace to tell the Luminary. At his age, few things spark his gratitude quite so much as avoiding polite conversation.

He shuffles forwards when appropriate, but is too distracted to be impatient. He clutches his field glasses in both hands and tries to recall the last time he went tatterwing watching. Three years? Five? Ten? He used to keep a diary – sizes, colours, wing patterns, going so far as to name those he spotted regularly. Another life, lived by another Berklum. A man more together, perhaps.

'Just younger,' he grumbles.

Younger, yes, less prone to grumbling, yes, yes.

He glares at no one and everyone, knowing he can't win this argument. This argument is with time, as much as with us, and both are inexorable.

But look, Berklum, see those children scampering up the ropebox shaft? Two boys and a girl. Anonymous in their youth: faces so smooth and lacking the character of years; voices unbroken; shoulders that don't know the weight of responsibility. They climb the vertical shaft with the same ease and gait of a Wayward horse on the flat. Wouldn't you want to feel that again? And no, not as a part of yourself that is already lost, but a part regained? Taken back, by your will alone. Look at the men and women about you. Look at their faces as they watch the children too. Look past the grimaces, the disapproval, to what's beneath. What do you see?'

'Want,' he says.

'What do you want, Berklum?' Newsands asks.

'Not just me. All of them. We all want that back.'

'You understand,' the girl says. 'You will help them, Berklum. Together, we'll help them.'

Help them you might, but they're staring at you now. Staring at the old man talking to himself as he holds his hand at an odd angle, almost as if he's...

'We all want more ropeboxes,' he says to them, 'more like the cone has.'

This elicits the expected tribal response: yes, more like the cone has, this old man understands. He's seen the problem right away, damn the cone to Silence, seen it right away despite his mumbling to himself and his stale smell. That's the kind of insight you get from experience.

And although they might not know it, they're thinking just the same as you, Berklum. They see those children with their hairy hands and feet, the freedom they have, innocent enough to make the Nodding Child sit up and listen. And then they see you. An old man. Fine, he may have plenty of stories for the Audience when he gets there, but for now it's only the Widow listening. Listening and waiting. She's patient; she waits for that same old story. So, they feel caught, Berklum, just as you do – caught between the Child and the Widow.

'More boxes,' he says again, those nearby mollified. 'The cone.'

When their turn comes, Berklum steps into the box as confident and steady as any man of the Rusting Mountains. For her part, Newsands sits on the side of the box, her feet dangling over the edge. He's surprised she gets in at all.

'What?' she says. 'Why bother flying when I can take the box up?'

This makes him laugh. After all that serious talk of freedom and innocence, youth and age, the girl with wings rides in the box too. And her expression, so earnest, only makes it worse. He laughs so much that everyone else looks away, looks anywhere but at him.

'I don't see what's so funny,' Newsands says, which does nothing to help.

By the time the box reaches the top of the shaft – the children climbing it long gone – Berklum is out of breath from his laughing. He clutches the side of the box and is the last to get off, under the glare of those impatient to go down.

'I hope you're quite finished,' she says.

He wipes his eye. He has no idea when he last laughed until it hurt. No idea at all.

Newsands pointedly walks on. There's something imperious in the set of her shoulders and how she looks ahead. No more handholding, Berklum. She looks as if she knows where she's going. He doesn't hurry to catch up but notes she is indeed going the right way.

They proceed this way, Newsands a good few paces in front and neither of them saying a word, for another upward winding street, another vertical ropebox, and two more streets besides. One more ropebox and they're nearly there. It is a good thing that watching bats involves a lot of sitting down – Berklum finds the journey more taxing than he cares to admit, even to himself.

'Is that so?' he mutters.

Come now, you know the most powerful lies are those we tell ourselves.

He refuses to waste any more precious breath on the matter.

This high up in the spire the streets and pathways are quiet. The houses are bigger, with more solid rock between them, and the shops sell more and more specific wares: whole businesses trading in duck down, or sweetbreads, or a kind of modification oil he's never heard of before. This is where anyone with a few marks to their name lives on the spire. Of course, being the spire, it means those folks don't have *that* much money – otherwise they wouldn't be here at all. They who top the spire are merchants. Successful, Seeder-connected merchants; but purveyors of this, that and the other, nonetheless.

All that means very little to Berklum. He has neither the imagination nor the natural bile to turn bitter. Perhaps he has been rescued from such petty feelings by his craft? A busy bonesmith has no time or need to ponder the lot of others. Except those lying on his tabletop, that is. No, it is simply a happy coincidence that at the height needed to watch tatterwing bats on the spire, the streets are quiet and the people generally keep to themselves.

It will surprise none of you to know that Berklum has a favourite spot for tatterwing watching. Nor will it be a great surprise to know he recalls the route even after all these years. This being the Rusting Mountains, and not a fancy Perlish manor house, there's no designated area for taking one's leisure as one enjoys the surrounding natural beauty. Berklum's spot is a wide connecting pathway that is open to the elements at the front and above, facing south, and is twenty or so feet below a tatterwing roost. It just so happens that, on the upper end of this pathway, the rock curves into a natural ledge to sit on, with a full view out into the Tear.

Perhaps other such enthusiasts have found other, similarly accommodating places, but Berklum wouldn't know. There's no

Rustan association or guild or group for the watching of bats and birds. Such an idea has never even occurred to Berklum; the Rustans are a less tribal people than others in the Union.

'I just like the peace and quiet,' he says, easing himself onto the rocky seat next to Newsands.

'Don't worry,' she says, 'I can be patient when I need to.'

He doubts this somehow but keeps that to himself. She's clearly still annoyed about the laughing. So let her be annoyed, he decides. He's here to watch bats and maybe, just maybe, learn something about wings.

Were you perhaps wondering what this was all about? Or had you, like Berklum, managed to put the pieces together for yourself? When he helped Newsands with the door of his workshop, he had no idea where she was going or what she wanted. And when she pushed his field glasses into his hand, the idea had just come to him, hadn't it? But why? Why had he gone from a feather floating over his hearth to watching bats at the top of the spire?

Yes, you understand, clever thing, you. This isn't your first story, after all.

The bats use the hot air of the Tear to fly.

Berklum raises his field glasses to his face. They have an arm on each side that slots directly into his temple. This is one of the bonesmith's few personal modifications, and it helps in all manner of ways with his work. Whether he needs his vision protected, or magnified for close work, everything is designed to click into place just above his ears. Helpful too, it is, for his old hobby.

The vista beyond the ledge is not unique, but no less impressive for that. You'll recall the spire sits at the northern edge of the Tear, it being the northernmost of the Rusting Mountains. So, to look south from the spire is to see the great chasm that is the Tear in all its broken glory. The ground – what can be seen of it through the thick clouds – is a rucked and buckling two-toned blanket. Those tones are the grey of cold rock and the piercing thread of Wit's Blood. From such heights, even large floes of the blood appear thinly stitched through the great Tear. Then there are the other peaks and mounds; few so tall as the chain that makes up the Rusting Mountains, but they make their own claims on the sky well enough. Too tall for the burrowing Torn, and too short for the Rustans, they're home to firecats and other creatures that prefer to be left well alone.

And then, beyond these peaks, is the horizon. A simple enough notion, but in the Tear simple things are the most complex of all. The southern edge of the Tear is a distant, hazy line that belies the pitted caverns and precipitous gullies that make a maze of it. And should you manage to navigate a way through such a nightmare landscape, what awaits you? Your map might claim there lies *The Great Southern Desert* or *The Shifting Sea* or, more simply, Desert. Simple, but complex.

This, and more besides, greets the roaming eye of Old Man Berklum, who is a bonesmith and that is what he is. He sees it all, and none of it, because he's looking for bats, remember? The ground and the horizon are no places to look for flight. The tar-black clouds are what fill Berklum's field glasses. Watching for tatterwings is like gazing at the night and hoping for a distant spark, a flicker of a lantern or the fleeting pulse of a star. No wonder it isn't a popular pastime.

'Well, we're here, and so are the bats,' he says, spotting a pair of large males in a break in the clouds. 'What now?'

Newsands, sweet little thing she is, has shuffled to the front of the ledge and is concentrating enough to furrow her lineless brow. 'Tell me,' she says, 'how do you think they do it?'

'By being born to it,' he says, still watching them.

'You weren't born to being a bonesmith.'

'My palla disagreed.'

'Just tell me what you see, all right?' she says. She can sound stern when she wants to. It's disconcerting. Best do as she says, Berklum.

'Two male bats, big ones, rising through the clouds.'

'Rising how?'

'Just ris—'

Something cuffs the back of his head, like his palla used to, and he loses the bats for a moment. How did that feel, Berklum? Different, wasn't it? When your palla cuffed you it was with rough, calloused fingers. This was a soft, dull thud. This was a wing, and she did it without even moving.

'Rising *how*?' she says again.

'They're not moving. At least, that's how it looks. They don't flap. They... circle,' he says, adjusting the focus of his glasses. 'It's small, but they tilt. The line of the span stays the same, but the angle changes as they come round.'

'There's more to a tatterwing though, isn't there,' she says – it's not a question, but an order to look closer.

He does so, picking out one of the males in particular. And in this way, with nothing else filling his vision, with no other distractions, he can finally see it. Something he'd not noticed in all his days of tatterwing watching. Or maybe he had and not considered it consciously, not thought it important, not cared for its significance. But if he'd ever had a tatterwing on his tabletop, like one of his recipients, he'd have seen it immediately – if not understood right away.

'Their wings, they're whole. Not in tatters.'

'Have we named them wrong, for so long?' she says.

No. He knows their wings have holes in them. He *knows*. But he *sees* them now, whole.

Until one of the males decides to stop rising. Then it turns to tatters.

They watch for hours. The comings and goings of bats. Their rise and fall. Mostly males at this time of day, but the occasional female too – darker in the wing and harder to see in the clouds. They feed on the Picknicker's own winged delights, those also caught in the hot airs of the Tear. This makes the bats popular with your average Rustan: each insect eaten is one fewer biting and buzzing in the middle of the night.

Not so long after the first sighting, Newsands nudges Berklum. He turns, forgetting his field glasses for a moment and sees nothing but red stone wall. The glasses don't come away easily. They catch in his temple, the mechanism thickened by lack of use. Still, nothing a little brute force can't clear. With his eyes his own again, he looks down to find Newsands offering him one of his small notebooks and a nub of charcoal. Now, just where does she keep these things?

Berklum ignores the question in favour of his notebook. He marks down, in a system only known to him, the different tatterwing bats circling in and out of the clouds. He has a keen eye – simply having field glasses is not enough – for the details that set individual tatterwings apart from one another. Scars are common, especially on the wings. As are damaged thumbs and fingers. Nips taken out of ears, the shapes and sizes of their noses, and much more besides.

But really his notes have a different focus: the wings. And in that focus, he begins to understand their workings. The outer wing membranes are peppered with holes. This is what gives the bats their name, tatterwing. Most Rustans assume this is a result of flying in the Tear – the hot rocks and ash in the air, the Jittery Wit's gift to the sky, must take their toll. It's a tale that makes enough sense to satisfy. But it doesn't explain why the *inner* membranes are not so affected. Watching them now, Berklum sees the truth of it. That every bat's membranes are only tattered on the outer, and not the inner, is too unlikely a coincidence. So he watches the ends of each wing closely and finds that they move in and out in a very clear, deliberate way – when the bat climbs, the outer membranes close in on themselves. When the bat descends the membranes open.

Yes, yes, you say, all very interesting for those interested in bat wings. But what does it mean for *our* story?

'They don't need to flap their wings,' Berklum says.

They don't need to flap. Understand now? No? Tell them, Berklum.

'Not having to flap the wings solves a great many problems.'

Newsands hops down from the seat. 'I knew you'd start to see it,' she says.

'Then why not just tell me?' he says, still looking to the sky. 'Could have saved us coming up here.'

'No, Berklum, you misunderstand. I *knew* being here would show you the way, not what that way was.'

Well then, the way seems simple enough: wings that catch the hot air to go up, and have holes that can be opened to go down.

'The saying is simple, the doing is something else.'

'That's wrong,' Newsands says. Her small, earnest face is tilted up at the old man. 'Don't underestimate how hard it is to say what has never been heard, to think what has never been dreamt.'

She turns to the open vista, to the clouds of the Tear, and the tatterwings circling.

'Enjoy your last days of dominion,' she tells them. This is what the little girl with rainbow wings tells them.

You're right to look worried, Berklum.

What follows is the work of the thing – what Berklum calls the doing. It begins again with paper. The rolls Berklum had filled and then discarded are suddenly blank – just as Unun found them – and ready to be covered in charcoal once more. Wing – size and shape. Mechanisms for opening and closing the outer membranes. Weights, measures, materials. Everything is considered, noted down, changed, improved.

Berklum does all this hunching over his tabletops. Candles burn down, sputter and fail, are replaced. Newsands comes and goes. Sometimes she sits on the high shelves, sometimes in his slipdog hide chair, and sometimes she is up on the tabletop with him. She doesn't interrupt. She doesn't fidget or play with anything. She isn't the nuisance she's named after. Her presence is as reassuring and companionable as the lit hearth, nothing more, nothing less.

And where, you may wonder, is Unun during these days back at the paper?

In exile, isn't that right, Berklum? Your own apprentice. Your own daughter.

He mutters something incomprehensible.

It was not a pleasant conversation, was it? He doesn't want to think about it, doesn't want to remember. But it is a part of the story worth telling, so you just carry on with your work, and we'll sate ourselves with familial conflict and tension.

★ ★ ★

Unun knows you're home. She heard the workshop door close behind you – not a door capable of closing quietly, that one. You're back from watching tatterwing bats, which is something you haven't done for years. She isn't sure what to make of that. But she's equally unsure what to make of you lying. The irony being that you haven't lied in years either, but she can't know that as we do. Hard as it may be to believe, you've had no reason to lie since your wife died. But back to Unun and her worrying.

She's biting her nails now, sitting on the edge of her bed. Everyone is picking up old hobbies. She knows you're home, but she doesn't want to see you. Instead, she's recalling the awkwardness at the house door earlier – she sneaking back in the house, you sneaking out of the workshop. She could barely look at you through the haze of guilt over Hassi's loan. Her friend's terms were reasonable, and she now has the money to pay off all your debts. It's stashed in the usual place, waiting to be distributed as necessary and with discretion. She doesn't want you to know what's happening until it's too late: too late for you to do anything about it, and too late for her to lose her nerve.

Chuuuuph.

Another fingernail falls victim to this story.

She needs to do something. She needs a distraction. Standing, she makes her way through the narrow corridor from their bedroom to the kitchen. A Rustan house is really a series of small rooms connected by thin corridors that the mountains begrudgingly tolerate. They are hewn painstakingly from the softer rock, which means rarely is a wall straight or a floor flat. Corridors slant up or down, kink one way or the other, as necessary. To Rustans this is entirely normal, so they are quite perturbed by northern homes with their characterless right angles and smooth planes.

Unun rushes about a kitchen she barely knows anymore. She finds oats, a little goat's milk, salt, and dried mushrooms bought from Seeder traders. This, and numerous variations of this, is evening porridge – a mainstay of the post-meiter, pre-Nibalt years when Unun and Berklum took turns to inadequately sustain each other. She heats the mixture until it starts to stick to the bottom of the deep pan and then spoons it into two bowls. Nibalt does not eat evening porridge.

She carries the bowls down the slanting corridor to the workshop.

'Palla?' she calls.

All noise beyond the internal door stops. She calls again, but you still don't answer. Putting one of the bowls down, she tries the door, but it's locked. She doesn't like that, never has, not since she was a little girl when she would howl from the high shelf to be let in. But this locked door has taken on a lot more significance since then.

'Palla, open the door,' she says, as she rattles the handle.

'No,' he says, muffled, small.

'You open this door at once!'

'No,' he says, firmer this time.

It's no good. She knows how stubborn he can be, so she tries a different approach. 'You have to eat, Palla. I have some porridge for you – mushrooms, how you like it.'

'Leave it there.'

'I will n—' She stops herself. She knows this is not a battle she can win. He has all the keys and can go days without eating when he's working. 'Whatever you're doing, let me help,' she says.

'I ... can't.' He's close now, standing just on the other side of the internal door. 'Not until it's finished.'

'Palla, I'm your apprentice. Let me *help*. Let me *learn*.'

'You can't see her. You can't know. Not this time.'

Her? Is that the recipient? Unun wonders. If it's a sensitive commission, she can be discreet. Far more than her palla. This little slip will give her much to think on in the coming days.

'Palla, please—'

'No, Unun. You have to go away now and leave me to work. You'll understand when it is all over.'

'You're sending me away?' she says, her voice thick with hurt.

There is a pause, a silence, in which every heartbeat feels like a dagger.

'Yes,' he says.

She stares at the heavy panels of the door. She can picture everything that lies behind it: the tabletops, the racks of tools, the hearth, the slipdog hide chair, everything. This is not just a room that is being denied to her, but a part of herself.

When she turns away, one bowl of porridge still on the floor, she doesn't flee. She strides away with renewed purpose – a purpose forged in the crucible of her palla's betrayal.

She may be exiled from the workshop for the time being, but it will be hers in the end.

Both of you know this. Both of you cling to this to justify what happens that evening.

My, my, you've been busy, Berklum. When we left you, there was just paper, but now look at this! This is... you've made a...

What is it, Berklum?

'A test,' he says.

Oh, of course. A test. But what *is* it? All we can see is a long stretch of material, many metal rods and something lumpy in the middle.

'It's not finished,' he mutters. He runs a hand along the material – hide, that much we can tell now. 'These, wings. This here? Weight. About that of a Rustan adult.'

It really is something, Berklum. A test. A step on the way to Rustans in the sky. It is auspicious, even if it's not so much to look at. But tell those listening, those who may not be so comfortable and experienced with such matters, what are you testing?

'Hot air and holes might work for the bats, but that doesn't mean the same will hold for us.'

But why ever not?

'First, the air might not be hot enough.'

The Tear not hot enough? Come now, we struggle to believe that!

'Then, even if it is, maybe we'll still be too heavy. And then there's all the complications of getting into the air, then finding the heat, then coming back down.'

So, a test. Very good, Berklum. A man of his craft. A man who takes care, takes the appropriate steps, doesn't rush into the dream but plots his route. And you've put this all together with what you had lying about the workshop?

'Only missing the rope.'

Rope? Yes, that makes a sort of sense. Rope to keep a hold of your test. You'll need a lot of it, Berklum.

'I know.'

You know, there's one person who deals with rope all day. A lot of rope. He might—

'I *know.*'

Ah, but how to ask Nibalt, that's the question. He's not home yet. And when he does get back, he'll be tired and, in all likelihood, irritable. His guard will be up as well as his hackles. No, better to wait until morning when he's too sleepy to be suspicious. Can your test – and your patience – stand such a delay?

'Yes, yes.'

He returns his focus to the tabletop, where his test lies incomplete. We have a better look at it now, over his shoulder, as he tinkers with this and that. Even for a crude and swiftly assembled model there is evident craft in the wing structure, its arms and its mechanisms. That is what it means to be a craftsman: no matter what they turn their hand to, it will exhibit a degree of quality.

These wings resemble a tatterwing's reasonably faithfully. Stretched hide makes up the membrane. Just what hide *is* that, Berklum?

'Goat, mostly.'

And the arms, wrists and fingers? What are they made of?

'Tin. Lightest I have to hand.'

Perhaps not all of my audience realised bats have fingers. At least, that's what we call their wing bones. Amusing, isn't it, how we feel so comfortable applying the names of our own constituent parts to beasts of all shapes and sizes? But then, bats cannot name their bones themselves, so who better to do it than a bonesmith?

This is why you were chosen, Berklum. This is why the girl with rainbow wings appeared to you, and you alone. You make bones, you prefer to make fingers – that's good work, you say – and here you are, making fingers. That has a neatness that all the Audience can appreciate.

'So you say.'

We do! We do say. You'll have more than enough stories for the

Audience when all is said and done. How long, do you suppose, it could take the Musician, and the Inker, and the Messenger, and any other you care to mention – how long might it take for them to grow tired of tales of Rustans flying through the air? Five generations? Ten? A hundred?

'I just make bones.'

'You do more than that,' Newsands says from some dark corner of the workshop. 'You do so much more. Even before this, you changed lives.'

She's right, as much as it pains us to admit it. The wincher whose palms blister and burn, the tailor whose sight is failing, the miner whose shoulder locks up – all these people changed by your modifications. And that's not even considering the countless accidents that leave people in need of your services. All those stories changed, helped, made more interesting.

Harrumph, he says, adjusting the tiny cogs that open and close a set of holes at one end of a wing.

There are many such adjustments to make as the night wears on. Moving parts need to be greased and oiled. His stitching isn't poor, but it could always be better. Everything is balanced and weighed and tallied on various papers. At some point, Newsands retrieves the bowl of evening porridge left by Unun. He doesn't notice her do it, the bowl just appears next to him, and he absently eats a mouthful every so often. Mushrooms, he thinks, but tastes very little. Dwelling any longer on this risks feelings of guilt, and he can't face those, not now. So instead he works until he sleeps.

He is woken the next day by Newsands shaking him, and the sound of the house door closing. Nibalt! Hurry, Berklum, you need to hurry with those locks and catch him. Remember your coin purse, now. We're after rope, lots of it, no questions asked.

Damn, if we'd just had more time to think it through, to know just what to say, and how to ask him.

Do you know how, Berklum?

Berklum?

You look smug as you hurry down the street. You've thought this through already, haven't you? Planned it while we were distracted by one thing or another. Maybe even talked it through with that multicoloured monstrosity. No matter. We can be patient when necessary. We can simply listen. There he is, just turning the corner, the hulking man who cooks your dinner and sleeps beside your daughter.

'Nibalt! Wait,' he calls.

Nibalt falters, mid-stride. He turns enough to see you, Berklum, and his shoulders sink. Just a little, but there it is.

'You're up early, Berklum.'

'Wanted to catch you, before work.'

'Well, here I am, caught,' he says, crossing his arms. Here we go, Berklum. Let's hear it.

'I need to buy rope.'

'Do I look like—'

'A lot of rope. A hundred feet,' Berklum says. 'I thought you, being a wincher, might know who supplies amounts like that.'

'A hundred feet of rope,' he says. He definitely wasn't expecting that. He's not only too sleepy, he's also too surprised to be suspicious. And yet, he still asks, 'Why?'

Here it comes. Settle in, everyone. We give you Berklum's great deception...

'I've been asked to make a kite.'

'A kite?'

'Yes, it's a frame with—'

'I know what a kite is.'

'—popular among the Seeders, especially.'

Nibalt sniffs then rubs at his nose. 'Nothing but bats fly in the mountains, every fool knows that.'

Every fool indeed, Nibalt.

'A kite is what they want, which means rope. Which means' – he pauses a beat here, like a master storyteller – 'I need your help.'

Bravo, Berklum, bravo. The change in Nibalt is so profound, we can't help but feel sorry for him. A grown man, weary and bitter and married, reduced to an eager boy.

'I might be able to lay hands on eighty feet,' he says. 'Won't be too cheap though.'

Berklum runs through the numbers and decides eighty feet should be fine. He'll need some extra twine, maybe some thick thread, but that he can buy elsewhere. From his coin purse, he takes out a mark and gives Nibalt the rest.

'This is too much,' Nibalt says.

'That's fine, I trust you.'

Nibalt cinches the purse shut and nods. 'Kites,' he says. 'Good work?'

'Could be. Could be.'

So, what to do while we wait for Nibalt and his rope? Oh, you have that planned already. Well, by all means, proceed, bonesmith. Perhaps you don't need us to tell your story after all, perhaps you can tell it yourself? No?

'No time for stories,' he says.

I hope the Audience didn't hear that, Berklum. They can be vindictive on the best of days. But we'll follow along; we'll follow this new sense of purpose.

He passes the door to the workshop, stopping just briefly to check he did lock it, and then he is off up the winding street. Shops on either side are busy opening. Owners are sweeping the night's dust and yesterday's custom off their steps, hoping for a fresh day. The old local bonesmith garners a few nods of recognition, a kind of grudging – but long-earned – respect. They may not like you, Berklum, but they know they might need you one day. If they haven't already.

At the vertical ropebox, he steps right in: no queue this early. The same is true at the box over to the ridge. We have a sense now, don't we, of just where he's going. Why else go to the ridge? Spine work's dangerous, but he knows someone he just might trust.

On the box ride over he stares out at the clouds. There are no bats to see, not at this hour, but plenty of other things swirl among the billowing black. Ash. Rock. Sparks and embers. A future. He holds out a hand, ignoring the concerned glances of the few strangers nearby. He holds out a hand and feels the wind. It pushes at him, insistent, as if it is saying, 'I'm here, I'm always here.'

He looks for the rainbow, but it isn't in the clouds. It's waiting for him on the ridge, right when he steps out of the ropebox.

She falls in beside him without a word. He wonders if it's worth telling her about the rope, about the test being almost ready, but decides she probably knows. When you're not sure if someone is real or not, it's difficult to determine their boundaries. What the extent of their power and their limitations is. You've wondered the same of us, haven't you, Berklum? He shrugs, but Newsands doesn't notice. Or doesn't care. She seems determined today. Her gaze is fixed straight ahead and her arms swing by her side as if she's marching into battle. A battle? No, you don't think Lanthan will fight you on this. She's a bonesmith who likes a challenge, likes good work, just the same as you.

You're lucky – maybe not so lucky as to tell the Latecomer – that Lanthan doesn't have a recipient on her table. Instead, she is at her forge, faceguard down, and turning something with her tongs. Her son, Acti, is on the other side of the heat and watching closely – as an apprentice should. Where's your apprentice, Berklum? Oh, you don't want to think about that, we know. But we won't be the only ones asking today, so you'd best have an answer.

When he clangs his metal fingers on the door, by way of announcing himself, neither bonesmith nor apprentice flinch. They don't even look up. Not until Lanthan is satisfied with whatever she's forcing from a comfortable orange to a blistering yellow. This she takes to an anvil and beats with a hammer, once, twice, ten times or more. Then with all the excitement of the workshop, she drops her tongs in a bucket of water and the hiss of steam fills the air. He waits at the door, respectful and patient because that is the only way he knows how to behave.

'Berklum,' she says, lifting her dull metal faceguard.

He takes that as permission to enter.

'I'd been meaning to send word. I might have some work for you soon,' she says. 'Toes.'

'Good,' he says. 'That's good.' He's thinking not of himself, but of his daughter. It is good she will have some solid, reliable orders when she takes over.

'You're alone,' she says.

He can't help glancing to the little girl beside him. Not his own daughter, but a girl who chose him. Lanthan sees the moment differently, of course. She feels something complicated, something hard for her to describe were she to try. Something close to pity, but pity edged with the knowledge the same will befall her, in her time.

'I'm here as a recipient, not a bonesmith,' he says, by way of explanation.

'Is that so.' She doesn't believe you, Berklum. Doesn't believe it's possible for a bonesmith to just be a recipient. Just as the Caskers' sangas make the worst patients, you will be a terrible recipient. Unless she puts you out cold, that is. But today is not the doing of the thing. Today is the planning, the designing, the negotiating the price. You have done all you can alone – now you need to discuss it with Lanthan.

'It's a modification.'

'And it's of a kind you can't do yourself,' she says.

It's hard to say, isn't it? Hard for you to admit you need help from another bonesmith – even one who has done that very thing herself.

'No, it isn't.'

'Why do I get the sense I'm not going to like this?' she says.

'It's your kind of work...'

'Go on.'

'But it's something new. Never done before.'

Her expression is one of confident scepticism. She doesn't believe there is anything new to be done with iron and copper in all the Rusting Mountains. One day she may be right. Not today.

'Show me,' she says.

Newsands gives him the roll of paper. We're used to this trick of hers by now, as is Berklum, but to Lanthan and her apprentice the paper appears from nowhere. One moment Berklum is standing there empty-handed, the next he is offering the roll to Lanthan. This is enough to distract her from the unsettling moment.

But not so her apprentice, Acti. He still bubbles with the curiosity of the young, still values the dream-like as highly as more practical matters. He shuffles over to Berklum and peers in front, behind and all around the old bonesmith. Without knowing, he has danced around Newsands too, danced a jig merry enough for the Companion. She watches on, stifling her giggles with a hand. But she has to be quick when he pokes the air, just where her head had been. A hop and a skip, and she's off, away into the workshop.

By the tilt of his head, Acti thought he heard something just then. Poor boy, we hope he's not the kind to worry at such a mystery.

At a table, his mother is worrying at a very different, but equally concerning puzzle. She's weighted down Berklum's paper at each corner and is now squinting at the contents. Bonesmiths have their own way of making their notations, of course – no two craftsfolk are the same, really. But she can read his measurements well enough. And just where on the body these modifications will be made is also clear as a Seeder sunset. But...

'What's it all for?' she asks.

'Does that matter?' Berklum says. He doesn't join her at the table, doesn't need to – he knows that paper better than he knows his own mind.

'It might. Will it hurt anybody else?'

Undoubtedly.

'Only if they get the same thing done to them,' he says.

'I respect you not wanting to tell me – a Rustan's modifications are their own business – but you know what that means; I might have to make decisions when you're on the table.'

'I wouldn't be here if I didn't trust you.'

She glances at the design. 'I use my own materials.'

'Of course.'

'And it won't be cheap. Spine work's—'

Dangerous.

'Dangerous,' he says, a beat after we do. See, we've learnt one or two things from this story, haven't we?

'Difficult,' she says, firmly.

'Whatever price you think is fair.'

'All right then,' she says. She points to the paper. 'What is this supposed to do?'

He joins her then, the deal done. They talk bonesmithery – a kind of talk heavy with technicalities of materials and measurements, stresses and forces, mechanisms and casual butchery of the flesh. Lanthan has her own thoughts on how certain things can be achieved on a man's shoulders, and how the movement of that part of the body can be best harnessed. Berklum listens to her expertise and, together, they improve the design in a number of ways. When they both straighten from looking at the design, Berklum does his best not to wince. He is pleased with their plans.

He is pleased with how his wings will soon attach to his body.

That evening, Nibalt returns home with eighty feet of rope and an empty coin purse. He's drunk. If he had the inclination to tell it, and Berklum had the inclination to listen, his tale would be one of Seeder spirits bought to grease the wheels of commerce. Barrooms up and down the spire, different but the same tacky floors, smoke-clouded ceilings and raised voices.

So it is that a drunk Nibalt pounds on the workshop door, with eighty feet of rope over his shoulder and the beginnings of a headache. He hands the rope over with a grunt, and that is that. None of the questions, none of the needling, none of the disapproval that Berklum had been steeling himself against. When he closes the workshop door, he can faintly hear Nibalt struggling with his keys for the house door. You're right to wonder what Unun will make of him, Berklum. Let us tell you. It's not how you imagine.

There's no fight, not even an argument between husband and wife. She makes him tea. Then she makes him evening porridge. He's grateful without the endless apologising of the drunk. Then they lie down together, neither speaking but neither able to sleep right away. Just together, companionably, as their world refuses to stop spinning – one drunk, one worried. In short, it's nothing like your marriage, Berklum.

'That's right,' he says, hefting the rope.

He gets to work and doesn't allow himself sleep until he finishes building the test. He packs the wings and the... body into a small hand cart – the kind allowed in the vertical ropeboxes – and finally, he slumps into his slipdog hide chair.

Newsands appears just as he is closing his eyes. Her serious face softens with a smile.

'This is good,' she says. 'I'm proud of you, Berklum the bonesmith. So very proud.'

He isn't up early the next day, but that is no matter. In all the spire, the Rusting Mountains and the Union beyond, there's not a single man, woman, or child who is impatiently waiting on Old Man Berklum or his discovery. How could they be, when they know nothing of it? Even the girl with rainbow wings has apparently infinite patience. What of the Audience, you say? Yes, perhaps you are right. Perhaps they are ready for this story to race towards a conclusion. But it is difficult to race so, when we're following an old man as he wrestles a cart along uneven streets.

The best we can do is skip over his trials and tribulations with the queue at the vertical ropebox, the many rest stops he takes leaning against his cart as he struggles for breath, and the curt answers he gives those idly wondering, 'What's in the cart, old man?' Let us skip to a rested Berklum at the same vista where he watched the tatterwings. He has napped through the midday heat, watched over by a girl who might not be there. The test lies spread out on the ground. He has checked the various fastenings, stitches and mechanisms and is satisfied. He is ready.

Newsands is also ready. For once, the girl is going to do more than speak in enigmas and produce Berklum's possessions from thin air. She is going to carry the test to the wind.

It will be a simple test really, for all its players, its workings and its moving parts. Berklum will stand firmly on the ledge the whole time, and he will hold the ropes connected to the test – as a boy holds string attached to a kite. Newsands's role is to fly out from the ledge, carrying the test with her, so as to launch it mid-air; it is too heavy to simply wait for a passing breeze as one would when launching a kite. And if the test flies, if it can rise and fall on the hot winds of the Tear, it will be a success. If it falls...

Berklum takes up his intricate lattice of twine and rope. Beside him is a coil, just shy of eighty feet. He nods to the girl. She lifts the test body as if the weight of a grown man is nothing to her little arms. She flaps wings that are a quarter of the size of those she is carrying.

Berklum holds his breath. Readies himself with the rope, hoping he is strong enough to keep control.

And then she is off. Her tiny wings beating at such speed the colours ripple and run together like water. She is clear of the ledge, carrying the test with her. She flies away from the spire and towards the black clouds of the Tear.

Mark this tableau, Berklum; who knows when you will see its like again?

'It's just a test,' Berklum mumbles.

Yes, but can we not appreciate the wonder of things when we see them? There must be more to such a story than the functioning of cogs and gears, of ropes and pulleys. And it is a wonder to see Newsands's brilliant colours in proper flight, not just hopping about your workshop.

He marks it, of course, not for the beauty but because he is concentrating. He already feels in his hands the tug and release of the wind. Even this bloodless test has a kind of life to it. The kind of life that is unsure of itself, that is difficult to control, and as unpredictable as the Audience.

And then Newsands, mid-air, lets go of the test.

Berklum cries out – not a word, just a feeling, and one that comes rushing up from his lungs to surprise him. It is a sound he recognises from the early days of fatherhood, when his daughter started to crawl up the walls. He braces himself. A not inconsiderable part of him is expecting to be dragged right off the ledge and out into the Tear. But the pull is not so great as to move this man of metal, flesh and bone.

The pull is not so great when the test wings start to drop. Or do they?

It is hard to be sure from where he stands on the spire. Newsands could be rising, he thinks, trying to use the girl as a reference among the swirling clouds. He checks his twines to make sure the wing holes are all closed. When he looks up again it is clear Newsands *is* rising. And he needs to make the test follow her – this was how they agreed it would work. He pulls the threads, and the wings jerk in response. Easy, bonesmith, easy – this isn't the forge. You're not bludgeoning elements of the earth into submission, but asking for the assistance of air. That's right, gently. See how the girl circles. Follow her round and up, up and round. Have faith when either your test or your guide slips behind the cloud.

'This is good,' you hear her say, as if she were right beside you. 'Now down.'

Is this the real test, Berklum? You can be satisfied the heat of the Tear is enough to keep a Rustan and their wings afloat, just as it does the tatterwings, but what about when that Rustan wants to come back to the mountains?

He plays cat's cradle with the twines and ropes in his hands, and far away, the wings twitch and convulse. The far membranes on either side reveal their holes to the Tear and the air. The stitched hide ripples with the rush of it. This time the test definitely descends. He can feel it as much as see it – there's a heaviness in his hands that wasn't there a moment ago. He counts to three slowly, so he is sure, and so he can judge just what a difference the holes make. More complicated work with the ropes makes the holes close. The test stops falling. He will have to find another swirl of hot air to rise but, although he can see Newsands in a position to guide him, he decides he has seen enough. He angles the test back towards the ledge, back towards its maker.

Could you have asked for more, Berklum? The air not only holds the weight but can also lift it, and the holes allow for a controlled and gradual descent. Are you pleased?

'Yes, yes,' he says, still concentrating.

Good. Remember that feeling.

Newsands isn't following the test back to the ledge. She is still circling among the clouds. Perhaps she is simply enjoying the freedom of real flight; it must be better than those short hops she makes onto tabletops or high shelves.

So she isn't there to help.

He guides the test in as straight a line as possible back to him. This may not have been the best idea. When the wings are only ten or so feet from the ledge, one is caught in a strong gust. It sends the whole thing spinning. Ropes and twine coil around each other. The test spirals downwards sharply.

Before he can even guess what might help, it's gone.

He has long enough to glance down at his hands before the ropes there are ripped from him. He hears a slap, and flinches as if struck. Despite our earlier suggestion, it is this sensation that he remembers most – the feeling he and his test had been slapped by someone. Someone with the authority to chastise him for what he attempted here.

The sound is, of course, the test colliding flatly, drily with the spire. It's a long, long fall to the Tear below. At least it cannot scream.

He waits though, and listens. He waits longer than he needs to. But he doesn't hear another sound, not until the tatterwings come out from their roosts. He doesn't want to watch them today. Turning from the edge, he readies the handcart for the journey home.

He is not so dejected as you might think. He has lost his test, yes, but it served its purpose. It proved that something so heavy could use the hot air to fly. The landing will be someone else's problem.

Newsands is standing in the entrance to the passage. He has

long since given up trying to understand how she gets from one place to another.

'It works, Berklum,' she says.

'I know.'

'You don't sound pleased.'

He sees what's coming, that's why.

'Rustans will own the sky here,' he says. 'I hope they're worthy.'

They walk home, both of them tired in their own ancient ways. Home, except there's no joy in the prospect, is there? Why don't you tell everyone listening – and we mean *everyone* – why you don't want to go home, Berklum?

'Unun,' he whispers.

He sneaks back into his own workshop. At least he is aware enough of this irony – of him having accused Unun of stealing back into the house earlier, only for him now to do the same. He closes the metal door behind him as quietly as possible. He all but tiptoes about the workshop until he can settle into his chair. Newsands disappears, reappears a moment later with a bowl of stew. He recognises the work of Nibalt when he smells it, but he's not hungry. He picks at the food out of habit. A habit of pleasing his daughter. A habit that will be impossible to maintain soon.

He waits. How long is hard to say in a room with no windows, when you sleep whenever you feel tired, and you only eat a mouthful here, a mouthful there. He is waiting for a certain sound. He hears its kind twice a day – the way to record time passing would be to count this, but what would that mean to an old man so singular in purpose? He hears its kind, but not *the* sound he is waiting for.

It is a test of wills, he realises. Which of them has the greater patience, which of them is the more stubborn of the two. Which of them has the most to lose. She may try, but he has no doubt he will win. She undoubtedly has more days to give, but she has more of a life to live in them.

Latecomer's luck, he's not sleeping when he hears *the* sound. The house door, softly, softly opens and closes. He can almost hear her holding her breath. He can almost feel the tension in her shoulders. He can almost see her waiting in the street, waiting for him to open the workshop and go to her. But soon she realises how cruel such hope is. She leaves for the market.

Hurry, Berklum, hurry out of your chair and into your home. Use this urgency to distract you from what you do here.

You know where she keeps it.

She may have lost the hairs on her hands and feet, but this part of her never changed: the room she grew up in is now the room she sleeps in with her husband. The room where, one day, her own child will climb up to the shelves and form habits that last a lifetime. You, however, can't climb.

Berklum drags his daughter's chest of drawers from one side of the room to the other. He at least has the wherewithal to take the drawers out first. As he is dragging the piece of furniture, he notices Newsands in the doorway. She won't come in, for some reason. It would be easier, wouldn't it, to have her fly up to the shelf? But that feels too sharp a betrayal. If someone has to do this, it has to be you. That's what you've decided.

With the chest beneath him, he manages to reach up, into the corner of the room. He can't see so well but he can feel the raised edge of the loose stone. He pulls it free and strains to reach behind it, to his daughter's hiding place. To where she keeps her most precious things. To where she keeps her money.

His metal fingers clunk against soft leather filled with coin.

His fleshy fingers know the feel of a coin purse well enough. To his surprise, he finds two more beside it. And they're all full.

He takes one down, careful, careful, and eases open the string. Where he expects pennies, he finds marks. He shakes his head. He knew his daughter had more of a mind for money than he did, but this is too much. She must have saved so hard, he thinks, gone without so much, and so often. What little is left of this old man's heart breaks there, as he stands atop his daughter's chest of drawers, her coin purse in his hands. He cries soundlessly, because he knows he cannot stop, and he knows he cannot blame anyone else.

Newsands is saying something. Words that are soft and consoling, but he hears only snatches as he stares down at the golden marks. Unun will forgive, she says, changed forever, she says, Rustan future, she says.

And Berklum, though he might hate himself for it, only thinks: one purse is not enough. The weight, the feel, what he can count. He needs more.

If he was not already broken, if that part of him had not already shattered into thousands of irretrievable pieces, he couldn't have reached up a second time. But he is, it is, and he does. He takes another purse, and then flees.

He leaves everything just as it is: the chest of drawers up against the wall; the drawers themselves on the other side of the room; the stone pulled away and sitting on the shelf. There's no use in hiding what he has done here.

He hurries out of the house, out of the workshop, and away from the spire.

Berklum makes it as far as the main street of the ridge before he stops. Here, he's not worrying about Unun finding him. That worry was a helpful distraction as he made his way up the spire and across on the ropebox. A distraction from what he'd done. Now, staring at the barroom doors, he seeks another escape from the heavy ache. And perhaps someone will listen as he tells the story of it.

The long, dark barroom is mostly empty at this time of morning. He sits at one end of the metal bar and clunks his fingers on the top to show he wants to do more than sit. The woman behind the bar has the kind of limp Berklum recognises as a modification.

'What're you after?' she asks.

A good question, isn't it? Without a better answer, he asks for Greynal. She raises a very weathered brow.

'Occasion, is it?' She turns and ratchets her leg up so she can reach the top shelves. It happens on only the one leg, and it could look ungainly if she wasn't so used to balancing like this.

'It's what she used to drink,' he says.

'Ah.' The woman doesn't need any more than that – she might not know the particulars, but she knows the story. She pours the Greynal, and he pays from his own small coin purse. No need to let the whole Union know he has a family's fortune about his person. The woman instinctively moves away and busies herself with something or other. This one, she thinks, doesn't need me to listen. He's here because he should be talking to someone else.

He sips at his drink and barely tastes it, this pride of the Seeders. Instead, he prefers to stare at the swirling depths of deep grey in the glass. Her hair went a similar colour, a year or two before the end.

'I haven't done that badly,' he mutters – not to us, but to *her*, if she's listening from among the Audience. 'We didn't do so badly. Unun's strong, and she has the talent.' He sends the Greynal swirling again. 'That has to count for something,' he says.

Oh, Berklum, we wish it was her voice you could hear and not ours. We wish she was here now, to say how right you are. It won't mean a thing coming from us.

'I just wanted to do good work. *Good* work.'

We know. She knows. The whole Audience knows. Such a simple dream, but those can be the most dangerous.

There's still time, Berklum. You could hurry home, put the coin purses back in the wall above the high shelf, tidy your daughter's room and be the only one to live with the shame of what you almost did.

'No,' he says, and we wonder if the word has ever had such finality to it? Such certainty of the ending that is to follow.

He stops staring at the drink and finishes it.

'I'm sorry,' he says. And maybe there's some value in the saying of it, even if those who need to hear are far, far away.

'Seems you've already made a start,' Lanthan says. She can smell it on you. That's no surprise to you though – you remember just what that's like.

Berklum is sitting on her table, his chest bare and his shoulders hunching as if he's trying to make himself as small as possible. But this will make you huge, Berklum, bigger than any man has ever been. Behind him, Lanthan is marking up his back – where to cut, where to graft, where to break, and where to mould with metal.

There's a tall glass of something waiting beside you. It won't taste as good as Greynal and won't listen as good as Greynal either, but it will take some of the pain. The part that's not self-inflicted.

The workshop is hot – hotter than usual – from Lanthan working the forge. He's had to wait as she finished with another recipient, though that was just an enquiry. And now there is more waiting as she sent Acti out for the materials she didn't have to hand. So she marks you up, in the manner you've done for so many modifications. But it's been years since you felt the charcoal press against your own skin. Despite everything, you feel the flutter of a thrill there, don't you? What *is* that, Berklum?

'Only a Rustan can know,' he says. 'To be modified, to change in such a way that your body is new to you again. Knowing that feeling is to be Rustan.'

Lanthan leans forwards to see you better. She isn't so much surprised by the outburst – she has heard all kinds on her table – but by the eloquence of it. 'It's why we're bonesmiths,' she says. 'We get to be close to that feeling every day.'

'But it starts then,' he says, nodding to the doorway. They both look, which makes the boy, Acti, stop. Slung over his shoulder is a heavy-looking sack.

'What?' he says.

The only answer Acti gets from either adult is an expression he knows all too well: pity blended with a kind of longing.

With the last of the materials brought by Acti, Lanthan returns to the forge and begins to turn orange heat to white. There, she can shape the lumps of metal into the intricate, interlocking parts that took two bonesmiths to draw. Berklum wishes he could help at this stage too, but he respects the craft too much for that.

Instead, like a good recipient, he drinks the hideous concoction given to him and lies face down on the table. He starts to dribble

– something he's aware of but has no power to stop. His whole body slackens. There's no way to stop now, if there ever had been. This is your story, Berklum, but is it *yours*? Do any of us have that kind of power, of ownership?

No, you're right, it's cruel to ask such questions when you can't answer.

Sleep now, Berklum the bonesmith, and when you wake, you'll find your body new to you again.

We watch what he cannot. Do you want to hear of it? Of course you do. Even those of the Audience who claim to be above such gratuities, or claim not to have the stomach for them, are just trying to deny their fascination. We suppose they have their reasons, and so might you. But we shall tell it, and you can decide how closely you listen.

Lanthan starts by making a wide circular incision – her word, not ours – on one shoulder blade. She is precise and she is careful, taking her time to ensure that, even in beginning, there is symmetry to her work. There is blood, but not as much as we imagined. It seems to be in no hurry to leave this old man, who is not much more than skin and bones and metal. In fact, there appears to be very little flesh removed before her scalpel strikes bone.

'See here, Acti,' she says, 'we're not following the shoulder entirely. Instead, part of the circular incision runs close to the spine on either side.'

The boy is next to her, watching even more closely than we are.

She drops the cut away flesh in a nearby bucket and wipes the wound as clean as such a thing can be.

'First, the base part needs to sleeve the shoulder bone.' From the forge she retrieves a thick metal disc that has raised walls but, importantly, a slot cut through one side. This, we are given to understand, will slide over the shoulder bone to 'sleeve' it, as she says. She uses tongs to carry the disc because it's still hot. She tests just how hot this is with her hand – too much heat and it will just burn a way through the man. But there needs to be some burning, if the metal is going to fuse with the bone, if the modification is going to take. Lathan knows this right kind of burning. She knows the touch of it better than she knows what it's like to run her hand through her son's hair; this heat is more familiar than the feel of sun on her skin.

Waiting until it's just right, she then slides the disc into place around the shoulder bone. There is some resistance, but her measurements were fairly accurate. She has to make one or two small adjustments by filing at the metal. Acti is ready with the suction bellows and assists with the clearing of any loose filings – such things can cause all sorts of problems later. Eventually, the shoulder bone nestles neatly against the inside wall of the disc.

Now comes the drilling.

Even we have to look away at first, but it does little to stop the sound. Lanthan stands on a pedestal, high above Berklum's exposed back, and rotates the handle of her drill as she presses her weight down. A slow grinding, churning of bone that rumbles like a landslide. And the squeal of the suction bellows does little to help. This cacophony, once heard, cannot be *unheard*.

Old and skinny he may be, but Berklum's bones appear solid enough. Lanthan is sweating, her arms slick with the effort, by the time she pulls the drill away and slides a thick pin through metal and bone alike.

The first base part is in place. She and Acti sit long enough for a drink of water and half an apple each, before they begin work on the second.

This is how a Rustan modifies their body.

This is how a bonesmith plies their trade.

It's nothing mystical or romantic. It's a lot of hard work and mess, and it's no surprise the rest of the Union leaves them to it.

He feels heavier. It's a simple, foolish first thought, but what else is there in those first moments? Berklum is still lying face down on a table, and it's as if someone is sitting across his shoulders. Sitting, not just because of the weight but because it's not moving and it's a constant. He can breathe and he can open his eyes, but his mouth and tongue are slower in coming to.

He can see his daughter, and the girl with rainbow wings. Unun is sitting forwards on a low bench, kneading her hands. This is what she does when she's somewhere she doesn't want to be. She hasn't noticed your eyes are open, Berklum, because she's looking away to the forge.

But Newsands sees you. She's on the high shelf and is as unreadable, in her old – young way, as ever.

'You're almost ready,' she says.

You'd laugh if you could. Is our bitter chuckle enough, do you think?

'You've been strong. You'll need to be stronger still.' And just like that, just as you blink, she's at the table.

'Palla?' Unun says. She hurries to kneel by your head. 'Are you awake?'

He manages to mumble. Manages a smile when she strokes his face.

'Oh, Palla, why didn't you just ask?' she says.

It's hard to hear the compassion, the love, in her voice, isn't it? But he doesn't shy from the pain. He knows he deserves it.

Unun tells him a story, and some of it is true. She tells him of coming home to find the mess he left in her room. The slow, crushing understanding of what was gone. And would you believe, she's apologising now. *She* is saying how sorry she is. She won't say why or what for. She is crying now as she cried then, as she replaced the stone above the shelf. She dragged the chest of drawers across the room and put the drawers back in the right order. She straightened the one rug in the room. In the mirror, she washed her face as best she could to hide the tears. She did this all before Nibalt came home and asked how her day had been, before he asked whether you were still locked up in the workshop. She didn't even need to check; she'd felt it as soon as she came home that day from the market. The house felt empty, as if the bonds that had been keeping it together had shattered in a way that could never be undone.

Still, she forced herself to listen and laugh and eat the meal Nibalt cooked. And when he fell asleep that night, she snuck out to look for you.

How did she find you? Were there so many places to look, really? You have no friends, no other family, no vices to indulge. But that was a challenge in its own way – where does a man go when he has nowhere to go? She wandered the spire, hopeless, until she came to the ropebox to the ridge. Then she knew.

She knew where, but she had plenty of time on the crossing to wonder *why*. A modification, perhaps, but you hadn't talked of wanting any more for as long as you lived. Did Lanthan have more work for you – but then why take the money? Were you trying to buy part of her business? Did she have something you wanted? Did you owe her money? Was something wrong with the fingers you made for her?

There were other, even less probable, ideas that occurred to Unun. But when she walked in and saw you on the table, she realised she'd been right with the first improbable thought.

You were covered, as you are now, and she respected that. She didn't even ask Lanthan, she knew better.

'You don't have to tell me, Palla,' she says. 'It's your body. But I want to know, why didn't you ask for the money?'

Berklum tries to work his mouth. He tries to form the shapes, make the words, explain his actions. For so many reasons, he can't, but he tries.

'You...' he manages, just a whisper, 'wouldn't believe.'

She can't look at you. Not like this, not right now, and not after what you've done. And there's no blaming her, is there? The money is only the start of it. The money is only a symbol we use, we who tell stories of our lives, to focus those feelings that have been there all the while. Love and hope – quick, hide them in purses above the high shelf, so one day they can turn to betrayal and despair. She can't look at you because she doesn't trust herself anymore. She doesn't trust her own feelings. That's the extent of what you've done, Berklum.

There's nothing to say, even if you could say it.

Something takes his hand. He can't see and can't move his head to look. But his arm slowly swings out and up. It's the girl, Newsands, and she has Unun's hand too. She has both of your hands in hers. And she brings you together.

A small but wondrous gesture. That's all we have left in our story.

★ ★ ★

In the days that follow, Berklum recovers in some ways more than others. His body heals as well as any Rustan, thanks largely to Lanthan's ministrations. Through an unspoken agreement, he lives in her workshop for these days. She makes sure the lockport – that's what they come to call them eventually – are secure and in working order. After the initial base was inserted, she worked tirelessly to craft the inner workings. Together, in the hours that Berklum can manage, they test those workings so that when he rolls a shoulder or stretches his back in a particular way his wings will respond.

For her part, Unun is just as busy. She has the workshop keys now, and she wastes no time making it her own. She uses what money she has left to clear some of her palla's debts and re-start the business. Work is slow to start with – and not 'good work', as Berklum would say. But word soon starts to spread that the spire's best bonesmith isn't a misery of an old man, but a young woman who listens, who understands, who wants to help. It's not long before she has more work than she can manage, and she starts to think, perhaps one day, of an apprentice.

So the days tumble into weeks in this manner. Which is much the same manner as they always do. It is only us storytellers who mark the time. The rest of you live it.

Finally, Berklum is ready. His lockports are finished and his shoulders fully healed. With the help of Lanthan, Acti and Newsands he has made his wings. He wears them in the workshop for hours at a time, so as to be used to the weight and shape of them. The membranes, made of slip-dog hide this time, are stitched by Acti – who, to the surprise of his meiter, has a gift with the needle. She decides he will stitch up all her recipients from that day on. He is most careful with the holes at the end of each wing. That is, once he understands why Berklum *wants* holes in his wings. That conversation takes most of an afternoon, and Berklum threatening to bring a dead tatterwing into the workshop, before the boy is convinced.

Which brings us here, to this now familiar ledge in the upper spire. Above us are the roosts of countless tatterwings. Below us, Rustan life, and lower still, the Wit's Blood and volcanic rock of the Tear. And out there? Hot air and dark clouds.

This is what Berklum sees, with his feet on the edge.

But he also sees Rustans in those clouds. Rustans flying back and forth between the spire and the ridge. And not just here, but between the cone and the sisters, the stack and the ring, and all across the Rusting Mountains. The air full of Rustan-made wings that harness the heat of their home. Wings made of hide that sail the mountains. That's what they'll be called, Berklum: hidesails.

'Our gift to them,' Newsands says. 'Every Rustan who knows the pain of losing the freedom they knew in childhood, they will have a different kind of freedom to look forward to.'

He can picture it all now but knows he won't live to see it. The future isn't his. But he's helped to shape it.

He steps off the ledge.

He flies. He flies far, and then he falls.

Unun straightens from the tabletop where her last recipient of the day is trying not to fidget. His discomfort is understandable – he broke two ribs some time ago, and they won't heal properly, which makes lying flat difficult. Unun won't keep him there long. She only needs to consider where she might make her initial incisions and take one or two measurements.

'It would be helpful if you didn't wash yourself tonight,' she says.

The man grins. 'I think I can manage that. But you might have to tell my wife.'

She helps him to sit. His breathing is somewhat laboured – his chest is tight, and he's doing his best to hide it. That's not because of Unun, it's just a habit he's acquired.

'First thing tomorrow,' she says.

'I won't know myself when this is all fixed up.'

How true. What is it your palla used to say, Unun?

'My palla used to say our modifications change us so our body is new to us again.'

'I'd like that,' he says, easing an arm into his shirt.

'Tomorrow, then.'

He leaves the workshop, and as the door is closing there's a rush of air. It circles the room, making the candles splutter – Unun has more candles lit now than her palla would use in a year. The sudden breeze stops her. It smells strange: dry, so very dry. A picture comes to her, from where she couldn't say: a picture of sand. Sand as far as any field glasses could see. And somewhere among the rolling dunes is a man. It appears he has fallen, with his heavy cloak surrounding him. Perhaps he's a Wayward man, they wear cloaks. But no. The closer she looks the more the seed of an idea starts to grow. An unbelievable idea. She smiles, bittersweet, and hopes that wherever her palla went, he's happy with how he got there. But she misses him. Every day.

The door clanks shut. She blinks, and she's back in her workshop. The candles settle once more. As she turns back to the forge, to tend the orange embers there, she glances at the high shelf. And for a moment, she sees a flash of it. So brief, but unmistakable in all the Rusting Mountains.

A rainbow.

All things are new once. All things have a first sighting, a first use, a first telling.

But we all forget, don't we?

Can you imagine a time when riding a horse was a far away dream? Or a time when fire only occurred beyond our control, like the wind and the rain?

Maybe you're disappointed that Berklum didn't soar through the Rusting Mountains to return a hero, lauded as the greatest bonesmith there ever was. But those ancient people who first sat on a horse, they fell. Time and time again they fell. Who knows how many were badly hurt, or worse, before we mastered the act of riding? And how many were burnt before we tamed fire?

Berklum was one such person. A man who fell, who was burnt, who flew from the mountains.

We Rustans tell the stories, year after year, of hidesails and how it feels to fly.

This was a story *without* Rustans in the sky. Because we take flight for granted.

Because we forget all things are new once.

Thirteen

The Rustan storyteller bowed, and the applause began immediately. That hadn't happened at the other stories so far in this election. For the Caskers, the Seeders, the Perlish and the Torn, the applause had come slowly, if at all, almost as if those listening were coming out of a deep sleep. But here in the Water Gardens, as the Rustan 'teller told the end of their realm's story, it seemed everyone had been hanging on their final word.

'Looks like you've got some competition,' Cora said to Ruth.

Her sister smiled. 'Of the best kind. The Rustans share our aims. But it's the Wayward story that will give the news of the Tear to the Union, that will ask them to make their choice.'

'The choice that lot makes is the first hurdle,' Cora said, nodding towards the masked voters now swaying back to the garbing pavilion. There they could finally remove their hot, heavy black robes, and the coloured masks of the Audience. And do the thing they were brought here for: choose between the black stone and the white.

Cora doubted their backs could be aching as much as hers

did from sitting on the fountain's edge. As she stretched, she thought of the old man in the Rustans' story, Berklum, him saying so often that spine work was dangerous. That hadn't stopped him getting his own spine modified in the end though. The first lockport. The story of how the Rustans got their wings.

'Adaptation in the face of grief,' Cora muttered to herself. 'The story was about finding a new way to be in your home.'

'And showing how that brings freedom, not restriction,' Ruth said. 'That's a message the Union needs to hear.'

'It's not without risk though,' Cora said. 'The old man flying off to Audience knows where. Lost in the desert beyond the Tear.'

'But look what he gave the people of the Rusting Mountains in return.'

Cora rolled her shoulders and felt an alarming series of clicks. 'You ever seen them fly?'

'Many times, but only when I've been in the Mountains, where the air currents are right for the hidesails. It's amazing to see. You should go, Cora, once this is all over, before…'

'Before the Tear swallows the Rusting Mountains?'

Cora was thinking of Serus. They could go together. *Once all this is over.* She'd been so focused on the Wayward story, keeping Ruth safe until the moment she spoke its first words, but there was a whole world of *after*. A world of Wit's blood.

There was a noise behind them – a kind of clap, then a shunt. Cora spun round.

But the noise was just the fountain starting up again. Water spurted from the mouths of the bronze kenna birds, and the air around Cora and Ruth was once again cool with spray.

The Audience were out of sight now, but no one else would be able to leave until the voting chests had been secured and were on their way. Harassed purple tunics were now explaining this to those in the public gallery trying to get out of their seats.

'We should slip away now,' Ruth said, 'while everyone's distracted.'

'Better to wait. Safer in a crowd.' Cora reached for her bindle tin. 'Want one?'

'Well, if we're not going anywhere for a while…'

Cora handed a rolled smoke to Ruth.

'This hat itches like it's lice-ridden,' Ruth said, rubbing at her forehead which, Cora had to admit, did look pretty red. 'It's the stuff it's made from. So coarse. I don't know how the Seeders put up with them.'

'Glad to hear you haven't been forced to use *Lowlanders*.'

'I'll call them that when their Chambers stops trying to kill me.'

'Speaking of which…'

Lowlander Chambers Morton came into view. She was a short woman, easy to miss in the crush of people milling around the Commission box. Her grey hair was cut into a jaunty crop, which was no doubt expensive.

'When I confronted her at the Assembly building,' Cora said, 'after I got back from the Tear, she said she'd known our parents, that she'd been to the house.'

Ruth drew deeply on her bindle. 'Don't you remember her?'

'I've tried but…'

'Morton was always first to arrive at the parties and last to leave. Until I found her on Father's lap. They were in the salon. Mother had gone to bed. It was late. I'd gone down to get a drink, probably woken by their ridiculous attempts to keep quiet.'

Cora stared at her older sister. 'You never told me this.'

'Why burden you with it?'

It was on the tip of Cora's tongue to remind Ruth how much she'd burdened her twelve-year-old sister with when she'd fled Fenest, selling the story of the Gorderheim embezzlement to the pennysheets on the way. But she didn't. What would be the point now?

'What were Father and Morton… doing?' Cora asked.

'Not much, thanks to me disrupting them. But I was old enough to know what they were *about* to do, and to understand that it wouldn't have been the first time. Something about their ease with each other, even when I was standing in front of them. Morton didn't come to parties after that, and not long after, she became Chambers anyway. She told Mother she was too busy. A helpful excuse – once someone puts on the brown robe and the manacles, they haven't got time to drink Greynal in ordinary salons with ordinary people.'

'But embezzlement isn't off the cards,' Cora said. 'Morton said she was the one who made the stolen money disappear. Used it to buy land in the Lowlands.'

Ruth dropped her bindle in the fountain. 'I know, but that's one silver lining of the Tear widening: Morton's land in the far south has gone, and the Gorderheim theft with it. Do you ever go back to the old house? Just to look at it, I mean. I know it was sold.'

'Never.'

'Good,' Ruth said. 'Looking back does no one any favours.'

Cora suspected her sister's words were chosen for another reason: Chief Inspector Sillian was now in view, chatting with Lowlander Chambers Morton. Morton's brown robes, the mark of the Chambers, were a sharp contrast against Sillian's deep blue jacket pressed and brushed to perfection. The two women were deep in conversation. What might that be about? Cora wondered idly. The number of cutpurse attacks since the election started? How the Assembly – in the last few days of being controlled by the Perlish – needed to consider extra police funding to sort out the leaks at the Bernswick station? Or perhaps Morton and Sillian were talking about a former detective and her ability to enter a tool sharpener's shop, then disappear.

As Cora watched, another brown robe joined them: one of the Perlish Chambers. There were two: the eastern and western duchies each demanded their own representation in the Assembly.

Sillian gave a low bow and stepped away, but then Morton called her back. Sillian did as she was bid, but not before her shoulders had slumped, her head dropped – small movements, but Cora saw them. Morton had some hold over Cora's former boss, something that kept her working for the Chambers.

'Don't think I don't know what you've given up for me,' Ruth said softly, nodding in the direction of Sillian and the two Chambers.

'Makes it easier when it turns out not to be the thing you thought it was.'

'You miss it, Cora, I know you do, and I—'

A cry went up, to Cora's relief, and then one whole side of the garbing pavilion opened. From within the deep shadows, a huge object was carried into the sunlight.

The voting chest.

It was borne on wooden poles, four constables carrying them, purple tunics pushing aside anyone unlucky enough to be in the path of the chest. Ordinarily, a constabulary coach would be standing by to receive it, but the nature of the Water Gardens made that impossible. So today the voting chest would be carried out by constables instead. One of them looked familiar: Cora would know those teeth anywhere.

Evidently Jenkins had landed herself on the security for the voting chest. She'd be pleased, Cora knew, though not if the posting was her mother's doing. Jenkins hated the system of favours and privilege that basically ran the Commission. It was something the constable shared with Cora.

'You know where they go?' Ruth said.

'Constables?'

'The voting chests. When they leave here, with the uncounted votes of a story inside, where are they taken?'

Cora shrugged. 'That's beyond my pay grade. Why do *you* want to know, Ruth?'

'I like to know the whole story.'

The constables set off at a cracking pace, and now that the voting chest was away, the purple tunics allowed the public gallery to empty. People rushed to speak to one another about the story they'd just heard, and their guesses at the votes. At the gates, the pennysheet sellers would be ready to ask those leaving the Water Gardens which way their vote would have gone, and the exit polls would be printed in the 'sheets within the hour. From the tone of the chat burbling all around her, Cora thought the Rustans would come out well. Perhaps she should have found some coins to make a bet.

Ruth was still looking in the direction that the voting chest had gone.

'Wherever the votes go,' Cora said, 'it'll have to be one of the safest places in Fenest. To keep the chests locked until all the stories have been told, no counting until you've said the last word of the Wayward tale—'

'No counting, or slipping a few extra white stones into a chest, taking out some black...'

Cora stared at Ruth. 'You can't really believe votes are tampered with?'

'In Fenest, anything's possible.'

'Never a truer word,' a man said.

Cora spun round to see who had appeared suddenly beside them at the fountain. It was a young man, tall and broad, dressed in Seeder clothes, as they were, but without the hat.

'Help you?' Cora said, her hand reaching into the folds of her coat for her 'dusters. If Ruth had brought her knife, now might be the time to produce it.

'Just wanted to wish good day to fellow Lowlanders. Not many of us here today.' He looked at the now emptying public gallery, everyone streaming down the various paths that led to the gates. 'Seems mostly Fenestirans got to hear the story.'

'No surprise there,' Ruth said, her gaze firmly fixed on the stranger.

Except, he wasn't a stranger. Cora recognised him, recognised his voice, but she couldn't think why. She glanced around the fountain. Still plenty of people about, plenty of purple tunics. No one was paying her and Ruth any attention.

'Aye, you're right, friend,' the young man said. 'The capital looks after its own. Only got to look beyond the south gate to see that, the way people are living...' He shook his head, as if dismayed at the thought, but Cora wasn't convinced.

'We must look to our Chambers,' Cora said, testing him. 'She'll protect the people of the Lowlands.'

He nodded eagerly, his eyes bright, and the change was striking: here was his real self. A supporter of Morton.

'The Union can't afford to neglect the Lowlands,' he said, stepping closer to the fountain. Cora got to her feet and squared up to him, but it seemed to make no difference to his eagerness. 'We feed all the other realms, after all.'

'That we do,' Ruth said. 'You did a good job of showing that, in your story, I mean.'

So *that* was where Cora knew him from: this was the Seeder storyteller. If he was surprised that Ruth recognised him, he didn't show it.

The area around the bandstand was all but empty now. The purple tunics had gathered at the garbing pavilion to take it down. Cora's plan had been to hide in the crowds leaving the Water Gardens, but at this rate she and Ruth were likely to miss their chance.

'We'll be making our way now, friend,' Cora said.

'Of course. Well, been good to talk to you both.' His gaze never left Ruth. 'I'll see you at the last story.'

He lingered for a moment too long – time to end this strange conversation. But then he was turning away, lifting an arm in farewell, and Ruth's hand stayed Cora's.

'He's no threat,' she said.

Cora let out a breath she hadn't realised she'd been holding. 'He was... unsettling.'

'Storytellers often are.' At Cora's glance she added, 'And I'd include myself in that.'

'I guess it explains why Nullan is always so short-tempered.'

The Seeder storyteller disappeared between two hedges, and Latecomer's luck, he'd gone in the opposite direction.

'Come on,' Cora said, 'we need to go.'

Her back was stiff, and by the way Ruth was moving, Cora guessed she was feeling the same. But she hurried her sister along, trying to catch up with the knots of people ahead, threading their way through the paths, around fountains and flower beds, over the little bridges.

'His name's Jerome,' Ruth said.

'He knew who you were.'

'Little doubt about it.'

'Was it a threat, when he said, "See you at the last story"?'

'That'd be a turn for the Audience, one storyteller killing another. But I can't believe that lad has got it in him.'

'I remember thinking when he began the Seeder story,' Cora said, 'that his voice wouldn't carry in Tithe Hall. He managed in the end though.'

'To have told the Seeders' election story, he must be the best the Seeders have, and yet he doesn't have an ounce of the brilliance of Nicholas.'

But Nicholas Ento would only be telling his stories to the

Swaying Audience now. No one in Fenest would ever hear him.

They'd come to the last of the narrow, humped bridges they needed to cross. Ruth went first, as always.

But then someone stepped in front of Ruth. He'd put on a disguise, just as they had, but for him it was Fenestiran clothes. His Wayward cloak, which would have been all too conspicuous in the Water Gardens, was gone, but Cora knew his shaved head, his arrogant glare.

Tannir.

He caught Ruth off balance, and she stumbled. To Cora – only a few feet behind Ruth – it looked as if Ruth fell into Tannir's arms, and onto the glinting blade in his hand.

Her sister let out a sigh, and then she was down, a crumpled heap at the end of the bridge.

Tannir made to check his handiwork, but Cora was on him then, grabbing his wool coat. He twisted free and hurried away, quickly lost in the crowds. Cora had to let him go, had to see to Ruth. She turned her sister over and saw the blood spreading across the pale blue cloth of her shirt, the vines now sprouting red fruit across her hip.

Tannir wasn't a coward after all. But he was a fool, and she wouldn't let her sister die at the hands of a fool. Ruth mattered too much for that to be her end; she was worth so much more. Not to the Wayward election delegation, not to the southern alliance – to Cora.

'Ruth, can you hear me? Ruth!'

There was a lot of blood. Her sister couldn't seem to focus, her eyes rolling in her head, sweat gleaming around her mouth.

'Ruth, I'm going to pick you up, and we're going to get

out of here. It's going to hurt, but I need you to try to walk, you hear me?'

A low moan was all the answer Ruth managed, but it was enough.

Cora pulled her to standing and then placed her coat over Ruth's side, where she thought the blade had gone in. 'Hold this, it might slow the bleeding.' And hide it too, Cora hoped, because being stopped by purple tunics now wouldn't help Ruth, not ultimately. Cora would have to figure this one out herself.

They began their slow way towards the old pie stall. There were still plenty of people around, but the looks they gave Cora and Ruth spoke of Seeders who'd had too much sun, too much drink, too much excitement at hearing an election story.

She grabbed a pennysheet girl who was shouting the new odds on the Rustan story and gave her a message. If she could get it to Bernswick station before the Poet's bells chimed again, there'd be an extra penny for her trouble. The girl baulked at having to leave her pitch, so Cora promised more – she'd give all she had in the world and that wasn't much. The girl set down her sheets and sped away. Cora asked the Audience that she be quick enough.

Fourteen

With Ruth slumped against her, Cora pushed her way into the whorehouse. The lad on shift welcoming the punters took one look at the two Seeders – one of whom was covered in blood, the other sweating and cursing – and hared off down the passage, crying for the madam.

Cora booted the door shut and went after him, struggling to keep hold of Ruth who seemed to be growing weaker.

'You still with me?' Cora said.

'You take me to all the best places…'

The joke gave Cora hope when the blood that leaked from Ruth's hip and her sister's semi-conscious state had all but taken it away.

The madam appeared in a doorway: a woman not much older than the oldest of the whores themselves, but she'd been in business for a while now. Better class of customer, this close to the Water Gardens. She was tall and slim, with black hair braided and piled high on her head. On the days the better customers visited, there'd be flowers woven into the plaits. Today was clearly only an ordinary day, even with a stabbed woman dripping blood onto the carpet.

'Haven't see you for a while, Detective.'

There was no time for corrections. 'The election's kept me busy.'

'Kept my lads and lasses busy too,' the madam said, and grinned. 'You'll be needing…'

'A room without a view, some peace and quiet.'

'Always happy to help you out, Detective, especially with my licence coming due.'

Cora licked her lips. Was now the time to say she wouldn't be able to help smooth the passage of paperwork through the Wheelhouse? Ruth gave a low moan.

'Just send a lad to Bernswick,' Cora said, and the madam smiled. There were none so unshakeable in Fenest as whorehouse madams – they'd seen it all, and their stories were surely favourites of the Audience.

The madam led them deep into the whorehouse, past closed doors, past the cries and laughter and much more besides. With each step, Ruth seemed to lean heavier on her.

Finally, the madam stopped at one of the doors. 'Get blood on any of my lads and lasses' things, you'll answer to them. Some of my lot are handy with their fists, but you'll remember that, won't you, from your previous visits.'

'Only too well,' Cora said to the madam. 'And I won't forget this either.'

Cora elbowed her way into the room which wasn't much bigger than the table standing at the centre, a few mismatching chairs with it.

There were no windows but a small pane of glass set into the roof. They must be right in the heart of the house, and this some kind of break room for the whores. She eased Ruth onto the table. Her sister's eyes were glassy and her skin cold yet sweaty.

'You want a stitcher?' the madam said from the doorway.

'No need,' Cora said, turning round. 'I've sent—'

But the madam had gone. A lad came along a few minutes later with a pail of warm water and cloths of soft, clean linen. He didn't hang around. Cora did her best to move the scattered shawls and feathers, shoes and even children's toys away from the table, and away from both their bloodstained hands.

Thank the Latecomer, Pruett made good time. The pennysheet girl Cora had sent had earned her coins.

'So this is your new job is it, Gorderheim? I've been wondering what you were up to. Must admit, even my *wildest* imaginings didn't involve a place like this.'

'Not even close,' Cora said. 'This is... temporary, and serious.' She ushered him to where Ruth was lying on a table. 'Stabbed.'

Pruett dropped his black bag and began to examine Ruth who lay still, glistening with sweat, silent as the Mute. Cora bit back her fear.

'I'm surprised you sent for me,' Pruett said, without looking up from his work. For all the jokes between them, Cora knew she could trust him with Ruth's care. It wouldn't be pretty work, but he'd do his best to save her. 'Surely a place like this has its own stitcher on the books. The scrapes people get into in whorehouses.'

'I got too used to your butchering, Pruett, what can I say?'

'Once you've been lucky enough to have me stitch you up—'

'You don't recognise any better.'

Pruett was in his shirtsleeves, which were as stained as ever. Cora had often wondered why the stitcher chose to wear white shirts, given that he spent his working life examining dead bodies in various stages of decay. Maybe it was a badge of his profession, all those bloodstains and smears. Audience knew what people made of him when he left the station's cold room looking like that. It was a surprise he'd never been reported to his own station as a cause for public concern.

'Take it you're not going to introduce us?' he said, nodding towards Ruth.

'Last time I checked you didn't need a name to stitch a body.'

'And there was me thinking a break from Bernswick might have softened you up. But I can see your troubles have followed you.'

'They follow us all, Pruett. That's why the Audience loves our stories.'

Pruett gave a grim laugh and lifted Cora's bloodied coat from Ruth's side, then he began to cut away what was left of her sister's Seeder shirt. The light blue cloth was now dark with blood. The small room stank of it. Despite the jokes, the Bernswick stitcher was tender in his examination of Ruth, careful not to disturb the flesh which, to Cora's eye, looked badly torn. As Pruett examined the wound, Ruth lay still and silent, staring at the smoke-blackened beams of the ceiling. If it wasn't for the fact her sister blinked once in a while, Cora would have thought she was dead. Moving her coat out of Pruett's way – the cloth warm as well as damp, the heat of Ruth's blood still there – Cora realised her hands were shaking.

'Just this?' Pruett said, gently pressing the flesh of Ruth's side, above and below the cut on her hip. 'No other injuries?'

'Far as I know.' Cora slumped into an old chair that had seen better days, and tried to roll a smoke. 'I chased him off as soon as I could.'

Pruett glanced at Cora.

'It's better you don't know,' she said.

He reached into the pail of water and wrung out a cloth, then set to cleaning Ruth's wound. Cora heard her sister's sharp intake of breath and looked up.

'You two are louder than the Brawler,' Ruth muttered.

'You're alive then,' Pruett said, dunking his cloth back in the pail. The water had turned a scummy pink. Cora sucked hard on her bindle.

'Just about.' Ruth gestured for Cora to hand her the smoke, then said to Pruett, 'Well?'

'Whoever did this,' Pruett said, 'the angle was bad – bad for him but good for you. Half an inch to the right and you'd have been dead before he'd wiped the blood from the blade. As it is, he missed anything important, and I've stopped the bleeding.'

Now Pruett had cleaned the blood Cora could see the wound: a curved cut of three inches that sat just above Ruth's hip bone. Ruth didn't have much flesh to cushion such blows. This really was a story for the Latecomer.

The stitcher rummaged in his black bag and drew out a fold of cloth. Within it were the tools that gave his trade its name: needles and thread. He set the cloth on the table and took something else from his bag – a squat bottle of dark glass with a fat cork. The contents sloshed audibly as he offered it to Ruth.

'Take the edge off while I close this up? It's no Greynal, but it'll do the job.'

Ruth shook her head. 'I'll need my wits about me when I get out of here.'

'Suit yourself. I know you won't want any, Gorderheim, but if you'll excuse a man drinking alone.' Pruett uncorked the bottle and took a nip.

'Anything to make your hand steadier,' Cora said. 'I don't want my sister losing any more blood when we get out of here.'

Pruett's hand had stilled as he chose his needle, and Cora cursed herself. The stitcher glanced at Ruth who returned his look with a glare.

'Sister? Well, well, Cora. You kept that quiet.'

Ruth grabbed Pruett's wrist. 'And I hope you'll do the same.'

The stitcher looked down at Ruth's hand, then at Cora. 'I came, didn't I? If Sillian finds out I'm helping you, and on police time—'

'I trust him, Ruth. There is such a thing as stitcher's code, remember?'

There was a long moment of silence, broken by the sound of a door banging somewhere, followed by laughter. Then Ruth let Pruett go and turned her face to the wall.

'Get on with it then,' she said. 'There's somewhere I need to be.'

Pruett went back to choosing a needle. 'As charming as each other, but your capacity for pain is better. Cora here screamed the station down when I fixed her up after the Hook barge.'

Was Ruth trying not to smile?

The stitcher licked a length of black thread and stuffed

it through the eye of a needle that looked to Cora thick as an ink nib. 'How *is* your leg, Cora? Want me to check how it's healing?'

'I'll take my chances.'

He bent low over Ruth's side and readied his needle. 'Sure you don't want that drink?'

'Get on with it!' Ruth said through gritted teeth.

'Brace yourself.'

Cora found she was pleased to hear Ruth scream.

When it was done, Pruett took his leave, and the madam called them a gig. A Garnuck's gig. The madam clearly thought Commission employee wages were better than they were. Cora hoped Ruth had some money stashed about her. The madam gifted her sister a blouse made of thin red cloth, discarded by a whore no doubt, but presented to Ruth as if it was a real hardship to give it away.

'With my compliments, Detective, for all your help in the last few years.'

Ruth shot Cora a glance, but Cora ignored it, just as she ignored the wink from the madam. The bloodied remains of Ruth's Seeder shirt were balled in the corner of the sad room when they finally left.

'Where to?' asked the gig driver, a young lad wearing a cap two sizes too big for him. Surely he couldn't be old enough to take a pair of reins?

'You know which safe house is next on the list?' Cora asked Ruth softly as they climbed up. 'You know where we'll find Nullan?'

Ruth put a hand to her side and winced. Beneath the whore's red blouse were several thick layers of bandage wrapped around Ruth's middle. 'That stitcher of yours—'

'He's not mine,' Cora said, and helped her to sit. 'And he usually works on dead people. He's not good with bodies that still have a pulse.'

'I can tell.'

'You know we charge by the time not the mileage?' the driver said. 'This ain't a Clotham's gig.'

'Then why's a scrawny kid like you driving it?' Cora said.

The driver gawped at her, revealing neat rows of good teeth. 'Look, we going to sit here all day or you got somewhere to be?'

'The docks,' Ruth said. 'The Murbick end.'

'Finally,' the driver muttered, shook his reins and the gig clattered off.

'You're going through with it then,' Cora asked Ruth, 'the trip upriver?'

'Of course I am. It's up to me to get the Wayward Hook, Cora.'

Ruth half sat, half lay on the richly embroidered seat of the gig. The pattern was the symbol of the Tear woven in red and orange wool on a cream background. It had been so long since Cora had caught one of the expensive Garnuck's gigs that she'd forgotten the seats bore the realm symbols. The flame of the Tear here, perhaps the horseshoe of the Wayward in the gig going the other way.

'Do you remember that game we used to play,' she said to Ruth, 'when we took Garnuck's gigs?'

'All the gigs we took were Garnuck's. Mother would hardly travel in anything run by Clotham, would she?'

'But the game. We had a score card to keep track of the seat designs.'

Ruth smiled, closed her eyes. 'I remember. There were always so many gigs with Seeder spades on their seats. What colours were they?'

'Green and brown,' Cora said.

'Of course they were. Seeders and Perlish. High numbers for those. Never any Wayward. You were so excited when we finally caught a gig with horseshoes on the seat.'

Cora stroked one of the red-and-orange flames on the gig seat. 'So were you.'

'Suspect I was humouring you. The way you went on about the scorecard.' The gig jolted over a pothole and Ruth cried out.

'You won't humour me now?' Cora said, her gaze on her sister who lay prone in the corner of the seat, her eyes screwed shut. She was clearly feeling every uneven cobble, of which there were plenty now they were nearing the docks. It wasn't just the roads that gave it away. The air changed too, carrying the sourness of the river here where people loaded and unloaded, sailed and docked, all day and all night.

'Cora, please.'

'You're hardly in a state to go sailing.'

Ruth kept her eyes closed, but her hand gripping the edge of the gig's seat was as pale as the wool. 'I have to get the Hook. To be back in time for it to be displayed according to the Commission rules, I have to leave today. There's no time.'

The gig rounded a corner and the oily expanse of the River Stave came in sight. It was at its dirtiest dockside. Lining the docks themselves was a jumble of barges and people swarming all over the decks, most of them inked.

'And Tannir?' Cora said. 'He nearly killed you today, Ruth. I should have—'

'Set us down here!' Ruth called to the driver. He did as he was bid but with more speed than Cora thought was right; the gig skidded to a halt, and the horse bucked in her traces.

Cora helped Ruth down. 'At least you've got some colour in you again.'

'See? Better already!' Her sister fished some coins from the Seeder trousers she was still wearing and tossed them to the driver. He opened his mouth to protest the lack of tip, but then took one look at the women and flicked the reins. The gig went haring off down the dockside, Caskers calling out curses as it thundered past.

'Some people are in too much of a hurry,' Cora said, shaking her head.

'Nullan's crew will be waiting for us. We've been waylaid too long as it is. Come on.'

To Cora's surprise, Ruth turned away from the water's edge and headed down an alley. Cora checked for anyone watching, before following her sister into the crate-strewn, puddled passage that ran between tall warehouses that had seen better days – blistered paint on warped wooden clapboard, windows cracked, some holes stuffed with rags. Attempts at painting the walls with pitch to keep the rain out appeared to have stopped halfway up the building fronts. This kind of dereliction wasn't seen at all the docks in Fenest, but it was true of the Murbick end where the gig had set them down. She'd walked this patch as a constable, but not for years now. Once she made detective at Bernswick, this part of town was someone else's problem.

In the thin strip of sky overhead, clouds had gathered.

The warmth of the day was still hanging around, much like the stink of the docks, but now there was rain on the air.

'Tannir,' Cora said, 'he should never have been able to get that close to you.'

'But he did. There's no use going on about it.'

She felt the first drop of water on the back of her neck. 'I failed you.'

Ruth spun round, wincing with the effort. 'You *saved* me, Cora! Without you I'd never have made it out of the Water Gardens. I would have bled to death on that stupid little bridge, surrounded by stupid little Perlish shrubs.'

Cora opened her mouth to argue but Ruth wouldn't let her, grabbing her arm.

'I know, I know – you want to protect me, stop murderous Wayward men from stabbing me in the first place, but they're pretty keen on that, let's be honest.'

Despite herself, Cora smiled. 'That I won't argue with.'

'Good. Come on.' Ruth carried on down the passage, but she kept hold of Cora's arm, leaning on it with all her weight. Not that there was much of it, but it was a surprise nonetheless.

'There's one good thing to say about Tannir managing to stab you,' Cora said.

'This should be interesting.'

'Tannir being the fool that he is,' Cora said, 'there's a good chance he believes he killed you today.'

The end of the alley was in sight: open water, the sound of wood being shunted about. Someone crying the price of fish. The raindrops came thicker, faster.

'Let's hope so. That would make for a quieter journey upriver.'

'I was thinking the same,' Cora said.

They stepped out onto the dock again – Ruth's cut-through, Cora realised now, having avoided an open corner of the quay that was crammed with Caskers and their wares. It was definitely raining now: a story for the Painter, beginning with Cora soaked through and staring at a barge.

It was wide, low-lying and tied up opposite the alleyway – and as barges went it had seen better days. The peeling paint and the cracked windows looked a lot like the warehouses they'd just passed. On the much-patched side was the remains of a painted design. Some kind of flower?

This wasn't the weather to take a closer look, and there didn't seem to be time either. Coming down the gangway towards them was a familiar figure: slight, wearing a cowl, throwing up her inked hands as if to say where have you been, what happened? Nullan hurried them onto the barge. Ruth was trying to explain, but Cora couldn't hear them over the noise of the rain drumming on wood, and everything around her was made of wood: the barge, the cart alongside, the last of the crates and barrels being loaded by three or four inked dockhands. There was another figure with them. He turned and looked at her. A welcome sight, his auburn topknot dripping with rain, his slipdog hide glistening with the same. Even his metal cheekbones looked shinier.

'I didn't think you'd come,' she said to Serus.

The Rustan shrugged. 'And miss a boat trip in this *lovely* weather?'

'Serus. This trip – it might not be safe.'

A cry went up from the barge. It was Nullan, calling Cora aboard.

'I guess it's time to find out,' Serus said, then frowned.

'Why are you wearing Seeder clothes, and is that blood on your shirt? Cora—'

'It's a long story.'

Serus offered his arm. 'My favourite kind.'

Fifteen

Nullan led them through the barge, explaining who was who, what went where, what not to touch, how not to get in the way of the crew – passengers in the wrong place at the wrong time were readily thrown overboard. Given the water seeping through the floor and dripping from the ceiling, the boat might sink and see them all in the water anyway.

They were making their way along a corridor that ran the length of the barge, cutting straight through the middle. Ruth had stayed behind, sitting in the alcove near the door. She was fine, she said, though her pallor suggested otherwise.

'This thing is bigger than it looks,' Serus said to Cora, practically shouting to be heard over the noise of the rain hitting the patched wooden roof.

'That's often the way with Casker barges,' Cora said. 'Searched a few in my time at Bernswick. They often seem like different vessels inside.'

'That sounds useful for a crew looking to smuggle cargo,' Serus said.

'They take a lifetime to search,' Cora grumbled. 'All the tiny cupboards and tables that turn out to be boxes...'

Serus looked pleased at this idea. 'Ingenious, really. Making use of every bit of space. I wonder if it's the same in Bordair, with their houses.'

Bordair – the inland lake the Caskers called home.

'I've never been. You?' she asked.

He shook his head. 'But I'd like to go. Perhaps, after the election, we could—'

'Watch yourself here!' Nullan called, and just in time – Cora saw the low beam and ducked. From the *thunk* and the groan behind her, Serus hadn't been so quick.

On either side of the corridor were small rooms – 'cabins' Nullan called them. Each had a narrow, hard-looking bed bolted to the wall – 'berths'. Evidently there was a whole new language to learn once you were staying on a barge rather than searching one. Cora counted four cabins, two on each side of the corridor.

The other rooms all had obvious purposes and less than obvious Casker names: the room with a stove and jumble of dented pans was a 'galley', the place to sit and eat the food cooked in the galley, with wooden benches built into the walls, was called a 'saloon', and then there was a windowless room packed floor to ceiling with ropes and hooks, casks, folded canvas, what looked like nets, poles.

'What's the name of this one?' Cora said.

Nullan looked at her as if she'd lost her wits. 'It's a store-cupboard, Cora.'

'Of course it is.'

She thought she saw something move, in a heap of nets near her feet. Cora stumbled back, bumping into Serus. His torso was solid: a wall of muscle.

'You get many problems with rats?' she asked Nullan,

but the Casker was turning away. Cora quickly shut the door of the storeroom without risking another look inside.

'Are you all right?' Serus said, but she waved away the question. These barges were a mystery.

'Now, as to sleeping, this is the Captain's cabin.' Nullan pointed to the berthed room that was slightly larger than the others and with an extra piece of furniture in the form of a desk, above which were pinned maps and charts – the Union, but with all the rivers marked. There was more blue than Cora had imagined. Nullan pointed to another doorway. 'Ruth and I will share this one, Harker is in this one, and you two will take this. Hope you don't mind sharing. We weren't expecting an extra passenger.'

Nullan shot Cora a knowing look, one that made the piercings in her eyebrows dance about.

To Cora's great frustration, she felt her cheeks growing warm. 'It's fine,' she said gruffly.

Serus, she noticed, was suddenly interested in the water-marked and scuffed wood panelling that lined the barge's gloomy interior. The rain thundered down and the dark, noisy corridor was at once too small and too full of embarrassment.

'What's through here?' Cora said, pushing past Nullan to open the door at the end of corridor.

Nullan reached out to stop her. 'Don't—'

Cora banged the door open and found herself in the open air, the rain louder, the air wet, though she was spared the rain thanks to a canvas canopy, which covered the front of the barge while being open on three sides. She vaguely remembered Nullan had said this was called the 'for'ard'. The space ahead was dominated by a large wheel and the woman standing in front of it, who spun round and was now frowning at Cora.

'If you're the sister,' the woman said, looking Cora up and down, 'you don't look like you're related.'

'You're not the first person to say that.'

Cora extended her hand, and the grip that met it was firm, hot and calloused.

'Captain Luine.'

Short metal bolts pierced the skin on the inside of the woman's ears. Her lips and nose were heavily ringed. One side of her face was inked with some kind of pointed design Cora hadn't seen in Fenest before, and her spikey grey hair reminded Cora of an old broomhead.

She looked well past seventy but might have been younger; a Casker's life on a barge aged a body almost as fast as the Wayward aged in the saddle. A short pipe was crammed into the corner of her mouth. There was a box of levers beside the wheel, and on top of the box was a cup of something that looked and smelt to Cora like lannat: a spirit the Caskers made while sailing. It kept well on barges, apparently, and was enjoyed by a certain kind of customer in the Dancing Oak – the hard-living kind of customer, because from the smell of it, lannat stripped the pitch from barge-boards too. The captain saw her eyeing the glass.

'Got to keep the chill off. This rain. Get you one?'

'She doesn't drink,' Nullan said from behind Cora.

Captain Luine's eyebrows shot up. 'They told me you worked for the Commission.'

'I did, but—'

'Those bean-counters!' Captain Luine wasn't listening.

'Would drive anyone to drink, working for them. All the bleedin' forms!'

'Can't argue with that,' Cora said.

'We're moving?' Serus peered out from underneath the canopy. 'I wasn't aware we'd cast off.' He turned to Luine. 'A smooth-running vessel you have here, Captain.'

Luine's pride was obvious, as was the fact Serus had just gone up in her estimation, even if he *was* an unexpected passenger. The captain slapped the wheel. 'That's the *Pretty Lilly* for you, my Rustan friend!'

Lilly. That explained the faded flower design Cora had seen on the barge's side as she'd come aboard. *Pretty* was a stretch though.

Captain Luine stared lovingly at her wheel. 'She might not be the newest barge on the river—'

'You can say that again,' Cora muttered.

'—but you can trust old *Lilly* here to get you where you need to go. Wherever that might be.'

The barge was making its way past the docks, close enough to the other craft moored there that Cora felt she could easily step right onto another barge. It seemed a risky course, but Captain Luine was making it with only half an eye on the river.

'Go on up if you want a better view,' Luine said. 'You're responsible for your own lives on this barge, but keep away from the edge of the deck, and you'll be all right.'

Serus needed no encouragement, and with a leap that reminded Cora of the Rustan children in the Seat of the Commoner, he was away and out of sight. Cora clambered after him, feeling a sharp pull in her leg: the injury from the Hook barge still giving her trouble.

'Here.' Serus reached for Cora's hand and pulled her up, out of the footwell where the captain had her wheel and levers, onto the deck.

It was possible to walk all the way round the barge on the deck, and over it too – rickety ladders leaned against the humped forms of the rooms, giving access to the roof where cargo was lashed down to keep it from rolling into the river. There were hatches between the bundles of cargo that meant a nimble Casker could drop down into the belly of the barge as needed.

Standing on the roof now, adjusting the stained and fraying sails, the rain sluicing off him, was a tall, slim Casker roughly the same age as her. His ink began on his chin and cascaded down his neck – a pattern of hatched lines. Cora guessed this stringy man must be Harker. He, Captain Luine and Nullan formed the crew of the *Pretty Lilly* to take Ruth upriver. Harker stopped his work to raise a hand. The inked hatching was on his palm too. As Cora returned the gesture she realised she hadn't let go of Serus's hand since he'd helped her up. He was smiling and she found she was too.

The weather was terrible, the air ripe with all the foulness of the docks, and yet she didn't want to go back inside. Serus didn't seem to want that either, so she hauled a crate to a partly sheltered spot, and they sat down.

'What made you decide to come?' she said.

'After I saw the distiller's, I got to thinking about what you said – about the need to ask questions.' Serus wiped the rain from his face and stared out at the warehouses slipping by. With the daylight beginning to leach away, lamps were being lit. Dockside almost looked pretty. 'I asked myself why the Commission didn't want me to file a report on that fire.'

'Any answers?'

He shook his head and drops spun from his richly auburn hair. 'This election… It's not been right from the start. First a storyteller gets murdered, then the Hook barge sinks, the Torn 'teller willingly risks his own life for his story and, with the last word, pays the ultimate price. And then when a fire guts a building, people are said to have died, but there are no bodies and any talk of an investigation is quashed.' He turned to her. 'And a good detective of many years' standing loses her job.'

'So?'

'So I filed the report on the cause of the fire. At least I'll be able to sleep at night. Figured I had nothing to lose.'

'Apart from your job,' Cora said.

'I didn't hang around long enough for the Commission to relieve me of my post. If it's going to happen, there's nothing I can say or do now to change that. So why not join you on this trip out of the city?'

'I can think of a few reasons.' Cora tapped a loose plank on the deck. 'This fine vessel being one of them, plus the woman I arrived with – you must have seen she was badly hurt, Serus.'

'But she had you to lean on, so things can't be too bad. She's your sister, isn't she? The one you mentioned at the distiller's?'

'Ruth. She's the new Wayward storyteller.'

Serus stared at her. The metal plates in his cheeks moved, though he said nothing. It was as if he was chewing over what Cora had said, and who could blame him? It was a lot to take in, and there was more.

'Ruth was never meant to be a storyteller,' Cora told him, 'but now she has to be. Nicholas Ento might be dead, but his story needs to be told. Ruth is the only one who can tell it.'

'I thought storytellers couldn't tell someone else's story?' Serus said.

'This is a… special case. A sad case. Ento was Ruth's son.'

There was silence between them then. The rain was easing, but the drops still falling from the ledges and overhangs on the barge were loud. The sails caught the rising breeze and flapped, and as she glanced up at them, she became aware of a figure crouched there in the gloom of early evening. She stiffened, then the figure moved, fiddled with something on the edge of a sail, and Cora caught the dull gleam of a piercing. It was Harker, of course it was, just doing what a Casker bargehand did. But Cora was uneasy – she'd forgotten he was there, and now she had the feeling he was listening to her and Serus. Then from the ever-darkening quayside came a burst of shouting and her thoughts were scattered. It had been a long day, and she'd nearly lost Ruth. That was all it was. They were underway now, sailing out of Fenest, leaving behind Tannir, Morton and the rest of it. Cora needed to stop worrying.

'You still haven't told me where we're going, Cora.'

'That's because I don't know. Ruth hasn't told me. But wherever we *are* going, the Wayward Hook is waiting there for her.'

'The Hook?' he said. 'So that's what this is all about.'

The lights of the dock were thinning out. They were

leaving Fenest, and as the city grew quieter, the river grew wider, louder – Cora could hear the water sliding past them.

'Well, that and I thought if we had some time together, out of the city…'

'Yes?'

'We could see where *we* were going.'

Serus was about to say something when there was a shout from inside the barge, followed by a second voice. The loud, unmistakable tones of a certain pennysheet girl.

Sixteen

Cora couldn't believe what she was hearing: it was Marcus. Marcus was on the barge. How was that possible? She rushed inside.

The barge interior was a blaze of light from the lamps swinging from beams, hanging under cupboards, set on the crates that were everywhere. After the darkness of being outside with Serus, it took Cora a moment to focus.

At the store cupboard, Nullan was hauling out a grubby leg at the end of which was a boot Cora recognised; she'd paid for the pair, after Marcus's previous ones had grown so full of holes they'd been practically sandals. But the trousers the girl was wearing... It was hard to be sure with the cluster of people in the way and Marcus flailing, but Marcus's clothes looked to be much better than any pennysheet girl could afford. Not just clean, better cloth too. Cora dismissed such thoughts for now. She needed to break up the fight, then find out what Marcus was doing here.

Marcus was wildly kicking Nullan. From inside the store cupboard came the noise of the pennysheet girl shouting and grabbing anything that came to hand. Many wooden things cascaded to the floor.

'Looks like we have a stowaway,' Serus said, and on hearing his voice Ruth turned. She was beside Nullan, leaning against the frame of the cupboard. Her face was set with tired resignation.

'This is your doing, I suppose, Cora? Paid her to sneak on board?'

'I had no idea she was here.'

'Really? After the trick you pulled in the Water Gardens this morning.'

'You know this child?' Serus said.

'You could say that, but I swear I didn't—'

'Throw a net over it!' called Captain Luine from somewhere.

Then Nullan took a boot to the cheek. Wincing, she motioned for Ruth to move back. 'If she should kick your bandage...'

But there was no room in the corridor *to* move back, not with Cora, Serus, Ruth and Nullan there. A wisp of smoke told Cora that Captain Luine was at the far end, looking on from her wheel but sensibly deciding not to get involved.

'Get your hands off me, you inky beast!' Marcus shouted at Nullan. 'I ain't done nothin' wrong!'

'Oh really?' Nullan said between gasps. The Casker's face was slick with sweat, and it *was* hot in the cramped space. The damp that had got into everyone's clothes earlier was now steaming.

Cora handed her coat to Serus and was about to help Nullan when there was a flash of movement above, and Harker dropped through the hatch. The shock made Marcus stop thrashing for a second, which was all Nullan needed to finally pull her out of the store cupboard. Between them, Nullan and Harker bundled Marcus into the saloon. Cora followed, and when Marcus saw her, the girl stopped struggling.

'Detective – get 'em off me!'

'You'd do wise to pipe down, Marcus,' Cora said.

The girl glared at Nullan. '*She'd* be wise to take her nasty inky hands and boil them.'

Nullan ignored this, and the two Caskers pinned Marcus in the corner as if she were an animal that might bite. As well she might. Marcus had survived on the streets of Fenest. Biting was probably a handy skill.

'Everybody out!' Cora roared, and roared again when no one moved. 'I said, everybody out. This place is too small to pretend you didn't hear me.'

Serus and Harker went willingly. Nullan left, panting and wiping the sweat from her face. She shot a parting glare at the girl. Ruth closed the door behind the Casker and then sank onto one of the benches that ran round the room – clearly Ruth didn't believe she was included in 'everybody out'.

'I'm looking forward to hearing this story,' Ruth said.

Cora grunted in reply then opened the saloon window. It did nothing for the heat, but it would mean her bindle-smoke had somewhere to go. She stayed by the window as she rolled two smokes. Marcus had lost her fighting spirit as soon as the others had gone, and now gazed around as if on some kind of Seminary trip. Her legs were too short to reach the floor, and she banged her boot heels against the wooden box of the seat. Cora was dismayed to see, through a rip in the girl's new-looking trousers, a gash in her knee. Blood was smeared down her leg.

'Can I have one of them smokes?' she said.

'No,' Cora said. 'So, you going to tell me what you're doing here?'

'Fancied a little holiday, didn't I? Ain't you always telling me to give the 'sheets a rest, Detective?'

'So that you can go to school.' Cora lit the smokes and handed one to Ruth who took it without lifting her gaze from Marcus.

Marcus shrugged. 'There ain't no school these days. It's on a break.'

'Really.'

'Yeah, it is, and I done you so many favours lately—'

'Which I paid you for.'

'—that I thought you wouldn't mind if I came along. To see them sights people is always going on about.'

Marcus's heels drummed the wood. The blood on her leg glistened in the lamplight.

'How did you know we were leaving on this barge?' Ruth asked.

Marcus shrugged. 'Heard it somewhere.'

Her sister sat back and stared at Cora. 'Did you now.'

'Ruth, I swear – this has nothing to do with me. Why would I need this ruffian on the trip?'

Marcus folded her arms. 'Well that's charming, that is – ruffian!'

'Marcus, this is important, *really* important.' Cora perched on the seat next to her. 'Who told you about this trip?'

The girl reached for Cora's smoke, so Cora tossed it out the window.

'When I picked up my morning 'sheets, first edition, people was talking about a storyteller going upriver.'

'Who?'

'Other 'sheet sellers. Young 'uns like me. I thought it was a story they was telling each other and it was a good one, so I listened. And then at the Water Gardens I was behind you for a bit, Detective. I was getting ready to do what you paid me for, to make life difficult for anyone in purple who give you trouble, and I heard you and her,' Marcus nodded at Ruth, 'you was talking about a trip upriver.'

Did she and Ruth talk about the trip while they were in the Water Gardens? She couldn't remember. It was possible.

'And I thought maybe it weren't a story that I'd heard from the 'sheet sellers,' Marcus said. 'Maybe it was true! So after the Rustan story I followed you to see if you was getting on a boat. Saw that bloke cut you,' she turned to Ruth and pointed at her side, 'saw him do that and the detective carrying you.'

'And then you waited outside the whorehouse?' Cora said.

'And then you come here.'

It was on the tip of Cora's tongue to mention the gig that she and Ruth had caught across the city to the docks. How had Marcus kept them in sight all that way? Clinging to the tailboard? It wasn't out of the question, but unlikely. Cora would have noticed her.

'And you really expect us to believe you're here for a holiday?' Ruth said.

'Why else would I be?'

'Because someone is paying you,' Cora said. 'Is that it, Marcus? Someone's paid you to come on this trip?'

The girl yawned. 'I wish! A holiday *and* getting paid for it – that's a good story, Detective. With selling 'sheets and all the jobs you give me to do, I ain't got time to sleep, let alone do *more* work. So don't you go asking me to do nuffin on this heap of junk.' Marcus eyed the peeling paint on the saloon walls and kicked a grubby cushion away from her. 'I ain't come to be a skivvy.'

'Given the state of the cupboard you've just emptied,' Ruth said, 'I doubt Captain Luine will be asking for any assistance.'

Marcus's grin slipped into another yawn, and Cora felt herself needing to do the same. Ruth rubbed her eyes. It was late.

Cora opened the door and made to call for Nullan, but found the Casker waiting outside where she'd clearly heard everything.

'Can we set her down here,' Cora asked Nullan, 'let her make her own way back to the city?'

'We're well past Fenest now. Had a good wind, and a good captain.' Nullan gestured in the direction of the for'ard end of the barge, where the figure of Captain Luine was visible beside her wheel. 'If you're happy to set the girl down here and have her take her chances in the scrub—'

'I'm not.'

'Thought you'd say that.'

Cora glanced back into the saloon. Marcus had stuck her head out of the window and was booming questions to Ruth: How fast does it go? Why doesn't it sink? Did you bleed a lot when that bloke cut you?

'Can you find her somewhere to sleep?' Cora asked Nullan. 'She's not that bad once you get to know her.'

'As long as she keeps her fists to herself, we'll manage.

The saloon seats can be folded out into something halfway decent.'

'I'm sure it'll be better than she's used to.'

'Or deserves,' Nullan muttered.

Ruth was heading for her cabin, her face pale, shadows making her eyes deep pools.

'Ruth – wait.' Cora kept her voice low. 'The fact that Marcus heard about a storyteller taking a barge upriver, that people were talking about it in the streets, that's not good. Morton's people might have heard too.'

'It's no good trying to talk me out of this, Cora. It's too late.' Ruth's hand strayed to her injured side. 'I have to collect the Wayward Hook, and we're on our way now. She's just a child. Nullan can handle her.'

'Ruth—'

But her sister shut her cabin door. From the saloon came mutterings from Nullan and louder protests from Marcus. She was too tired for anything more tonight: dealing with Marcus, trying to talk Ruth out of danger. Cora went to her own cabin, eager for some rest.

'Where did you find that child?' Serus said. He was sitting on the narrow bed, leaning against the wall. His slipdog coat was folded neatly beside him and his tunic was open enough to reveal the softest part of his throat and the auburn curl of hair that clung to it. And the barest hint of metal?

'I get asked that a lot.' Cora sat next to him, and that took up most of the bed. 'Marcus has had a rough life.'

'I could have guessed that bit.'

'Her stories had enough danger to interest the Partner back when I found her, living in an abandoned printworks not far from the Assembly building. Marcus could see the glass dome from her bed of pennysheets. I got her fixed up selling the 'sheets instead of sleeping in them, working for one of the better bosses, paid for her to attend the city school. Now it's the Messenger who hears Marcus's stories.'

'And you hear them too?' Serus said. 'She seems a useful person for a detective to know.'

'I have a habit of finding them.' Cora put her hand on Serus's leg and leaned towards him, but he was moving away, getting up. Her hand slipped to the rough, stained weave of the bed's blanket.

'I don't want to rush this, Cora. I... This means too much to me.' Serus gestured towards the narrow bed. 'I don't want us to take things further just because there's only one bed in here.'

'Neither do I.' Though she was disappointed, she understood. And the sight of him standing awkwardly in the small space of the cabin, his fingers fretting at one of his metal cheek plates, made her take pity on him. 'I guess I could bunk in with Marcus in the saloon.' She made to get up, but Serus stopped her.

'There's no need. While you were talking in there, I had a rummage in all the cupboards and drawers, and I found this!'

With a flourish that would work for a street performer, Serus produced an armful of rope from somewhere on the floor. At Cora's lack of excitement, he explained, 'It's a hammock.'

'If you say so. Looks to me like a fishing net that's seen better days, just like the rest of this barge.'

'There are some hooks to tie it to on the deck. Captain Luine showed me, said it's going to be a dry night so...'

'So you'll be under the stars, Serus.'

He smiled. 'I will. But I won't be far away.' He bent and kissed her, and it was long and good and she wanted more of him, but he was heading out the door.

Weariness overcame her then. She lay on the bed, and something cool and soft grazed her neck. Serus had forgotten his slipdog coat. She got up with the intention of taking it out to him on the deck but the smell of him was on it: smoke and spice. So she lay down again and used it for a pillow, to have some trace of him with her.

Cora's last thought before sleep overtook her was that the barge had stopped moving. She could feel the difference – the slight tremor through the wooden structure had gone, and the sway of the barge she hadn't noticed until it stopped had been replaced with something gentler. Perhaps she was becoming something of a bargehand already. It was worth considering as a trade. She'd need something to do after all this was over.

Seventeen

When Cora stepped onto the deck the next morning, the sky was cloudless, the air already warm even though it was still early. The deck and everything on it were dry. The rain must have held off overnight, just as the captain had told Serus it would.

The river had widened, the banks on either side further away than Cora felt was comfortable. When she'd gone to sleep, the last lights of Fenest were still in sight. Now the city was a small hump on the horizon behind her, and on either side of the river stretched the winding roads and small towns of Perlanse. West Perlanse, to be precise. When she and Jenkins had gone to investigate what befell the prisoner transport that was carrying Finnuc Dawson to the Steppes, they'd gone in the other direction, east. To Cora, this landscape looked just the same. If there was a difference between the two duchies, as the Perlish were always harping on about, Cora couldn't see it.

The captain called out good morning. She'd been at the wheel when Cora had turned in the night before, and was in the same position now. Had she left her post at all? She must have. But so far on this trip, Cora had only ever seen the captain here, at the wheel, pipe in mouth, a glass of the Casker spirit lannat close to hand.

'Morning,' Cora said in return. 'We're making good time, I hear.'

'That we are. The Bore's wind has been good to us.'

'Long may that continue.'

'It's the making of a good story, isn't it? With a worthy ending, with a worthy prize.' Captain Luine glanced at the rushing water. Nullan claimed to have found a trustworthy crew, but what that meant these days was anyone's guess. The Audience would likely have a few ideas. Trustworthy didn't seem to equate to waterworthy.

'Helps to have a bargehand who knows his canvas.' Captain Luine nodded towards Harker who was once again on the roof of the barge, involved in a complicated business of undoing and tying down the flapping sails.

'What about the return journey?' Cora said. 'Wind'll be in the wrong direction for us, won't it?'

The captain sucked deeply on her pipe. 'I don't think you'll be needing to worry about that.'

'Oh? And why's that?'

'Nullan paid me for upriver miles only. I got a cargo of my own to collect, once you lot disembark.'

'But we'll have to get back to Fenest. Ruth has to—' Cora stopped herself just in time, just in case.

Captain Luine shrugged. 'I got my sailing orders. Just doing what I'm paid to.'

They were drawing near another barge moored on the opposite side of the river. The captain seemed to know the crew and shouted over. Cora took her leave of the for'ard part of the barge and headed onto the deck proper.

Everyone else had got up before her and were making the most of the fine morning after the rain the evening before.

'Suspect it suits him, being in the air,' Ruth said, appearing beside her.

'What?'

Ruth pointed along the deck to where Serus was rolling up his hammock. 'Not a bad bed for a Rustan.'

'I guess not.'

'So are you going to tell me why the Chief Fire Investigator of Fenest is with us?'

'The clue's in his name, Ruth. Safety first. That pipe of the captain's has got to be a risk.'

Ruth shook her head, but she was smiling. 'He's handsome, and you deserve some happiness, Cora. Audience knows, we all need to find it, with what's happening in the south.' Her sister's smile had gone. 'We need to grab any chance we get.'

'How are you feeling?'

'Better.' She was at once brisk and business-like. 'Nullan took out the stitches this morning and says the cut is healing cleanly. That Pruett didn't do too bad a job.'

'I won't tell him. He thinks too much of himself already.'

Nullan herself appeared at that moment. With a nimbleness Cora could only wonder at, the Casker stepped onto the deck while carrying a tray well-laden with a blackened cooking pot and a stack of chipped, mismatched bowls. Steam curled from the pot, and Cora caught the smell of hot milk with spice. Pastries were a luxury left behind in the city, but maybe Casker cooking wouldn't be so bad.

'As none of you were coming inside for breakfast, I've brought it out here.' Nullan set the tray on a crate, and people started to help themselves, Marcus elbowing her way to the front with well-practised form.

Cora hung back to roll a smoke – she wouldn't be able to stomach breakfast without a bindleleaf before it. She joined Serus sitting on the other side of the deck, and as she caught sight of his face, she laughed.

'What's so funny?' he asked.

Cora reached out and ran her thumb lightly over his forehead. 'The hammock's given your face something besides those metal cheeks. Printed you with its pattern.'

Serus smiled. 'The price you pay for a good night's sleep. And you?'

'I was asleep as soon as I'd taken off my boots.'

He offered her a forkful of his breakfast – some kind of porridge, by the look of it, and the barge without enough spoons to eat it with.

Cora shook her head. 'Once that lot have had their fill, I'll get mine.'

'The way that child is eating, there might not be much left.' They both watched Marcus peering into the porridge pot, the long-handled spoon unwieldy in her hand. Harker lifted her up to get a larger spoonful from the bottom. 'That's her third serving,' Serus said.

'She needs it more than me.'

'And you, Cora – what do you need?'

Cora leaned back against the side of the cabin, feeling the damp of the wood seep into her coat. 'I'd say I've got all I need right here. Got my smokes, got the sun, got a Rustan beside me, and I seem to have finally shaken off the people who've been on my tail since I left the police.'

'Maybe you were right,' he said. 'This will be a holiday after all.'

'A short one. We have to get the Hook back in time for the Wayward story. If Ruth's not there, others are waiting to take her place.'

'And the Hook itself – you still don't know what it is or where on the river your sister will pick it up?'

'No, on both counts.'

Serus set down his bowl. 'Aren't you tempted to ask her?'

'Don't you think I have? Ruth's as tight-lipped as a Perlish merchant's coin purse.'

'But she must have told the Caskers where we're headed.' Serus was looking at Nullan and Harker who were deep in conversation as they secured what looked to be fishing poles off the back of the barge. 'Why not tell her sister too?'

She had no answer to that, other than a swift stab of frustration that he should say what was already on her mind. 'Why are you so interested in our journey plans? I thought you were here to spend time with me.'

Serus looked wounded. 'I am. Cora, I was only—'

'Well, don't.'

She went to see what was left of breakfast. Not much, but that didn't matter. She had even less of an appetite now anyway.

Marcus was seated cross-legged nearby, head bent, entirely concentrating on something in her hands. It looked to Cora like a bit of twig.

'Tell me you haven't snapped that off something important,' Cora said.

The girl looked up and grinned. She held up a V of wood, with a thong of leather tied between the two prongs. A slingshot. 'Harker gave it to me. He's going to teach me how to use it.'

'I dread to think what for.'

'For stoning birds, the ones that nest in the banks. They stone 'em, and then they fish 'em out of the water with nets and roast 'em.' Marcus turned to look at the fast-flowing water. 'Not here. He said the birds nest on parts of the Tun. I got time to practise because we haven't reached that yet. This is still the Stave.'

'Been looking at the charts, have you?' Cora took a forkful of cold porridge and made herself swallow. 'Starting to wonder if you've got some Casker blood in you.'

'Harker showed me them maps. Says we should reach K'stera Point this time tomorrow.' She pulled the slingshot's strap tight as if to test its power. 'Give me your fork, Detective.'

'I don't think that's a good idea. And what's K'stera Point?'

'It's the river junction! Where the Stave splits into the Tun and the Cask.' Marcus sighed. 'Don't you know anything?'

'I know that you've got new clothes and that you weren't wearing them when I saw you at the Water Gardens yesterday morning.'

It wasn't just the trousers. Now that she could see Marcus in the daylight, it was clear the girl's jacket was fine too – far better than Cora had ever seen Marcus wear in the years she'd known her. Green velvet with richly brocaded panels in black and silver thread. Fenestiran bordering on Perlish, and though Marcus was now sitting on it, the quality was unmistakable. Even Cora could tell *that*, and she knew next to nothing about clothes.

'Well?' Cora said. 'Where did you get them?'

A pause, and then the girl said, 'Took 'em. I was passing the laundry on Gweek Street. There were bags of clothes going in, coming out. The washers stopped to have a chat and a smoke, and I had a rummage, didn't I?'

'That's a good question: did you? Or did someone buy you these new clothes?'

Marcus gave Cora a look that said Cora was the biggest fool in the Union. 'And who would be buying me nice clothes?'

'You tell me. You sure no one told you to be here, to see what I'm doing with the new... with the crew? Someone who bought you clothes as payment?'

Marcus snorted. 'You're the only who buys me things, and it wouldn't be this kind of fancy stuff, would it?' As if to demonstrate, Marcus grabbed a handful of her new finely woven trousers.

'So, I guess you just got lucky outside the laundry then,' Cora said, 'finding clothes that fit you so well.'

'Being named on Drunkard's Day, the Audience owes me some luck.' Somehow the girl had got hold of Cora's discarded porridge fork after all – pennysheet sellers were as light-fingered as they were loud, practically cutpurses in the making. Marcus put the fork into the slingshot. 'I had to go through almost the whole bag of clothes,' Marcus said. 'Chucked loads into the gutter before I found this stuff.'

'A bad day for the laundry,' Cora muttered.

'And anyway, you should be more worried about *your* clothes, Detective.'

'Oh?'

Marcus looked her up and down. 'Them Seeder things don't suit you, and the blood on your shirt looks something nasty.'

Cora glanced down at herself. Marcus was right: she was still wearing the clothes she'd worn to hear the Rustan story, which were marked with Ruth's blood. All at once, she could smell herself, too. Sweat and staleness. No wonder Serus hadn't wanted to share a cabin with her. She'd have to see if Nullan had something in store she could borrow. Changing from a Seeder to a Casker. She was less and less herself these days.

She stood up, and while Marcus was distracted by her new friend Harker climbing onto the roof of the barge to see to the sails, Cora whisked the fork away. She quickened her step to outrun Marcus's loud protests and was heading for Nullan at the back of the barge, still doing something with the fishing poles, when she saw it. Them.

Him?

A figure was watching the barge. They were standing on a low hill on the north bank of the river, a few houses and the spire of a Seat between them and the boat. Too far for Cora to see a face, or much of anything beyond the hood they wore and a dark coat, despite the sun. But she could feel the intensity of the gaze.

'Cora? What is it?' Ruth joined her at the edge of the deck.

'Someone's watching us.'

Ruth shielded her eyes against the sun. 'Where?'

Before Cora could direct her sister's gaze, the figure had gone, back down the far side of the hill.

'Don't tell me you're worrying about livestock,' Ruth said, and shook her head. 'Not everything in the Union is out to kill me, and certainly not the beasts the Perlish keep to make cheese.'

Cora kept her eyes on the hill in case the figure should reappear, but there were only the goats, brown dots ambling across the green, the bells at their necks tinkling softly. It would be a beautiful sight, if it weren't for the dread creeping up Cora's back, wrapping its fingers around her neck.

'I saw someone, Ruth. And they were very definitely looking at us.'

Ruth turned away. 'People are allowed to look at the river, Cora.'

'But there was something about them…'

Ruth took her by the arm and pulled her away. The sunlight was too bright, the way it flashed off the river, off the barge windows. Her vision was spotted with dark shapes. The figure. The goats.

'Come and sit down,' Ruth said, steering her to a crate set with a grubby cushion, beside an already seated Serus. 'Nullan is going to tell us a story.'

'Is she now?'

'We might as well make use of having a storyteller on board.'

'Does that mean you've got a tale for us as well, Ruth?'

'I'm saving mine. But after the election, who knows?'

Eighteen

'Hope this is a cheerier tale than the one you told for the election,' Captain Luine shouted from the wheel.

Nullan smiled, for possibly the first time since Cora had met her.

'Who could tell a sad story on a day as beautiful as this?' Nullan called back, lifting her inked arms to the sky.

'I'm sure you'd find a way,' the captain muttered, and Cora tried to hide her own smile.

Nullan stood at the edge of the deck, her back to the water, while everyone else, bar Captain Luine, took up seats facing her. Harker stayed on the barge roof, and when Marcus tried to climb up to join him, the Casker took hold of her shirt collar and hauled her up as if he was plucking a fish from the river. She sat cross-legged beside him, triumphant yet still as grimy as ever. Not that Cora could say much about that, the state of her clothes. She'd been about to ask Nullan for something to wear from the barge's stores when the figure had appeared on the hill.

Cora looked back at that bank. Nothing. No, that wasn't true. There were people on the road that ran next to the river, people on the grassy slopes that led away from the road, people beyond that, in the fields. West Perlanse was full of people, none of them paying any attention to the barge sailing past.

'Got somewhere to be, Cora?' Nullan said softly.

Cora turned. The Casker storyteller was waiting to begin, her audience sitting ready, waiting, staring at Cora. Even though they were far from Fenest, and not in anything like an official story venue – with no purple tunics in sight, no garbing pavilion, no black-robed voters wearing the masks of the Audience – even without all that, the special hush of the election had descended. That was what happened when you spent too much time with storytellers. At any moment, they could change the air around you into something almost hot with expectation.

'Sorry,' she mumbled. With a quick glance at Serus beside her, she knew she was forgiven for snapping at him earlier.

Nullan closed her eyes. The world quietened, even the river beneath them. The creak of the barge's planks – a constant since they'd got underway – stopped. The birds criss-crossing the rich blue of the sky above were silent, only shapes. And Nullan began.

'Ralli's tea kettle was famous. Upriver and down, those who sailed the Cask, the Stave, the Tun, from shore to shore at Bordair, the tea kettle was known to them all. People said, if anyone had ever managed to cross Break Deep and were still living on the other side of that graveyard then they, too, would have heard of Ralli's tea kettle. They might even risk the crossing back if they knew they could drink the wonders it brewed.

'And the reason Ralli's tea kettle was famous on every waterway in the Union?' Nullan said. 'It was known that tea brewed in Ralli's kettle had the power to make two good hearts fall in love. If two should drink the same brew made in the kettle, share the same cup to drink it, then as soon as they next looked into each other's eyes, they would be bound together, a love match until the day they joined the Audience.

'There were many happy couples who owed their happiness to Ralli's tea kettle. Her family claimed a long line of water-readers. That was how the kettle had come into the family in the first place. A storm, predicted by a child who no one else believed, blew down from the Rusting Mountains. It caused a great wave to rise from Bordair itself – an inland lake with no current, no wildness in its water, and yet this wave ripped through the eastern parts of Bordair, upending huts and tearing up 'walks. Before it had blown itself out, the storm had sent a fleet of fishing smacks to the bottom of Bordair and dumped the tea kettle at the feet of the water-reading child.

'The powers of the kettle were discovered soon after this – the story of how is known only to the Devotee whose sightless eyes see such mysteries better than we ever can. But from the first time the tea kettle brewed a love match, Caskers came from every riverway to ask for its aid in matters of the heart.

'Ralli was the great-great-great-great-great-grand-daughter of that water-reading child who'd predicted the storm that brought the kettle which had been handed down through the generations. Like all in her bloodline before her who had been custodian of the kettle, she asked no payment for the teas she brewed, though by then the kettle was so famous across the Union that she could have been a rich woman. Rich enough to leave the smoky, sweaty boardwalks that cling to the edge of Bordair, given that people came almost daily to the door of her hut to ask her to brew them tea they could take away and share with the object of their desires, to ensure a love match with the tea-buyer. Ralli could have left all that behind and moved back from the water, into the cooler streets and fine-timbered houses that look down on Bordair's back. But she didn't take so much as one penny for her teas.

'And though she took no payment, Ralli did have a condition of another sort. When someone came to her door professing love for another that was breaking the visitor's heart, Ralli questioned them as to the match. If in the course of these conversations it became clear that the intended lover was completely uninterested in the visitor, say if they loved another, or had decided love had no place in their already contented life, Ralli would refuse to brew tea for the visitor to take away and share with the object of their desires. This angered people, of course it did, especially those who'd travelled far to ask for help, but Ralli was firm. If there was no returned spark of love in the story the visitor told her, she would not help them.

'But if the story told of thwarted love, of cruel captains standing in the way of crew transfers that would allow couples to sail the same barge, of other suitors who forced their affections where they weren't wanted, of parents refusing permission, thinking only of the earnings another match might bring, then Ralli would act. She set the tea kettle over the fire in her hut, heated water from Bordair with a sprig of this herb, a cutting of that, no names of the ingredients ever uttered, and gave the visitor a cup to take back with them. Once shared with a willing lover, the obstacle to the match would cease to cause problems. Cruel captains changed their minds. Unwanted suitors found others to pursue. Money-minded parents saw the error of their ways. But if the visitor asking Ralli to brew them tea should lie to her about their match, if they took the tea and gave it to someone who did not love them, had them drink the love potion from the same cup unknowingly, then bad luck would fall on the visitor. Caskers don't take such warnings lightly, and so no one risked a lie to Ralli.

'Then one day, a Perlish woman came to the door of Ralli's hut. She said she'd heard wonders of the tea brewed in the kettle and needed some herself. As with all who came asking for the help of the tea kettle, Ralli asked her visitor for the story of her love. The Perlish woman had fallen in love with a seamstress, a woman of great talents with her hands but who was herself in love with another. The seamstress and her lover owned a shop, a pair of happy women – the seamstress sewed the dresses and her lover made hats. It was clear to Ralli that there was no room in that union for the Perlish visitor to her door, so Ralli did what she always did in such circumstances: she told the Perlish woman she couldn't help her.

'As you would expect from a Perlish, the woman tried to argue with Ralli, offered her not just pennies for the tea, but marks – lots of them. And when Ralli refused even that, the Perlish woman grew angry and snatched the tea kettle from the flames. She would have burnt her hands had she not been wearing a fine pair of leather gloves.

'The Perlish woman made off with the kettle, scuttling down the boardwalks, thinking herself very clever to have stolen the kettle because she could hear liquid sloshing inside: the dregs of the last tea to be brewed. When she thought herself far enough from Ralli's hut, she quickly emptied the kettle into a flask she had brought with her, kicked the kettle into the waters of Bordair and took herself back to Perlanse as swiftly as she could.

'The kettle didn't sink. It bobbed around near the boardwalk until someone spotted it, fished it out and returned it to Ralli, because everyone in Bordair knew what it was, who it belonged to. Ralli cleaned off the dead leaves and the salt marks, tipped out the minnows that had swum into the spout, then settled back to wait for her next visitor, because her life would carry on as before, she knew that, just as she knew the Perlish woman would soon know the cost of her actions.

'As soon as she was back in the small town in which she lived, the Perlish woman went to the shop owned by the seamstress and her lover, the hatmaker. Through an underhand contrivance that befits such a person, and which we needn't concern ourselves with, the Perlish woman found a way to have she and the seamstress drink the tea from the same cup. The Perlish woman waited for something wonderful to happen, for the seamstress to fall into her arms, to kiss her, to pack a trunk of finely worked dresses and move into the Perlish woman's house.

'But nothing like this happened. Instead, the seamstress thanked the Perlish woman for the tea and said she had to get back to work. There were a lot of orders waiting. The hatmaker came out of the back room and the seamstress's eyes lit up, not just as they had done on all the other occasions when the Perlish woman had gone to the shop, but even more powerfully. The two women were more in love than ever! How could it be possible! The seamstress and the hatmaker embraced, and they didn't let go of one another. Instead, they began to undo one another's clothes, though the shop had several customers, beside the Perlish woman. These customers blushed and averted their eyes, until the women were rolling on the floor, barely dressed, and modesty was no longer possible.

'The customers fled, including the Perlish woman, who went back to the lonely house she had hoped to share with the seamstress, and cursed Ralli and her tea kettle. When her cursing was done and she had reached the point in her anger when she was vowing revenge, she made to go to bed, and so she went to pull off her gloves – the very pair that had saved her from being burnt when she'd snatched the tea kettle from the flames, and which she had worn every day since leaving Bordair and travelling back to Perlanse.

'But now she could not remove the gloves.

'No matter how hard she tugged, they would not move an inch. When she took scissors to them, she shrieked with pain for it felt as if she was cutting her own skin, and indeed she was. The same was true when she resorted to the open flame of the stove to burn the gloves away. All she achieved was to blister skin that was already sore from the cuts she had made with the scissors. The gloves would not come off, and because the woman was too proud, and too frightened, it must be said, to seek help, the wounds she had inflicted on herself were given no care, and so they went bad, and in a matter of days her blood was poisoned, and she was dead.

'The seamstress and the hatmaker went on being happy

for the rest of their lives and forgot all about the woman who used to come to the shop and run her hands across the fine bolts of cloth more vigorously than was thought seemly in that part of Perlanse.'

The clapping came at once, and louder than Cora expected. How could their barge make so much noise? It was then she realised that it wasn't just their barge that had been listening. The boat had stopped moving, and all around them were other barges which had stopped their sailing too to hear Nullan. And why wouldn't they? It had been such a good story, Cora herself had stopped paying attention to anything but Nullan's voice. There were even Caskers from other barges, right there, on the deck of the *Pretty Lilly*. She hadn't noticed them, hadn't noticed that the barge had stopped, and that meant she hadn't been keeping an eye on the riverbank. Or the figure she'd seen there before Nullan began her story.

'That was racy at the end,' Marcus crowed from the roof. Several of the Caskers on the moored barges winced and glanced over to find the cause of the noise.

'Maybe *too* racy for your young ears,' Harker said.

'That's nothing compared to the things I hear on the streets or at Beulah's place.'

Harker helped Marcus climb down to the deck.

Cora was trying to see the bank, but people were in her way. The Caskers from the other barges were talking with Nullan and Captain Luine. Someone took Cora's hand. It was Serus. She'd forgotten he was even there, but the look he gave her told her the same wasn't true for him.

'A story about true love,' he said.

'Seems so.' There were too many people in her way, and

all of them broad as well as tall. Nullan had to be the only small Casker in the history of that realm.

'Cora, I wanted to say…'

If she could just get to the edge of the deck then she could see—

That was when the attack came.

Nineteen

A young Casker woman with inked waves across the bridge of her nose and cheekbones gave a small gasp then crumpled into the arms of the bargehand she was talking to. Before he could call for help, Cora was striding over.

'Make room!' she shouted, shoving aside the walls of inked and sun-warmed Casker flesh that was now on Captain Luine's barge.

The woman was limp in her friend's arms, and he was just about holding her up in his confusion.

'Sanna? Sanna, wake up!'

'What happened?' Cora said, helping him lay the prone woman on the deck.

'I don't know. One minute we were talking about the story, and the next, she dropped like a stone.'

Others had begun to notice, and a circle of anxious faces formed around the fallen Casker, a murmur of speculation and panic growing louder – a noise Cora knew from too many crime scenes.

The bargehand was pawing at his friend's face. 'Sanna!' The woman's mouth was slack, and her breath had a creak to it, though at least she still *was* breathing. 'She never gets ill,' the bargehand said. 'Never!'

Then Sanna jerked, thrashed her arms, and her breath became a rattle. Her eyes opened but seemed unable to focus on anything. She was gasping for air. Her friend began to whimper.

Cora knelt beside them and felt something under her hand – cool, hard, as well as somehow soft. She grabbed it, and held it up.

A thin spear of metal, half as long as her hand, one end a needle tip and the other decked with feathers. Black-and-white feathers.

Those around her saw it too, and cries went up.

'A dart!'

'Sanna's been poisoned!'

'The shot – where did it come from?'

The barge was at once a riot of rushing bodies, thumping feet. The deck lurched beneath her. She caught sight of Ruth amid the chaos and grabbed her sister's arm.

'Get inside – now!'

For once, Ruth needed no convincing of the threat and hurried to get under cover, grabbing Marcus as she went. Then Nullan was there, kneeling beside the fallen Casker Sanna, her small hands busy checking the woman over in a way that spoke of stitcher training.

'If this is what I think it is, she's a dead woman,' Cora said.

'Not if I can help it,' Nullan said, without looking up. 'Leave her with me. You need to find out who's firing poison darts at us.'

Cora dropped the dart by Nullan's side. 'Keep that safe

for me.' And then she was running, forcing her way to the edge of the deck where all was movement.

In every direction, Caskers were jumping back to their barges, and Cora wondered at how light they were on their feet, despite their size. Mooring ropes were flying through hands as the barges were set free, anchors hauled up, sails untied and shaken loose in a heartbeat. Were these crews going to flee? She'd never taken the Caskers for cowards. And where was Captain Luine when she was needed? The captain had barely left her post since they'd set sail and this was the moment she chose to leave the wheel?

Another Casker dropped – a man this time, right in front of Cora, caught as he was jumping from her deck to another. She glimpsed the black-and-white of the feathers that tipped the dart, and then the man was sliding into the river between the barges.

Cora grabbed his arm, but his weight was colossal. He was pulling her down into the narrowing space as the decks surged closer to one another in the bucking river. She slammed into the other deck, which hit her full across the chest. When she cried out, her mouth filled with water – the taste of earth, of old things, somehow – and then she was hauled clear, many hands around her, before they reached for the Casker who'd gone down first. His crewmates dragged him onto the other deck, and Cora fell back on hers, gasping for air, the pain in her chest – it was like a hot brand. But then she was on her feet again as quickly as she could stand, desperately searching the bank for the hooded figure.

The traffic on the road that flanked the river had ground

to a halt. People stared from their gigs, pointed, some even laughed at what was unfolding on the river before them, as if the Caskers were telling a funny story for the delight of the Perlish onlookers. From somewhere deep within her, Cora found the energy to hate the Perlish even more than she already did.

And then she saw him. Tannir. He was watching from the shelter of a wagon, but he was so close now, she could see him lifting something to his mouth – a thin pipe. He was making ready another dart.

'There he is!' Cora shouted. 'There – by the wagon! The one in the cloak. That's who's firing!' But she couldn't seem to get enough air into her lungs to shout and no one was listening. 'Look! There – he's there!'

She doubled over coughing and could taste river water again. But then there was an arm around her and a face close to hers, metal cheekbones cool against her hot skin. She managed to croak to Serus about Tannir, and at once he roared the information to the Casker crews. The noise around her changed. The panic was gone, replaced by purpose, and she realised the barges hadn't been preparing to sail away – they were turning in formation towards the bank.

Something sailed overhead, and for a moment, her heart stilled – another dart. But it was going the other way, towards the bank. A scream went up from the parked vehicles, and then it was the riverbank's turn for chaos as all those who'd stopped to watch now tried to flee. More volleys left the barges, and Cora spun round to see what was happening.

Harker was on the roof of the barge, a slingshot angled

towards the bank – bigger than the one she'd seen Marcus with earlier. That had been a toy, fashioned to keep a noisy stowaway quiet. This was a weapon, one the Caskers clearly knew how to use, given how quickly the rocks were being fired at the bank.

The Casker crews directed their attention to the bank in one combined assault, and Cora sucked in air, each breath refilling her lungs more deeply.

'Ah, that explains it,' Serus said to himself.

'Explains what?' Cora asked, her gaze never leaving the bank which was now under a constant hail of stones. With the scattering traffic her view was obscured again. She couldn't see Tannir, and thumped a cask in frustration.

'Last night when I put up my hammock,' Serus said, 'I came across a store of rocks. I couldn't understand what they were doing onboard as they don't seem burnable for fuel.'

'A weapons cache,' Cora said, and spat something greenish onto the deck.

'Are you all right?' Serus said.

'I will be once that snake Tannir has a hole knocked in his head.'

Serus looked to the bank. 'Tannir – the Wayward who wants to replace Ruth? Who burnt down the distiller's?'

'The same.'

Serus whistled, and it took Cora a second to realise the sound was coming through his metal cheeks. The number of slingshot volleys was lessening, and the various Casker crews surrounding the barge were directing their craft to moor at the bank. Some disembarked and searched the long grass, the ditches. They called back their findings: no cloaked figure lying prone. No sign he'd ever been there. Tannir had escaped.

The other barges began to take their leave, resuming the journeys that they'd paused to listen to Nullan's story. With backs slapped in farewell, pretend insults traded as to who could use a slingshot and who would be better off sticking to the cooking, the Caskers departed.

The last crew to leave was that of Sanna, the woman who'd been hit by the first dart. Harker found some unwanted sail canvas and, with the help of the dead woman's crewmates, wrapped her body tightly. But not before Cora had seen her purpled face, her eyes protruding. A familiar poisoning.

Nullan tucked some dried herbs inside the canvas. 'I tried... I tried, but I'm no sanga. I'm sorry.'

As the sail was pulled tight over Sanna's ruined face, all on deck murmured, 'Widow welcome you, friend.'

When the body had been safely stowed inside the other crew's barge and the two boats were drawing apart, Cora asked Harker about the herbs.

'To keep her fresh as they can on the trip to Bordair,' he said, watching the other barge on its downstream journey.

'She'll be laid to rest in the water there?' Cora asked.

'That's right. Sanna's with the Audience now. For those she leaves behind, there'll be a chance to say their goodbyes once the barge reaches the lake.'

'With fire?'

'Aye. A burning raft in the middle of Bordair is the best we can hope for, us who sail.'

'Where *is* Captain Luine?'

Harker frowned at Cora. 'You get your vision knocked about in all that fuss, Detective?'

'I'm not a... Never mind. And I can see just fine.'

'Then I don't know how you can miss the captain.'

Harker nodded towards the wheel where Captain Luine was indeed standing, once more looking out over the river.

'She'll be in need of a sup, I should think,' Harker said. 'I'd better fill her glass or we won't get underway. Doubt you'll be wanting to hang around these parts much longer.'

Harker loped away, and Cora wondered at Luine's presence. She'd looked for the captain during the attack and hadn't found her. Everyone else on board the *Pretty Lilly* had been around – Cora had seen them at one point or another. And yet Luine, captain of the vessel under attack, was nowhere to be seen. It could just have been chance that Cora hadn't seen her. The Audience knew, there had been a lot going on, all those other Caskers thumping about, and Luine might have decided she was safer inside. Still, there was a worm of doubt twisting inside Cora, and it was connected to Tannir on the bankside.

But mulling all this over out here on deck wouldn't help anyone. She needed answers.

Everyone but Captain Luine and Harker gathered in the saloon. In the middle of the table was the dart that had hit Sanna. The sharp end had a greenish edge to it. The feathers had lost their lustre and been knocked about, but their colouring was unmistakable. Black-and-white. The colours of the election, and of too many other things left on the bodies of those who'd died for it.

'Well?' Ruth asked.

'Two dead. Neither from this barge, but it easily could have been.' Cora stared at the dart. 'These things are hard to fight.'

'Did you see how it flew!' Marcus lunged to grab the dart, but Serus caught her.

'I think Harker needs some help with those fishing poles you set out earlier,' he said. 'Let's go and find him, shall we?'

Without a word of protest, Marcus did as she was bid: the power of a new friend. As Serus escorted the pennysheet girl out of the saloon, Cora gave him a look of thanks.

Then it was just her, Nullan and Ruth.

Cora pointed at the feathered end of the dart. 'This a Wayward thing?'

Ruth shook her head. 'Never in my life have I seen something like this.'

'It's not Casker either,' Nullan added.

'And it's not something I've seen in Fenest.' Cora leaned back in her seat. 'But the way the poison works, that I *have* seen before. It's Heartsbane. The same poison used to kill Finnuc Dawson and the prisoner transport on the way to the Steppes.'

At the mention of the Casker killer of Nicholas Ento, Ruth gripped the table edge. Nullan spat on the floor.

'And the feathers,' Cora said. 'The same were left on Finnuc's body.'

'Like the black-and-white laces that Dawson used to sew my son's mouth shut.' Ruth's voice was low but strong.

'So, you're saying this is the work of Chambers Morton?' Nullan asked.

'I'm saying it's Tannir using Perlish methods.'

Ruth stared out of the saloon window, and Cora followed her sister's gaze. The water was streaming past. They were moving again, and again Cora hadn't noticed.

'I just…' Ruth shook her head. 'I can't believe it.'

'Even after he burnt down the distiller's?' Nullan said. 'You have to face it, Ruth. There are those in your own realm who want you dead so badly that they'll stop at nothing. It doesn't matter who else goes down with you.'

'But I'm not Wayward.' Ruth wiped a smudge from the window. 'There are some head herders who have never approved of my place in their circle. From the first days of my marriage, they've viewed me with distrust.'

'It's one thing to distrust someone,' Cora said. 'It's another to want them dead at all costs. You have to realise you're not safe on the river, not now.'

Ruth sighed. 'You can't be about to suggest we go back, abandon the Hook. I've come too far to—'

'I wasn't going to say that.' Cora took out her bindle tin and was dismayed to find the contents damp. She tossed it on the table next to the dart. 'But it's clear that word got out before we left Fenest. How, I don't know. What we've got to worry about now is Tannir coming back to try again. Because he will.'

'If we can just reach the Hook,' Ruth said, 'we'll have protection.'

'Oh really? It's a big metal shield, is it?'

Ruth smiled. 'It's a shield against Morton's plans. A shield against the building of walls across the Union. But no – the Hook won't protect us in Perlanse. The Wayward herd waiting with the Hook, now *that* should be helpful.'

'How many more days' sailing?' Cora asked Nullan.

'Two at most. With a good wind, we'll reach K'stera Point by tomorrow morning, then the site of the Hook the following afternoon.'

'Well, until then, we need to set a watch at all times,' Cora said, 'and we'll need to keep the barge moving. Tell Captain Luine we sail through the night. No lamps.'

Nullan laughed. 'You're not serious, Cora?'

'Of course I'm serious. You saw that poor woman, Sanna, and the other Casker who was caught by a dart. Do you want that to be someone on this barge, their eyes forced from their head with their choking?'

'But sailing at night... No Casker does that, even with lights. It's not safe!'

Cora stood. 'Stopping this barge isn't safe either. I'll leave you to give Captain Luine my instructions. But before you do, tell me: How well do you know the captain?'

Nullan frowned. 'She'll do her best to make this ridiculous plan work.'

'That's not what I asked.'

An awkward silence fell, but Cora wouldn't be the one to break it.

Ruth sighed. 'Cora, you're starting to sound like Mother. Seeing enemies everywhere.'

'That's my job.'

'And it was my job to charter a barge!' Nullan said. 'Luine is a first-rate captain. She likes a drink – who on a barge doesn't? And I know the *Pretty Lilly* isn't exactly a first-rate vessel—'

Cora scoffed.

'—but Luine has been at the helm of a barge since she was eighteen,' Nullan said, 'one of the youngest captains in our history. The Commission have the records. Why don't you go back to your precious Wheelhouse and look it up?' The saloon table rocked with the force of Nullan's anger.

Ruth reached out to her friend. 'Nullan, please—'

'I said, how well do *you* know Captain Luine?' Cora said, not to be deterred. 'You personally, Nullan.'

Nullan slumped into her chair. 'I met her for the first time the day we set sail from Fenest. A friend put us in touch.'

Ruth withdrew her hand. 'You didn't tell me that. All these weeks we've been planning how to get the Hook, you made me think Captain Luine was a good friend.'

'She's a reliable captain!' Nullan shouted. 'That's what matters!'

'No, Nullan,' Cora said, and grabbed her bindle tin from the table. 'What matters is that we can trust her.'

'You think Luine's working with Tannir?' Ruth said.

Cora shrugged. 'I don't know. But I'm beginning to wonder, and that's bad enough. I'll take first watch.'

Twenty

'If you're going to be out here,' Serus said, shaking the pile of bunched rope that was the hammock, 'you might as well be comfortable.'

They were on deck, towards the back of the barge near the fishing poles. Cora had wanted to be as far from the captain's wheel as she could be, while still having a good angle to watch the riverbank. She found herself wishing for a sign of Tannir so that Harker's slingshot could fire a stone right between his eyes. Preferably a sharp one.

Serus went to attach the hammock to one of the hooks on the cabins' exterior walls, but Cora stopped him.

'Too comfortable, and I won't keep my eyes open.'

'I thought that was where the smoking came in, to keep you awake.'

He gestured to the saucer full of bindle ends beside the crate she'd been sitting on for the last few hours.

'I could smoke in my sleep. Sometimes think I do.'

He reached behind him and produced a bowl. 'You need to eat as well as smoke, Cora.'

'Surprised Nullan would save *me* anything.' She took the bowl and sniffed the contents: some kind of fish stew.

She'd seen Harker pull in the twitching fishing poles earlier that afternoon, heard Marcus's loud excitement at the fish dangling from the lines.

'What is happening, Cora?' Serus asked, sitting against the cabin wall. 'Nullan and Ruth have been holed up in the galley since you came out here, apart from when Nullan went to talk to the captain, and then there was all kinds of shouting.'

'That I heard.' Cora took up what she hoped was a spoon but found it was another fork. How was anyone meant to eat anything on this riddled old boat? Instead, she used the fork to poke a floating bit of fin in the bowl.

'I don't think Nullan poisoned it,' Serus said.

Cora dropped the fork back into the bowl.

'I was only joking!' Serus said.

'That's not funny.'

She huddled deeper into the borrowed Casker clothes Harker had found for her – trousers and a shirt, each needing a complicated system of folds and buttoning to put on. The clothes weren't clean, but they *were* cleaner than the bloodied Seeder clothes she'd had on since the Water Gardens. And at least the previous owner had been close to her height. She tucked her hands into the wide sleeves. The day's warmth had all but gone and the last of the sunlight would soon follow.

'You look exhausted, Cora. I've told Ruth I'll take the next watch, and I don't mind starting now.'

'You sure?'

'Given that I'm sleeping out here anyway.' He caught the look she gave him and was quick to say, 'Don't worry – I'll stay awake.'

'I can leave you my bindle tin if you want.'

Serus shook his head. 'You might want to ration that. Who knows when there'll be a chance to restock?'

'With any luck we won't stop again until we get back to Fenest with the Hook, and if that means I have to go without smokes, so be it.'

She rubbed her eyes and tried to blink the riverbank into sharper focus but she was too tired, there was no doubt about it. They'd just passed a small town that looked to have three Seats, going by the spires, but even that feature hadn't been enough to stop her eyelids dropping.

A noise from the other side of the barge made her turn, but it was only another boat going down river. The captain of that barge called out a greeting to Luine, but when no reply came, the captain of the down-river barge called out a curse instead.

'I hear we're not stopping tonight,' Serus said. 'Night-sailing, it seems.'

'And did you also hear it's dangerous to do so?'

He picked up the stew and somehow began to eat using the fork.

'There was some mention of it,' he said. 'Our crew seem... unconvinced that it's the best plan.'

'I don't see we've got any choice.'

'Fortunately, your sister agrees with you—'

'First time for everything,' Cora muttered.

'—so the crew have agreed. Though Captain Luine says she won't leave the wheel.'

At this, Cora merely grunted. She was overwhelmed by tiredness all at once and pressed her hands over her face.

'Cora,' Serus said gently. 'Get some sleep. You don't have to do this all by yourself.'

She stood, no energy left for words, but enough to kiss him.

On her way to her cabin, Cora caught a glimpse of Ruth and Nullan in theirs, the door ajar. The Casker was tenderly unwinding the bandage from Ruth's side, while Ruth had her eyes screwed shut, her mouth a hard knot. When the still-healing wound was visible – a red-and-purple crescent, the flesh all around it bruised – Cora turned away.

Finally in her own cabin, she fell asleep at once. Not even Marcus in the galley shouting about fish guts could keep her awake.

At first she thought she'd dreamt the noise. A thump and then a shout. But then there were more noises. Feet running, voices calling. Voices she knew. Serus. Ruth.

They were in the saloon. In the light of the single lamp, the windows shuttered to keep the glow sealed inside, Cora found Serus and Ruth looking at something, their heads close together.

'What is it?' Cora said.

'A near miss, fortunately,' Serus said.

'You had all the Latecomer's luck tonight, Serus,' Ruth said. 'If the course of that thing had been even slightly different...'

'Here.' Serus handed Cora his slipdog coat, bunched into an untidy package with the collar on top. And sticking through the collar was the barbed tip of another dart. As before, the point had a green tinge and the other end was feathered black and white.

'Tannir seems to be one step ahead of us at every turn,'

Cora said, 'and given he's on foot, that makes no sense –
how does he keep up with the barge?'

'He must be travelling by horseback when he's not right
at the bankside,' Ruth said.

'And all the while, we're out here on the water, a barely
moving target on an unchangeable route.' Cora pulled the
dart clear of Serus's collar and tried not to think of the coat
as the Rustan's neck.

'A metal addition I wasn't keen to try,' Serus said. His
tone suggested he was trying to make a joke, but even in
the poor light, his face showed the strain of what had just
happened.

'Where does the captain keep her drink, that lannat
stuff?' Cora asked Ruth. 'I think some of us could use a nip.'

'The galley,' Ruth said, wincing at the pain in her side as
she stood. 'I'll fetch it.'

As she stepped into the corridor, she made a sound of
surprise which was swiftly followed by the gruff tones of
Marcus.

'Why is she not in bed?' Cora asked, then realised she
had no idea of the time. She glanced at the saloon's clock – a
little after two in the morning.

'Well, her bed *is* currently in use,' Serus said, and gestured
to a small heap of blankets that had been squashed into the
corner of the saloon's seating.

'But she wasn't asleep before you and Ruth came in
here?' Cora asked.

'Not that I saw. I'll admit, when I first came inside, I
wasn't thinking clearly. The dart coming so close… Marcus
might have been in here. I didn't—'

'It doesn't matter.' She put her hand over his. 'You're

all right, that's the important thing.' Ruth returned with a bottle and glasses, and Cora removed her hand. 'And besides, Marcus lives in a games house. She keeps the hours of the chequers and their customers.' Cora looked up at Ruth pouring the drinks: only two glasses. She'd remembered.

'What have you done with her?' Cora asked Ruth.

'Who?'

'Marcus!'

Ruth glanced at the open doorway, and Cora noticed how much her sister's hair had grown since Nullan had cut it. It was curling at her ears, like their father's had done. A thought that was good and hard at the same time.

'The girl's fiddling about with something,' Ruth said absently. 'She's in the storeroom. Whatever keeps her quiet is fine with me.'

Ruth handed a glass to Serus who sniffed it, winced, then put the glass down.

'The captain drinks *this*?' he said. Ruth downed hers in a single gulp.

'Lannat is good for shock,' Cora said, 'if not for your insides.' And pain relief too? Ruth was already refilling her glass.

Serus took the tiniest sip. The curse that followed was a new one to Cora. She looked at him with fresh eyes, while Ruth clapped him on the back.

'The watch?' Cora asked.

'Nullan's taken over,' Ruth said, 'but from a safer position. After what happened to you, Serus, it's clear we need to take more care. That Tannir should try to harm us at night...'

'Which brings me to two questions,' Cora said. 'How did

Tannir know we were still sailing, and how was he able to keep up with our course when we're sailing in the dark without lights?'

The only answer Serus and Ruth had was to drink Captain Luine's lannat – one downing a third glass, the other still sipping at his first. Cora's answer was to roll a bindleleaf, her papers having dried, thank the Bore.

'You take the cabin,' Cora said to Serus, and when he looked like he would protest, added; 'I can't see myself sleeping for a while. Go on. You deserve a night in a bunk.'

'If you're sure?' He squeezed her shoulder, and she did her best not to lean into him, not with Ruth there. Whatever was happening with Serus, it was theirs, no one else's. She closed the door behind him.

'It's at K'stera Point the river splits, yes?' she said.

'The Stave becomes the Cask and the Tun there.'

'So it's like a fork in the river?'

'I guess you could call it that, though no doubt the Caskers have a technical—'

'Which side of the fork is the Tun?' Cora said.

Gingerly, Ruth rose to her feet. 'Let me get the charts from the captain.'

Cora grabbed her arm. 'Not now. I don't want anyone else hearing this, Ruth.'

'Who don't you trust here, Cora?'

Another question without an answer.

'Which side of the fork is the Tun?' Cora asked again, slowly.

'The right,' Ruth said. 'We'll bear right when we reach K'stera.'

Cora used the saloon's lamp to light her bindle, and

though it took a few deep draws to get at the smoke, after the tin's dunking earlier, it was better than nothing.

Ruth was frowning at her. 'What are you thinking?'

'So far, Tannir has always appeared on, and attacked us from, the south bank. Once we're past K'stera Point he'll at least have to cross the river to keep up with us on the Tun.'

'So you think we'll be safer from then on?'

'Possibly. But we can't count on it, which is why you and I should get off the barge for a spell.'

Ruth had been about to pour another drink but her hand stilled. 'What? Why?'

'Tannir's getting more desperate, Ruth. He took on crews of angry Caskers today, and now he's firing darts into the dark. He knows he's running out of time to stop you telling the Wayward story. We know he's happy to kill others in the process. He set fire to the distiller's. What's to stop him swapping poison darts for burning ones? From the bank he could set the barge alight and have us all burn to death in our sleep.'

'You really did bring Serus along as Fire Investigator. That's a shame. He'll be disappointed you don't want more from him.'

'Ruth, I'm serious! Once we're past K'stera and well on our way on the River Tun, you and I need to get off and make part of the trip on foot.'

'Won't that be more dangerous than staying on board?'

'Not as I see it. Tannir will keep attacking the barge, and that'll likely get worse. If we can't stop him, then our best bet is to find another way to the Hook. It's too risky for you here.'

'Risky too for those who stay on the barge,' Ruth said, meeting Cora's gaze squarely.

She shrugged. 'We can give you a better chance of getting to the Hook in one piece, that's all. We'll go overland for a stretch then re-join the barge just before we reach the Wayward herd. Until then, we need to keep Tannir guessing.'

Cora decided not to mention that the trip overland would also give her the chance to test a theory that was taking shape. A theory that the leaks on this barge didn't just involve water.

Twenty-One

Now that Ruth had agreed to Cora's plan to go overland for part of the journey, Cora needed the maps, but there was a problem. She wanted to keep that plan a secret for as long as possible, which meant she didn't want to ask Captain Luine for the maps, and neither did she want to be caught in the captain's cabin taking them. But there was someone she could ask for help. Someone who could be found there without anyone asking questions.

Though it was now well into the early hours, Marcus was still awake, sitting on the small patch of the storeroom floor that was clear of Casker gear.

'Your sister gone on watch has she?' Marcus said when Cora appeared in the doorway.

'She wanted to, but with her wound healing... Harker will take over from Nullan.'

At the mention of her new friend's name, Marcus was on her feet and ready to wake him, dropping whatever it was she'd been so engrossed in the moment before. Probably a slingshot.

Cora caught her by the collar of her new jacket. 'Not so fast. I have a job for you.'

Marcus sighed. 'When don't you, Detective?'

'Shh – keep your voice down. While it's empty, I want you to go into the captain's cabin and get the chart that shows in detail K'stera Point and the path of the two rivers once the Stave splits. But get it *quietly*. I know you can be silent as the Mute when you want to be, as well as light-fingered. The owners of the laundry know that all too well.'

'What?'

'Your new clothes.'

'Oh. Yeah, well, if they will leave bags of the stuff in the street...'

Marcus shook herself free of Cora, kicked aside the slingshot and trotted off to the captain's cabin. As Cora turned back to the saloon she noticed that what Marcus had kicked away, half-hidden under sacking, wasn't a slingshot at all. It was a scrap of paper and a lump of charcoal. Could Marcus *draw*? Perhaps she wanted to make her own maps, inspired by those Harker had shown her. Wonders would never cease.

Once Marcus had done as she was asked and retreated to the storeroom, Cora closed the door to the saloon and looked at the map. K'stera Point was a sizeable landmark by the look of it: some kind of building perched on a rocky outcrop. The River Stave divided itself in two either side of the rock, becoming the Cask on the left and the Tun on the right, just as Ruth had said. Ruth had also said that the current would become faster once they were past K'stera Point, so she and Cora would need to take a route that ensured they didn't get left behind. And the longer they spent on land, the greater the chance Tannir would cross the two rivers and find them without the support of the crew.

But it looked like they were in luck.

'Another good tale for you here, Partner,' Cora murmured as she looked at the path of the Tun. From K'stera Point, the river snaked round to the east, a long bend that Cora and Ruth could cut off on foot. According to the map, the land looked as if it was criss-crossed by lanes, so they should have some cover then. It might work after all. She was about to roll up the map and hide it in one of the many drawers built into the saloon walls, when her eye caught something marked on the map.

A bridge.

That could be a problem, but according to the map it was the only one for miles and was a little way before K'stera Point. In fact, they might be sailing under it right at this moment. If Tannir stayed on the south bank of the River Stave until K'stera Point then to reach the Tun he'd have no choice but to retrace his steps back to the bridge, and that would take him a while, even if he did have a horse. By the time he was on the north bank of the Tun, where Ruth and Cora would be on foot, they might well be deep into the lanes, and almost at the place the Hook was waiting for them.

Of course, Tannir should have no way of knowing that Cora and Ruth were even planning to leave the barge. Unless Cora was right and someone on the barge *was* feeding him information. She and Ruth going overland for a spell might reveal the truth, as long as they didn't both end up with a poison dart in their neck. The way

Heartsbane acted on a body, it would be a swift end to such worries. For both of them.

Cora was on deck with Serus when K'stera Point came in sight early the next morning. They were at the back of the barge, sharing the watch behind a length of stained canvas strung between two old fishing poles – Nullan's invention to protect those on deck from any more darts that might be fired from the bank. Of Tannir himself, there had been no sign. The dart that had pierced Serus's coat had been the last to reach the barge.

The sun was high enough to reveal a tower, incredibly tall but thin, no wider than the rocky outcrop dividing the river on which it was perched. As the barge drew closer, the walls revealed themselves to be made of white stone, which glittered in the day's first light, and what had first seemed just soaring, uninterrupted stone shooting up into the clouds became countless windows.

'How in the name of the Audience did the Perlish manage to build that... thing on that bit of rock?' Cora said.

The barge lurched, and Serus overbalanced, falling into her shoulder. Cora caught him but didn't let go of his waist once he was steady again. The solid weight of him against her hip felt good, and he didn't move away.

'Ruth says the current will get faster now K'stera Point's in sight,' Cora said.

'She's not wrong.' Serus was looking at the water. 'That's the first time I've noticed any change in the river's surface. Those little ridges.'

But Cora wasn't looking at the water. She was staring

at the approaching tower, at its windows. There was something troubling in them. 'I can't have had enough sleep,' she muttered.

'I keep telling you, Cora, the hammock is much more comfortable than that bunk in the cabin.'

She blinked a few times, but the sight before her didn't clear. 'I'd swear there are people in that tower.'

'That's hardly surprising, is it?'

'What's *surprising* is there are people in every one of the windows. Must be hundreds of them!'

Serus took a sharp breath. 'And they're all watching the river,' he said.

The back of her neck prickled. They were sailing ever closer to the rock on which the tower perched. Cora had to strain her neck to see the windows. Just as she said: in every one, there was a face turned to the water below. Cora could feel their gazes like a hot brand.

'Might want to get hold of this as we pass the point,' Harker said, joining them. He handed them the end of some rope coiled on the deck. 'Gets a little rough.'

The Casker wasn't wrong. The barge was rocking more than ever now, as the river swept them closer to the huge stone mass ahead. Harker made his way to the front of the barge, himself as steady as if he were walking on land.

'What will be the story of today, I wonder?' Serus said, having to raise his voice over the loud churning of the river.

Cora passed him a rope and kept hold of it for her own balance. 'Hopefully not a story of drowning.'

'Or poison darts,' Serus said.

There was no sign of Tannir on the riverbank. That wasn't necessarily a good thing. Her hope had been that when the River Stave split in two and their barge sailed down the northern fork, the Tun, Tannir would be stranded on the wrong side of the parallel river, the Cask, his only choice to retrace his steps to the bridge now behind them. The current here was surely too dangerous for other barge captains to offer transport from one side to the other. Cora wished she'd thought to check that with Harker before he'd gone to join Captain Luine, but that would have revealed more to the bargehand than she thought wise.

It was all action at the front, with Luine at the wheel shouting orders to Nullan who had charge of the levers and was hauling them back and forth. Harker leapt from the deck to the roof and back again in an endless dance with the sails and ropes, then he grabbed a rod and stabbed at the water. Cora guessed there must be a sandbank, impossible to see from the barge, but Harker seemed to know exactly where it lay. Other barges were in front of them and behind, making the same trip, but the captains kept a good distance between them.

Ahead, not far from the stony face of K'stera Point, a huge pole rose from the water, painted in red and white stripes that twisted sleekly down the wooden surface. As each barge neared this pole, they made their choice: River Cask to the south, River Tun to the north. Cora took another look at the bank where Tannir had appeared so often on this trip. Still no sign of him.

Their barge was now the closest to the striped pole, and at a shout from Harker back on the roof, the barge lurched, dipping so low in the water, Cora was sure they'd all slide right in. As she held her breath, she had time to wonder if Marcus and Ruth were stowed inside, and whether they'd have a better chance if they came out on deck – at least then they could swim, not be trapped in the shuttered saloon—

And then the barge righted itself, and they were sailing hard for the northern channel: the River Tun.

'I think we can let go of this now,' she said to Serus, holding up the rope.

'No harm holding on a bit longer...' His usually golden face had a definite green tinge.

'I didn't know you got water-sickness,' Cora said.

'I don't.' And then he brought up his breakfast all over Cora's boots.

The current stayed fast-moving as the barge rounded the white bulk of the tower. Behind it was a steep slope that led down from the tower walls to the level of the river. A large town, or even a small city, was packed into the V of land formed by the two rivers diverting. This was K'stera, Harker told Cora and Serus. The Casker was back on the roof of the barge, managing the sails. The man had no fear, exposed as he was up there.

'Who was that back there, in the tower?' Cora said. She couldn't get the faces at the windows out of her mind.

'You don't need to be minding them,' Harker called down. 'They got no eyes in their heads.'

'I'm not sure that's particularly comforting to know,' Serus said.

The Casker laughed. 'It's figures of the Washerwoman you saw, and too many to count. The ones at the windows, they're the only ones we can see, but they say every room of that tower is filled with them. Each one's made different, got to be unique. Made of every material you can think of – wood, stone, metal, sand, cloth, even ice in the winter. I heard a story once of a cake baked in her shape.'

'Who makes them?' Cora asked.

Harker waved to the city they were sailing past. 'The people of K'stera. Every household, every year, they make a new one, and in it goes. It's different with the storyteller of course. Only one of them. There's always a 'teller in the tower. They go in when they're a child. Their life's work to tell the Washerwoman tales of the river they can see from the windows.'

'Their life's work?' Cora said. 'And don't tell me – they get no choice in the matter.'

'You're right there, Detective. Well, far as I know anyway. Someone from K'stera told me, years back this was, that their council draw a name from a cask. Twelve you have to be, to have your name in the cask. If you're picked, you go inside the tower, and you don't come out.'

'What keeps the storyteller in there?' Cora asked.

A call came from the front of the barge. It was Nullan, signalling that Harker should join her and the captain at the wheel. He stood and stretched. Cora could hear the clicks in his back from the deck below.

'Being the Washerwoman's storyteller is said to bring honour to their family, who get all kinds of gifts from the council – fancy house, good horses, council membership. All the things Perlish people care about. And if the storyteller won't do it, won't go into the castle and spend the rest of their days telling the Washerwoman stories of the river below, their family have problems, for generations, they say. Goods seized. No marriages. Exile from Perlanse.'

'From the whole realm?' Serus asked. 'Even the western duchy?'

'So I hear,' Harker said. 'The duchies got some kind of special treaty about that, they say. And if the storyteller should take their own life, if there's even a suspicion of it – if they stop eating, that kind of thing – then the family have the same fate as if their child had refused to go into the tower in the first place.'

'A storyteller is in there until they die?' Cora said.

Harker swung himself down to the deck. 'When you've got no more stories to tell the Washerwoman and you join the Audience yourself, a new name is drawn.'

'That's a particular kind of Perlish cruelty,' Serus said.

'Always thought that was a talent of theirs. That's how they grow so rich.' And with that, Harker sloped off to join Nullan and Luine.

Neither Cora nor Serus spoke for a while after that. The barge was still rocking in the stronger currents that washed past K'stera. The buildings of the town were made of the same white stone of the tower, but here and there were glimpses of yellowish rock, as well as red and sometimes a grey-blue. Cora would have called K'stera pretty, but after learning of the indentured storyteller kept in the castle, the place held a deep ugliness. Beyond the settlement, a plain of land stretched away, widening as the two rivers drew further apart, and with roads and lanes criss-crossing its expanse. But Cora's eye was drawn to the other side of the river, to the north bank.

The River Tun began to snake round, just as the map had shown, and Cora soon spotted the clump of trees she'd been looking out for. It was there she'd told Ruth they should leave the barge, as quietly as possible, and make their way overland to a meeting point further upstream, just before reaching the Hook, where they would re-join the barge. And if the Partner had any favour for this story at all, Tannir would be miles and miles behind them.

'To spend your days watching other people's journeys and yet never go on any of your own,' Serus said at last. He placed his hand over hers. It was warm, she noticed, and heavy. 'I hope, for the storyteller's sake, their stories take them away from their captivity. And what of ours, Cora?'

'Hmm?' She was doing her best to lean into the barge's wild movements.

'Will we soon step off this barge? Is our destination close?'

'So I'm told. Should reach it tomorrow afternoon.' It was on the tip of her tongue to tell him that she and Ruth would be stepping ashore sooner than he would, but she didn't, and she didn't like the reason why.

Twenty-Two

Cora found Ruth in the storeroom. She, too, was now dressed as a Casker and was filling a knapsack with rope and a roll of canvas. Cloth-covered packages at her feet told a story of food supplies.

'Do we really need all that?' Cora asked, glancing behind her. The corridor was empty, but the voices of the others hummed through the thin wooden walls. Nowhere felt entirely safe from being overheard. She turned back to Ruth. 'We'll only be away from the barge for a night.'

Her sister placed the cloth parcels in the bag and drew it shut. 'You don't know that, Cora. If something should happen to us out there, and we miss the meeting point—'

'We won't.'

'—we could be on our own in Perlanse for Audience knows how long.'

'Shouldn't you be fine with that, what with you being Wayward these days?'

Ruth pushed past her. 'That's the problem. We won't be on horseback.'

'Keep your voice down!'

Ruth rolled her eyes, and all at once they were back in

the house, the old house, where they'd grown up, the years fallen away and the squabbling quick to their tongues. How was it that Ruth was able to do that to her?

'Why all the secrets, Cora?'

'Because I don't know who we can trust.'

'I know I don't trust this plan.'

Cora grabbed her arm then regretted it, seeing how Ruth winced and clutched her injured side. But Cora had to make her point. 'You have to trust me now, Ruth. This might keep you safe just a little bit longer and tell me if there's someone aboard this barge selling you out.'

'You think it's Luine, don't you?'

Cora glanced down the corridor, all too aware of the captain beyond the partly open door, still at the wheel. But before she could answer, Ruth was off again, having seemed to have lost all sense of caution.

'And the reason you think it's Luine is because it was Nullan who hired her,' Ruth said. 'And you're jealous of Nullan. Jealous of our closeness.'

'Ruth, I—'

'Devotee hear me,' Ruth said, and leaned heavily against the wall. 'She was my son's partner. Nicholas and Nullan had been together for years. She's like a daughter to me, Cora, and family don't betray—'

'I hope you're not about to tell me that family don't betray one another, Ruth.' Cora took the knapsack from Ruth's shaking hands. 'You of all people should know that's not true. And here's something *I* know. Tannir is tracking us.'

Ruth sighed. 'I don't believe someone on this barge is helping him. I just don't, Cora. I think you've lost your way here.'

'Then why did you agree to get off the barge, agree to going overland?'

'Because you asked me to,' Ruth said simply, and that took all the words from Cora's mouth.

She felt the barge slowing.

'Time to go. You've got your knife?'

Ruth nodded. 'And you?'

Cora slipped on her 'dusters.

'Then let's go,' Ruth said. 'I will admit, it will be good to be on solid ground again.'

Cora had arranged things as tightly as she could. Ruth had asked Captain Luine to draw close to a copse of trees that would come in sight not long after passing K'stera, claiming there'd be a messenger waiting there. Ruth told Luine she'd be off the barge and back within ten minutes. This lie had been delivered at daybreak that morning so there was little time for Luine, or anyone who overheard, to communicate as much to Tannir.

With the plan in place and the trees now drawing close, Ruth did as she and Cora had agreed: going to the wheel and standing ready to step down onto the bank. As the barge came alongside the trees, there was no sign of unease or expectation from Luine. The captain was talking to Harker about the best way to set fishing poles, one hand on the wheel, the other holding her cup of lannat, half an eye on the river and the ever-nearing bank.

It was only when Cora jumped off after Ruth that anyone said anything, and it wasn't Luine.

It was Serus.

He was on watch at the back of the barge and called out. 'Cora? What are you doing? What's happening?'

There was concern in his voice, *that* she could recognise, but the panic there – did that speak of something else? A plan gone wrong? She wasn't going to hang around to find out and ducked under the trees, out of sight from the water. She heard Ruth calling back to the barge.

'Change of plan, Captain. I'll be on foot a bit longer than I thought, and Cora's coming with me. Keep sailing and we'll meet you a little way upriver. Nullan knows the place. Tomorrow at noon, we'll be there.'

Silence then, too long to be comfortable, before Luine answered in her usual disinterested way. 'My job is to captain this barge. No concern of mine who's on it, who's off.'

Then Ruth was coming under the trees. She marched past Cora. 'Time to enjoy this stroll in the countryside, I guess.'

Ruth had decided their course, and that was fine with Cora. Wayward sense of direction was legendary in the Union. Though her sister had been born and raised in the narrow streets of Fenest, the sky so often hidden by upper storeys leaning drunkenly towards one another, by lines of washing and by makeshift bridges between roofs, she had no trouble working out the direction they should take now, in West Perlanse.

Cora had offered to sketch Ruth a map from memory, after Marcus had silently returned the charts to Captain Luine's cabin, but Ruth had said there was no need. She would use the sun as her compass and the lie of the land as her map. When they'd travelled south to see the widening Tear, it had been the same. Cora had had her own map for her own purpose, but Ruth had seemed to just follow her nose.

They walked away from the river, and though the copse of trees wasn't large, the trunks swallowed all noise of water, so that within minutes there was no sense the River Tun was anywhere near them. Cora found herself thinking of the trees outside Fenest, and the Seeders hanging there. The smell of rotting bodies rose around her. The day was warm – warmer than she'd realised. The movement of the barge must have given a false breeze. Through the treetops, only the barest scraps of clouds were visible. The smell of the dead sat heavy on the hot air, though it was a memory, wasn't it? A memory she couldn't shake, and maybe that was right, given how terrible it was that the people of the south should take their own lives from despair. It was a relief when the trees began to thin, then she and Ruth came to a gate. Beyond it was a lane.

'We follow this until we reach a Seat,' Ruth said. 'It's the Dandy's, I think. There should be a crossroads there.'

'We could stop at the Seat, see if the Dandy wants to hear a story of two women in borrowed clothes.'

'Ah, but Cora, you know the Dandy also likes stories of what happens in bed. Perhaps you have one for him?' Ruth gave her a sly look. 'A story involving a certain Rustan fire investigator...'

'Not yet.'

Ruth clasped her about her shoulders. 'I like your optimism.'

Cora could feel the heat rushing to her face and she

wasn't going to let Ruth mention *that*, so she took out her bindle tin to distract Ruth as much as give Cora something to focus on.

'Roll me one?' Ruth said, just as Cora had known she would.

There were tall, wide walls on either side of the lane. In the event that Tannir *was* on their trail, the walls of the lane would give them some protection. The stones in the walls were neatly placed, all the same size and colour – a uniform white. There was nothing ramshackle about this landscape. On top of the walls were coloured stones, reds of all different hues, one set every five feet or so along the road. Red, the colour of the western duchy of Perlanse.

'Do you think someone from the Commission comes along each night and measures the distance between those red stones?' Cora said, pointing at one with her bindle. 'Checks no one's moved them out of place?'

'Wouldn't surprise me,' Ruth said.

'For the wall Morton wants to build, she'll need an even number of red and blue stones to keep both Perlish duchies happy.'

'She will, won't she,' Ruth said. She slowed her pace then stopped walking altogether. 'Give me a leg up, Cora.'

'Are you sure you're up to that? With the cut Tannir gave you, it might not—'

'It's better, don't worry.'

It hadn't looked better when Cora had caught sight of Nullan changing the bandage, but Ruth didn't look in a mood to change her mind. So Cora did as she was asked, making a cradle of her hands for Ruth's knee, then lifting her level with the top of the wall. Her sister was light – light enough to fling over the wall if Cora had a mind to. When they were children, they'd done this the other way around, Ruth lifting her younger sister to reach the sintas in the neighbours' trees. Now the frailness of Ruth was almost too much to bear.

But for a frail-seeming woman, Ruth still had a fair bit of force in her. She shoved one of the red stones off the wall and into the pasture on the other side.

'That'll give some officious oaf something to do,' she said, as Cora lowered her back to the ground.

'Bound to be a specific Commission log to record such vandalism,' Cora said, and Ruth laughed – a bark that sounded too loud in the quiet of the sheltered lane.

The Perlish woman on horseback coming towards them apparently thought so too as she gave them a wide berth and a scowl as she passed.

'Two Caskers without a barge,' Cora said. 'We'll be logged too.'

'Not for a while, I hope. Map suggested we wouldn't be passing any towns.'

'Ah, but the Commission has eyes in every part of the Union.' Cora spread her arms wide. 'No dusty lane in the middle of nowhere goes unnoticed by the eyes of the Wheelhouse.'

She'd meant it as a joke, but Ruth was frowning at her. 'You miss it, don't you?'

'Who in their right mind would miss paperwork?'

'Who in their right mind would work for the Commission in the first place?' Ruth said.

Cora shrugged. 'People born in Fenest. People whose parents could afford to send them to a Seminary that *makes*

Commission staff. People like you and me, Ruth. If you'd stayed—'

'I'd never have got involved in that corrupt monster.'

Cora made to flick her bindle end away but was surprised to feel bad about the idea, given the pleasant countryside, so pinched the end with damp fingers and stowed it in her pocket instead. 'Given that you *did* leave, guess we'll never know, will we?'

'*I* know,' Ruth muttered.

They rounded a corner and the spire of a Seat came into sight. It wasn't a tall one, but the building looked fine: the same smooth white stone of the tower at K'stera Point. Would there be an indentured storyteller stowed inside?

'One thing's for sure,' Cora said, 'I'd never have guessed that you'd end up coming back to Fenest as an election storyteller.'

'It was never meant to be this way,' Ruth said, her voice hard. 'If Nicholas was still alive...' She shook away the end of that sentence. 'But my job is nearly over. Once the Wayward Hook is in Fenest I have one more thing to do, and then it'll be finished.'

'Big thing still left on that list though,' Cora said, 'telling an election story. The risk too.'

'That I won't deny, and if Morton should take me, Cora, if she uses my life—'

'She won't.' Cora kept the spire of the Seat of the Dandy in sight. Wouldn't look at Ruth in this moment. Couldn't. Then she felt Ruth's thin arm snake through hers.

'Morton's already managed it once, after the Seeder story at Tithe Hall. Look at the lengths she's gone to since then.'

That Cora couldn't argue with. Hadn't she been telling

Ruth about the risks since the day she'd left the police and thrown in her lot with the southern alliance?

'It's important we talk about this,' Ruth said, 'and I've been meaning to, but on the barge...'

'It's a bit crowded?'

'It is, isn't it? I wasn't expecting Serus or Marcus to join us.'

'Neither was I.' Cora used her coat to wipe the sweat from her face.

'But what I wanted to say, Cora, is that it doesn't matter what happens to me. Once I've said the last word of the Wayward story, my own story can end.'

They were almost at the Seat of the Dandy, and Cora could see the crossroads Ruth had said would be there. A crossroads, just as they were talking of a life's purpose. The Audience might doubt how those things came together, consider them too neat. But that was the way of life sometimes. At least there was something to break the perfection – a pennysheet seller was shouting his headlines somewhere close.

'Is that what you want?' Cora said. 'To tell the story and then give up?'

Ruth gave a deep sigh. 'Part of me gave up when Nicholas died. A large part, Cora. The part of me that's kept going... It's the story that's done that. And you.'

Cora squeezed and released her bindle tin, squeezed and released. 'You think your life has no other purpose than to tell a story?'

'Maybe it does, but this story is—'

'Bigger than either of us. I know. But—'

'There are no "buts", Cora.' Ruth drew her arm from

Cora's and stood square in the lane, blocking her way. 'My task is to tell my son's story. Your task is to help me do that, help me stop Morton dividing the Union and condemning countless people to a terrifying, painful end as the Tear consumes the south. Will you do that, Cora?'

'I'm here, aren't I? Gave up my badge in the process.'

Ruth was studying her face. 'But when it comes down to it, to a moment of choice, which will you choose, Cora?'

Sweat was beading round Cora's mouth. The bindle tin was slippery in her hand. She stepped away and started walking. 'Every choice I've made so far has been to help you, Ruth. I wouldn't start doubting me now if I were you.'

'We'll all be tested, Cora,' Ruth called after her. 'I wonder if yours is still to come.'

The pennysheet lad was on the steps of the Seat, shouting his headline and proffering pages to those coming in and out of the Seat, which was busy, despite there not being many houses in sight. The large double doors were like no doors Cora had ever seen, more like gates – thin wooden poles held in a frame but with gaps between them. Woven through those gaps were ribbons of all colours, and within *those* were poked flowers. The smell was enough to make Cora's nose itch, but would the Prized Dandy expect anything less at his Seat, especially a Seat in Perlanse?

'Here.' Ruth gave the 'sheet seller a penny, which was helpful, given that Cora had no coin at all.

Cora took the pennysheet and quickly skimmed it. 'Looks like a local paper. You got anything from Fenest?' she asked the lad.

'Sold 'em all,' he said. 'Always go quick, the Fenestiran 'sheets.'

Apart from having a sheaf of printed sheets over one arm and an appraising glance that Cora recognised, this pennysheet seller looked nothing like those of Fenest. He was washed, for a start, and his clothes, though lacking the usual finery of Perlish stuff, were clean and unpatched. Perlish pennysheet sellers were a different animal entirely.

'Leaving out that useless rag *The Spoke*, can you remember the headlines of this morning's Fenestiran papers?' Cora asked him.

'I can,' he said slowly, his brown eyes wide beneath his green velvet cap. 'But that'll cost you extra.'

Not so different to the capital's 'sheet sellers after all. Ruth gave him another coin and then he drew a deep breath. Cora was about to tell him he didn't need to shout the headlines – she was right there in front of him – but there was no stopping him. Another habit that couldn't be unlearned.

'*Wayward Hook will be greatest yet – huge crowds expected. Will the Commoner have room?* That's *The Fenestiran Times.*'

'For once, they're not wrong,' Ruth said.

Before Cora could ask her what she meant, the lad drew a deep lungful of air and yelled, '*Talks to choose final story venue collapse. Wayward blame Commission.*'

'Let me guess,' Cora said. '*The Daily Tales?*'

He nodded.

'Sounds like the head herders are doing a *great* job in my absence,' Ruth muttered.

The lad drew breath again. A man leaving the Seat had stopped to watch. Short and round, sweating beneath what looked like a wig of blueish curls. Perhaps he thought this was the start of some loud story, told outside a Seat for a change, rather than inside. Whatever his motives, it wasn't good to have company.

'Make it quick,' Cora told the boy.

'*Black Jefferey suspected in south gate camp. Perlish Chambers tell Commission to dispel the destitute.* That's—'

'—*The Stave*,' Cora finished for him. 'I know their way of reporting human misery. Another penny for his trouble,' she said to Ruth, and when the lad had pocketed the coin, she leaned close to his ear and said, 'We were never here. Now, keep that one there busy until we're out of sight.'

He began his loud sales patter on the man who'd stopped to watch, while Cora and Ruth set off again, taking the left-hand lane of the crossroads.

As before, the lane was flanked on either side by high walls of white stone, topped at regular intervals by the red stones. But from the narrowness of the way and the weeds peppering the gravel, it seemed they were on a less well-trodden path than before. That was no bad thing, and neither were the trees that sprawled over one side of the lane, giving welcome shade.

'I was enjoying not knowing what was going on in Fenest,' Ruth said. 'Why did you have to remind me?'

'Because we'll be back there soon enough, and I'd rather know what was waiting for us.'

'Sounded like the usual Fenestiran politics to me. Southerners are bad, they spread disease, so don't let them come anywhere near us. Commission falling out with the realms they're meant to serve.'

'And excitement about a Hook,' Cora said, rolling a new smoke. She guessed she had enough bindle left for three more so she and Ruth would have to share. 'Will the Wayward Hook live up to it?'

'It'll do more than that.' Ruth said. 'But it's not excitement people will feel when they see our Hook. It's fear.'

'Not sure the pennysheets will know how to write about that – a Hook doing something new.'

'They'll have to find a way,' Ruth said. 'With the Tear widening, all our stories will be different.'

'Mine already is,' Cora said. 'But yours—'

There was a grating sound behind her, but somehow above too. Cora spun round, but she was too late.

Too late to stop the hooded figure leaping from the wall towards her.

Twenty-Three

The force of the impact knocked Cora to the ground and took the air from her lungs. As she struggled to breathe, she was dimly aware of Ruth charging to her side, the glint of the sun on her sister's knife.

Tannir was on top of Cora, his knee pushing deeper into her chest with every lunge he made at Ruth – he had his own knife. Of course he did. Darkness was swooping at the edge of Cora's vision. She tried to push it away. Her hands found cloth and that was dark too. Had night come when she wasn't looking, and did it have buttons? That made no sense, but she couldn't breathe, couldn't breathe, couldn't…

Pain in her cheek. Raw, hot, slicing. He'd cut her face, and it hurt like nothing else ever had. Then there was a cry from Ruth, her sister's arms shoving – she was so much stronger than she looked – and then the black cloak was falling away, falling to the ground. Air raced back into Cora's body, but too much, too fast. It hurt to breathe, and she could taste blood. Her cheek rested on gravel, and now she could see the tiny grains. They were rough against her skin because her face was cut – Tannir had cut her, and she was coughing.

Then there was another sound: Ruth. Ruth saying, *No, no. I won't let you. No. You can't stop me. No. Get back.*

Cora scrabbled to her feet to face the tumbling figures. Her body felt heavy and it still hurt to breathe, but she had to move, and quickly.

Ruth was on her knees. Tannir stood over her, his back to Cora, but she could hear Ruth's choking, knew what he was doing to her sister. Her sister who needed her voice more than she needed any other part of her body, and Cora needed to be quicker, lighter, as she stumbled to the wall, but her legs were as heavy as the red stone she grabbed from the top of the wall. And the stone was itself a terrible weight and she wasn't sure she could carry it but she was doing it, she was lifting it, somehow, and when she slammed it down on Tannir's hooded head, she felt light as the breeze that had come from nowhere, now cooling her face.

It was Tannir now, who was the heavy one. He was lying across Ruth, silent but twitching. Cora picked up the stone again and found it was easier to hit him the second time, and she used more force. He stopped moving then. The stone's red surface was streaked with new shades. She tossed it to the ground and tried not to see the same colour all over her hands.

'Cora – help me.'

Ruth was attempting to push Tannir off her. Cora grabbed his shoulder and pulled. Together they flipped him onto his back. His hood had fallen over his face but the blood from the ruin that Cora had made of his skull was trickling down his chin and onto his chest.

'I was wrong,' Cora said, then her mouth filled with

blood so she spat. 'We should have stayed on the barge. Ruth, are you hearing me?'

But Ruth was bent over Tannir, fumbling to push back his bloodied hood.

'Wait – are you sure Tannir's dead?' Cora said.

'It's not Tannir, Cora.'

She slumped against the wall. 'What? How can that...'

'All the time we thought it was him following us, shooting those darts. But we were wrong. I should have realised, after the Water Gardens... Cora, help me uncover him – there's so much cloth.'

Cora checked the lane in either direction. There was no one in sight, but how long would that last? She didn't want to be talking to any constables about a dead man and her own bloodied hands. She knelt on the other side of the body. Ruth reached under the dead man's neck, as gently as if he were a child she didn't want to wake, to lift his head from the ground. With the cloth free of the weight of the head, Cora could properly push the hood clear of his face.

The face of the Seeder storyteller.

Jerome. That was what Ruth had said he was called, back when they'd encountered him at the Water Gardens, just after the Rustan story had finished.

Ruth sat back on her haunches and stared at the dead storyteller. 'He must have decided that his own story wasn't meant to end with the Seeder tale. He had more to do before joining the Audience.'

'At Morton's bidding,' Cora said. She couldn't help thinking of Nicholas Ento, seeing him for the first time dead in the alley, blood all down his chest, just like this man. But Ento's blood had dried by the time he'd been reported to the police, and his lips had been sewn shut with bootlaces. Morton's hand was all over the dead of this election.

Cora pushed the folds of the storyteller's cloak aside and began searching his clothes.

'What are you looking for?' Ruth said.

'He knew where to find us. No matter all the ways we've tried to outrun him, confuse him, how we've changed our plans – he was always ready. I need to know how.'

Jerome's trousers had more pockets than a Wayward cloak. Ruth went to help Cora search him, but Cora stopped her.

'We need to keep as much blood off ourselves as we can. Two Caskers in the lanes of Perlanse are conspicuous enough.'

Ruth fell back and let Cora work. It seemed to take an age. The sun was fierce on the back of her head and her cheek was throbbing. She could feel the blood there stiffening in the sun, but there was no time to do anything about it now. Finally, her fingers closed around a scrap of paper. She drew it out, and even before she'd opened it, she knew who'd given it to Jerome: the paper was a torn corner of a pennysheet.

'Well?' Ruth said, looking over her shoulder.

Cora took a deep breath, then let herself confirm it. On the scrap of pennysheet, written in the grubby mess that could only be charcoal – of a kind she'd seen Marcus using in the storeroom – were notes about their trip overland. The point they'd leave the barge, and where they'd pick it up again.

'I didn't know she could write,' Cora said, tucking the note into her pocket.

'Barely, given the spelling.'

They stood in silence for a moment. Flies had begun to settle on Jerome. Ruth touched Cora's arm, gently, kindly, which was so much more than Cora deserved that she thought she might be sick, right there in the lane. Instead, she stirred herself to action. There'd be time for blame later.

'We need to get him out of the lane,' Cora said, 'and quickly. If he's found before we're back on the barge, we'll have trouble.'

'And how do you suggest we do that?'

Cora looked up and down the lane again. Just the gravel and the walls, the spire of the Seat of the Dandy. And the trees on the other side of the wall.

'If we can lift him, we'll tip him over and hope the trees will hide him for long enough that we can reach your Wayward herd. Are you up to it?'

'We're both cut, and we'll both lift,' Ruth said firmly.

'Then let's move.'

Cora wrapped the cloak around the body as best she could, to save from getting any more blood on their own clothes. Then with Cora at the head, the heavier end, and Ruth at the feet, they raised the body of the Seeder storyteller above their own heads. There was a moment when Cora's arms started to tremble and she could see Ruth was pale and sweating, a moment that she thought they'd never do it, but then they both seemed to find strength in the same instance. With a shared grunt they pushed Jerome onto the flat top of the wall. It was Ruth who gave him the final shove over to the other side.

'Let's hope no one comes by any time soon,' Cora

said, once they'd both got their breath back. 'In this heat, Jerome'll stink before too long.'

'Time for us to get moving then, but I'd better clean you up first.'

'What?'

'Your face, Cora. You're covered in blood. Given that cut in your cheek, I'd say most of it's yours. Though the force you hit him with the stone…'

With deftness that spoke of many injuries in her life crossing the Union, Ruth took a water bottle and a cloth from the knapsack and cleaned Cora's face. Her cheek stung worse than the moment Jerome had cut her, but Ruth told her it didn't look too deep.

'When we get back to the barge, Nullan can stitch it. You'll have an impressive scar.'

'Not sure who I'm meant to be impressing,' Cora said.

'Any of your old constables?'

And Cora thought of Jenkins. How much better would it have been to have the constable on this trip rather than Marcus? Marcus who was in Morton's pay. She picked up the knapsack, and they carried on up the lane.

They didn't speak for a while, and that was fine by Cora. She rolled a smoke. Her hands were steady, which surprised her, given that she'd just killed a man.

'When we were in the Lowlands, going down to the Tear,' Ruth said, 'and those two people traffickers attacked us, you wouldn't kill them.'

'I wouldn't let *you* kill them, Ruth. There's a difference.'

'Fine. But the end result would have been the same. You

insisted we keep them alive, tie them up and leave them to be found by their friends.'

Cora handed Ruth the shared smoke.

'And yet I just watched you kill a man by braining him with a rock. What's changed?'

Cora licked her lips, looked up at the sky, and thought how to answer.

'Nothing. Everything. I was in the police when that pair attacked us in the Lowlands. I was meant to hunt down murderers, not do the killing myself.'

'And now you're just like the rest of us: subject to the power of the Commission, the Assembly.'

'I was still subject to them when I had my badge, Ruth.' She took back the smoke and drew deeply.

'If you've done it once,' Ruth said, 'you can do it again.'

'Speaking from experience?'

'The girl. Marcus. She's betrayed me. Put everything we've worked for at risk.'

Cora stopped. 'You can't be serious, Ruth. You want me to *kill* Marcus?'

'I'm completely serious,' Ruth said, and from her cold, calm tone, Cora knew that she was. And she also knew, in that instant, that the person standing before her in a lane in West Perlanse wasn't the person she had grown up with. Ruth was right – Cora had changed, but she hadn't changed as much as her sister.

'If you won't do it,' Ruth said, 'I will. Make your choice. You've got until we reach the barge to decide.'

Twenty-Four

As the barge reached the meeting point – a ruined cottage that had all but slid into the river – Cora could see Serus, standing with Luine at the wheel. He had spotted where she and Ruth had been waiting, half-hidden by the remains of the cottage chimney breast. That he'd been looking out for them was clear, but there was no smile on his face. In fact, he looked grim. Cora hadn't thought she could feel any worse than she already did, given what she'd learnt about Marcus, but seeing Serus did just that. How could she have ever thought it was him feeding Jerome information?

With her usual laconic efficiency, Captain Luine sailed the barge close enough to the bank that Cora and Ruth could step aboard without the barge having to completely stop and tie up. Ruth marched past Cora without a word, going inside. Nullan glanced at Cora, frowning, then went after Ruth. The truth would be out in no time, and Cora still didn't know what she was going to do.

Serus was still looking glum, but on seeing the cut Jerome had given her, that turned to concern.

'Cora – what happened to your face?'

'It's not as bad as it looks. The one we thought was

Tannir, the one following us. Turns out, it wasn't him. It was someone else. The Seeder storyteller. He found us and took a swipe at me.'

'Stitcher hear me!'

'But he's... gone now. We don't have to worry about him anymore.'

The guarded look returned to Serus's face. 'Well, that's some good news at least,' he said, 'isn't it?'

'It is, but...' She was trying to see past him, catch sight of Marcus before Ruth did. A yell from inside the barge told her she was too late.

'I have to sort something out. Something important. I'll explain later, I promise.'

With a nod to the captain and Harker, both of whom were at the wheel and looking confused, Cora went inside, following Marcus's shouts to the saloon. There she found Ruth struggling to get a rope round the girl's wrists. From the dazed look on Nullan's face, Ruth had just told her about the pennysheet girl's betrayal. To Nullan's credit, she looked as disappointed as Cora felt. But Nullan wouldn't hesitate to carry out Ruth's bidding, however unpleasant it was. Cora had to find a way to stall.

'You said you'd let me decide,' Cora shouted over the noise.

On hearing her voice, Marcus looked over to the doorway, and the relief on the girl's face was clear.

'Detective! What happened to your face? No – that don't matter. You got to get this sister of yours off me *now*. She's lost her wits! Tying me up!' Marcus made to bite Ruth but her sister dodged it, managing to tighten the knots that now bound Marcus.

'And have you decided, Cora?' Ruth said.

'Let me talk to her, find out why.'

Ruth shoved Marcus back against the bench, to a loud *oi* from the girl.

'And you think that'll make a difference?' Ruth said, her voice rising. 'My son, my only child, *died* for this election, and this wretch thinks she can make that sacrifice be for nothing?'

'She's only a child herself,' Nullan said, putting her hand on Ruth's shoulder, but Ruth shook her off. She was crying now, tears coursing down her cheeks, but that wouldn't soften her. From the silence now emanating from the bench, Marcus had finally grasped the seriousness of the situation.

'That girl knows what she's about,' Ruth said, her gaze on Cora. 'You've got half an hour. After that, she goes in the river. I'll fill her pockets with stones myself.'

Ruth stormed out, with Nullan close behind. Cora grabbed the Casker storyteller by her inky wrist. 'If there's any way you can get me more time—'

Nullan shook her head. 'I'm sorry, Cora, but there's no reasoning with her when she's like this. I've seen it before. When this is done, come and find me. I'll stitch your face.'

Cora shoved the door closed, then kicked it. Her boot left a mark but the wood held. It might be old, but it was tough. Just like the captain who had charge of this old floating tea chest. Another person Cora had wrongly suspected when the truth had been right there in front of her.

Marcus was trussed up on the bench, trying to undo the knots Ruth had tied.

'You going to help me here, Detective?'

'Not sure I am. You've not been helping me much on this trip.'

'I dunno what you're talking about.' Marcus gave up on the knots and leaned back on the bench. Her gaze was on the ceiling.

'I think you do.' From her pocket, Cora took the note she'd found on Jerome, then tossed it onto the table. 'You've been giving the Seeder storyteller our plans.'

'Is *that* who he is?' Marcus said. 'She didn't tell me nothing about him. Just to get word to him about what you was going to do.'

'And by "she" you mean Chambers Morton.'

'You think a Chambers would talk to *me*? You've really lost it since you left the police, Detective.'

Cora ignored the jibe. 'So, if it wasn't Morton that put you up to this, who was it?'

'It was the grumpy one at Bernswick station. The one you never liked talking to. Stayed on the top floor mostly.'

'You can't mean Chief Inspector Sillian?'

'I dunno her name but her hair is all strange and flat.'

With her bound hands, Marcus did her best to flatten her hair into a vicious parting, just as Sillian wore it. Of course she'd do Morton's dirty work, save Morton the embarrassment of having to talk to a grubby pennysheet seller.

'When I was leaving the Water Gardens after the Rustan story,' Marcus said, 'that one with the hair, she got them purple tunics to catch hold of me and take me to her. Then she told me what she wanted me to do, what she'd pay me. I got half the money then, and I'll get the rest once we get back to Fenest.'

'I *knew* you didn't have time to follow me and Ruth from the Water Gardens to the barge,' Cora said, 'and that you couldn't have found out what we were planning just by keeping on our trail that day. And as for the story about thieving those clothes from the laundry…'

'I do do that, you know,' Marcus said. 'Sometimes.' She pulled at the collar of her fine new jacket, much as she was able with her hands tied. 'But I've never found nothing like this.'

'It was Sillian who gave you the clothes.'

Marcus nodded.

'And Sillian who told you about the trip upriver.' Cora covered her face with her hands. 'You lied to me, Marcus. I asked you, outright, if someone was paying you.'

'Yeah, I did lie. But I ain't been all bad.' Marcus hopped off the bench and came to stand before Cora, her bound hands held out in a gesture of pity. 'The one with the flat hair, she didn't know where you was leaving from, what dock it was. She didn't know the time neither. It was true what I told you when you found me in the storeroom – I worked it out from what the other 'sheet sellers were saying, like you do.'

'What do you mean, "like I do"?'

'A detective! I was being a detective.'

Cora groaned. Audience help her. Marcus's small, eternally grubby face peered up at her.

'I found out the barge you was getting,' Marcus said, 'and what time you was leaving, and I didn't tell her, the one with the hair. If I had, she'd have got one of her people to go straight to the dock and get your sister.'

'If you do manage to survive this in one piece, Marcus, you might not be a bad bet for a detective.'

'I don't think you know much about betting, Detective. Beulah says—'

'Never mind about my chequer debts.'

There was a noise in the corridor. Cora went back to the door. There was no lock, so she leaned against it again.

'All right, so you didn't betray us to Sillian before we left Fenest, but you've been doing it ever since. This note to the storyteller. It's not the only one, is it? You've been sending him messages the entire time, using those new slingshot skills.'

The girl grinned.

'And I didn't even know you could write,' Cora said. 'Reading, yes. You can't be a pennysheet seller without being able to read the words you're selling. But to write a note like this—'

'You're the one who said I had to go to school.' Marcus shrugged. 'Ain't my fault you don't know what I can do.'

'You're right. It is my fault. I underestimated you, and even worse, I trusted you. After all I've done for you.'

'Sillian paid me more than you do. Lot more. That's all.'

'So that's what this is about – money?'

'Isn't everything?'

There was no resignation in Marcus's voice, and no guile either. Just a simple statement of fact. This was truth as the girl saw it, and who could blame her for that, the life she'd had? Cora knew she should have done more for the girl. That she was partly to blame for Marcus being an easy target for Morton's schemes.

'I gave you a head start, didn't I?' Marcus said. 'And I only fired a few notes to the man sent to catch your sister.'

'You're claiming you did enough to get paid but not enough to actually betray me?'

'Got it in one, Detective.'

'Well, you won't be sending any more notes to anyone,' Cora said.

'Because your sister's going to throw me in the river?' There was the barest hint of fear in Marcus's voice, and Cora was pleased to hear it, because if Marcus believed the threat then she might fall into Cora's plan to save her, and quietly for once.

'Not just that,' Cora said. 'He's dead. The Seeder storyteller. I... He's dead.'

Marcus grinned. 'That's good. I didn't like them poison darts. Harker said I couldn't sit with him on the roof because it was too dangerous. But now it's your sister who's the dangerous one.'

'Ruth's not dangerous, she's just... sad, and angry. And there's something she has to do that's really, really important. I don't suppose Sillian told you why we were making the trip upriver, or why the Seeder storyteller was following us?'

'She only told me what I had to do. And I done it!'

'I wouldn't get too excited, Marcus. You're not going to be able to collect the rest of your pay.'

'You could untie me, let me climb out the window and swim to the bank.'

'*Can* you swim?'

'It can't be that hard. Or help me get to the captain's wheel. Luine will sail close to another barge if I ask her, I know she will. I'll jump across, and you can tell that sister of yours you had no idea.'

The girl's voice was babbling, but it was no use. The barge was slowing. From the look on Marcus's face, the girl could feel it too. Before Cora could say anything more, there was a thump on the door to the saloon – a thump so forceful, she felt it in her spine.

'Time's up, Cora.' It was Ruth.

Marcus scurried to the corner of the saloon. There wasn't much room to hide, but she did her best to crouch in the shadows. Cora took a deep breath and opened the door.

Twenty-Five

'Well?' Ruth said.

'It should be me that does it,' Cora said. 'Marcus is my fault. If I'd taken more care of her—'

'None of that matters,' Ruth said. 'It's only the punishment I care about now.'

'Leave it to me. I'll see to it.'

Ruth looked like she would say more, but then there was a noise from the bank. A loud noise, an unexpected noise, but of course it shouldn't have been.

It was a horse, calling to another of its kind.

The effect on Ruth was as if *she* were the one being called, because she turned away and rushed down the corridor towards the captain's wheel.

Cora stuck her head back into the saloon. 'Come on!' she called to Marcus.

The girl didn't need telling twice, and her trust made Cora feel sick to her stomach. The corridor was empty. Cora pushed Marcus into the galley and there found a knife to cut the girl's bonds.

'Thanks, Detec—'

'Shh. In here, quickly.' Cora led Marcus into her cabin.

The only sign of Serus was his slipdog hide coat lying on the bed, which made things easier. 'Get under that bunk and stay there until I come for you. If Ruth finds you, you're dead.'

As soon as Cora stepped on deck, she could smell a change in the air. Gone was the freshness of the river, replaced by something ripe and slightly sour. A smell she'd caught on Ruth every so often, and of course on nearly everyone who'd been in the safe houses back in Fenest. The smell of horses. And it was no wonder, given how many of them were on the riverbank.

Having moored the barge, Captain Luine had joined Harker on the roof of the barge where both Caskers were smoking and staring at the sight before them. Nullan, too, was transfixed, leaning on the captain's wheel. Cora went and joined her, the breeze stinging the cut in her cheek. The Seeder storyteller had sliced her deep.

Horses crowded the bank – all kinds of them. Some black and glossy, like the special paint the Commission used for depicting the spoked wheel. Others were brown as mud, some with patches, some with spots even. Greys that ranged from the colour of pebbles to almost blue. Creamy hides. Yellow hides. Tall ones and short ones, some in harnesses and some without any kind of rein on them at all, just wandering around as if they were dogs.

The row of tents behind the animals suggested the herd had been here at least a day or two. This was nothing like the camp outside Fenest. That was full of despair – frightened people unwanted where they'd pitched up but with nowhere else to go. For the Wayward whose whole existence was to wander, this place was just one stopping point on the journey of their lives. Cora couldn't think of anything worse than trudging across the Union in all weathers, sleeping on the ground. But that was the life they chose, that Ruth had chosen too.

There were people everywhere, most wearing Wayward cloaks. Men, women and children, every one of them looking busy as they carried saddles, cooking pots, logs, sacks, pails of water filled from the river.

'I know Ruth said the herd we were meeting was big,' Cora said, 'but that's a *lot* of Wayward.'

'It's because of the Hook,' Nullan said, her gaze fixed on the herd. 'They've come from all over the Union to work on it, under the direction of... Well, I'll let Ruth tell you that part.'

Cora turned to look at Nullan. 'You know what it is, don't you?'

'Only a few details. I'm excited to see it.'

'Will we be allowed to, given we're not Wayward?'

'From the little Ruth's told me,' Nullan said, 'there's no way we *can't* see it.'

That didn't make a lot of sense, not that it mattered right now.

'Speaking of Ruth,' Cora said, 'where is she?'

'Didn't even wait for me to tie up the barge,' Captain Luine called from the roof. 'First cry of 'em ponies and she was jumping onto land. Like one of 'em little 'uns the Rustans had as their Hook, jumping around the Seat of the Commoner.'

'Didn't think she had it in her,' Harker added.

'She's among friends here,' Nullan said. 'Makes a change not to have to worry someone will kill her.'

'Don't get used to it,' Cora said. 'As soon as we're back in Fenest, Morton will try again. She's running out of time.'

'Morton or Ruth?' Nullan said.

'Both.'

Nullan had put her hand to Cora's face, making her jump.

'Your cheek,' Nullan said. 'It doesn't look like it needs a stitch after all.'

Cora stepped away, onto the deck. 'Thank the Audience for that. My face hurts enough without you poking a needle into it.'

Serus was there, sitting on the deck, his back against the barge rooms. He seemed to be ignoring her, and her spirits sank. Ruth might be safe for the moment, but she had other things to worry about.

Cora made her way over to him, and at the last moment, he looked up. The sun was in her eyes, but she could still see his gloomy expression, just like when she and Ruth had returned to the barge.

Cora gingerly put her fingers to her torn cheek. 'Thought this might be a good opportunity to try something new. Thought you might be able to help.'

He said nothing, just looked at her.

'Reckon this gash is the perfect site to try a metal plate.'

She was joking, but he wasn't laughing. Or even smiling.

'Only a small one,' she said. 'The teaspoons in the galley might work.'

'So there *are* some decisions you trust me enough to share.' He looked back across the bank to the ever-changing

landscape of horses and Wayward people. 'That *is* good to
know.'

'Serus, what is it?'

'Oh, I don't know, Cora, just the fact you didn't tell
me you were leaving the barge with Ruth. That you were
risking your life.'

'I'm sorry, but I couldn't...'

'Couldn't what, Cora? Couldn't trust me?'

'Serus, I know this trip hasn't given us much time together
but—'

'Oh, I think it's given us more than enough time together.
Time enough to know how you really feel about me. If
we'd stayed in Fenest that might have taken another three
months, so at least we've reached the truth quickly.' His
metal cheek plates were grinding over one another, and the
noise was awful – she'd never heard this from him before.
Nor his anger. 'I guess I should thank your sister for that.'

Cora grabbed his arm and pulled him close to her, their
hips pressed together. He wanted her, she could feel it, and
the Devotee knew she wanted him too.

'I'm sorry I didn't tell you,' she said. 'Truly. I needed to
find out who was giving away our plans.'

'And you thought it was me?'

Not wanting to answer that, she kissed him, hard and
long. He kissed her back, despite his anger, and for a moment
she thought she was forgiven, but then he was pulling away,
and she couldn't keep hold of him. He was a few feet away,
at the edge of the barge, his back to her.

'I can't do this, Cora, knowing that you doubted me like
that.'

Her blood was hot, and she wanted him like she'd never

wanted him before. Was it partly the relief of knowing Serus
hadn't betrayed her? She'd been holding herself back, and
now she was ready, but her hesitation had spoiled things.
She had a strong desire to break something. But instead she
found her voice and asked him to watch Marcus.

'Ruth can't find out she's still on the barge.'

Serus turned to face her. 'Do you truly believe your sister
would kill a child?'

'I don't want to risk finding out.'

'You Gorderheims are really something. The pennysheets
were right all those years ago.'

So he had read the stories. He did know her history. Well,
at least that was out in the open now. Maybe it was better
they didn't take things any further.

'Will you keep Marcus in the cabin?' she asked him.
'Keep her quiet until I get back?'

'Where are you going?'

'Just tell me if you'll do it, Serus. It's the last thing I'll ever
ask of you.'

He stared down into the river. 'Of course I will, Cora.'

She moved back along the deck to draw level with the
barge roof where all three Caskers were now gathered.
Harker and Captain Luine were playing cards. Nullan had
her face turned to the late afternoon sun, her eyes closed.

'What's Ruth's plan now?' Cora called up.

'We're to wait until the Hook's ready to be transported,'
Nullan said, 'then join the herd and head back to Fenest.'

'There'll be horses for us?' Cora said.

'Well, I'm not walking.' Nullan's piercings glinted like
fine jewellery.

She looked exhausted – the loss of her lover Nicholas,

telling her realm's election story, doing her best to keep Ruth safe so that she could tell her story. Nullan had had a tough few weeks, and Cora had barely given her any thought. Now, the strain was clear on Nullan's face, mixed with the relief at the chance she now had to relax, even if only briefly. A murky bottle of lannat was set between the three Caskers. Time to leave them to themselves, and Cora had enough to do.

She needed to find out how long she had until the herd began the journey to Fenest, and that meant finding Ruth. And seeing the Hook? Despite all the things on her mind at that moment – Serus's anger, what to do about Marcus – she felt a flicker of excitement at the thought of seeing the Wayward Hook. She jumped onto the bank and headed into the herd.

With the huge numbers of Wayward and their horses, Cora feared it would take all afternoon to find the Hook, and Ruth with it. Might as well get started on the hunt, she thought, spying a pair of young women filling buckets next to the barge. Hoping for some luck, Cora asked them where the Hook was and was surprised to find that they knew. One of the women pointed over the heads of the surrounding horses to a large blue tent in the middle of the camp. Cora set off, but she soon lost her way amid the bustle and mud, and couldn't see a path between the ropes and wagons to reach the blue tent. Fortunately, everyone she asked knew where the Hook was, and knew the way. Nullan's words came back to her: whatever the Hook was, it couldn't be missed. Before long, Cora was standing before the blue tent that housed it.

It was nothing like the garbing pavilion used at the election sites – that was a spotless wall of white canvas, no doubt regularly scrubbed by purple tunics under the direction of whoever had replaced Jenkins's mother as Director of Electoral Affairs. The garbing pavilion had always struck Cora as being a hard, sharp thing – all angles. This Wayward tent was a smooth dome, and the deep blue canvas – if it was made of such stuff – was spattered with mud and horse grease and Audience knew what else. A working structure, put up and taken down regularly. The Commission's garbing pavilion was as much about show as it was anything else.

Cora glanced back to the river. It was barely visible with all the herd between her and the barge, the last of the afternoon's sunlight leaching into early evening. Had Marcus done as she'd been told and stayed on board? If she had, there was still a chance. Cora pushed her way into the tent.

And found herself in a different world.

Twenty-Six

She closed her eyes and opened them again, but that didn't change what was in front of her. With just a single step inside the tent, she'd gone from the muddy riverbank in West Perlanse crammed with Wayward, to a very different land. Gone were the grass and the trees beside the river, the rushes and little flowering plants she'd never found time to ask the name of. Instead, she felt she was standing on rock, and before her were cracks, ash and an orange fissure, within which were islands of rock, caught with the lake of Wit's Blood – a lake that was hot. She wiped her forehead, but her hand came away dry. No sweat, and yet she was on the edge of the Tear. Wasn't she?

'It should excite even the most jaded of Fenestirans, wouldn't you say?'

Cora turned to the man who'd appeared beside her. He was tall and with more muscle than his bones seemed able to bear, bunched and corded visibly beneath his skin. His face was lined with the effects of the sun, like most Wayward, but there was something familiar about his eyes, bloodshot though they were, and the shape of his nose.

This man looked a lot like Nicholas Ento.

'You're in shock,' he said, and it was as if Ento was speaking, something he'd never been able to do in Cora's presence, given how his lips were sewn by the time she'd found his body. Given the fact he'd been strangled. 'Seeing it for the first time, everyone is,' the man said. 'And that's the idea of our Hook, of course. Shock first, action after.' His hands were covered in orange, brown, grey. The same colours as the view ahead of her, and then she realised.

She hadn't somehow stepped from West Perlanse to the edge of the Tear. She was looking at a painting. A painting of the Tear made by this man standing beside her, smiling at her shock. She turned to face the Tear again, and now she knew what it was, she could marvel at the scale of it. The painting was colossal – at least thirty feet tall and just as wide, if not wider. The headline the pennysheet seller had told her that morning, about the Seat of the Commoner not being large enough to hold the Wayward Hook, there had been some truth in it.

'Just wait until you see the whole thing put together,' the man said.

Cora dragged her gaze away from the orange of the Wit's Blood before her. 'There's more?'

'Oh yes. Three canvases that fit together. The other two are finished. This is the middle. I had to do some final touches.'

At this, he frowned and moved closer to the canvas – so close, it looked as if he would step into the Wit's Blood, such was the powerful effect of the painting.

There was movement at the edge of the canvas. It was only then Cora noticed the ladders propped against it and the trays of brushes, pots of colour. Other Wayward were in the tent too, packing up the materials, though the paint splashed across their hands and clothes spoke of their work on the Hook too. Nullan had said people had come from across the Union to make the Hook, and now, their work was done. They'd head back to their saddles, while the Hook set out on a journey of its own.

The painter turned back to Cora. 'This middle section shows how the Tear has looked for centuries,' he said. 'It's the "stable" Tear, if you'll pardon the pun.' He smiled at Cora, but it wasn't a smile of happiness or peace: he looked like he hadn't slept in weeks. Cora recognised as much from the gaming houses.

'And the other parts of the painting?' she asked him.

'The start and the end. The Wayward Hook will take the eye on a journey,' the man said, his body once more turned to the canvas, as if he couldn't look away from it for long, let alone leave its side. 'We will show the land before the Tear opened, when the Rusting Mountains rose into the sky without clouds of smoke and ash surrounding them. Then we will show the rent in the earth when first it split open.'

'And then the state of it now,' Cora said. 'You'll show it's widened.'

He swept his arms before the painting. 'There'll be no denying the truth once we've shown the Union this Hook.'

The blue wall of the tent opened, and Ruth appeared. She'd changed out of the dirtied, bloodied Casker clothes and was now wearing a long, dark dress Cora knew to be a Wayward riding habit.

'I see you've met Frant,' Ruth said, joining them in front of the painting.

He opened his arms wide and bowed, then moved away to speak to the Wayward packing up the materials.

Cora leaned close to Ruth to whisper. 'Is he—'

'You see it too then, the resemblance?'

'Hard to miss it,' Cora said.

'Don't mention our son's name in front of Frant. He's… struggling.' Ruth said this as if she hadn't suffered herself, as if she was speaking of someone else's child.

'He's your husband?' Cora asked.

'Not in the way any Fenestiran would understand, but in the Wayward way, yes – we were bound.'

'Not any more though?'

'Frant and I had chosen different paths years before we lost Nicholas. It's not uncommon in Wayward relationships. When your lives are shaped by the movement of herds, the weather, which season you find yourself in the Rusting mountains, which season back on the Steppes, couples pull apart. They don't always come back together again. Frant was… upset when I decided I was happier alone, but he still had his son. Since we lost Nicholas, the painting has become Frant's world.'

'It's soon to be everyone's world,' Cora said, 'given what's happening in the Tear. How are we going to get this to Fenest?'

'The wagons are being readied as we speak,' Ruth said in a low voice. 'Once we can convince Frant to put down his brushes, this last canvas can join the others, and we'll set off. This is why it had to be me that came for the Hook. He'll struggle to let it go.'

'How long has he been working on it?' Cora asked.

'Two years. He only accepted help from the apprentices

when time grew short.' Ruth looked over at the other Wayward packing up the materials with quiet, deft movements. 'I dread to think how he's treated them.' She cleared her throat then called over. 'That's your last brush stroke, Frant.'

The painter shuddered, as if Ruth's words were like cold rain suddenly pelting his shoulders.

'There's no more time,' Ruth said. 'You know this. What good is the most powerful Hook the Union has ever seen if it doesn't reach the capital in time to be displayed?'

Frant hung his head and stepped away, but his eyes were still on the canvas. His hand that held the brush reached up, as if working independently of the painter. Ruth strode forwards and grabbed him, all but dragging him from the painting.

'Some help here, Cora?'

Cora took Frant's other arm, and together she and Ruth walked him out of the blue tent, into the deeper blue of early dusk. Lamps had been lit, and for a moment Cora thought she was back in a city. Then she heard the horses calling to one another, smelt them on the warm air, and remembered.

With the tent's folds resettled behind them and the painting out of sight, Frant had at last stopped looking back. All the air seemed to leave his body, and he fell to the ground, weeping.

Ruth eyed him sadly then dropped to her knees in the mud beside him. She spoke into his ear. Cora didn't catch the words and was grateful for that. This was too personal a moment for a stranger to step on. She moved away, keeping the couple in sight but well out of earshot. But in doing so she stumbled upon something else.

'... and then the mare pawed the ground until she'd dug a hole. Your tale.'

'The mare picked up the shell and the four leaves with her teeth, and dropped them into the hole she had dug. Your tale.'

'And with the shell and the four leaves, the mare dropped a bucket. Your tale.'

The voices were those of children, and they were coming from a wagon a few feet away. An awning had been stretched from its side and held in place by a sturdy wooden pole, making a roof to shelter from the sun that had now all but left the sky.

Cora glanced back. Frant was in Ruth's arms, and she was attempting to comfort him, but there was something restrained about her. From the looks of things, Cora had at least a few minutes to see if she was right about what was happening at the wagon.

Beneath the awning, an old man was seated on a barrel. A circle of children surrounded him. Each was taking a turn to say a line of a story, deciding what it was as they went round the circle. A Wayward school.

It might work.

'Can I help you?' the teacher said. Twenty small Wayward faces turned to look at Cora.

'I hope so,' Cora said, and ducked under the awning.

'It's a bit late in life for lessons,' Ruth said. At the sight of her sister, Cora took her leave from the teacher. There was no sign of Frant.

'You're always telling me I need to learn new ones,' Cora

said, stepping carefully along the muddy byways of the camp.

'True, and one in particular, about trust. The girl – is it done?'

Cora made sure to look Ruth square in the eye. 'Yes.'

Ruth looked right back, clearly checking for any sign of a lie. But thank the Audience, someone called Ruth's name, and then she was striding towards a large covered wagon next to the blue tent. One enormous roll of canvas had already been laid on the wagon bed, and a team of Wayward men and women, sweating despite the cool evening, were attempting to load another fat roll beside the first.

Ruth conferred with the small huddle that surrounded her and gave some orders. When there was a gap in the people wanting to talk to her sister, Cora managed to ask where Frant was.

'He's gone to his bed, with stories only for the Child.'

'Will he come with us to Fenest?'

Ruth shook her head. 'He needs time to grieve. Better he does that without me.'

Cora found that hard to believe, but then what did she know of what Ruth and Frant had experienced?

'The election is what matters now. That's what my son died for. I have to tell his story.'

'And if I have anything to do with it,' Cora said, 'you will. But it'll still be dangerous when we get back to Fenest. Tannir will be there, and anyone else Chambers Morton has paid to stop you.'

'Just a few more days,' Ruth said, her face barely visible now in the shadows of evening. 'Can you keep me safe for a little bit longer?'

'I'll do my best.'

They watched the last of the three canvases join the others on the wagon.

'We start at first light,' Ruth said. 'Tell Nullan and Serus to gather their things and be ready to leave the barge. Your horses will be on the bank.'

'You're not sleeping on the barge tonight?' Cora asked.

'When I can be back under canvas, a saddle for a pillow?' Ruth smiled. 'I won't spend one more minute on Captain Luine's old wreck if I don't have to.'

Ruth would be off the barge tonight – Cora's plan might work. If she could just make sure that Nullan—

'Cora, are you listening?'

'Hm?'

Ruth shook her head. 'I *said*, Luine has her orders. Once you, Nullan and Serus are on horseback, our contract is ended.'

There was no more mention of Marcus. As far as Ruth was concerned, the girl was dead. Her sister trusted her, and she had lied. As Cora made her way back to the barge, she thought about the bargain she'd struck with the Wayward teacher, and hoped she could trust him.

Twenty-Seven

Marcus had nothing more with her than the clothes she stood up in. At least they were new clothes, and decent, thanks to Chief Inspector Sillian. Cora doubted that even back in Fenest, Marcus had many more possessions. Not much to abandon, but still – Cora hadn't wanted things to go this way.

Marcus was sitting on the bunk in the cabin, with Serus beside her. The girl was swinging her short legs back and forth, her feet nowhere near the floor. It was well past midnight, and Cora was listening for movement on the barge, one ear pressed to the door. She caught the lap of the river, the occasional stamp and whinny of the horses, and laughter – distant, distracted laughter. On the barge, all was quiet. The three Caskers had drunk the *Pretty Lilly* dry of lannat.

'Time to go,' Cora said, turning around.

'Time for an *adventure*,' Serus said, doing his best to give Marcus a reassuring smile.

He hadn't been convinced by the plan when Cora had explained, but he'd agreed it was the only option – Cora couldn't well smuggle the child back to the capital in a saddlebag. And besides, if it did work, Marcus's life would be much better than what she was leaving behind in Fenest – sleeping in Beulah's games house, shouting pennysheet headlines day in, day out. Cora kept telling herself that. She thought she'd done right by the girl in the years she'd known her, but now she could see she hadn't done enough. It was Cora's fault as much as anyone's that Chief Inspector Sillian had been able to bribe Marcus. Ruth might not have much pity left in the pockets of her Wayward cloak, but the world had been too hard on her sister. Marcus deserved another chance.

'Teachers never mean adventures,' Marcus said sullenly.

'But the teacher is just helping us, remember?' Serus said. 'He's bringing the Wayward couple who are going to take you to the Steppes.'

'So you say.' Marcus's legs swung more wildly. 'How do I know this isn't some trick to get me to go to school?'

'Because this is serious,' Cora said. She opened the door and, after another heartbeat of listening, beckoned Marcus and Serus into the passage.

'Don't say a word until the barge is out of sight,' she whispered to Marcus.

'Where are we—'

Cora clamped her hand over the girl's boom. 'Just follow me, all right?' she whispered.

Serus picked up the sack of provisions he'd scraped together from the galley. With a nod from Cora, they headed out.

Marcus managed to keep silent until they were on the bank. 'I need to say goodbye to Harker.' Marcus's voice had a tremble Cora had never heard before. All words left her.

Serus stepped in. 'Harker told me to tell you, he's sorry not to be here right now, when you're leaving.'

'He said that?' Marcus asked.

'And he also said I should tell you that he's up and down these waters all the time with Captain Luine. He says he'll see you soon, when you're passing this way with the herd.'

Marcus thought about this for a moment, and Cora exchanged a glance with Serus.

'All right,' Marcus said, and started walking away from the barge. 'Tell Harker he'd better be ready to show me them birds' nests he's always talking about.'

Cora breathed a sigh of relief. 'Thanks,' she said to Serus, reaching for his arm. She thought better of it when she saw the look on his face: this was just business. So be it.

'Cora?' came a voice from the dark hump of the barge behind them. It was Nullan, weaving towards them with a lantern. 'What's going on? Is Ruth all right?'

'Go – I'll keep her busy,' Serus said, and before Cora could answer, he'd dropped the sack of provisions and was heading for Nullan. 'Cora can't sleep,' she heard Serus say loudly. 'You know what these Gorderheims are like – always chewing over something.'

Nullan laughed. 'You can say that again.'

'Seems best to leave them to it,' Serus said. 'Have you any of that lannat left?'

Nullan's groan and Serus's words faded as the pair went back inside.

Cora nudged Marcus forwards and they were on their way again, heading for the tree where she'd agreed to meet the teacher.

They had no lights with them, Cora wanting to keep as

low a profile as possible, but the lanterns dotted about the nearby tents gave just enough light for them to avoid sliding into the river or turning an ankle in the mud. Neither would be a good start for Marcus's journey.

As the tree came in sight, Cora's heart sank – there was no one there. The teacher had changed his mind, or the couple had decided against the plan. Maybe Ruth had caught wind of it...

Then the darkness appeared to move, and a shadow stepped forwards. It was the teacher. This might be a story for the Latecomer after all.

Marcus's steps faltered. Cora gave her another nudge and then felt a small hand slip into hers. Together they walked to where the teacher was standing, two other shadows just behind him. The night was warm and the air had some kind of sweetness: the tree was in blossom. It could have been a beautiful night, if Cora hadn't been about to send a pennysheet girl away with strangers.

'I wondered if you'd had a change of heart,' the old man said. His braid was silver as the moon and his eyes had all but disappeared inside his wrinkled cheeks.

'Likewise,' Cora said.

'I think you can count on this pair,' the teacher said.

He turned and beckoned. A man and a woman stepped forwards. They looked around thirty-five, which on a Wayward face meant they were probably ten years younger. They wore the cloaks of their realm, and each had a long braid – the man's black, the woman's red. They seemed nervous, glancing about them, but when they saw Marcus there was a longing there. Cora could almost feel it.

'This is the couple I told you about,' the teacher said,

then added in a whisper, 'The Devotee hasn't heard any stories of youngsters from them.'

Cora gave the pair a nod. They clutched each other's hands.

The teacher knelt next to Marcus, his knees making so much noise of protest that Cora feared he might not get up again.

'So you're the young Fenestiran who'd like to see the Steppes,' the teacher said.

Marcus kicked the dirt. 'I guess so.' Her voice was the quietest Cora had ever heard it. 'But I'm not Fenestiran. My mother was a Lowlander. My father... He was a bad sinta, my mother said, so he was probably from a Lowland farm too.'

'I didn't know you came from the south,' Cora said.

Marcus shrugged. 'There's a lot you don't know, Detective, and you won't ever know it, now we're saying goodbye.'

'Try not to think about it like that,' the teacher said, getting to his feet again, more nimbly than Cora had thought possible. 'We Wayward have a phrase for goodbyes that aren't forever.'

'Oh yeah?' Marcus said.

'*When our reins lie still, our horses will find the same path*,' the woman said.

The man beside her nodded. They looked like they might cry. Marcus was dry-eyed, but she hadn't let go of Cora's hand.

'The child will be well-cared for, I promise you,' the teacher said to Cora. 'They have wanted a child for some time.'

'I hope they don't mind loud noises,' Cora said.

The teacher looked uncertain. Cora thrust the sack of provisions at the couple.

'For the journey. We didn't want you to go without, given the unexpected mouth to feed. That's the only payment I can offer.'

'None is needed,' said the man. 'We are the ones rewarded.'

Cora turned to Marcus. 'You'll have plenty of stories,' she told the girl, 'riding with the Wayward.'

'I s'pose so...' Marcus kept her eyes on her boots. 'Do they read pennysheets on the Steppes?'

'They do, but you won't be the one selling them. Isn't that a good thing?'

'How am I meant to eat?'

'You don't have to worry about that anymore, I promise.'

Marcus seemed to mull this over, then gave Cora a stern look. 'What will you do without me, Detective?'

'I really don't know.' It was the truth, and it stung. 'But it won't be forever. Let the reins lie still, remember?'

'I'm sorry about telling that Seeder bloke everything.'

'It doesn't matter.'

'You sure?'

'I'm sure,' Cora said.

Then at last Marcus let go of Cora's hand and went over to the couple. 'Be seeing you, Detective,' she boomed.

'Make sure you do,' Cora said.

The teacher, the couple and Marcus slipped between the tents. Cora leaned against the tree and smoked until she couldn't smell the blossom anymore.

Twenty-Eight

The journey back to Fenest took half the time it had taken to reach the herd, even with the weight of the Hook that the covered wagon bore. Partly it was the speed of being on horseback instead of on the barge, which Cora knew was faster, but it was the pace Ruth set too. The Hook had to reach the capital in time to be displayed for the regulation three days before the Wayward story was told. If it arrived late, the Commission might decide it couldn't be displayed at all. Cora had seen such pettiness from the Wheelhouse – rules were rules. It didn't matter if the trouble was an incomplete form to change the name of a whorehouse, or an election that could determine the fate of the Union. Ruth knew that as well as Cora did. There were some parts of being a Gorderheim that had stood her sister in good stead.

They rode from dawn until dusk, stopping only to let the horses drink from the river. Any needs of the riders had to be met then. Cora became so stiff that she felt worse climbing down from her horse – a sleepy-seeming grey – than being in the saddle. When she started to think about sleeping on her horse instead of in the tent that an obliging young Wayward man put up for her each evening, she knew she was in a bad way. But there was nothing to do except hold the reins and look ahead. At least the cut on her face was healing, and Nullan had found her something to smoke, filling Cora's empty bindle tin with a coarse Wayward leaf that apparently grew well on the Steppes. It wasn't what Cora would choose to smoke, given the roughness of the leaves which made her chest tighten more than was comfortable, but it was better than being without.

Though it was Ruth determining the pace, her sister tended to ride in the middle of the herd, beside the wagon carrying the Hook, rather than at the front. Cora rode near her, and the safety of the other riders around them meant she didn't have to worry quite so much. That, too, helped the journey go faster.

About half the herd had come with Ruth and the Hook – Cora guessed it was about two hundred Wayward in total. The rest had their own paths to follow, so Ruth had told her – some taking the breeding pairs to their plains, others taking the expectant mares north to the Steppes. And then there were those who would melt away to find work across the Union. Among them was the couple who'd taken Marcus.

Every so often, Cora looked around to find Serus in the herd, but apart from the occasional glimpse within the mass of people and horses and wagons, she didn't see him. He was the one who'd decided to put distance between them and now didn't seem the time to try to change that. He'd helped Cora get Marcus away, and for that, Cora would always be grateful. If that was the last thing they did together, at least it was a good act.

On the second day of the journey they came to a small

town, which Cora remembered seeing from the barge. As had happened everywhere the herd went, people came out of their houses and their shops, their Seats and their schools, to see the long line of Wayward pass by. Nullan's horse came alongside Cora's, and the Casker passed her some dried meat.

'Don't tell me this is lunch?' Cora said.

'And dinner. Don't eat it all at once.'

'I think I can manage that.' The meat was hard and almost sharp in Cora's hand. She had no idea what animal it had been originally, and she didn't want to know. Her back twinged, and she made an attempt to stretch awkwardly.

'Not too much further now,' Nullan said.

'I'll need to lie down for a week. Not that there'll be much chance of that until after Ruth's told the story.'

'Do you know what'll you do,' Nullan said, 'after you've finished lying down?'

'See if they need any security guards at the Assembly. Open a coffee house. Join a wall-building crew if the Seeders end up winning and Morton blocks off the south.'

Nullan took a bite of the dried meat she held, which involved a lot of yanking with her teeth. 'I'll take that as a no, you don't know,' the Casker said through forceful chewing.

Cora shrugged. 'Can't think any further ahead than Ruth telling the story. But I can't go back to the police. Maybe I should just quit Fenest altogether.'

But even as she said these words, she knew she wouldn't, couldn't. Just as she knew Marcus would make her way back to the capital someday. Fenest was more than just a city. It got into your blood.

'What about you?' Cora asked.

The Casker's answer was delayed by a small child shouting with excitement and running in front of the horses at the head of the herd. With practised skill, the riders pulled their mounts neatly out of the way, and the child was soon back in his father's arms, bawling and laughing at the same time, it seemed.

'It's long past time I went back to Bordair,' Nullan said. 'If it weren't for Nicholas, for Ruth, I would have gone back as soon as my story was finished.'

'Going to see that woman with the tea kettle?' Cora said.

'Seems as good a strategy as any to work out what to do with a life. You could come with me, Cora, see if Rilla can help you with your Rustan.'

'That's one of those matches she *wouldn't* help with,' Cora said, and the truth of it was so sad, she had nothing else to say all the rest of the miles back to Fenest.

But she did make some decisions.

When the north gate of Fenest came in sight, Cora assumed the herd would disperse. She thought the wagon bearing the Hook would continue to the Seat of the Commoner where it was to be displayed, with one or two outriders at most to see it safely there. But the Wayward herd gave no sign of falling away, and so it was that several hundred horses entered the city's narrow streets – a river of animals surging forward. Coaches and gigs found their way blocked, foot traffic came to a chaotic halt, and the noise of hooves on cobbles made for a relentless din as it echoed off the surrounding buildings. People stopped what they were doing and stared, open-mouthed, at the spectacle.

Now that they were back in the city, Cora had to be on the alert again. Word that Ruth was still alive could have made it back to Fenest already, and so Morton might even now be setting her next move in motion. Cora checked on her sister. Ruth was riding close to her, but not close enough, as far as Cora was concerned. The herd had had to thin out to make its way through the streets so there was only one other rider on either side of Ruth now, and Cora was two lengths behind. If the Latecomer was paying attention to this tale, he'd surely see that, with any luck, the chaos of the herd would keep Ruth safe for now.

And chaos really was the right word for what was happening. If Cora had still been at Bernswick, this would have been a nightmare. She could picture it now. People would pour up the front steps of the station to report the city being overrun by Wayward horses, which would soon turn to complaints about the disruption and the increasing levels of mess the horses left behind them. The desk sergeant would be overwhelmed as he tried to get everyone to fill in the appropriate form in the small space by the main doors. As constables tried to fight their way out, Jenkins in the lead, Sergeant Hearst would skulk off to the roof where, along with his beloved birds who nested there, he could look down on the streets filled with horses. From her window on the top floor of the station, Chief Inspector Sillian would look on with horror at Fenest grinding to a halt, and guess that her attempts to stop Ruth had failed. *That* thought cheered Cora up and gave her renewed strength to stay in the saddle just a bit longer, and to ignore the knocks her knees were taking as the horses pressed together in the narrow space.

The Commoner's love of crowds meant that his Seat had been built in the middle of a large open square. So when the herd arrived there, not only was there space to spread out but also to actually dismount too. Scores of constables were there to meet them, sent from the parts of the city that hadn't yet been blocked off by the steady stream of horses. But no one from the Commission seemed to know what to do, given the unexpected arrival of the herd. That was no bad thing.

When Cora's feet hit the ground, she thought the rest of her might join them in a heap on the cobbles, but then Nullan appeared from somewhere and caught Cora by the elbow.

'You got a place lined up for us to stay?' Cora asked the Casker.

'Of course.'

'Then let's get going.' Cora lurched out of the way of a horse's hindquarters as it swung around, too close for comfort. 'It's not safe being out in the open like this, and not just because of the herd.'

'I'll let you tell your sister that.' Nullan looked at the wagon bearing the Hook, which had Wayward crawling all over it. 'Ruth wants to see it installed in the Seat. Frant gave her a whole list of instructions for hanging it straight.'

'Then she can give them to someone else. Someone who isn't a target for a murderous Chambers.'

'After you, Detective.'

The title felt more like it belonged to Cora again, now

355

that they were back in Fenest. Not that this was the city she recognised, it being full of horses.

She pushed her way to where Ruth was directing the men and women unloading the rolls of canvas. A guard of Wayward had formed outside the open doors of the Seat of the Commoner to block the view of the growing crowd of gawkers – mostly pennysheet sellers who could slip beneath arms and duck low to the cobbles. Purple tunics were dashing out of the Seat and adding their noise to the chaos.

Cora reached through the press of bodies surrounding Ruth, her hand grazing the stiffened hide of Wayward cloaks, and caught Ruth's arm. Her sister spun round, tense as a fighting dog who thinks they're being attacked. Cora was pleased at the reaction: Ruth hadn't let her guard down. If anything, she looked more alert and determined. Certainly less tired than she had in the last few days.

'Ruth, it's not safe you being here.'

'But—'

'Only so far you can test the Latecomer's patience,' Cora said, pulling her, gently, away from the wagon. 'Don't make this Hook another dead storyteller.'

Ruth's fingers drifted to her side, where Tannir had stabbed her. She nodded, and gave some instructions to a grizzled Wayward woman who had lost most of her teeth. Then together they headed to where Nullan was waiting for them in the shadow of a coffee house flanking the square.

As they dodged between the horses, Cora stole glances at Ruth. There was a look on her sister's face that Cora recognised from their days in the Seminary: Ruth was ready to stand up and say her piece. But instead of challenging teachers about the fairness of the Union, she'd be standing before the Union itself to tell that story. A new version of the one she'd first told Cora on the night she'd left Fenest all those years ago.

'Does it seem different to you?' Cora asked. 'The city, I mean.'

'I've not been back here often since I left,' Ruth said, 'but every time I set foot in Fenest's streets, I get the same feeling.'

'Overcome with love for the old place?' Cora said dryly, dodging a drinker caught between gawping at the Wayward herd and bringing back up his day's ale.

Ruth covered her nose against the drinker's less than pleasant aroma. 'It's as if I never left. Joining the herd, marrying Frant, having Nicholas... It's like none of that happened.'

'There was plenty that came before that,' Cora said. 'You stealing the papers from the study, selling the story of the embezzlement to the pennysheets. Or does it feel like that never happened either, Ruth?'

'You make it sound like I was in the wrong, Cora! It wasn't me who stole from the trading halls.'

'Or me, but the years that followed...' Cora was all at once weary. The days in the saddle catching up with her, leaving Marcus behind, Serus... And it was so much more than that too. It was thirty years of not knowing what had happened to Ruth. Of living with the shame of their parents' theft.

She was so, so tired of it all.

'I should have gone with you,' she said.

'I should have stayed to see that you were all right, Cora.'

'I doubt Mother would have let you keep your old room, not after you exposed them.'

Ruth's laughter brought her closer to Cora. 'True. I was ready to leave that house anyway. But I could have found a way to stay close by. Help you out, after Father—'

'Too late for any of that now,' Cora said.

Ruth gave a deep sigh. 'I'm not so sure. Morton made a lot of money from what our parents did in the trading halls. Arrani said that played a big part in Morton becoming the Seeder Chambers. If we can stop Morton's plans, we can put right one wrong, at least.'

'The Gorderheim wrong.'

They stood aside for a gang of constables rushing to join their fellows in the chaos of the herd.

'You know what always surprised me?' Ruth said. 'Why you never changed your name. "Gorderheim" will always be associated with our parents, the money. When you joined the police you could have started over, become someone else. Why didn't you?'

Cora swallowed, the words hard to find, but if not now, then when?

'I thought if you came back... I didn't want to make it hard for you, to find me, I mean. But you didn't.'

'Cora, I'm sorry. I—'

'Made a good story for the Drunkard,' Cora said.

'I'm here now, Cora.'

It was all Cora could do to keep walking, to stay upright, to stay focused. She checked her pocket: Beulah's key was still safe. She'd need the underground routes to get Ruth to whichever new safe house Nullan had in mind. Keeping her

358

there for the next three days while the Hook was displayed, that would be harder.

As Cora and Ruth reached Nullan, Cora caught the hood of a pennysheet lad, stopping him mid-shout. She already had the words of the message she wanted him to take, had been working them out all the way back to Fenest. The conversation with Ruth had made up her mind to send that message. Time could get away from a person. With a coin begged from Ruth, Cora paid the 'sheet seller for his trouble, and he hared into an alley. Whether it would work, she had no idea. But she had to try. Nullan had asked what she'd do after the story. It was about time she started thinking about her own future, as well as the future of the Union.

'Ready?' Cora asked Ruth.

'Guess I'm paying for a coach.'

'No need for that,' Cora said, 'as long as you two are up for a walk, stretch the legs after all that time in the saddle?'

Nullan frowned. 'Cora, you keep saying we need to keep a low profile, not be out in the streets.'

Cora led them into an alley. 'We won't *be* in the open. Time you two got to know the other side of Fenest. The one that runs beneath us. Nearest door is in the games house round the corner.'

'What are you talking about?' Ruth said.

Cora started down the alley. 'You'll see. And if we're lucky, we might even get a hand of cards in before we go below.'

Twenty-Nine

The next morning, Cora was back outside the Seat of the Commoner. She'd travelled beneath the ground most of the way, but the Seat was on her route and curiosity had got the better of her, so she'd climbed back up to ground level through an obliging butcher's shop. Now, as she stood in the shadow of one of the large trees in the square, she thought she could smell blood. Had she caught her coat on one of the many hanging carcasses on her way out of the shop? She couldn't find any spots of blood.

The queues outside the Seat were long – the longest she'd seen for any Hook in this election. In any election. And the headlines shouted by the pennysheet sellers who strolled the length of the queues told her why: *Wayward Hook paints picture of destruction! What do changes in the Tear mean for the south?*

She didn't allow herself to think about Marcus, instead studying the faces of those in the queue. They were worried. There was nothing like the excitement she'd seen in those waiting for the Rustan Hook. And the expressions of those leaving the Seat this morning were even more grave than those waiting to go in. Even the purple tunics managing the site looked sombre too. News of the Wayward painting would be spreading through the city, and the whole Union. Preparing the voters for the story to come, and the choice they would have to make.

Cora stepped aside for a couple walking past her, their heads bent close together in hurried conversation – she didn't think they'd even seen her. They were young, the woman with a stack of pennysheets tucked under her arm, the man worrying at the patchy beard he was trying to grow.

'But it's so different from the first canvas to the last,' the man said. 'What else could it mean?'

'Not that,' the woman said. 'It can't mean that. The ground can't simply just *open*.'

'It did once before, didn't it? When the Tear was made, and now it's—'

'Don't,' the woman said. 'I can't bear to think it's true. Those people in the camps...'

The couple continued down the street, their voices replaced by others all saying variations of the same thing as they crossed the square in front of the Seat of the Commoner: the Tear is widening. What would the Wayward story tell the Union of this catastrophe?

A fresh pennysheet headline came booming across the square to distract her: *Wayward lose battle with Wheelhouse: story to be told at Easterton Coach Station.*

This was news to Cora, and troubling too. The coach station wasn't on the map of Beulah's underground routes. There were few buildings on the site which meant there were no obvious places to emerge. No obvious places to hide, either, from a Wayward with a knife, sent on a mission to kill a storyteller and step into her place. Which raised the question of just how to get Ruth to the point she'd seen all the other realms' 'tellers reach: standing in front of the audience, taking a deep breath, uttering their first line. That moment felt both uncomfortably close and impossibly far away.

She'd left Ruth under the watchful eye of Nullan in the new safe house – three rooms on the top floor of a lodging house, not far from Easterton Coach Station, which was now apparently convenient. Nullan must have had some idea that venue was possible, even if it wasn't the head herders' choice.

Of all the places Nullan had found for Ruth to hide in, the ones Cora had seen at any rate, this was the most comfortable. It had proper beds for a start. The Child knew, they could all do with some rest.

Ruth didn't seem to think so though. She had been sitting in the corner of her room when Cora had gone to sleep in the adjoining one, and was still there that morning. It looked as if she'd been facing the wall all night. More of her tanketting: practising her story, making her memory strong. Cora had left her to it, but not before she'd made Ruth swear on all the Audience members, including the Mute, that she wouldn't leave the lodging house. The head herders had no idea where she was and, hopefully, that meant neither did Tannir.

Just as she was about to leave the square, Cora saw someone who might shed light on Tannir's whereabouts.

Jenkins was out of uniform, heading for the back of the queue: an ordinary Fenestiran wanting to see the Hook, like anyone else. The Poet's bells had only recently chimed the half hour, which meant Cora had time before she was due to be somewhere. She went after the constable, falling into stride beside her only after having to break into a jog. It wasn't just Jenkins's long legs that had her walking faster. It was having young lungs free of bindle-smoke damage.

'I've seen it, can save you the bother of the queue,' Cora said.

Jenkins whirled round. 'Detective!' Her grin was huge, and real. It was hard not to feel good about that, and Cora didn't bother to correct the constable. There were worse things to be called.

'Quietly now, Constable. We don't need to tell the whole Union we're here, do we?'

Jenkins's over-sized teeth disappeared, and she nodded solemnly. Cora led her to an alley that looked onto the square, and they went as far as the first bend, which kept them out of sight of the queue and anyone coming up the other way.

'Have a lot of horse mess to clean up yesterday?' Cora asked her.

'Enough to fill all the flowerbeds of Fenest. Some divisions are still moving it.'

'Hearst got you on other work, I hope?'

Jenkins fidgeted, warming her hands in her pockets. She was wearing a long navy coat that had an expensive-looking cut, even to Cora's untrained eye. Even out of uniform, Jenkins favoured a blue jacket.

'The sergeant said I should keep tailing that Wayward, the bald one.'

'And?'

Jenkins's gaze dropped to the puddle at her feet, and Cora's spirits dropped with it.

'I've lost him, Detective. It's been days since I've seen him. I was wondering if he'd followed you, wherever it was you went.'

'I had other problems than Tannir. Do you think he's still in the city?'

'I suspect so. I last saw him two days ago near the Wheelhouse, but lost him when a group of coaches arrived at once. I've been trying to find Marcus to pass the message on but—'

'No need to worry about that anymore, Constable.'

'What do you mean?'

Cora waved the question away. 'Keep looking for Tannir. Any news, send it to the Dancing Oak.'

'My mother'll be pleased.'

'Donnata spending more time over that way, is she?'

Jenkins sighed. 'Now she's discovered the Oak, she doesn't want to leave.'

'Happens to the best of us. I saw you at the Rustan story. You got the voting chest detail?'

'I did.' The constable's face brightened. 'I'm down for the same at the Wayward story too.'

A sound from along the alley: water splashing, a low voice muttering. Cora's hand went to her coat pocket. Jenkins, too, was alive to trouble, in a way Cora hadn't seen before. Somehow, without her constable jacket, she looked more at home in the streets. Perhaps there were the makings of a plain-clothes detective in her yet.

The source of the noise came into sight – an old whore splashing through the puddles, not seeming to notice the water landing on her rouged cheeks and on her wig of black curls. The woman stomped her way past Cora and Jenkins, giving each a glance that spoke of disgust, then she was gone, into the square.

'So you finally know where the voting chests go,' Cora said. 'Like mother like daughter, eh?'

'People say that, but—'

'But you're your own woman.'

Jenkins met her eye. 'I am, Detective. I really am.'

'Good. You'll need to be in the months and years to come.'

'You mean with the Tear widening?'

'With what comes next.'

The Poet's bells chimed again, and Cora knew she had to leave to make her meeting on time. Whether he came or not, she had to be there. She had to give this a chance.

Before taking her leave, she gave Jenkins a message to take to the Assembly so that the Torn Galdensuttir would know where to find them.

'Will I see you at the Wayward story?' the constable asked.

'I'll be there but...'

'But I shouldn't see you.'

'Not this time, Jenkins.'

'*After* all this, I hope?'

Cora waited until Jenkins's blue coat had passed out of sight, back into the square, then turned and headed in the other direction.

She reached the tailor's on time. The pavement outside the shop was empty. Not of people – there were plenty passing on the street, plenty stopping to look at the clothes in the window. But it was empty of the person she wanted to see, the person she'd sent the message via the pennysheet lad. She looked up and down the street. She waited, watching the tailor's from the other side of the road. Watched everyone who climbed down from a gig, everyone who climbed into one, those who went in or out of the adjoining shops.

There was no sign of him.

The Poet's bells chimed another quarter hour. They were louder somehow, though she was no closer to the Seat, as if the Poet himself was trying to tell her to give it up. As the noise of the last peal quietened, she decided to listen to the Poet's advice and turned from the tailor's shop, heading back the way she'd come.

'You thinking I need a new coat?' Serus was behind her, staring over at the tailor's.

It took her a second or two to find her voice. 'Well, that coat is pretty old.'

'It's a classic of its kind.'

He ran a hand down his arm and Cora's skin prickled, as if she were touching the soft slipdog hide, feeling the firmness of his body beneath it.

'Just like its owner,' she said, walking over to him, but not too close. She still didn't know how he felt about her, but then he closed the gap between them, and she felt it would be all right.

'All the way back to Fenest, you never once tried to speak to me,' he said.

'I figured you needed some time to be angry.'

'I did.'

'And now?' Cora asked.

'Now I'm wondering what we're doing here. You could have come to my place, Cora.'

'Not until after the election.'

He frowned. 'You still think your sister's in danger, even with that dart thrower being... Well, with him staying in Perlanse, shall we say.'

'None of us are safe until after the election, Serus, but I couldn't wait until then.' She stepped close, and she could smell the metal of the plates built into his flesh.

'We've waited too long already,' he said.

Cora took his hand and led him across the street to the tailor's.

'Where are we going, Cora? Really?'

'I trust you, Serus,' she said, looking him square in the eye. 'Do you trust me?'

'With every bone in my body – the metal and the parts I was born with.'

'Then don't worry.'

There were two men behind the counter, so similar looking, despite their age difference, that they had to be related. They both looked up from their work when she and Serus entered, but as soon as Cora held up the key, their gazes fell back to the cloth they were cutting.

'There's a curtain next to the sink,' the older of the two said. 'Door's behind it.'

Cora thanked him and headed for the back of the shop, Serus close behind her, but not close enough. She wanted to have his skin pressed against hers, and she knew he felt the same. The feeling stretched between them like a lightning strike.

She pushed aside the heavy green curtain, and there was

the door – narrow, low, but the key worked, just as it always did when following Beulah's map of secret routes. This one in particular was special: it led to a whorehouse, a decent one, so Beulah promised.

'Cora, where in the Audience's name are we going?'

'Somewhere with clean sheets. You and I are too old to roll around in alleyways.'

'I like the sound of that.'

She kissed him, and it was all she could do not to tear his clothes off there and then. But from the corner of her eye, she saw the younger of the two tailors was craning his neck to see what they were up to. An elbow in the ribs from the older man made the younger snap back to attention, but it was time to get going. She and Serus wouldn't have long, and she was determined to make the most of it.

Cora opened the door and lit the lamp from the supplies left there. Then she headed down the stairs, Serus close behind her, his hand on her back, just where she imagined his lockport was on his body. At last, she would be able to see every inch of him, new and old.

Thirty

The day of the Wayward story, Cora woke to the sound of rain. As she lay in bed under the eaves of the safe house, she listened to the water striking the roof. How fitting that on the day of a story whose Hook was a giant painting, the Lazy Painter was listening, and sending his rain to show it. Surely this was a sign of favour for the Wayward story? Whether it would make it any easier to get the 'teller of that story to their venue, Cora wasn't so sure.

Rain, and heavy rain by the sound of it, tended to make everything more chaotic in Fenest. Tempers frayed, journeys across the city took longer as more gigs and coaches were on the road, and potholes became swimming pools. At least the cutpurses tended to stay home. The thieves of Fenest were a fair-weather bunch, their stories favouring the Devotee and her love of the sun. But it wasn't thieving that Cora was worried about. It was getting Ruth inside Easterton Coach Station and in front of the voters without a knife finding its way into her back, her throat, between her ribs.

Cora threw back the bedcovers. Such dreams had plagued her all night. Ruth had fallen, again and again, into Cora's arms, and the warmth of her sister's blood pouring over her had woken her so often that Cora felt she'd barely slept at all. By the time she went to bed tonight, it would be all over, one way or another. The Wayward story told. And then? Only the Audience knew, and they were keeping their cards close to their chest.

There was a knock on the door – not the door to her room but the one that led to the stairs, on the other side of the landing. She checked the time: not yet eight. The visitor was earlier than expected, but that was no bad thing, given the rain. As Cora crossed the landing, she could smell tornstone.

Galdensuttir, the Torn who worked with Wayward Chambers Arrani, was soaked. As Cora led him to the small sitting room, water dripped from the Torn's glass mouthpiece onto the floor.

'Is good to feel this,' Galdensuttir said, patting the water on his cheek. 'In Fenest, your air is too thin, but your rain – it leaves no trace but the cold. In the Tear, the Painter sends fire from the sky.' Galdensuttir's finger ran along a deep scar that bit into his cheek, and Cora thought of the Torn election story, the girl Aris who bred beetles. 'I do not need to hide from rain here,' Galdensuttir said, 'so I walk in it. I get wet!' He laughed, making the tornstone in his mouthpiece flare, and the room was filled with the sulphuric smell. 'But I do not come to tell you of rain.'

'You've got word from Arrani, about where Ruth needs to be?'

'I have.'

'Let me fetch her,' Cora said. 'Make yourself comfortable.' With a heavy sigh and a wet *thwump* of his soaked canvas tunic, the Torn threw himself into an armchair. Cora crossed the landing to the room Ruth shared with Nullan.

For a second, she was back in their childhood home, standing outside her older sister's door after Ruth had left Fenest, wondering if she would ever see Ruth again. Cora remembered many such moments, wanting to go in to see her sister's things: her angry Seminary notes, her clothes left on the floor, her unwashed glasses. Nothing special, yet all made precious by Ruth's absence. Her mother had told the maid to clean the room, but Cora had screamed that she mustn't – so unusual an outburst that her father had intervened, talked her mother down. That was unusual too.

Now, on the landing of the lodging house on the day of the Wayward story, Cora put her hand to Ruth's door and remembered doing the same thirty years before. But back then she had never been able to open the door. She'd lain down beside it and stayed there, night and day, for a week. By then, her mother's impatience with Cora and anger with Ruth won out. The maid was finally sent in. Her father died that night.

Cora knocked on the door.

It was Nullan who opened it. Cora could see, over the Casker's shoulder, Ruth asleep in bed.

'Great weather for it,' Nullan said, and managed half a smile.

'Glad to see Ruth didn't do her memory testing all night.'

Nullan glanced behind her. 'She said she'd done as much as she could. Like the rest of us. Is that tornstone I can smell?'

'Galdensuttir's here,' Cora said.

Nullan was already turning away to wake Ruth. There was no going back from this moment. It had begun.

Ruth and Nullan took chairs beside the Torn. Cora stood under the small skylight in the roof to watch the rain.

'First,' Galdensuttir said, 'let me say this: I am sorry you have to tell your story at the place of the coaches. It is... a poor draw for the Wayward.'

'This weather doesn't help,' Ruth said. 'I remember Easterton Coach Station having little in the way of shelter.' She looked to Cora who nodded in confirmation.

'When it was first mentioned as a venue,' Nullan said, 'Electoral Affairs said they'd put up tents.'

'Fitting for the Wayward,' Cora said.

'And for Fenestiran voters,' Ruth said. 'It'll make people think about the camps outside the south gate, finally see that the suffering is already here, on their doorstep.'

'My fear,' the Torn said, 'is that the rain will annoy the voters. The rain drips on them and their fine Audience robes.'

Nullan pinched between her eyes. 'That's why the head herders were petitioning for somewhere else. Anywhere else!'

'That didn't seem to go too well,' Cora said. 'Why am I not surprised?'

'Because the Assembly is still controlled by the Perlish,' Nullan said, 'and the Perlish help the Seeders, and the Seeders—'

'The Seeders want walls,' Ruth said. 'Morton very likely had a hand in the venue choice for the Wayward.'

At this, the Torn inclined his head. 'From what I have heard in the Assembly, this is so. The open nature of the site – this, too, is deliberate. To make you more vulnerable, Mistress Gorderheim. But Chambers Arrani, he fought hard to find a different venue. He still supports his storyteller. He wants no other. He told me this himself.'

'What about the head herders?' Cora said.

'Arrani has not spoken to these traitors since the Bird House. He gives me this to give to you, Mistress Gorderheim, to prove his trust.'

From another part of his tunic, Galdensuttir pulled out what looked to Cora like a short, thin stick. Ruth gasped, and the Torn handed it to her. Nullan craned forwards to see what it was. Ruth's fingers closed around the stick – which had to be more than that, given the look on her sister's face – but whatever it might be, this wasn't the time to find out.

'Chambers Arrani will meet his storyteller in the small tent that stands for this purpose only,' the Torn said. 'I come to tell you it will be red, the canvas – the only one of its kind there.'

'Do you know where it'll be,' Cora asked, 'this red tent?'

'Electoral Affairs, they say the red tent will stand between the garbing pavilion and the Commission box.'

Nullan exhaled deeply. 'So you'll be right in the heart of the danger, Ruth.'

'Not much to be done about that,' Ruth said. 'Storytellers always meet with their Chambers just before the story. You know that better than anyone, Nullan, and we can't risk doing things in a way that will upset the Commission.'

'Or draw more attention to you than is necessary, Mistress Gorderheim,' the Torn said.

Cora stared at the raindrops snaking their way down the glass, each finding their own path. 'Will the Commission open any extra gates into the coach station?' she asked the Torn.

He shook his head, and a small puff of tornstone left his mouthpiece. 'There will be one way in and out only – the main gate. All will enter there. Including the storyteller.'

'And the place within the coach station where I'm to tell the story?' Ruth said.

'It is... an unusual choice,' Galdensuttir said slowly. 'Though perhaps not, given the venue. I do not like it. Chambers Arrani, he does not like it either.'

Ruth and Nullan exchanged a glance.

'I think you'd better put us out of our misery here,' Cora said, looking back at the raindrops again, the way they moved. A plan was forming in her head.

'Electoral Affairs say the Wayward storyteller must stand on the roof of a coach to tell her story. They have put it in place, I am told, in front of the voters' seats. All others with wheels will be moved away, to the edges of the coach station. But this storyteller's coach will remain in the open.'

'A coach.' Ruth ran her hands over her shorn hair. Not even she could have anticipated such a thing. 'The risks—'

'Thank you, Galdensuttir,' Cora said, striding over to shake the Torn's scarred hand.

Galdensuttir looked briefly confused at this abrupt end to the conversation, as did Ruth and Nullan, but then the Torn shrugged and stood to leave.

'Let me walk you to the stairs,' Ruth said, and escorted the Torn from the sitting room, thanking him for his service to the Wayward cause on the way.

Nullan watched them go. 'She wants to talk to the Torn privately about Arrani.'

'There's something between Ruth and the Chambers, isn't there?' Cora asked.

'Good to know you're not completely blind to romance, Cora.' Nullan gave her a shrewd look. 'What happened between you and Serus when we got back to Fenest? He seems good-hearted, kind. I saw the way you—'

'That thing Galdensuttir gave Ruth – the stick. You know what it is?'

Nullan gave the briefest of nods, but that was all. Cora guessed the token from Arrani was something to do with Nicholas.

'Perhaps we'll hear about it in the story,' Cora said. She shut the door to the sitting room, making sure they were alone for what she was about to say. 'Nullan, I need you to do something for Ruth, and you're not going to like it.' Cora licked her lips, took a breath, took another one.

Nullan perched on the arm of a chair. 'Well, come on. Out with it, Cora.'

What she had to ask Nullan, it wasn't an easy thing to say, but it was the only way. Since the Torn had mentioned the place Ruth was to meet Arrani, Cora had gone round and round in circles trying to think of other options, but she'd always come back to this.

'The venue for the story being Easterton Coach Station,' Cora said, 'it's not going to be easy for Ruth to get to the top of that coach safely.'

'You think Tannir will be waiting for us?'

'We have to plan for that, which is why we need something to throw him off the scent.'

Nullan fiddled with one of the piercings in her eyebrow. 'You make him sound like a bloodhound, Cora.'

'He's not that clever, but he is persistent, I'll give him that. This is his last chance to replace Ruth. We know from what happened at the Water Gardens that he's not afraid to get his own hands bloody. We need a diversion.'

'Have something distract him while Ruth sneaks in somewhere out of sight?' Nullan said.

'Some*one* needs to distract him. Someone who could be mistaken for the real target.'

Nullan's hand fell away from her face, and she looked up at Cora. Looked up because she was shorter. She was thinner, too. The same build as Ruth, and with her piercings taken out, her inkings covered, she could be the decoy. And from the look on Nullan's face, she knew it.

'It'll be dangerous,' Cora said.

'I know.'

'We'll do our best to protect you, but you need to know the chances—'

'I *know*, Cora. Nicholas died for this election, and at the Water Gardens we nearly lost another storyteller. You don't need to tell me this is *dangerous*.' Nullan all but spat that last word. Then she sighed and opened the door to the landing. 'Guess I'd better find something suitably Wayward to wear and get dressed.'

'But you are dressed,' said Ruth, coming back to the sitting room in time to catch Nullan's last words.

'I...'

'Nullan?' Ruth said. 'What's going on?'

Cora made to speak, but Nullan cut her off.

'I'll tell her. Get yourself ready. We ought to be leaving soon – the rain.'

Thirty-One

For a day when an election story was being told, the streets were quiet. Five stories had been told so far, and each time, Fenest had all but ground to a halt, thanks to the number of gigs and coaches making their way to the story sites. Then there were the multitudes on foot who would never get a place in the limited public gallery, but who wanted to be nearby to feel the atmosphere, tell their friends and neighbours they were *there*, in the presence of an election storyteller. More likely, four streets away from that storyteller, but still, close enough for a story of their own.

But this morning, it was different. As Cora, Ruth and Nullan splashed through the puddled alleys between the lodging house and the venue for the Wayward story, Cora blamed the rain as well as the place they were headed: Easterton Coach Station. There could hardly be a more different venue to the other story sites. Tithe Hall and First Wall hadn't been as fancy as the Water Gardens or Z'anderzi's Kantina, but they'd had their own kind of charm and interest. Patron's Mount, where the Caskers had told their story, right at the start of the election, had the benefit of a raised position over the city, and the sun had shone, of course. People had brought picnics, she remembered. Easterton Coach Station was a muddy pit full of wheeled contraptions, as well as the bad-tempered men and women who drove them, and it stank of horses.

The lack of traffic in the streets meant fewer people to see Ruth make her way to the coach station, but it meant fewer people to hide among too. So often in this election, crowds had helped Cora, and she'd told plenty of stories to the Commoner in thanks. But this morning, it seemed he'd stopped listening.

The Poet's bells chimed. All three of them picked up their pace.

Nullan was wearing Ruth's riding habit and had covered her head to help the disguise, replacing her usual cowl with the kind of hat Cora had seen some Wayward wear. With the hat pulled low and her cloak collar turned up to cover the inkings on her neck, and with her piercings removed, Nullan was a good likeness. To anyone who would be watching the Wayward storyteller make their way to the red tent to meet Chambers Arrani, there should be no reason to believe this wasn't Ruth.

Ruth herself was back in her Fenestiran clothes, like Cora. She'd been so quiet on the journey to Easterton, Cora half wondered if Ruth had gone back to doing that tanketting even while walking, checking she knew every word she needed. Every word that would have been said by Nicholas Ento: the man who should have been telling this story. If he was on Cora's mind now, he was surely on Ruth's too, and Nullan's. But thinking of a dead storyteller was no help to anyone, not when the job at hand was to keep one alive.

379

To take her mind from dead storytellers, Cora decided to go over the plan with Ruth and Nullan again as they headed to the coach station. She didn't care if they were sick of it, sick of her. This was too important to get wrong.

'Remember, we all three go into the coach station together. Being with a storyteller, we should have fewer problems getting in. Once we're inside, Nullan, you head straight for the red tent to meet Arrani. Don't look back at me and Ruth. Pretend you don't know us.'

'That doesn't sound too hard,' Nullan muttered.

'Ruth, you and I will—'

'I know, Cora, I know,' Ruth said. 'While Nullan goes to meet Arrani, you and I head to the other side of the storyteller's coach.'

'And we need to hide ourselves as best we can,' Cora said. 'Purple tunics will be all over the site, as usual, and if any of them think we're in the wrong place, we'll be chucked out of the venue. We need to use the coaches parked around the edge of the station for cover. And then—'

'Then we wait for the Master of Ceremonies to appear,' Ruth said. 'Once he's said his part, Nullan will head for the coach in plain sight, while I make my way there from the other side of the station.'

'Staying hidden for as long as possible,' Cora added. 'We can't risk making the switch until the last possible moment.'

The idea was, to those watching in the Commission box and the public gallery, and the robed voters themselves, it would look as if the Wayward storyteller was making her way to her rightful place, and all eyes would surely be on her. No one should notice the woman dressed in Fenestiran clothes who was also drawing close to the coach. At the last minute, Nullan would duck sideways, and Ruth would climb up onto the coach. Once she was in place, standing before the great and the good of Fenest, including half the police constables of the capital, she would be safe.

'What am I meant to say to Chambers Arrani when he realises it's me?' Nullan said.

'You're a storyteller,' Cora said. 'I'm sure you'll think of something.'

'Tell him my sister made me do it,' Ruth said.

They rounded a bend and the alley began to widen. Noise drifted in: voices, for the first time that morning. And one particularly loud voice. It was a pennysheet girl, calling her headlines. Not a voice Cora knew, not that one, not as loud, but she couldn't help thinking of Marcus. Cora could only make out one word, shouted over and over: *Wayward. Wayward. Wayward.*

'Sounds like Marcus has a new rival for loudest pennysheet seller.'

Cora felt Ruth's gaze on her and realised her mistake, but it was too late.

'*Has?*' Ruth said, coming to a halt. The rain dripped from her cherry-red soft hat. Her velvet coat glittered with water. '*Has*, Cora? Why would you be talking about that child that way?'

'I...'

'Marcus is meant to be at the bottom of the River Tun, not round the next corner, ready to stick a knife into my side.'

'She's not in Fenest,' Cora blurted. Nullan wisely stepped away to leave them to it. 'Or she shouldn't be. The people who took her, they said—'

'You're too soft, Cora. Staying in Fenest all these years.' Ruth shook her head. 'I knew you wouldn't be able to do it.'

'Then why tell me that I had to?' To Cora's own ears, her voice was too loud.

'Because I had no other choice,' Ruth said. 'The girl had betrayed me. She not only put the Wayward story at risk, she also risked the rest of the Union. People died on the river because of her, and more would have done so in the years to come if they'd stopped me telling my son's story.'

'But you didn't want me to kill the girl, did you?' Cora said. 'Not truly. You wanted me to rid you of the bind Marcus had placed you in, and it didn't really matter how that was done.'

Ruth started walking again, and that was answer enough for Cora.

'I knew you were up to something that night before we left the herd,' Nullan said. 'When Serus was there, asking me for a drink. I could tell he didn't really want one, that he was covering for you.'

'But you didn't stop me,' Cora said.

'Because I'm as soft as you are. Come on.' Nullan wiped the rain from her face as they headed after Ruth. 'What are the chances Electoral Affairs have rigged up some shelter for a storyteller?'

'I wouldn't get your hopes up, but it sounds like there might be *some* good news.'

The voice of the pennysheet seller was getting louder, and clearer. By the time Cora and Nullan reached the end of the alley where Ruth was waiting, the girl was in sight. Her words were sharp: *Wayward story odds on favourite to win. Landslide expected.*

*

The alley led onto a main street, and on the other side was the coach station wall. There were more people now, all streaming down the street towards Easterton's entrance. From beyond the coach station wall, a hum of noise rose over the persistent sound of the rain. Cora caught sight of the banners that flanked the Commission box below, snagging in the wind. The spoked wheel plus the realm symbols were a furious mess of fabric.

They joined the crowd, keeping close together to reach the main gateway. Usually this was a dangerous place to be on foot, with carts, coaches and gigs racing in and out of the station. But today, the traffic was all people – rained-on people, keen to hear an election story, but their tempers soured by the weather and the mud.

The purple tunics, too, were harried, struggling to keep order, and that was helpful. As soon as Nullan presented herself at the gate, claiming to be the Wayward storyteller, she was rushed over to a senior staff member, identifiable by the deeper purple of their uniform. Cora couldn't hear their exchange over the noise of the rain and the crowd, but whatever Nullan said, it worked, and she was being escorted into the coach station by a pair of tunics. Her two Fenestiran companions went overlooked, just as Cora had hoped, and all three of them were safely inside.

At once, the tunics melted away from Nullan – shouting suggested a crisis about the voting chest entering the site. The other tunics in sight were struggling to direct those seeking a seat in the public gallery.

'Time for me to go,' Nullan said.

She and Ruth embraced, then Nullan pulled away. Her eyes were wet. The Casker squeezed Cora's shoulder before heading for the red tent without a backwards glance. She soon disappeared in the heaving mass of people and the gusting rain. Ruth seemed to have forgotten where she was and simply stared at the point Nullan had vanished. Cora grabbed her sister and pulled her in the other direction, close to the wall of the site where the coaches and gigs had been moved. There was no order to it, the vehicles all jammed together this way and that. It would be a nightmare to free them, but it did give the cover Cora was hoping for as she and Ruth picked their way towards the storyteller's coach.

The rain was even heavier now, limiting visibility – it was an each-way bet as to whether that was good or bad for Ruth's safety. But there was no time to think about it. The coach station was chaos. As best she could in the weather, Cora scanned the muddy square that made up the site. The business of the election was in full swing – the white expanse of the garbing pavilion bright and strange against the mud of the coach station. Rough matting looked to have been put down for the Commission box and the voters' seats, but in the public gallery, already full, people had to make do with the puddles at their feet.

'They did put up some shelter,' Cora said, nodding to the canvas sails that even now teams of purple tunics were securing with ropes.

'It's the least the Commission could do,' Ruth said. 'There's the coach.' She pointed across the site at a lone, large coach that had been left directly in front of the voters' seats, a ladder leaning against it. This was where

Ruth would tell her story. As long as she could reach it safely.

'What the...'

Ruth spun round. 'What? What is it?'

Cora swallowed her words away, shook her head. She couldn't tell Ruth what she'd just realised.

The coach – it was familiar.

The size of it, the black paint and the spoked wheel picked out in white: it was one of the old Commission coaches. One of those too large to pass through the streets of Fenest and so rarely used, grown shabby. Nicholas Ento had been killed in such a coach, strangled with a curtain cord before being dumped in another part of the city. The choice of an old Commission coach had to be deliberate. They weren't even stored at Easterton anymore. Cora's investigation had shown her that. So someone had brought this one here, to challenge Ruth and Cora, to show their power, and to make them quail before it.

Lowlander Chambers Morton.

Cora glanced at the Commission box. It was full. Cora could see the brown robes, and what looked like the uniform of Chief Inspector Sillian. The voters' seats were still empty, but from the hush growing over the coach station, the Master of Ceremonies would soon appear.

When they drew level with the coach, twenty feet or so of open space lay ahead of them. Cora said they should stop and wait, keeping hidden behind a Clotham's gig that needed a wash – even the rain couldn't dislodge the mud that caked its paint-peeling sides. Cora looked back at the tents and seating areas.

'It all looks calm. No sign of any trouble so far.'

'Can you see Nullan?' Ruth said.

Cora squinted across the open space. 'There are too many people. The rain. I'm sure she's fine.'

Cora wasn't sure at all, but there was nothing she could do now. Nullan had agreed to take the risk. Cora just hoped the Widow wouldn't be hearing any stories about the Casker today.

A bell rang.

The voters began leaving the garbing pavilion. To see the Audience there, in Easterton Coach Station, making their way through the mud, the gigs and coaches lining the walls around them, was one of the strangest sights Cora had ever seen. And she had seen some things, working the streets of Fenest.

The fifty voters, wearing their over-sized coloured masks, took their seats. Silence fell over the coach station. Even the rain seemed to grow quiet. A single figure had climbed onto the coach facing the Audience: the Master of Ceremonies.

'Audience, welcome.' His voice was just audible, carried on the wind. 'In this, the two hundred and ninth election of our realms...'

Cora looked towards the red tent. There was no sign of Nullan.

'She should be coming out now,' Ruth said, voicing Cora's thoughts.

'She's probably waiting until the last minute,' Cora said, 'keeping hidden as long as possible.' But she wasn't sure she believed this.

Ruth was straining to see, looking out over the site. 'What if she didn't even make it to the tent? What if something happened on the way? Anyone could—'

'There she is!' Cora almost shouted the words as, on the other side of the coach station, a figure in a Wayward riding habit was heading for the coach. For a heartbeat, Cora thought she was seeing Ruth, but her sister was still beside her, safe. For these last moments, safe.

Nullan.

She was heading for the coach. The Master of Ceremonies was extending an arm to her, believing this was the real Wayward storyteller.

'Time I was going,' Ruth said.

Cora felt the ground pitch. She had to fight herself not to reach out and grab her sister, hold her back, keep her safe. But she couldn't. This was what it had all been leading to. Whatever happened next, Ruth had to get to that coach. The Audience was waiting.

Ruth kissed Cora's cheek. 'I'll see you afterwards.'

'See that you do,' Cora muttered, though 'afterwards' was the thing they'd never settled on. There was only the story.

Ruth was walking away, heading for the lone Commission coach. Her path took her between the scattered gigs and coaches, giving her cover until the last moment.

Nullan's pace had slowed: she was giving Ruth time to appear. From Cora's angle, she caught glimpses of Ruth weaving between the gigs.

There was a flash of movement from the public gallery, and then someone was running towards Nullan. Gasps went up from those watching, even as Cora felt the air drain from her lungs.

It was Tannir, running straight for Nullan, nothing to lose now.

Nullan had realised something was wrong from the noise of those watching, and was turning, but too slowly. Tannir leapt upon her, and Cora saw the glint of metal in his hand before the two bodies became a tumbling heap of cloth and arms, mud and shouts. Two purple tunics were sprinting over, and on their heels were constables. Cora was running herself now, but not to save Nullan.

She was running to Ruth.

She caught Ruth just as her sister was emerging into the open next to the coach she was to tell her story from, wrapping her in her arms and not letting go.

'What's happening?' Ruth cried, her eyes wide, straining to see over Cora's shoulder, to fight her way free.

'It's Nullan. Tannir attacked her.'

Ruth went limp. 'Is she—'

'She's fine,' Cora said.

But there was no way of knowing, given the churning crowd that had formed around Nullan. Too many people, too much movement. Ruth buried her face in Cora's shoulder.

They stayed like that until order was restored, with Cora telling Ruth a story of what she could see, Ruth keeping her face pressed into Cora's shoulder.

The Audience had been swept back into the garbing pavilion by purple tunics as soon as Tannir had struck. Now the purple tunics worked to quieten the public gallery and make everyone return to their seats. A line of constables formed a protective ring around the Commission box. Inside it, Lowlander Chambers Morton would no doubt be expressing shock and sadness to the dignitaries around her, even as she believed she'd finally silenced this Wayward story.

But Tannir would have no chance to tell *his* story, Cora thought, watching a handful more constables leading the Wayward away, his hands cuffed. The bruise on his cheek was visible even from a distance. Who did Morton have waiting? Who was her back-up 'teller, now that Tannir had over-played his hand? The head herders were likely to have helped with that – without a Wayward story, the whole election was void, and the Commission would assume control of the Assembly until a new election could be held. All this, Cora murmured to Ruth. Except one last part, as a constable scooped up a limp figure from the ground, her head fallen back over his arm.

Cora changed the story. In the tale she told Ruth, Nullan was on her feet, shaken, but walking. The plan had worked. All was well. Ruth gave no cry of joy. She must have known it wasn't true, but they would keep the fiction for now. It had to be done: the Audience were returning to their seats.

'The Master of Ceremonies is climbing back onto the coach,' Cora said.

At this, Ruth finally looked up. Her eyes were red raw from crying and her chest heaved.

'This has been a most… irregular occurrence,' the Master said. 'I thank the Audience for their forbearance and ask that the Commission rule the election—'

'Suspension or delays will not be necessary,' Chambers Arrani shouted. He climbed onto the coach beside the Master of Ceremonies who bowed his head in deference. 'The Wayward storyteller is here,' Arrani called to all in the coach station, 'and she is safe.'

The crowd gasped. Cora wished she could see the face of

Lowlander Chambers Morton in that moment, and Sillian beside her. Their plan had failed.

Ruth stepped into view. Cora had hold of her hand. To let go, it was the hardest thing she'd ever had to do. Ruth squeezed it, then she was gone.

'This is the rightful storyteller,' Arrani boomed. 'Let no one in the Union say otherwise!'

The Master of Ceremonies was so shocked, he froze atop the coach. Arrani gave him a firm push towards the ladder, and all at once, he remembered himself and scuttled out of the way. Arrani's leave-taking was more dignified. Evidently, a Chambers was always self-controlled, no matter the crisis.

Ruth took a deep breath then climbed onto the roof of the coach. Would she be able to tell her story, after all that had happened? Cora wasn't sure, but then Ruth opened her mouth, and her words came, strong and clear.

'This is my son's story.'

The Wayward story

This is my son's story. It is *his* story. Although he didn't always know it.

The Wayward have many traditions and rituals that other realms deem... unusual. One such tradition concerns those wishing to marry for the first time in their lives. The reasoning behind this particular tradition is to give any two people a chance to gather memories and stories, together, before taking their vows.

It also determines if their love can survive living with each other.

Nicholas didn't want to be there. He hardly knew the bride, and the groom was at most a friend of the family: his father had driven herds decades ago with Nicholas's father and apparently that was enough – here they were, on a long table at the wedding. It was just the way of things, when families and their herds moved across the Steppes at the whims of the seasons and their cattle. Anyone within a few miles was suddenly an old friend of someone, or someone's second-cousin, or known to be a reliable hand and good company after a drink.

So, under the biggest tent for miles around, Nicholas found himself at the end of a table, eating tasteless meat and surrounded by children. At least he'd been allowed a proper drink. What exactly, he didn't know, but it was milky – probably goat – and it kicked as rough as the animal itself. He was determined to make the one cup last the whole evening. There'd been no promise of more.

'—and in the winter we went even *further* south. Really, really far.' The little boy sitting next to Nicholas kept talking, whether Nicholas was listening or not. 'We saw the More-wall Mountains. Have *you* ever even seen them?'

Nicholas looked down at the earnest face staring back at him. Grease smeared across one cheek, all the way to the boy's ear. How had he even...?

'The Moral Mountains. I've seen them.'

Disappointment came and went in a flash, as the boy evidently realised they now shared something. What followed was a litany of place names and landmarks progressively further and further in the south. Nicholas considered lying – yes, he had seen the Tear with his very own eyes – but decided it would be too much effort. Beyond the boy there were maybe ten or so other children at the wedding, all corralled together as far from the adults as decently possible. That way, the adults could drink and curse and sing as much as they liked, knowing the older children, like Nicholas, would make sure none of the younger children choked on a bone or wandered off too far. Though he had no direct brothers or sisters, at seventeen years old he wasn't the youngest in their herd, so he had plenty of little ones to be watching. Keeper hear it, it wasn't fair. Whenever real grown-up work needed doing out on the trail, Nicholas put his back to it like the rest of them. He should be at the other end of the long table, spilling his drink on the next man's beard, swaying to the songs and bellowing the rude words.

Instead, he wiped the grease from the boy's ear – who surprisingly didn't put up a fight.

'Well, do you?'

'Do I what?' Nicholas said absently.

'Want to have a wedding one day?'

Nicholas blinked. 'A wedding one day. I guess—'

'Move up, will you?' a woman said. This woman – no, a girl, no, a woman; he couldn't tell really – she didn't wait, just pushed her way onto the bench. She had more grease across her face than the boy did. Her dark hair was tied back, though it hadn't escaped unscathed, and where there wasn't grease, there was smoke. 'What are you two staring at?' she said, without turning from her plate. She ate like the meat might get up and walk away if she wasn't fast enough.

'I... nothing.'

'We've seen the Moral Mountains,' the boy said, beaming.

'That so.'

'What have *you* seen?'

The woman – she was at least as old as Nicholas, he decided – wiped her mouth with the back of her hand. 'Cooking fires,' she said. 'Enough that I'll be seeing them in my sleep too.'

'That's not—'

'Can't someone eat in peace?' she snapped. The boy suddenly found his own plate very, intensely, interesting. From the wetness edging his eyes, he was doing his best not to cry in front of his new, older friend.

Nicholas waited a little while before he said, 'Peace? At a wedding?'

'Wedding. Hah!'

'What do you mean?' he said.

'Have you even looked at the bride and groom? Plenty to tell the Companion already, I'd say.'

Nicholas didn't want to admit he didn't even know what they looked like; he hadn't been there for the binding ceremony. He'd been tending to the goats. 'What's your name?' he asked.

'Odette,' she said, with a note of a challenge. The kind of note that came from years of comments and judgements on something as simple as her name.

'Nicholas,' he said, and held out an arm. They shook, wrist to wrist, a little awkwardly sitting next to each other. Seeing her properly, despite the grease and smoke, she had big eyes and a slightly rounded face. 'What did you mean, they have plenty to tell the Companion?'

'Look at them,' she said, pointing with a half-eaten chicken leg. 'Barely even talking to each other.'

The crowd of drunken adults had parted just enough for him to see a man and woman at a table. They looked about as alone as anyone can when sitting next to someone. And there was something else, a tightness to them, as if they were both straining against something.

'It's as if they both need to piss, but aren't allowed to leave,' Odette said.

It wasn't quite how Nicholas would put it, but he could see what she meant. He tried to think back to the other weddings he'd been to – maybe this was just how people were at their own weddings? But he'd evidently paid little attention over the years, which was hardly surprising from the end table with all the children.

'What's really wrong, do you think?' he said.

She shrugged. 'Maybe after five seasons tramping around the Union they don't love each other anymore.' It was Wayward tradition for all couples wanting to get married to spend five seasons together, travelling across the other realms. If their love survived that, it would survive life on the Steppes, or so it was supposed to go.

'But they're getting married.'

'And one herd trades yak hides for a few iron tools. Beautiful, isn't it?'

It took him a moment to piece together what she was saying. But when he did, the veil lifted, and suddenly he heard an edge to the adults' laughter, saw a restlessness about their eyes, and more than a few tight grips on drinking horns.

'I'm sure they still love each other,' he said.

'Oh, you're *sure*, are you?'

Nicholas was busy thinking of a witty rejoinder when an old man who was as smoke-smudged as Odette barked something incomprehensible in her direction. She stuffed as much meat into her mouth as she could, apparently deciding she'd chew on the way, and left. Nicholas watched her cross the tent until she disappeared into the crowd. She didn't look back once.

'She's mean,' the boy said. Nicholas had all but forgotten him, but it seemed he'd been listening the whole time. Listening better than Nicholas, perhaps.

'She might be,' he said. 'She might be.'

As the spring night descended proper, lanterns were lit up and down the great tent. The general noise grew as the adults drank and the children became wild. Any semblance of control that Nicholas and the few older ones had was well and truly gone, and like trees in a storm they kept as still as they could while chaos raged around them. He sipped his fermented goat's milk and tried to ignore being poked and prodded and climbed over. He remembered having that kind of reckless blood pumping through him. That kind of wild abandonment which came with being fearless and ignorant of such things as consequences.

At least his parents hadn't bothered to find him. He couldn't face them as they tried to hide condescending smirks, their empty platitudes. He didn't care who he'd have insulted – he didn't want to come to this wedding. Or any wedding for that fact.

When he wasn't dealing with one crying child or another, he watched the supposed adults run amok in their own way. In the light of the lanterns, men grinned through braided beards and women roared with laughter as stories were swapped between draughts from horns. Somewhere, there was music, though Nicholas only heard snatches of drums and the occasional piercing high note of a fiddle. He was able to see the dancers. Pairs of them swirled and churned until it was hard to tell them apart. He wondered if Odette, the woman he'd only just met, was there somewhere. If she'd had a chance to get rid of her apron, change her dress and wash her face. He tried to remember just what that face looked like. Big brown eyes, that much he remembered. Dark hair. Was it straight or curly? He found himself hoping for curls and was surprised by the feeling. What did he care what a stranger's hair was like?

From the dancers, his gaze slid towards the shadowy eaves of the tent. There, shapes were even harder to be sure of, but mostly he found people still and close to each other. A few were doing more than talking, and he looked away quickly. He hoped his parents were drinking or dancing in the decent light – he didn't want to accidentally find them in the shadows...

'You're still here. Where they keep the children.'

He looked up to see Odette. Same apron, same dress, though her face was clean – mostly. There was still a line of something at the edges.

'Where would I go?' he said.

'Anywhere? Anywhere but here?' She made it sound like an invitation.

He drained the last of his drink. 'Anywhere with more drink,' he said.

'I think we can manage that.' She led him away from the table, ignoring the whines and protests that followed in their wake – the other older children questioning just why he was allowed to escape. Nicholas had to admit he'd wondered the same, in the moment he stood up and tried not to look so awkward removing himself from the bench. The answer was simple enough: he was being rescued. And the rescue involved two flagons lifted from a table beside the tent door.

Before he knew it, they were outside with the quiet darkness rushing towards them. The sky was patchy with clouds, stars peeking through in places. The moon, nearly full, made showy entrances and exits. These were the things he noticed as he walked alongside her, carrying one of the flagons, the light and noise softening behind them. These were the things he noticed, because he daren't look at her. Not yet. He wasn't sure why, but he felt like she might decide she didn't want to be outside with him after all. That she'd rather be dancing, or eating, or whispering with someone else in the shadows.

The vastness of the Northern Steppes was all around them. The rolling grasslands, the craggy outcrops, the thin winding rivers – Nicholas could sense it all, and in the darkness, it felt never-ending. He could keep walking from right there and never see anything but the Steppes. He shuddered.

'Cold?' Odette said.

'A little.' The lie was easier than trying to explain the feeling.

They came to the top of a gentle rise. The moon-brushed grass rolled out below them, as still as a painting. Odette sat down without a fuss and took a slug from her clay flagon. He hesitated and something happened to the air between them, a small shift that he didn't understand. He drank just to be doing something. The bitter ale was a shock after the sweetened goat's milk, but she didn't seem to notice his wincing. He couldn't believe all the adults drank so much ale; it was like rinsing your mouth with ashes or licking sun-bleached rocks or—

'You sitting down? Or you have somewhere else to be?' She gestured at the dark horizon.

He slumped down right where he was standing, suddenly more aware of himself than he'd ever been before. It must have been the ale; his legs didn't normally feel so long, or his hands so big, and why was he grinning?

'Tell me your story, Nicholas.'

'I'm no good at telling stories,' he said.

'That's a shame.' She sounded genuinely disappointed.

'But I'm a good listener,' he said quickly.

'That's all you need to be a good storyteller. One day I'm going to have the best stories to tell,' she said. 'I just need to get away from all of this.'

'You want to leave the Steppes?' It was his turn to sound disappointed.

'Of course! Where are the stories here? There's just grass and the animals that eat it. I want more.'

'So do I,' he said.

'That so?' She was looking right at him. With her brow furrowed she looked as stern and serious as his mother.

'I want to make my own way, not just follow along at the back of the herd.'

She nodded, as if she understood. But how could she when he didn't understand himself, not really? It was just a feeling that was getting stronger in him each day, each time he got into the saddle, every time someone told him where to be, what to do.

'Tell me a story then,' he said, 'if you're going to be such a great storyteller.'

The moon broke free from the clouds, she smiled, and suddenly he was glad he'd come to a stranger's wedding.

'Last winter,' she said, 'when we were as close to Perlanse as my father ever gets, a storyteller came riding into our camp. Perlish, he was, and anyone could tell that from the dainty ankles on his horse and the floppy hat he wore. He even had a bare chin and an oiled moustache that curled at the ends. Somehow he wasn't soaked to the bone, despite the Painter doing his best to wash away the Steppes.

'This man was welcomed into the camp, as any storyteller should be, but most of my family weren't too happy about it. A Perlish 'teller once stole away one of my uncles, but that's a different story. This teller was too old for that sort of thing. When he entered our main tent, which he did with a flourish of his cloak, he was met by a circle of blank faces. Someone in the back cleared their throat, but otherwise, the cackle of the fire was the only sound. If he was expecting applause, he recovered himself quickly enough.

'He had a bag with him. Not like our leather ones with string ties – this had all kinds of shiny metal fastenings and clasps. He

399

produced a little key on a chain to unlock it. Even my family weren't immune to such a curiosity, and I wasn't the only one leaning forwards to see what such a fuss was about.

'He took out five objects, one at a time, and placed them carefully on the floor before my father. He asked the whole tent to choose an item, and he'd tell us a story about it. He asked the whole tent, but everyone knew it would be my father – as head of the herd – who would choose. My whole family was looking at him, everyone except for me.

'I was looking at the objects.

'I didn't recognise a single one of them.

'It sounds silly, doesn't it? But I had no idea what they were. There wasn't a blanket, a saddle, a pot, a flagon or drinking horn among them. No jewellery carved from wood. No clothes I recognised. Nothing to do with tents or horses or herding cattle. Five things I didn't know the name of, let alone their purpose or use. They might as well have come straight from the Audience.

'Apparently, my father, at least, knew more of the realms. He barked a word – I was too absorbed in my own turmoil to hear what exactly – and the 'teller swooped on a shiny circle. A story followed, maybe the only story in my life that I can't remember at all, not a single word.

'See, the 'teller had left all the other things on the floor of the tent. I suppose it was a kind of reminder of what we might have chosen. For me, it was a reminder of how little of the Union I knew.

'I decided then, if I was to be a storyteller, I had to see the realms for myself. I had to find my stories.'

She drank from her flagon – long enough for Nicholas to come back from last winter, her family's tent, back to the night-draped hillside.

'Last winter?' he said.

'I'll get there,' she said, her voice firm. 'You'll see.'

'Best not wait too long.'

There was a quiet then, and it stretched and stretched. He wondered if he'd said the wrong thing – or lots of wrong things. He stole glances at her and wished she'd say or do something. But she just stared far into the distance and drank. He did the same, and imagined what she might be looking for. At least the taste of ale wasn't so bad after a while. At least he wasn't stuck on a table with screaming children, as his parents danced and kissed and all the rest. At least...

She didn't laugh when she helped him up. Standing was harder than it should have been. They meandered their way back to the tents, and the next thing he knew he was lying face down on his furs. That felt right.

'Best no rate you long,' he mumbled to one of his boots. He couldn't see the other, couldn't move his head, couldn't remember what he was looking for.

He fell asleep frowning.

'Will you marry me?'

The voice came from nowhere. There hadn't been voices in his dream up until then – just clouds, the Audience, and a moon that eluded him. A moon that, try as he might, he couldn't understand. But he didn't want to open his eyes, he knew that much.

Being shaken was harder to ignore. Someone was shaking him by the shoulder. He opened an eye then quickly shut it because it was too painful. His tent had become some kind of forge that was too hot to look at. Or maybe it wasn't his tent, maybe the sun had fallen from the sky and landed just above him. Either way, it hurt.

'Hey, Nicholas, wake up!'

'No.'

'No, what?'

'No, the sun... and it's hot... and just... no.'

Suddenly he was rolled onto his back and slapped hard enough to open both eyes.

'There, now we can talk,' Odette said. She was standing over him, in a fresh dress and apron, hunching a little under the roof of his tent. A woman, in his tent.

'How did you— Why are you— You just hit me!'

'Do I need to do it again?' she said, raising her arm.

He wiped the dribble from his chin and worked his jaw. 'No, it's still stinging.'

'So, I say again: Will you marry me?'

Squinting up at her, it took a long time for each of those words to settle at the back of his head, individually at first, and then together to form the unbelievable. A question he thought was part of his dream.

'Well, will you?'

With some effort, he glanced to one side, to the furs he was lying on, fully clothed, trying to remember. 'Why, did we do...?'

She made to hit him again, but he raised his hands quick enough this time.

'This is serious!' she said.

'We only met last night – I think.' Through a milky-ale cloud, he started to remember. 'We talked, away from all the noise. You told me a story. It was nice. Look, I know I'm handsome for a cowhand, but you need to think about this.'

She groaned. 'You don't understand. If we say we're getting married, we can get away from here. Now, today.'

'Get away?'

'Yes! Just like those two dullards who can't look at each other now they're properly married; they had five seasons wandering the realms, with their parents' blessing, as goes the tradition.'

He was struggling to keep up with her. That was the way, ever since they'd met. 'You. You want to spend five seasons out in the Union. With me?'

'Well, we wouldn't have to be together the *whole* time.'

'And when we get back, we have a wedding? Like last night?'

'Maybe, maybe not,' she said. 'Maybe we don't even come back.'

'Maybe we don't *even* come back,' he echoed.

'It's like you said, we can't wait too long. I can't face another year, another roll of the seasons, out here on the Steppes.' She grabbed the ridge of his tent and shook it. 'Another year sleeping in the same old tents, herding the same tired cattle, cooking the same meat on a spit.'

'But... married?'

'It's only the excuse. I need to be out there, finding my stories. Don't you see?'

He was starting to. Yes, even in his addled state he was beginning to put the pieces together. He didn't realise, until that very moment, this was exactly what he had been looking for: a way to leave his family without hurting them. Something his mother and father would accept. A reason they couldn't argue with.

But they did argue.

★

'What's this girl's name? Who is she?' his mother said.

'She's my daughter, that's who. And she's not riding off with some milk-eared goat-herder,' a large man said, pointing at Nicholas. Odette's father was as big as the bison he drove, and just as hairy.

Nicholas and Odette stood, eyes lowered, in front of all four parents like two thieves awaiting judgement. In the hours that he'd known her, he hadn't seen her act in any way meek. When she had finished slapping his face and explaining why they needed to get married, he'd assumed she would take the same tone when they told their parents. Instead, she had let him talk. As if this was his idea.

Around them, the different Wayward herds that had attended the wedding were gradually breaking camp in the weak light of morning. Men and women moved about the business slowly, deliberately, as if even the simple task of taking down a tent was an enormous effort. Others carried their belongings to wagons as if wading through water. Nicholas's father kept pinching the bridge of his nose and wasn't so steady on his feet. His mother was having no such problems. She prodded the large bison-man in his chest.

'Your *daughter* has clearly seduced my boy, with her hussy ways. He hasn't so much as looked at a girl in that way before today.'

The man arched a brow and, having taken in just what she had said, turned to Nicholas. 'What's wrong with him then?'

'Nothing! He's just a *boy*!'

'I'm n—'

'Stay out of this, Nicholas.'

'Call my daughter a hussy again,' Odette's mother said. She shrugged free of her shawl and started to crack her knuckles. The bison-man found himself caught between two glaring women ready to do each other harm.

'From sense to madness, all of you,' Nicholas's father said. 'I've got a camp to clear. Let them marry if they want, just... do it quietly.'

'Frant!'

But he waved his wife away and meandered back between the tents.

'It's tradition,' Nicholas said, lowering his eyes again when they all looked at him.

'I told you to stay out of it.'

'But he's right,' Odette said. 'You have to let us go.'

'I don't have to do any such thing.'

Odette's father cleared his throat and spat on the ground. 'The children are right. If they're so determined, there's no stopping them. No Wayward is caged on the Steppes.' He turned to his wife. 'You still want to punch her?'

The woman did appear eager. But Nicholas's mother just shook her head and went to stand in front of her son. She lifted his chin until he was looking right at her.

'Do you really want to marry this girl?' she said.

He didn't have the wherewithal to lie. 'I don't know.'

'Ha! I knew—'

'But I might in five seasons.'

At that, Odette came to stand beside him and took his hand. A touching moment that even his mother couldn't ignore.

'We're ready, Mother,' he said.

'Ready? What do you know of "ready"?'

'We know as much as anyone,' Odette said.

'So she *does* have some fire in her,' his mother said. 'I was starting to doubt these were really her parents.'

Nicholas smiled. His mother had no idea.

The Wayward camp was gone almost as swiftly as it had appeared. The only marks it left were a large area of flattened grass and, in a few places, earth churned by feet and hooves alike. In every direction, wagon trains and their herds snaked across the Steppes. It was a bright, clear spring day, and not too hot for those nursing sore heads or spirit-scoured blood. Still, there was no hurry among the herds to be away from a good spring wedding. The same could not be said for the last few stragglers, and two in particular.

'You'll need your cloak come winter,' his mother said, checking his saddle knots and cinches. 'Don't be fooled by the southern heat; a Fenestiran winter can be just as cold as it is here. Trust me.'

'Yes, Mother.'

'And your little pipe? You know how much you enjoy playing that of an evening, when you're far from camp.'

'Mother!'

He envied the straightforward goodbye Odette received from her parents: they shook hands, promised to see each other in five seasons, and told her to come home with stories worth hearing.

His father was clearly keen to be on the move too. He had looked Odette up and down and said, 'She's prettier than you deserve. But then, we've always had the Latecomer's luck in that regard.' Then he left them to attend the herd's goats.

All of which were acceptable Wayward farewells. It was just his mother who lingered. She kept fussing, kept saying, 'Oh, my boy,' and taking his face in her hands. Until finally, even Nicholas could take no more.

'Mother! We need to make the most of the light.'

'Yes, yes of course.' But she hugged him once more. 'I do understand. You want to find your own ways, both of you. I understand more than you know.' She pulled back and smiled at him, tears in her eyes. 'Something foolish enough to tell the Drunkard: I never readied myself for *my* child heading out into the realms.'

'It's only five seasons, Mother.'

'No, Nicholas,' she said, smiling again. 'It's a whole lifetime. You'll see.'

She walked over to Odette who was already in the saddle – and had been for some time. She looked up at the girl, this girl who had tempted her son away with her big eyes and a bigger horizon.

'Don't tell my son stories,' she said. 'Not if it comes to love.'

Odette could only nod.

Nicholas mounted, and with final farewells, they were away. They rode side by side, heading south away from their herds, their families and everything they'd ever known. The temptation to look back grew with every plodding step of their horses. Odette was strong, stronger than him. He turned in the saddle to see the figure of his mother, alone in the flattened grass. He waved but couldn't tell if she saw him or not.

After some time, Odette took a deep breath and asked, 'What did she mean about winters in Fenest?'

'That's a long story,' he said. 'And I barely know the half of it.'

Salt water was not something Nicholas was prepared for. It didn't make much sense *as* water – it felt coarse somehow, and dried you out even though it was just as wet as any other kind of water. It left a taste in the mouth even without drinking it. He couldn't get used to salt water, even working in it day after day.

He and Odette had ridden south until they reached the coast and the high cliffs where the Steppes met Break Deep. As beautiful and stupefying as the views were, they had both seen the sea before at such a distance. And growing up on the Steppes readied a person for an endless horizon stretching out in front of them. But that vista was as close as either of them had been to the waters of Break Deep. That was, until they rode the coast south, and further south still, during the lengthening days. At night, they ate dried meat, fed their horses, and sometimes they'd light a fire. They slept in their own tents. Odette didn't want to start their five seasons in Perlanse, her reason being it was the realm closest to home – the realm they knew most about already. She was hungry for what was different, the more the better. Nicholas had no reason to argue – it was all the same to him – so they crossed the Stave Basin and into the Lowlands.

Nicholas lifted the oyster out of the brackish water, ignoring how much was sloshing about inside his heavy leather gloves, and quickly checked it over. Satisfied he didn't need to chip this one with his little hammer, he tossed it in the basket beside him. The tide was low, but not so low for him to be working on the beach and out of the water. In those first days he'd been given high boots that were covered in some kind of fat that was supposed to help keep his feet dry. But the truth was, after an hour or so of working, every part of him was wet to some degree.

Odette was a little way along the shore, with her back to him. They'd proven to Mr Samuels they could work together well enough – he had to split up some couples. Too distracting, he'd said with a wink. Mr Samuels ran the oyster farm that spanned the few miles of this small stretch of Break Deep. He always needed more workers, what with Lowlanders often heading home for spring planting and the harvests that followed.

'Wayward always welcome here,' he'd said when they'd presented themselves at his shack. 'Your people know the value of hard work.'

That value, for Mr Samuels, came to seven pennies a week, two meals a day – one of which being oyster stew without fail – and a bed in the bunkhouse if they'd care for it. They kept to their tents, which they pitched a little way from the ramshackle buildings. When Mr Samuels had seen their separate tents he just shook his head and kept his questions to himself.

'Chipping hammer. Fat-covered boots. We shuck oysters. Shucking. In the shallows...' Odette did that sometimes, just ran through lists of things to herself, her voice carrying in snatches on the wind. Nicholas didn't mind. The softness of the way she made each sound. That he never knew when she would start a list. It was strangely soothing. He knew what she was thinking about.

'I'm almost full,' he said, loud enough for her to hear.

She glanced at her basket, then round at him. 'So am I.'

He reached down into the murky, cold water again and lifted out a mess of jagged edges and unusual shapes. He knocked off the hard sediment around the oysters – he was quick in learning how to recognise this – and figured that would be enough to satisfy those at the shucking tables. He stood and stretched. Those first few days he had ached all over, like the first days in the saddle, but now it wasn't so bad.

Picking up his basket, he made his way carefully onto the stony beach. His boots were too big, so he had to bring his foot high out of the water and be ready for a slight give with any footfall. Odette was even less steady on her feet.

'You all right?' he said, waiting for her.

She glared at the smooth rocks as if they were in the pay of the Liar himself. When she made it to him, she steadied herself using his shoulder. Her wet gloves sent a fresh wave of saltiness through his nose and up to his eyes.

'You're light,' she said, nodding to his basket.

'There's more in there than it looks.'

'Save it for the shuckers.'

They trudged up the beach to where the stones gave way to long, reedy grass. All along the shore, others worked in just the same way, hunched over and pulling oysters from the rocky shallows. Any that were too small were tossed back. Mr Samuels and the rest of the regulars got all kinds of angry if you brought them anything small.

At the shucking tables, Nicholas and Odette emptied their baskets separately. If he really was light, it wouldn't be worth getting them both in trouble. But the woman with the knife said nothing as she set to. Half the table was worked right there and then, the other half put into buckets of cold water and run back from the beach still in their shells.

As soon as he realised he wasn't going to be scolded, Nicholas's attention drifted. But not Odette. She watched the shuckers work like it was her first day. That no longer bothered anyone, that was just Odette – no harm to anyone, if you didn't mind being stared at.

The morning was dragging on. But it would be another three or four baskets before they could take a break – either wander together further along the cove or, as Nicholas preferred, far inland enough to smell something other than the sea.

'You're done,' the shucker woman said, and Nicholas blinked at the now cleared table. All that remained of his hard work was a slimy runoff of water and a woman cleaning her knife. He waited for Odette. Maybe she did have a few more in her basket.

'That was three of yours, and five of mine,' Odette said as they walked back down towards the waterline.

'What's that?' he said.

'That many gone bad in the shell.'

'Nothing anyone can do about that, far as I see.' He held up his bucket. 'I just take them out of the water.'

'Harvest them,' she said, but she wasn't paying attention to him really. She was looking up and down the beach. 'That's the way the Lowlanders say it.'

'Well, they should know.'

Odette craned her neck to call to the foreman, back by the shucking tables. 'Going far end.'

'What?' Nicholas said. 'But then we have to carry them twice as far!'

'More time walking, less time bent double.' She didn't wait for a witty response – which Nicholas was so obviously thinking his way towards – and set off for the southern end of the beach. Their previous spot, a prime location so close to the shucking tables, was seized almost immediately by a pair of Lowlander women, moving crab-like across the rocks. He hurried to catch up with Odette.

They worked the rest of the day there, in the shallows of the southern end. They didn't speak much beyond the necessary, but it was an easy, companionable kind of quiet. The softness and economy of words when at work. Nicholas soon lost himself to the rhythms of the task: hands in and out of the water; the shells clattering against each other in the basket; the tension and awareness of walking across pebbles. At the shucking tables, Odette was as hawk-eyed as ever, but it wasn't until their final basket of the day that she spoke up.

'Eight bad in the shell, each of us,' she said. 'Eight to a basket at least since we moved down to the end. It's worse there.'

The shucker, Anna her name was, dropped her knife. It clattered on the tabletop. Anna looked down at it as if she'd just let go of a Steppes viper.

'Not here, fools,' Anna hissed. She made a face Nicholas found hard to understand, but she was serious – he could tell that much. Maybe even scared. 'Bunkhouse porch, after dark.'

'What—'

'All done here,' Anna said loudly. 'Not a bad day from you two, all told.'

So dismissed, they took their empty baskets and put them in the pile at the foreman's feet. The burly man grunted, which was all the permission they needed. Bone-weary, they made their way back from the shore. Nicholas followed behind Odette, her shapeless, thick trousers bulging over her boots. Her wet ponytail slapped between her shoulders like a marching beat. Loose planks had been laid – some many years ago – as a path to the collection of shacks and huts that made up Mr Samuels's domain. Already, Nicholas felt he could find his way back to the tents with his eyes closed. The days had tumbled into one another – quick, quick, slow, and now the Steppes felt like someone else's memories. It was ridiculous, really, they'd only been gone a few weeks. Was it six, or seven? Putting one foot in front of the other without thinking, he tried to count the days he'd been picking oysters. *Harvesting* them. Too many days, too much the same.

The final climb to the tents was the worst; the slight incline became a mountain to match the Rusting, after a long day's work. His cold toes pressed to the front of his boots, the salt water pooling at his heels, he bit back a useless complaint. Instead, he focused on her. The curve of her neck. Her strong shoulders. The way she carried herself as if life's hardships were no different from its gifts.

On the lines outside their tents, they hung their gloves and, after emptying them, their boots and socks. Inside, Nicholas fumbled at the buttons of his shirt with numb fingers.

'Left hand, third knuckle, big enough for a penny,' he said, loud enough for her to hear from her tent.

There was silence for a moment.

'Right hand, first and second, I might try a mark,' she called back. They were comparing cracks in their skin.

'Think that'll impress the regulars?'

'Only if I punch one of them with it.'

'Feet?' he said.

'Worse than my grandmother's.'

Changing into dry trousers, Nicholas caught sight of his own feet but couldn't bear to look for long. That they swung wildly from numb to stinging to throbbing heat was something he'd come to accept – when the feeling felt as distant as anything attached to him could be. But to see them, properly see them, would be to admit too much.

They came out of their tents almost at the same time, wet clothes ready to hang, set in this routine that felt so old to them, but was really so new. That was perhaps one of the strangest things for Nicholas – how quickly he'd become used to this place, this way of living, this being 'married'. Some of that had to be because of the work, but then work had been hard out on the Steppes. Drier, yes, and with less salt everywhere, but hard, nonetheless. Looking after a herd was just as demanding on a body as hauling shells out of Break Deep.

'You've got that look about you again,' Odette said.

Nicholas blinked. He was standing in front of the tent line, his clothes in his hands, and she'd already finished with hers.

'I was just thinking about... Never mind.'

'I'm thinking about food,' she said.

'Another oyster stew – a story to make both the Glutton and my stomach sick.'

'Do you remember beef?'

'Don't.'

'How earthy, how thick it tasted.'

'I remember having to chew food,' he said.

When their turn at the stew pot came, all thoughts of complaints or beef were gone, replaced by the hunger of a day's work. They ate together, but alone, sitting at one end of the long table. In some ways it reminded Nicholas of how he first met Odette, at the children's end of a wedding table. But then the murmur of conversation snatched between mouthfuls and the clunk of wooden spoons against wooden bowls gave the whole thing a softness, a calm. Other workers drifted to the pot, to the table and away again without the frenzy of a wedding.

When Anna, the woman from the shucking table, walked past, she didn't look at them. She didn't sit near them, either, once she had her stew. Nicholas didn't know where to look. He wasn't accustomed to keeping secrets, or people confiding in him. Sneaking around just wasn't worth it on the Steppes – there was always too much to do, always somewhere else to be moving on to, always another animal that needed tending. If there was a problem between people, they had it out at the fireside: words, fists and, on the rare occasion, knives. Simple.

Odette appeared more comfortable though. She ate her stew and talked of coming spring rain as if it was just another day at the oyster farm. Perhaps it was all those stories she listened to, those stories she wanted to tell one day. Stories so often had secrets at the heart of them. When they finished eating, Odette herded him away from the table, a hand firmly on his shoulder. They weren't to speak to Anna, or to look at her even. Not until after dark.

'Play for me?' Odette said as they neared the tents.

Nicholas looked down at his hands – the cracks and split skin across his knuckles, the callouses all along his fingers. Playing his little herder's pipe was uncomfortable these days, sometimes outright painful. But despite all that, he played when she asked.

They each sat in the mouth of their own tent, and Nicholas played the long, slow herder melodies that were meant to fill the hours. Between notes, between breaths, he occasionally heard the roll and roar of Break Deep, or the sounds of the other farmworkers. The sun set, the moon rose, and on he played. He played until her hand stilled the pipe.

'Thank you,' she said.

His hands throbbed and his mouth was dry, but he smiled up at her. 'For a while, when I'm playing, it feels like I'm back there. Back on the Steppes.'

'We carry it with us,' she said, 'no matter where we go.'

'Do you miss it?'

'Already?'

'At all?' he said.

'A little. But I want to see more. I want to see it all.'

'You want to see what Anna has to say.'

She glanced towards the bunkhouse. Maybe there was a

shadow there, deeper than the others. 'There's a story here, and I don't like knowing just a part of it.'

He stood slowly, feeling the aches of days and weeks in the shallows. 'You can't hear every story. Not even the Audience hear *every* story.'

'No, but I *will* hear those right in front of me.'

The lamps in the bunkhouse had been doused, but the night was still a bright one. Anna was sitting on the front of the porch, just a woman seeking small solace in the quiet of the night. But when she saw them, she stood and, without a word, started walking.

As they followed her, Nicholas couldn't help worrying if he should be worried. He had his shucking knife, but then everyone had a shucking knife. Anna led them away from the huts and shacks, and back towards the beach. But not by the usual paths. She was taking them further south, and higher, up to where the reedy dunes topped out as small cliffs. A fall from those cliffs wouldn't necessarily prove fatal – there was a lot of sand and scrub below – but breaking a few bones would be the end of their time at the farm. Nicholas wondered just how he felt about that idea.

But for all his wondering and worrying, when Anna stopped a ways from the cliff's edge, there was no one else out there with them.

'Can't be too careful,' Anna said. 'Mr Samuels has more than two ears, if you catch my meaning.'

'Is this really about bad oysters?' Nicholas said.

'For now,' Anna said. She hugged herself against the night's chill. 'But you ain't the first to notice.'

'Notice that more oysters are going bad in the shell,' Odette said.

'That's right. And not just bad. But smaller too. Make the mistake of saying something to Samuels, and he waves it away as just a rough season. But it's not been just one season. We regulars know.'

'What do you know?'

'It won't feel it, not to you newcomers,' Anna said. 'But the water's warmer.'

Nicholas sniffed. He hadn't felt properly warm in weeks.

'And warm water's no good for oysters?' Odette said. 'What's causing it?'

'That's why Mr Samuels doesn't want folk talking about it. He's scared, see.'

'Scared of what?'

'You want to know – you *really* want to know – walk along this cliff line for an hour or so. Then you'll see.'

'See *what*?' Odette said, clearly losing her patience with all this secrecy. So much for the storyteller's love of a good secret – maybe that was something Odette had yet to learn.

'You'll know,' Anna said. 'Not even you wool-headed Wayward can miss it.'

'But people like Mr Samuels can deny it.'

'They try.'

Without so much as a goodbye, let alone a thank you, Odette marched off south along the clifftop. Nicholas tried to apologise, tried to say thanks, but Anna just shrugged.

'No good will come of it. But she's the curious kind, isn't she? I knew she wouldn't leave it alone.'

He hurried to catch up with Odette, glad of the clear sky and the bright night.

*

They walked side by side, but said little. There was no talking Odette back from this, no suggesting they come out another night – or perhaps on one of the rare days they didn't work the shore. She needed to see what Anna was talking about, and she needed to see it now – that much was clear. *Why* Odette felt this way was what occupied his thoughts. Why did she feel so strongly about this, about anything? He didn't share those feelings at all. Was there something wrong with him, something deeper than the aches and pains of a day's work? He understood good and bad things happened to people, and that those things made up the stories they told the Audience. There was no stopping those events, no controlling them; that was just the way of life – the way of Nicholas's life, right up to when a woman he'd just met asked him to marry her. That was just another thing that happened, and a story he'd told the Companion many times since. But he didn't go out seeking such stories; he didn't burn with the kind of curiosity that blazed in Odette – blazed bright enough for people like Anna to see. Where was his fire?

'You don't approve,' Odette said. Her voice cut across the soft rustle of cloth and their dull footfalls like a pealing bell.

'What?' he said.

'You've been huffing and puffing since we left Anna.'

'I'm just tired.'

'You were grinding your teeth too,' she said.

'I was?' He opened and closed his mouth, checking his teeth were all present and accounted for. 'I was just thinking how different we are. That's all.'

Evidently, she didn't have anything to say to that. So they kept on walking. The cliff trail rose and fell, rolling like the hills of the Steppes. But that's where the similarities ended. The ground underfoot was too soft, too sandy. The grass too long and reed-like. The air stank of salt, was just heavy with it, not like the fresh crispness of home. The constant noise of Break Deep could almost be the wind blowing across a rocky outcrop under which his family had camped for the night. Almost.

He found it strange that, given how much he'd wanted to get away from his home and his family, he often thought of them now.

'Is that smoke?' she said.

He looked up. There was definitely something in the air, but he couldn't smell smoke. At least, not a smell he thought of as smoke.

'It's not... right,' he said, not having the words to explain.

'No. Something is burning. Just not wood.'

The 'smoke' was billowing up and away from the cliffs in the distance. On a stormy night, which they'd had a few of since arriving at the farm, it could have been the spray from the waves. But that night was still, and Break Deep was as calm as it ever was. The smell grew stronger the closer they went. It not only stung the nostrils but also made him smack his lips to be rid of the taste.

'It's like a pot burning,' he said, thinking back to the times he'd been in charge of cooking as a child.

'It's salt,' she said. 'Burning salt.'

He shook his head. Not for the first time, Odette wasn't speaking sense. There weren't any villages or farms on this part of the coast. Maybe someone had set up some tents, other Wayward perhaps, and had left their cooking pot. But that was a lot of smoke-that-wasn't-smoke.

'Odette, look.' He stopped, lifted his boot then pressed a toe firmly into the ground. Or tried to. The sandy soil was gone. They'd been so busy looking up at the sky, they hadn't noticed the ground ahead of them. And now they were walking on it. Hard, rocky, the kind of ground you avoided with your herds. He knelt down and touched what his eyes were struggling to see in the night. It was solid, slick in some places, rough in others, with a grime that came away on his fingers. But there was something else too. He pressed his palm to the ground.

'It's warm,' he said.

She knelt beside him, not believing, or maybe she just wanted to feel it for herself. 'Clear skies today,' she said.

'Summer sun, sure, but what we had today wouldn't leave this kind of heat.'

'Warm water, warm earth.'

'Something burning on the air.'

They stood and made their way slowly up the next rise. What greeted them there was the answer to one question, but the cause of so many more.

At first, Nicholas did not understand what he was seeing. But the overwhelming feeling was of something terribly, terribly wrong.

He recognised the individual parts of what lay below, just in the same way he'd recognised Break Deep for what it was, even when seeing it for the first time. But he could not connect these pieces together into any story that made sense to him. He felt the heat. The smell of burning salt, of burning metal, was growing stronger and stronger.

'Have you ever heard...?' he said.

She didn't answer. She just kept staring straight at it.

Straight at a river of Wit's Blood flowing into the sea.

The colour was impossible to believe. The brightest yellow, hard to look at directly, merging into pulsing oranges. Harsh, bitter shades of red that seemed to grumble and groan as they churned. All those colours moving in a way they never did, never should. Water moved that way, nothing else. Rivers and streams and, sometimes, even lakes on the Steppes moved that way – but all of them were greens or blues or complicated versions of the two.

And there was more. Not just one stream of Blood, but others along the dip in the cliffs. Some flowed over the edge in broken waterfalls, thick and in bits like porridge from a spoon – searing hot globules that hissed when they met the water, and then were quickly gone. The only trace of them a billowing steam that buffeted the cliff side.

'This isn't supposed to be here,' Odette said. A simple thing to say, but one that cut right through all his confusion and cluttered thoughts. 'The Tear does *not* reach Break Deep.'

'But here it is.'

Perhaps it was the walk, perhaps it was weeks of hard work, or perhaps it was the strangeness of the scene that made him dizzy, but he had to sit down. He felt the warm rock through his trousers. Rock that days, weeks ago had flowed across this hillside and swallowed everything in its path. It had settled here, now cooled. For how long? How long could the Wit pour his Blood from his veins and into the sea?

Odette remained standing. Her whole body appeared tense, as if she were fighting herself – fighting the desire to know more, to poke and to prod places that were not meant for the likes of them. Fighting the desire because she knew better. She was a Wayward, not a Torn. So instead, she could only watch, as they both did, mesmerised by the meandering, flowing stone. The beauty of it undeniable. The presence of it unbelievable.

'This isn't supposed to be here,' Odette muttered to herself every so often, alongside more descriptive utterances. This, he'd realised, was her way of being sure of her memory. Of remembering the small and the big, anything that wasn't itself a whole story but might be part of one.

He didn't know how long they stayed there, not talking, just staring. Time struggled to mean anything when faced with rivers of stone. Eventually, it was Odette who decided they'd watched long enough. She turned and started walking back to the oyster farm. He followed in her wake.

She waited until they were a good distance from the Wit's Blood before she said anything. But even before that, he could tell she wanted to – it was in the set of her shoulders, and how every time she took a breath, it was like she was readying the words. But they needed time. And they needed to be away from that place.

'It won't just be the oysters,' she said, loud enough for him to hear. He came beside her. 'It will be bigger, the changes bigger, I... I can't even think about it properly.'

Again, even when struggling to do so, she found words for what they had both been feeling. He marvelled at that, at her face in the moonlight, and that she had chosen him to share this with. Even if neither of them was certain just what it was they were sharing.

Back at the farm, they made their way between the rough-shod wooden huts where Mr Samuels toiled with his papers, where the various workings of the farm were stored, and where the oysters were boxed up to send along the River Stave. And once they were finally beyond all these Seeder buildings, their story found a new way to amuse the Audience.

Their tents had been turned out.

Their scant belongings, just as much as two horses could carry between them, were scattered across the ground. Those horses were themselves still hitched to the post, calm as could be – that they were untouched was as clear a message to leave as the mess around them. Nicholas's cloak was sprawled on the ground, its many pockets pulled out and emptied. Their saddlebags were open and screaming their own stories. In the full moonlight, everything looked the same – dark, colourless shapes among the scrub and the grass. Nicholas almost didn't recognise anything. Part of him understood what he was staring at, but these didn't look like *his* things. *His* waterskin was tucked neatly inside his tent. *His* bindleleaf tin was in the fourth pocket, inside his cloak, for the rare times he wanted to taste the smoke. *His* working gloves had been hung on the line. But no one else slept in tents on the farm.

He went to start picking things up, but Odette stopped him.

'Nothing's broken,' she said quietly. She didn't sound angry or upset. She could have been talking about a haul of oysters or the state of the stew. 'Nothing.'

She still had a hand on his arm. And the more he looked, the more he realised she was right. The tents themselves were fine, just as they left them, no slashes or tears along the hide; on the Steppes, that's the first thing you'd do if you really wanted to hurt someone. Even the tents' lines were undisturbed. Looking closer at their clothes and their cloaks, there didn't seem to be any damage – not a stitch. Yes, things had been opened, yes things had been scattered across the ground, but seeing it now – as Odette did – it almost looked like it could have been done carefully. Deliberate and slow.

Evidently deciding she'd seen enough, committed enough to memory, Odette picked her way through the mess. She stopped every so often to check a pocket or lining. She ducked inside her tent which had been cleared entirely. She came back to him, hefting two small purses in her hand.

'Two left here, two missing, and two still on me,' she said.

'Left here?' he said.

'Had to be. Whoever did this would have found all my purses. But they only took two.' She pursed her lips. 'Took the smallest two, as well. What about yours?'

Nicholas didn't need to go searching among his belongings. He just patted his pocket to be sure.

'You don't hide your coins?' she asked.

'No, why would I?'

She opened her mouth but clearly decided it wasn't the time for that particular conversation.

'So, what do we do now?' he said.

'It's too late,' she said. Then she started gathering up her things, not hurrying but not caring too much what went where. She just wanted it all off the ground and in her tent. He did the same. When they were finished, dawn was still some hours away. Nicholas was bone-tired, but sleep seemed unlikely.

Odette hesitated at the entrance to her tent. 'You can sleep in here tonight,' she said, not looking at him. 'If you want.'

He nodded. He understood what she was saying and appreciated her saying it. Sleeping alone in a tent after it had been turned out wasn't too appealing. He took his bedroll and his one coin purse and ducked into her tent. She was lying down on one side of it, the implication clear. He settled with his back to her. It was good to be lying down, his body finally easing in places that had been tense or worked hard that day. But his eyes were wide open.

'Are you all right?' she said.

'I think so. Are you?'

'I'd had enough of salt water any way.'

He rubbed his cracked knuckles. The smell of burnt salt smoke heavy about him. Odette was right; spring was almost over.

In the morning, they ate one final meal at the oyster farm, breaking their fast with porridge they'd paid for in more ways than one. Nobody would meet their eye, not the man ladling out the pot, not the folk they passed on the bench and not even Anna who gulped down her porridge desperate to be away. But there wouldn't be a ruckus. Not started by either of them.

Mr Samuels was waiting for them when they finished. The portly Lowlander had his pocketwatch in his hands. He had a habit of rubbing the brass cover with a thumb, as if that might wind back the minutes somehow. Or perhaps, Nicholas thought as they approached him, Mr Samuels was hoping those minutes would speed on past without him. Either way, the man rubbed his watch when he was nervous.

'I heard what happened,' Mr Samuels said.

'Strange,' Odette said, 'nobody's talking about it here.'

'No, no. That's right. I'm sorry, but maybe it's time you two were moving on.'

Odette glanced at Nicholas then back at the Lowlander. Would she make Mr Samuels twist and squirm? Nicholas wondered. Would she make the man say it?

'Chasing us off won't stop what's happening here,' she said. 'It won't change your oysters going bad.'

Mr Samuels's eyes swivelled as if seeking their own kind of escape. 'Our oysters are—'

'It's only going to get worse. More will notice, those that haven't already.'

'Just go,' Samuels hissed, his nerves taking a turn to the nasty.

But he needn't have bothered himself. They knew when they weren't welcome. They were Wayward, after all.

* * *

The hardest part of being in the Tear was sleeping at night. First, Nicholas wasn't really sure it *was* night when he crawled onto his blanket; it felt as if the sky was a long way away from Erdan-Har. He was used to thin hide, stretched across wooden poles, being the only thing between him and the stars above. Here, there was so much rock above him he didn't even have the right words to describe it. He stared up at the solid, uneven black rock of the ceiling and imagined miles and miles of the stuff between him and the night air. The stars, the moon, clouds, even the sun had started to lose their push and pull on his days almost as soon as he and Odette had arrived.

They had wandered the Tear proper for three days. Three days without seeing a single living thing. It was a dead land, or so Nicholas felt. No birds to greet the rising or setting of the sun. The only rivers and streams were Wit's Blood, and nothing could live in that let alone swim in it. The air was clear of the Picknicker's buzzing and bothersome favourites that followed every animal on the Steppes. To his surprise, Nicholas found himself missing the tales of bites and scratching at various itches. More than once he swatted at the air in front of his face, but found nothing but heat there. They sold their horses before leaving the shores of Break Deep, knowing enough to know the Tear was no place for any beast with hooves. After three days, it didn't seem a place for *any* beast. But the Wayward marriage tradition was to visit *all* the realms, not just the easy or inviting ones, and Odette was still determined to find her stories.

Then, on the fourth day, they finally found Erdan-Har, and the eastern-most Torn.

They'd heard stories of this, the nearest Torn har. He was content to just listen, but Odette always pressed the 'tellers for details. He was glad of it then, as she had as good a sense as anyone of how to get to the eastern-most settlement in the Tear.

Even those days walking across rolling hills of cold rock, avoiding crevasses and canyons and the more serious climbs, felt very distant to him now, as he tried to sleep in his stone bunk inside the har. He'd asked, then pleaded, for the top bed hewn out of the rock wall. Odette looked embarrassed, but the others in the dormitory just shrugged and let him have his way. Anything to be a little closer to the sky.

It wasn't just the miles of rock above him that made sleep hard to come by, deep in the bowels of the har. The heat was constant and oppressive. The air throbbed with it. The Torn didn't seem to notice, barely broke a sweat, but he and Odette were drenched all the time. The worst, he quickly decided, was sweating from the eyelids: no matter how hard he blinked, his eyes stung. Odette hated sweat behind her ears, and she soon understood why the Torn shaved their heads. The sweat was bad, but breathing was worse.

He wore a mask all the time. Even when sleeping it was the only way to come close to breathing comfortably. Cloth masks that covered his mouth and nose, and tied behind his head. Inside the cloth, tucked in like a hand slips into a glove, were potho vine leaves. Potho vine being about the only plant that grows in anything like abundance in the Tear – and even then, only in the higher reaches and away from the Wit's Blood. Fortunately enough for northerners like them, the leaves helped with the harsh, ash-tainted air. But eventually, the leaves would succumb, turning black and slimy, and the whole mask needed to be washed and new leaves put inside. It was one small routine among many since they'd arrived. Odette didn't sleep with her mask on. She tried, at first, but kept waking up and thrashing about – not a good idea in a stone bunk. Apparently, the mask felt as if someone was pressing down on her face, on her mouth, trying to smother her. Some in the dormitory were sympathetic, others looked at her as if she was broken in some way. But they were mostly Torn, so everything the northerners did and said was strange to them.

Odette woke most mornings coughing and spluttering, and spat a black mess on the floor. That was until someone put a battered copper pot next to her bunk. A pragmatic people, the Torn, and sometimes that extended to kindnesses.

So, for weeks now, they had lived and worked and tried to sleep in Erdan-Har, in the east of the Tear. Tried to sleep despite the weight of black rock, the heat of Wit's Blood, and masked against the very air they breathed.

Tossing and turning as he sweated into the blanket beneath him, he found himself thinking about Break Deep. Not just the work there, where the waters had shrivelled then cracked his hands from all the salt. But he thought about the reason they were forced from the oyster farm: what they saw when Wit's Blood met the sea. At the time, he had been too stunned by what was happening, too in awe of what was right in front of him, to even hope to understand it. On nights like this when he struggled to sleep, he would return to that image: the molten stone steaming as it flowed into the water. The unnatural hiss and splutter of it.

Wit's Blood where it was never meant to be. Out of place, like a Wayward trying to sleep in a Torn har.

He needed to sleep before the day's hard work ahead of him. Lately, he'd hauled blood rock to and from a distillery. At first, they'd tried him in the mines, but the air was so bad and the heat so fierce he didn't last long there. But he would work, the Torn saw that, so he put his back to whatever needed doing to make the awful drink they called mutters, which was so popular in the har. When it wasn't blood rock it was moving Seeder grains from store to store, or cleaning out the great vats they used, or fuelling the fires. He didn't ask many questions, just listened when they told him what to do and where to go. Odette was the one who asked questions. By the end of the season, he was confident she'd be able to make her own mutters, as good as any in the Tear. Not that Nicholas would drink any of it.

'You're grinding your teeth again,' Odette whispered up to him.

He opened his mouth wide – he couldn't stop himself; he did it every time she mentioned it, as if that would make a liar out of her. 'I was just wondering how I let you talk me into this,' he said.

'I got you drunk.'

'That much I remember.'

'You looked so surprised when I sat next to you,' she said. 'As if I was the first girl that had ever done that.'

'You were. Still are.'

Someone in the dorm snored themselves to a peak, loud enough to silence even Odette, and then a heavy quiet followed. Nicholas was so tired.

'You haven't played your pipe since we got here,' she said.

'It's hard in the dorm.'

'That can't be it. It can't be just that.'

She was right, of course, but he hadn't given it much thought until just then. 'I don't like how it sounds in the har – so harsh, somehow, surrounded by all the stone.'

'Then play outside,' she said. 'Lilja says we should leave the har more. She says she'll take us.'

This was Odette trying. And he appreciated it, he really did. He didn't want to be the one to ruin this... whatever this was... for her. However hard it was to remember, he'd made his choice back on the Steppes, and now here he was.

'That's good of her,' he said. Lilja was as close to a friend as either of them had made since they left their herds. The first person to look at either of them as more than a hard worker or a curiosity. Though it was obvious she had to fight the urge to stare at their hair, worse still to touch it.

'What are you working tomorrow?' she asked.

'Rocks. Always more rocks.'

He could almost hear her wince. Unlike with the Seeders' oyster beds, here they'd found different work between them. Odette worked with what passed for animals in the Tear. Despite what she thought, Nicholas was glad of his rocks – they didn't have pincers or too many legs to count. Apparently, the animals had names, and each one was a character in some way. He'd keep to goats and horses and bison, all the same.

'What are *you* working with?' he said. Seconds passed. 'Odette?'

He leaned over the edge of his bunk. In the dull light of the low candles he saw she was asleep, her mouth half open and sweat glistening along her hair line.

'You're why I'm here,' he said, quiet enough he could deny it – even to himself.

*

The next day was hard, but no more so than any other when he'd snatched only a few hours of sleep the night before. What helped was to find a rhythm, a way of letting the body manage the work without having to tax the wool sitting between his ears. With blood rocks that wasn't too hard. Someone else swung the pickaxe, deep below ground, someone else sifted the rubble to separate the usable rock from the almost identical unusable kind and someone else worked the winch to bring the rocks up. More than one Torn had tried to explain to him what made for good blood rock and what made for bad, which was all about tiny gaps in the rock that let water through. No matter how many blood rocks he put into his handcart, which was his part of this whole glorious process, he couldn't see any with gaps in them; but the Torn were adamant they were there, so into his cart went the rocks.

When it was full, he wheeled the cart carefully back towards Erdan-Har. This part of the job did need his concentration – at best, a spill would mean time wasted and a scolding from whoever was in charge that day. At worst... well, with that kind of accident he wouldn't be working the rocks or any other kind of job under the Audience then. No, then he could sit back and listen to all the other poor fools down here. As tempting as that might be, he gave his rickety wooden cart his full attention.

Today, he was carting for the Er-jun mine. It was to the north of the har, though not by a long way. He took a break at the top of a smooth rise to rub his hands dry and adjust his mask. From the whiff that came with every breath, his pothos leaves didn't have much life left in them. He looked north. The high cliffs of the Tear loomed on the horizon, huge and dark and stern. At least, that's how they looked to him – like the faces of every strict elder he'd ever known. All old things were severe, all old things were cracked, all old things knew better than him. He ducked his head at those ancient cliffs, by way of showing his respect. It was the kind of gesture Odette would scoff at and then describe out loud so she'd remember for one of her stories. But Odette wasn't there.

She was waiting for him at the har.

He wasn't trusted to wheel the blood rock through the winding tunnels and halls of the har itself. Not after he got lost. Twice. And there was the time he wheeled right into a family's kitchen, spilling rocks on their dinner table. At least they had *almost* finished their meal. At the gates, he handed over the cart to a Torn born at Erdan-Har, who knew the difference between a tunnel and the corridor of someone's home. Odette was there, just inside the gate, with a lunch for them to share.

'You look terrible,' she said. She was sitting on a stone ledge, her hair tied up and a bright purple stain across her smock. As much as he felt the urge to ask just what made that kind of colour, he knew he wouldn't like the answer.

Slumping beside her, he gratefully accepted the pastry parcel she gave him. The Torn loved their pastry – at least, what *they* called pastry. It was much drier and crumbled as soon as you looked at it. With no herds to produce milk and butter, they'd had to be quite creative. Nicholas was fairly sure insects were involved – another question he knew better than to ask.

'Thanks,' he said, finishing the parcel. The insides had been mostly Seeder turnips, which was a relief.

'You can thank me twice: you don't have to work this afternoon.'

'What?'

'We're going to see more of the Tear,' Odette said. 'Lilja said she'll show us – she's on her way.'

'But how?' he said.

'How? Oh. It wasn't hard. I just told your foreman to take a good look at you and that wheelbarrow.' She wiped her hands on her smock, expertly missing the slashes of purple. 'He soon agreed it would be best for everyone if you took a break.'

'Thank you,' he said, feeling a kind of relief spread through him. Just the thought of an afternoon away from the mine was enough to loosen tight muscles and ease aching bones.

Odette seemed surprised at his sincerity. She cleared her throat, grimaced at what that produced, and turned her head to spit. 'Sorry,' she said.

'That can't be doing you good.'

'No.'

'You should wear your mask when you sleep.'

'Yes.'

They lapsed into a companionable silence, happy to watch the comings and goings of Erdan-Har as they waited for Lilja. Sitting just inside the gate, at perhaps the widest and tallest part of the cavernous entrance, the har was as busy that morning as he'd ever seen it. Traders from the western hars had arrived only a few days before, and they'd brought more than just goods. Erdan-Har was bustling with old friends and family bearing stories of relatives, events big and small, and new opportunities. And in the Torn fashion, everything began and ended with the raising of a glass. The distillery had been working all hours to meet the demand. It was just as well mutters didn't need to be aged like some Perlish and Seeder spirits.

'What are the big ones called again?' he asked, as a huge beetle carrying rolled rugs lumbered past.

'Trumpet beetles. They make an awful—'

It was hard to say which came first, the ground-shake or the noise from the beetle.

The beetle was louder than any whicker or call from a herd, and not nearly so soft. It cut across everything – a sound to make your teeth ache, no matter how you tried covering your ears. As well as making its call, the beetle retracted its legs and hunkered down, right there in the middle of the thoroughfare.

The shake was a small one, and over almost as soon as it started. But evidently the beetle wasn't taking any chances. It had to be coaxed back to its feet with promise of a... of a...

'Is that a dead rat?' Nicholas asked.

Odette sat forwards. 'Could be. Not a trumpet beetle's favourite, but easy to come by.'

'Another ground-shake,' he said. 'More stories for the Trumpeter today. She's as jittery as the Wit lately.'

'My father used to say every story is one more success for the Trumpeter, and one in the eye for the Mute. He liked his stories, my father.' She turned to look at him. 'When did you last go to a Seat?' she said. 'Or stop at a shrine, even?'

The beetle was finally up and moving again, and its owner dusted herself off as if the shake had covered her in something. Together, they made their way out of the gate. Everyone else had similarly recovered themselves and was going about their business once more.

'Nicholas?' she said.

'Do they have Seats here?' he asked, only half in jest.

'You need to tell the Audience your stories. It's important.'

'So everyone tells me.'

'I mean it!'

'You're starting to sound like my mother.'

'No, that's just what sense sounds like,' she said. 'Now, promise me.'

'Promise you *what*?' He was struggling to keep his voice down. There was a lot of noise in the entrance cavern, but it was strange what it picked up and sent echoing around the black rock.

'That you'll visit a Seat tonight.'

She wasn't going to let this go. She could be as stubborn as the bison she grew up with. Well, he grew up with goats and they weren't too keen on being told what to do either. But they did make way for bison when they had to. *That* was what sense sounded like.

There was a shrine near the dormitory, though he couldn't remember what Audience member it was for.

'A shrine. I promise I'll stop at a shrine.'

'Tonight,' she said.

'And there's no danger of you letting me forget.'

She smiled, clearly pleased with herself. That irked him. If he'd had the wherewithal, if he'd had more than a couple of hours sleep the night before, he'd have found a way to puncture that feeling of hers. But he was too slow, the moment passed, and then she was standing up. She waved towards the milling Torn in their heavy robes.

One waved back, Lilja, and suddenly he found himself holding a small glass of mutters. A drink, before even a 'hello'. He raised the glass, lowered his mask and threw his head back. The only way to take that awful stuff, as far as Nicholas was concerned, was to bypass the mouth entirely. Get it straight into the throat and down into the stomach. It scorched everything as it went, sure, but at least it was burning without the *taste* of burning. And to think he helped produce such a terror with these people – helped in his tiny, insignificant way.

Lilja shook her head. 'Such waste.' She and Odette sipped theirs. 'Did you feel the shake?' she asked.

'A little,' Odette said. 'It startled a Trumpet beetle at the gate.'

'Should we really be leaving the har?' he asked. 'What if there's another shake?'

Lilja waved away his concern. 'Where is the Wayward daring in you, with such a question?'

It was standing there, in a cavern surrounded by Torn, with a woman who had demanded they should be married the day after they'd met. That was as daring as any Wayward he'd ever known, but he didn't think it wise to say so.

Lilja took his silence for acceptance and pocketed their empty glasses. 'You will like the Gilded Fields, Nicholas. Today will be a story to tell your children.' She grinned, as mischievous as he'd seen any Torn. Then she was off, heading towards the gate.

'Children?' he said.

Odette shrugged, but he could tell she was just as perturbed by the idea.

They followed Lilja out and away from the har.

It was another cloudy day in the Tear. The weather was always the same there, because it wasn't really weather at all. The clouds were mostly ash and other spluttered gifts from the Wit. Sometimes, above the ash were real clouds, and sometimes, those clouds held rain. It had happened perhaps twice since Nicholas had arrived. It was not good rain – everything in the Tear seemed to burn somehow. Rarer still was a full break in the clouds, when a glimpse of a blue sky felt like a gift from the Audience.

As they walked, single file and quietly concentrating – the only way to walk in the Tear – he realised he'd not been ready to miss the sky. What little he knew of the Tear growing up could be spoken in a single, short breath: there was no grass. What could be more horrifying? What could possibly raise so many questions, and give so many answers, all at once? It made the Tear an impossible place to imagine, dreadful and exciting in his young ignorance.

But that excitement didn't twist and bloat into an obsession. In his idle moments, which were rare enough themselves, he hadn't thought of the Tear. He had thought of hunting bows, how big he might grow to be and how to avoid his older cousins. When the Tear was mentioned, he had shuddered at the idea of a grass-less landscape. Perhaps he would have done more than shudder if he'd known it to be a sky-less place as well.

But here he was, walking along ledges and through dry canyons – some paths worn to a dark grey by many boots, others fresh and slickly black. Both had their dangers, in this realm without grass or sky.

Best he could tell, they were headed west, because the northern wall of the Tear wasn't getting any closer. He wondered what could be so special about these Gilded Fields. Like anyone from the Union who wasn't Torn or Rustan, he'd been suitably stunned by the searing beauty of Wit's Blood. Seeing it for the first time, as it flowed like a river into the sea at Break Deep, that would never leave him. And seeing it pool in lakes near Erdan-Har was like staring at the sun from twenty feet distant, as if someone had buried the sun beneath the rock but made a poor job of it. But as days had turned into weeks, the blood became just another part of the background. He found it difficult to imagine what would constitute a landmark in the Tear.

They stopped for a short rest at a sheltered spot where a rock wall was hollowed out and formed something of a natural roof.

Nicholas loitered just outside, preferring even a cloudy sky to yet more rock overhead. Evidently, people had rested, and much more, in that very spot before.

'A shrine?' Odette said. Her voice sounded odd after a silence long enough to interest the Mute. The question was a fair one – Torn shrines looked nothing like those on the Steppes. No ribbons, no strips of paper, nothing like that would last here. Instead, they were piles of rocks adorned with the one thing most Torn carried about their person.

Lilja knelt and added one of her drinking glasses to the hundreds that were piled up on the ground and anywhere that was flat for a few inches. 'Anyone has a story?'

As if by some unspoken agreement, both of them turned to him.

'Me? I don't—'

'You promised,' Odette said.

'But that was—'

'I want to hear your story,' Lilja said.

He sighed. Outnumbered, this wasn't an argument he could win. 'Whose shrine is it?'

Lilja frowned. 'The Keeper, of course. See the stone cage?'

Amid more glasses than you'd find in a Perlish barroom, he could make out a knee-high column of stones piled one on top of the other. Looking closer, there may have been more of them, perhaps even enough to make the shape of a cage. Nicholas didn't think it worth arguing over, not when the two women were expecting a story from him. Cages, justice, fairness. Maybe he had something to say about the last one. He took a glass from Lilja.

'My first week working in the distillery,' Nicholas said, not looking at either of them but instead talking to the shrine. 'I helped with the filters – still blood rocks and hot. There are so many fires set in the distillery, there was no escaping the heat. I worked with Detlev, if you know him.

'The filter case held only so many rocks, and they needed to be changed out regularly. And they need be checked over before they go into the case.

'Detlev would leave me for an hour or two a day. He liked to talk to a woman who worked in the market. One such time, I got it wrong. Or someone else got their job wrong, and I didn't notice. There was a blood rock that was cracked or unstable somehow. I put it right in the case, right at the bottom in fact, then piled other rocks on top. Closing up the case, I opened the valve and let the wash through. Nothing unusual, until I saw the master distiller running right at me.

'He's not a young man, but he barged me out of the way and slammed a shoulder against the valve. He was too angry to explain. "Open it," was all he said. I did, and at the bottom of the case was a layer of mud or sand or the like.

'The rock had broken down and was seeping through into the spirit safe with the mutters.

'I lost that week's pay and was moved out of the distillery – the master refused to work the same floor as me. Detlev said, compared to some accidents, it was nothing. Far as I was concerned, getting out of the distillery was a good thing; you know how I prefer the outside, even in the Tear. But Detlev felt bad. He gave me half his pay that week. I didn't ask him, he just thought that was fair.'

Nicholas put the glass – it could have been the one he'd drunk from earlier that day – on one of the smaller stacks. Broken glass crunched under his boots. It covered the ground around the shrine and caught the grey light of a day in the Tear – a sparkle that spoke of all the stories offered to the Keeper over so many years. That was partly why Nicholas didn't like to tell stories: they all felt so small, so unimportant.

'That was terrible,' Odette said, adjusting her mask.

'To me it was good,' Lilja said.

'What is it like in the distillery? What does Detlev look like? How did it feel to be in trouble with the master distiller? That's what makes a story – the details.'

'I told you I was no storyteller.'

'Odette is too harsh.' Lilja touched his arm and smiled. 'Some in the Audience prefer a mind spoken plainly. No tricks, just feelings.'

'Nonsense,' Odette said. 'Now, how far are these fields?'

'Not so far.'

They continued, single file, across a landscape that looked just like every other he'd seen in the Tear. Every so often, Lilja would turn back to them and smile. For a woman with wonky, yellowed teeth, she smiled a lot. The third or fourth time she did this, Odette also turned to him with a questioning look, her eyebrows raised. He wondered why they were both looking at him in such different ways. He almost turned round himself, thinking there might be someone or some*thing* behind him worth staring at.

'Tell me the story of you being married,' Lilja said as they walked.

'Again?' Odette said. He'd not known Odette turn down a willing audience.

'Yes, again.'

Odette told the story, much of which he didn't recognise or remember. She described the wedding of another couple – where he was a guest, she was working the cooking pits. How she'd seen him at a table full of children and took pity on him.

Though he bristled at that, he didn't interrupt. She made the wedding seem both wild and a chore. The sounds, the smell... in her telling, it came alive until it was more real than the night itself. Then came their agreement. As she told it he was a co-conspirator, rather than the slightly stunned billy goat being driven on from comfortable grazing. The argument with the parents became quite the spectacle, with heroic and villainous moments on both sides. Odette gave an impassioned argument for the rights and freedoms of young love. When challenged on said love by Nicholas's wicked mother, Odette kissed him in such a way that could leave no doubt. Her story ended with them riding south, hand-in-hand if it could be believed, as the sun set over Break Deep.

The tale over, Lilja stopped walking, so they all had to stop. She glanced between the two Wayward.

'You have not kissed,' she said, with a bluntness only a Torn could manage.

'Well...' Nicholas said.

'We've seen Break Deep, broken bread with Lowlanders, and now we're walking in the Tear. That was why—'

'Not kissed.' Lilja gave a small shrug.

She led them up a rise on a fairly well-worn track – at least, what constitutes a track in the Tear. It gave Nicholas a chance to think without either of the women staring at him – for some reason they made thinking difficult. He understood why Odette had said they'd kissed: it made for a better story. Even he knew that. But he was less sure why Lilja seemed to find it so important.

What would kissing Odette be like?

He'd kissed girls, of course he had. Well, one girl, and when he was honest with himself, he would say she did the kissing. He had stood stock still and hoped he didn't do anything wrong or dangerous, just like when faced with an angry bull. It would be the same with Odette, he was sure. She would take charge, and she would decide when they should kiss. *If* they should kiss. Should they kiss?

He bumped into her. The women had stopped at the top of the rise and were looking down at something. Odette didn't even scold him for his clumsiness.

Then he saw for himself.

Below them, and stretching for a mile or more in every direction, was a huge lake of Wit's Blood. Perhaps it was the distance, but the blood appeared so still it could have been solid ground or even a painting. If there were currents or waves or the like, they were impossible to see. And above this stillness was a latticework of stone arches and walkways. They crisscrossed the lake, reaching various heights and all connected in one way or another.

It was like no field he'd known. That certainly wasn't the word that came to him then, but words such as lake or pool didn't fit either.

'Come,' Lilja said.

'Closer?' Nicholas said, but even as he did so, he was already following the Torn.

The Gilded Fields were surrounded on every side by higher walls of rock, formed as a caldera – Lilja's word for it. But as they descended towards the stone walkways, Nicholas was surprised to find it was no hotter there. Either he was becoming accustomed to the heat of the Tear, or everywhere was just so hot that the blood below made no difference.

He hesitated at the point the solid ground – at least, what he had assumed was solid ground – gave way to a wide bridge of stone that arched upward, leaping out over the blood. The bridge was so wide he'd have had no trouble herding his goats through such a space, but somehow, he doubted the goats would have been happy about it. Stepping out over Wit's Blood was not a sensible thing to do, it was that simple – simple enough a goat would know it.

'What is wrong?' Lilja asked from the arch. 'Are you sick now, Nicholas? You look sick.'

'He's not sick. He's scared.'

'No,' Lilja said, flatly refusing to believe such a thing.

Of course he was scared. Terrified, even. Why wasn't Odette?

'Just... I'm just changing my leaves,' he said. The potho leaves in his mask were no more than half done, but he didn't mind wasting a few. Not when it gave him a chance to focus on something, to busy his hands, so he didn't keep imagining the weightlessness of falling. And what an end to that fall.

As they waited for him, Odette was asking question after question. The whys and whens and hows of such a place. Lilja did her best to keep up. Until Odette asked why it was called the Gilded Fields.

'Ah, that you will see,' Lilja said. 'That is why we are here. But come, we must hurry.'

'Did you hear that, Nicholas? We have to hurry.'

'Unbelievable,' he muttered. He kept to the middle of the walkways, where they were at their widest, and never so much as looked at an edge let alone over it. He couldn't look at the others either, when they rushed from one edge to the other and pointed down at the blood. He stared straight ahead so as to be sure of where he'd be going next. One tentative step at a time.

Lilja took them to the centre of the field, crossing from one arch to another. Nicholas did not like the narrower walkways, or the steeper ones, or the smoother ones, or the... well, there were many he did not like. Eventually, Lilja turned them round to look back the way they'd come. Nicholas couldn't believe they hadn't gone further – it felt as if they'd been on the field for hours. Through breaks in the cloud, they could see the sun was a good way lower in the sky. And as it descended more still, something happened.

A gold stream washed over the tops of the walkways.

'The blood!' Nicholas said. 'It's changing—'

'Is okay, is just light,' Lilja said.

'But...'

'Crystals, up there in rocks and down here under feet.'

With every passing moment, the rock of the walkways turned from the black of the Tear to a gold only the Keeper would believe.

'This is amazing,' Odette said. 'Can you imagine a story that had such a thing?'

'Is no story, is here.'

They didn't have to wait long until the golden light washed over them and on towards the far shore of the lake. Odette lifted her boot, delighted to find gold underneath. She skipped away, trying to keep up with the line where dull turned to shine.

'Careful!' Nicholas called after her.

Suddenly, Lilja was very close to him. 'This special place,' she whispered into his ear.

He jerked away, but she was there again.

'I bring you here, to special place. How will you say thank you?'

Nicholas coughed. 'Thank you?' he said.

She pursed her lips. 'No,' she said. She lifted his mask and kissed him.

It was tacky, and it was dry at the same time. As before, he stood statue-still and waited for it to be over, waited for this bull to realise he was no threat, he wasn't going to run, and there was no chase here. Nothing to get excited about.

She drew away and pulled his mask back down.

'What—'

'What are you *doing*?' Odette said, to the both of them. Maybe she'd come back to rescue him.

'I see why you no kiss him yet,' Lilja said, grimacing.

'Lilja!'

'Shame, he's *my* husband now. Old Torn tradition – even older than your fool Wayward one. Keeper's kiss.'

She must have been joking, but with the Torn, it was hard to say. They both stared at her, Nicholas's mouth wide open behind his mask. He had an idea Odette's would be the same.

Lilja just laughed and walked along the golden archways.

'Odette, I didn't... It was... She...'

'Later,' she said, her voice the coldest thing that far south. 'We'll talk later.'

True to her word, they spoke little on the way back to Erdan-Har. Lilja made a number of jests, calling Nicholas 'husband', apparently trying to lighten the mood. But it only made matters worse.

Nothing in the months he and Odette had been travelling, making one long story for the Partner, had suggested she wanted to kiss him, or cared who he kissed. Or cared who kissed *him*. In fact, there'd been absolutely no mention of kissing the whole time he'd known her. It wasn't part of their arrangement. But now, even he could tell she was angry.

Such thoughts were swirling around in his head when the ground-shake came.

It was a strong one, much stronger than what they'd felt in the entrance to Erdan-Har – and even that had been enough to startle a trumpet beetle. One after the other, they fell to their knees, as if to make themselves smaller as the world around them shook. The air was suddenly full of dust and ash, far worse than even the bad days in the Tear. He could only just make out Odette and Lilja, a few feet away.

It is hard to describe a strong ground-shake to someone who hasn't felt one for themselves, especially in a place like the Tear. Everything, everywhere you look, is ground and rock of some kind. Which means it all shakes.

'Nicholas!' Odette was there, her head close to his, doing her best to cover herself against the pelting of stones and cinders. Somehow, she'd crawled to him to check he was all right. She always was the strong one.

There was nothing to say, nothing to do other than hope. There was no shelter nearby – and what shelter could be trusted when the very ground turns against you?

And then, just as suddenly as it came, it went. The ground stilled. The only shaking was his arms and his legs and every other part of him that had been tensed the whole time. Without realising, he'd been gripping one of Odette's hands – so tight it hurt, but he didn't let go, not at first. The air hadn't cleared and was a close, thick cloud. Even through the masks, it was hard to breathe. Lilja wasn't faring much better – he could hear her coughing, even though he couldn't see her.

'Nicholas, my hand,' Odette whispered, as if worried a loud noise might set off the shake again.

'Sorry.' He let go, and they both rose to kneeling. He wasn't ready to try standing just yet.

Her face was covered in dust and grime, except for tear tracks. He hadn't heard her crying. He wondered if he'd wept too, if his face looked the same. She was shivering with shock.

'Nicholas.' She swallowed hard. 'We shouldn't be here. What are we—'

He leaned forwards, pulled both their masks down, and kissed her. Amid all the dirt and mess, he found her lips, and for once, he was the one doing the kissing. He touched her cheek and felt her trembling. And then she was kissing him back. The whole thing was very different with *two* properly involved. He didn't care that she tasted like ash. Months may have passed since they met, but this felt right. Now. Here. After what they'd been through together.

He took a breath, their foreheads close to touching, her eyes eclipsing everything else.

'We're here to find stories,' he said. 'Remember?'

'I remember.'

Lilja coughed, waving an ineffectual hand in front of her face as she stumbled towards them. 'Keeper's kiss,' she said. It was supposed to be a joke, but nobody laughed.

The three of them managed to help one another up and along the path towards the har. The going was slow and treacherous, and more than once, one of them would have tripped if it weren't for the support of the others. It was hard to see much beyond their own feet, as if they'd gone from sunset to deepest night in a matter of moments. Lilja was doing the best she could to cover her mouth, and Nicholas was more grateful than ever for his mask.

When he wasn't struggling to stay on his feet, he was very much aware of Odette beside him. The press of her. The heat of her, even fiercer than the heat of the Tear. And the kiss. The kiss...

'Nicholas, look,' Odette said. She was pointing ahead, where the air was starting to clear. There were lights in the distance. He had to squint against the ash and the dust to be sure, but then he saw the har. Solid rock gates, ledges and balconies, spires – so much black rock in a landscape that had nothing else. And yet it could not be a more different, or more welcome, sight.

Without a word, and without risking too much with each step, they picked up their shuffling pace. Home – of a sorts – was not far now. Just to be inside, safe under a roof and breathing air as clear as the Tear could offer. It sparked a kind of hope.

That was, until they heard the first cry.

It was so clear and so close that Nicholas thought Odette or Lilja had stepped on something, or twisted their ankle. But a quick glance told him that wasn't the case. That, and the weight of agony in the wail. There is a cadence to pain, if you ever really stop to listen to it. And growing up on the Steppes, around so many animals, Nicholas had learnt the difference between a bruising, a breaking, and a pain that was worth mentioning to the Widow. The cry they'd heard was the last kind, and it was followed by more.

Somehow, they'd taken a winding path back from the fields that put Er-jun mine between them and the har. The thought occurred to Nicholas to skirt the mine, give it a wide berth and do his best to close his ears to the screams. A hard-hearted path, yes, but would anyone have blamed them? Would anyone, except for they themselves, have known? But instead, together, they stumbled on towards the mine.

They came to the dead first.

Rows of bodies, laid out neat and still as only the dead can be. But as they drew closer, those bodies told stories that were anything but neat. Limbs ended in messy stumps, or missing entirely. Clothes little more than shreds and patches among the blood and bone. More than a few skulls had been crushed or made almost unrecognisable. Men and women alike, lifeless and broken.

'Ransu,' Nicholas said, stopping at one of the bodies.

'You knew—?'

'Basti. Bengt. Peska.' He pointed to each in turn. There were more, many more, who he knew – at least by their name, at least to look at, even as they were now. They'd all wanted to talk to him once, the Wayward boy working their mine with them. Not unheard of, but not so common either. And now they were dead. As the air was beginning to clear, the ash and dirt thrown up by the ground-shake was settling once more. It was starting to coat the mine's dead in a layer of ash, as if gently burying them one flake at a time.

Lilja had left them. She was wandering between the rows, slow, careful, looking at each person in turn. Then, without warning, she dropped to her knees. Her shoulders shuddered as she wept. They gave her a moment alone.

Nicholas looked about the outskirts of the mine. The cries they had heard before were coming from those pulled alive from the rubble that now covered the mine's entrance. Crews of people were doing their best to clear the rocks but such a thing could only be dangerous. Those they found among the rocks were either put on makeshift stretchers and carried to the har or brought here, to the rows of the dead.

'We have to help,' he said.

Odette took his hand. 'Lilja first.'

Their friend was cradling the misshapen head of a man in her lap. She was smoothing the skin of his cheek down, down, so as to cover his back teeth. They waited, but she didn't notice them. Eventually, Odette touched her shoulder, and she gave a start.

She looked up at them, her eyes red, and said, 'My uncle.'

'I'm so sorry,' Odette said.

'He and my mother argued. Bitter, bitter arguing because of borrowed coins. Long time I have not spoken to him. I took her side. I took her side.' She shook her head and started to weep again. It was clear she wanted to be alone with her grief.

Nicholas and Odette left the dead to help the living. They crossed the rocky open ground, a distance of respect as much as a practicality, and approached an older woman Nicholas didn't recognise. She was organising those who carried the stretchers, all of whom looked exhausted.

'We want to help,' Nicholas said.

She took one look at them, then waved to where a man lay groaning.

They stood beside the stretcher, and for a moment, all they could do was stare. The man's eyes were closed, but his face was wracked with pain, from what they could see through the blood and the grime. But what they really couldn't ignore, couldn't look away from, couldn't properly understand, was that the man had no feet.

'Odette,' Nicholas said softly. 'Odette, look at me.'

He had to say it twice more before she did.

'We're going to carry him back to the har.'

'But, he has no—'

'We're going to carry him. You and me. We both know the way, don't we?'

She gave a small nod.

'You're going to go first, at the front, nice and slow,' he said. He moved to the other end, where the man's feet should have been. He'd spare her from being close to those stumps, and from the temptation of looking round. And he'd spare her from the fact he knew this man's name too.

When they picked up the stretcher, it felt unsettlingly light. He told himself it was because of all the days he'd wheeled lava rock from the mine. The grim irony that the miners now carried one another along the very same path was not lost on him.

As they walked the stretcher towards the har, the last of the ash thrown up by the shake was falling like the snows of late winter. He would see those snows on the Steppes again, and when he did, he'd appreciate them all the more for where he'd been and the stories they brought back. A story that began with a gift from the Keeper, was thrown into turmoil by the Trumpeter, and ended – as so many do – with words for the Widow.

* * *

'I don't care how safe they say it is, I'm not getting metal hands.'

Odette pushed him back onto the chair. 'Well, sit still then. You need the ointment.'

'But it stings!'

'I'll get the bonesmith, shall I?'

He shuddered. He had tried to keep his prejudices to himself since they left the Steppes. He'd known enough of the Union to know the Torn spoke funny and none of them had any hair, and he didn't have a problem with that. But the Rustans with their modifications were something else entirely. He couldn't walk down one of their winding streets without staring at someone who had metal where there should have been skin. And that was just the adults. He'd heard stories about Rustan children, but never believed they could be true...

He held out his hands and winced as she rubbed the foul-smelling mixture onto his palms. Even with the heavy leather gloves he'd been given, working the ropeboxes was tearing up his skin. He was starting to think no matter where you worked in the Union you wore a pair of gloves. At least, if you were Wayward. Growing up, his hands were tough enough – calloused by years of herding from the saddle. And that had helped some, but there was no accounting for the salt of Break Deep or the constant burn of winches. Odette was right in some ways: the best thing for it was to have a bonesmith replace his palms with metal plates. And maybe a finger or two while they were there, for better gripping. That was how most of the men and women working the cone's ropeboxes managed. But he was only there for one season. Surely, there wasn't any need for something so extreme?

'Ow!' he said, trying to pull back. But Odette had him now.

'Stop squirming.'

'You're enjoying this,' he said. 'Seeing me suffer.'

'Rubbing ointment onto blistered hands... Best part of my day.'

Through gritted teeth, he said, 'So tell me about your day. Tell me a story.'

'Hold still,' she said.

'Not until you tell me a story. Come on, you want to be a storyteller. Here's your audience.'

'Here's my audience,' she said. Somehow, she made those words sound mournful. 'Fine. Work today was the same as the day before, and the day before, and every other day. I move numbers from one column of parchment to another. Sometimes the numbers go up, sometimes they go down. A *really* exciting day is when I get to rule a line through a name. That means someone has either died or paid off their debt. I guess which based purely on their name and the size of the debt.

'But I have to guess quickly, because if Vana notices I've stopped writing for longer than it takes to scratch my nose, she bangs her desk with a cosh she's kept from her collecting days. She usually barks a word or two as well, but I can't understand anything through her metal teeth. Vana only gives those working the ledgers one candle each, so I'm working in near-darkness most of the day. Why do so many people in the Union hide away from daylight? I will never take the open skies of the Steppes for granted again.

'All of that is to say, when my working day is done, I hurry along to one of the high ledges of the cone. I try to catch the last of the sun on my skin and do my best not to look down at the swirling clouds below. I breathe deep what passes for the cleanest air in the Tear. And then I wait until the stars spread across the sky.'

'No wonder you're back so late,' Nicholas muttered.

Odette ignored him, fully in the telling now. 'On each of the ledges I go to there's a shrine to one of the Audience. The Inker is popular with the east-facing ledges, for obvious reasons. But there are shrines to the Hawker, Devotee, Student and many others besides. Since we came to the Rusting Mountains, since the shake... well, since I've spent my evenings on those ledges, I haven't told a single story to a shrine.

'Don't look at me like that. I know that's the kind of thing I berate you about. It's bad, I know. But worse, it scares me. I've always told stories at shrines. Always. Always, except for one time.

'Do you know the Mernberry Rings, in the far north of the

Steppes? Do they herd goats that far? No? Well, my family spend the late weeks of summer there grazing the bison. In truth, they will have only just left the hills, with the weather having turned colder. Do you remember what it's like to feel the cold? Anyway, one of the many shrines at the rings is for the Critic. My family makes sure we tell a story at every shrine before we leave, but some years we have to hurry because of weather or problems with the herd.

'On one such year, we'd had no luck with saddles. My mother took me to one side and told me to visit every shrine around the rings and quickly tell a story while the rest of the family broke camp. Nothing fancy, she said, just enough to appease the Audience. No election sagas. I did my best to keep each story short, but some stories take on a life of their own. And it's hard when facing a shrine – it's not like a Seat, which is so big as to make you feel like you might slip away unnoticed, just one among many under the Audience. No, a shrine is just you and the member, as close as you are to me now.

'The last shrine I came to was that of the Critic. My father was bellowing over the hill, impatient to be away. The bison echoed his calls, and I could see my mother waving to me. Everyone was waiting. But so was the Critic. His stone carving was severe. A long, sharp nose and a flat mouth that would never turn up into a smile, not for me. People had left the Critic various offerings, but the carving was unmoved. Somehow, even though I was just a young girl, I had the sense that few stopped to tell him their stories for fear of critique. I started to feel the same fear. A leaden, weighty thing in my legs that started behind my knees and rose until my whole body slumped under it.

'But I wanted to tell the Critic a story. And not just because my mother would take a switch to those heavy legs of mine if

454

I didn't. I wanted to tell him a great story, the *greatest* story. I wanted to make his long, dour face laugh, cry, sing and for all the Audience to sit up and take notice. I would be a storyteller for the ages. Election-winning.

'He just stared at me, and for the first time in my young life, I could not think of a story. Nothing, not even something short about one of my annoying sisters or a time my father broke wind which would rival the waft of a bison. There was a gap, a blankness, like a cloudy, moonless night's sky, where there had always been stories. And that *really* frightened me.

'I haven't felt anything like that since. Or, more truthfully, I hadn't until we left the Torn har. Now, I can't even look at the shrines on those ledges. There's nothing there anymore, Nicholas. There's... I just stare at the sky and then come back here, to this room, to you.'

'But you just told me a story,' he said.

She let go of his hands. 'I knew you wouldn't understand.'

Their room was small, barely bigger than their tents, but at least they didn't have to share with anyone else. There was a small window out onto the street, two pallets up against the walls and the corridor had a communal privy. The Rusting Mountains was not a place of wide open spaces, inside or out. The streets were narrow and spiralled tightly about themselves. There were no open markets or caverns like the Torn fashioned in their hars. Everything was so very close, and Nicholas constantly felt as if he was about to bump into something, or someone. The Rustans favoured small, private places compared to the dorms and camps that he was used to. And of course, you couldn't pitch a tent anywhere.

Apparently, he and Odette had enjoyed the Latecomer's luck in finding work and a room at all. In travelling west from Erdanhar, they had come to the cone first. They had briefly considered pressing on, deeper into the Rusting Mountains, but were too tired. Nicholas had wondered if the mountains were really so different from one another. But the story they found at the cone soon drove this ignorance from him.

The streets of the cone teemed with Rustans at all hours, and more were winched up from the Tear every day. They all looked as surprised as anyone to find themselves there. Those Nicholas worked with said it was the ground-shakes. Had he felt them? They had badly hit the spire and the ridge, so bad, people were abandoning their homes. It made life on the cone hard, but what could they do? What if the shakes had ruined the cone? The fact that could still happen went unsaid, but it haunted the eyes of the men and women who winched the ropeboxes. Once he knew what it looked like, he saw the very same in the faces of every Rustan he met. Or worse.

The next morning, when he and Odette walked to work, they had to wait in a queue for a vertical ropebox. Some days were better than others, but normally when they had to wait, Odette made a joke about lazy Wayward winchers. Every time they shuffled forwards he expected her to say something, but she was silent. She was staring at a shrine.

At first, Nicholas hadn't recognised what it was – Rustans had so many confusing customs. He thought it was a tailor or the like showing off their wares. The shrine was a trellis attached to the wall of a building, but only as high as the first floor. Tied to this trellis were hundreds of brightly coloured scraps of cloth. No, looking closer, he realised it was silk. Scraps of silk for the Whisperer. Expensive offerings, but what could be more expensive than the truth?

'There's more silk on that wall than in the whole of the Steppes,' he said, but Odette wasn't listening. She was staring at a woman sitting at the foot of the shrine. The woman's head drooped forwards, lolling as if drunk, and she was speaking but too quiet to hear.

'We should ask if she's all right,' Nicholas said.

Odette gave a start. 'What? No.'

'But she's—'

'We'll lose our place,' Odette said. 'We'll be late for work.'

He frowned. She didn't normally care about being late. In fact, sometimes he wondered if she saw it as a challenge: how late could she be without being told to leave? He started towards the shrine of silk.

'Nicholas, stop,' she hissed.

He knelt by the woman, not too close as to startle her, and asked, 'Are you all right there?'

She raised her head slowly and blinked many times, as if struggling to see him. But she didn't smell of spirits; nothing Seeder- or Torn-made that people of the south typically drowned themselves in. If she was drunk, it was on something else.

'Nicholas!' Odette said from the line. The rest of those waiting for the ropebox were studiously ignoring him and the woman at the shrine. Evidently her suffering was her own business, and besides, on the cone there was more than enough suffering to go round.

The woman was Rustan, that much was clear from the metal on her arm and the way she clunked and clanked when she breathed. She was older than him, but by how much was hard to say. Her hair was loose to her shoulders and greasy. In her lap, she was holding a scrap of dirty silk. She held it up, as if to show him.

'I think you're supposed to tie that on, when you tell your story,' he said.

'I know,' she said. Her voice was deeper than he'd been expecting, and hoarse with use. 'But I can't stop.'

'Stop what?' Odette asked, finally joining them.

'Telling her story. Every time, I tell it wrong. So I start again.'

'Whose story?' Nicholas said.

'My sister. She's gone, and this is all I have.' She rubbed the silk between her fingers. If she kept doing so, she wouldn't have even that for much longer, but Nicholas couldn't say as much. 'I reached for her, when the shake came. I reached for her, and this was all I got.'

The woman proceeded to tell her sister's story from the beginning. The *very* beginning, with her sister's birth in their home on the spire.

Odette stood, and when he didn't join her, she all but dragged him away. 'What's wrong with you?' she said. They re-joined the queue for the ropebox, though much further back this time.

'I was about to ask you the same,' he said. 'That woman had a story to share.'

'And we don't have the time. You want to hear her story, come back later – doesn't look like she'll be going anywhere.'

He glanced back to the shrine. The woman was still telling her story, and still handling the scrap of silk. 'Not so long ago you would've memorised her every word.'

'Not so long ago? Is that how it *really* feels to you?'

They shuffled forwards in the queue, until they were beyond the shrine and the Rustan woman.

He didn't understand what Odette meant, not at first. It was only their third season away from the Steppes. He could still count the weeks – let alone the months – without too much trouble. They'd been places, met people, worked in all kinds of jobs, seen and heard things that couldn't be forgotten – all experiences they'd never have had at home. Perhaps that was what Odette was talking about; maybe she was different from the woman he'd ridden south with, and he'd just not noticed. As the ropebox carried them up to the next street, he tried to remember what she was like with the Torn – if she'd been as keen as the Musician to find their stories and memorise them. He could recall her being like that in the early days and weeks in the har. But after that, it was harder.

He was still chewing that over when they arrived at his winching station. He wasn't all that late; another wincher was only a few paces ahead. She held the metal door for him.

'Nicholas,' Odette said.

He turned back to her.

'I'm... Take care of your hands today.'

It was clear, even to him, that she wanted to say more, to tell him something else. But instead, she gave a small smile and left.

He was distracted all day. He kept thinking about Odette and the idea she had changed so much without him even noticing. His winching partner had to shout at him more than once to take his weight. Winching wasn't complicated, but it did require timing as well as brute strength.

The centre of the problem, he decided, was just how little he'd known Odette in the first place. It had all happened so fast – one starlit night sharing a flagon of ale and then they were off to see the Union. He really knew nothing about her. She'd only made one thing clear: she wanted to find her stories out here in the realms. What he'd been looking for wasn't so clear, at least not to him. Thinking about it now, he realised he just wanted something different. A change. To know there was more to his story than herding his father's goats. Did Odette see that in him? Is that why she chose him, and not another unmarried Wayward man?

'Nicholas!'

'Sorry,' he said, focusing back on his work. But it didn't last. His attention wandered all day as he chased these thoughts up and down, as regular as any ropebox. But in all that mess of thoughts and memories, he kept coming back to one new idea, one thing that hadn't occurred to him until then:

Maybe he hadn't noticed Odette changing because he was changing too.

When his shift was finally over, he had decided on a course of action. It was a relief, in many ways, to have made a decision; he wasn't used to looking inwards with such intensity. It was unsettling. And when his winching partner said they were lucky they'd had no accidents that day, he agreed.

Leaving the winching station, he didn't turn for home. Instead he wandered the streets looking for a barroom. He didn't have to wander far.

The barroom was full of men and women making their various offerings to the Drunkard. Nicholas had to wait a good while to even reach the bar, and then for the barman's attention. It took three attempts to make it clear he wanted the whole flagon, and that he'd not be drinking it there and then. If Nicholas hadn't so evidently been a Wayward, the barman likely would have simply refused. Instead, the barman consulted a small woman with the air of someone in charge about her, and then named an exorbitant price. Nicholas paid it.

Then he went looking for Odette.

The higher he was on the cone, the fewer people he saw. He took ropeboxes when he could, but they stopped well before the top. The highest streets were narrow as a goat trail and had few houses or buildings of any kind. They felt more like the corridors deep within the Torn hars than the bustling Rusting Mountains. But the top of the cone *was* full of the viewing ledges that Odette had talked about. He found shrine after shrine, but they were all empty. He was beginning to understand why she sought out such places. They had a quiet, a privacy, that he'd forgotten was even possible over the last few weeks.

As he wound round and round the cone, every so often he saw the sun sinking towards the horizon. He lingered at those ledges a little longer, and when they had shrines for the Inker, he muttered about the changing colours or the way the light caught the wispy clouds.

But when he found Odette, she wasn't watching the sunset. Instead, she was sitting on a stone bench on a ledge that faced north. There was a small carving of the Devotee in the opposite corner, a blindfold covering her eyes, and about her feet was a scattering of dried flowers and fruit pips.

'I shouldn't have told you,' Odette said when she saw him.

He stopped, mid-stride. 'I'll go if you want.'

'No. You're here now. And you brought ale.'

'I did.' He put the flagon on the bench then gazed out from the highest place he'd ever been. But wait, was that right? The clifftops far in the distance, where the Tear stopped and the Lowlands began, wasn't that just the level ground he'd walked on his whole life? Weren't even the lowest hills on the Steppes higher than this mountain? Knowing that must be the case didn't stop him feeling giddy as he looked down at the clouds swirling between the mountains, obscuring the rivers of Wit's Blood and cold rock below.

'Hard to believe, isn't it?' Odette said. 'Hard to really understand.'

'As a boy, I never believed the stories. I just couldn't imagine a place like this.'

'It's changing.'

'What?'

'Can you *imagine* that?' she said. 'Easier to *remember*, maybe. The Tear isn't supposed to reach Break Deep. And it's supposed to end a mile short of the cliffs you see out there. A mile more of the Tear, a mile less of the Lowlands. You see, the Rustans remember. Especially those from the spire.'

'The ground-shakes.'

'They call them earthquakes, and I guess they should know.'

'A mile more of the Tear. But that means...'

She waited for him to say it.

'And a mile less of the Lowlands, that means it's growing. And fast.'

'It means a lot more than that. It means more of what we saw at that Torn mine.'

That he *didn't* want to remember. He turned to her. 'You're missing the sunset.'

'Have you noticed they're always the same in the mountains? Beautiful, but every day the same.'

He sat down, the flagon between them. 'I did wonder why nobody else was here,' he said. He rubbed idly at the callouses that covered his hands. 'It's not what you wanted, is it?'

'The sunset is the Inker's business, I don't—'

'I didn't mean the sunset.'

'Oh.' She took a swig from the flagon and then offered it to him.

The ale was flat, weak, and a delight. After the burning spirit of the Torn and the fruity stuff the Lowlanders drank, he hadn't realised how much he missed ale.

'I didn't know what I wanted,' she said, 'not really.'

'What do you want now?' he said.

'I want to go back to not knowing. I want to go back to when anything and everything seemed possible. All I had to do was go out and find them.'

'Your stories.'

'He had no feet, Nicholas.'

'I know.'

'I still hear the screams. And the moans. And the sound of falling rock.'

'Odette, you should—'

'The rows of the dead. I thought it couldn't be any worse than that. But what we saw at the har...'

'Odette, look at me.' He took her hand in his. She had smudges of charcoal on her fingers – just like when they'd first met, and she was working the cooking fires at the wedding. 'I saw two Wayward helping a child find his father. I saw two Wayward hearing the last story of a woman, to pass on to her family. I saw two Wayward carry water to so many thirsty mouths. That's what I saw at the har.'

'Do you know what makes it worse?' she said, as if she hadn't heard him. 'Every time I think back to that day the memories are all jumbled up. I remember when we... when you kissed me. And then I remember everything else.'

'I've thought about that too. Keeper's kiss, Lilja said.'

'She said it twice.'

'But only one time meant something,' he said. 'Only with you. Can I kiss you again?'

'You didn't ask the first time,' she said flatly.

'No. I'm sorry for that.'

'And what then? Would it be more than just a sunset in the Rusting Mountains?' she said. She was looking at him intently, their faces inching closer. 'Is that what you want?'

'I don't know. But it could be.'

'It could be,' she said.

He leaned forwards, closed his eyes and hoped he was doing the right thing. Everything stopped. He held his breath, his heartbeat seemed to cease and his mind was empty. In that moment, he didn't feel like he was there, not on the mountain, not anywhere.

Until he felt her lips on his. Gentle, then more insistent. She had her hands in his hair, and she pulled him closer. Then she was pulling at his shirt.

He lifted his arms, but when the cloth was clear, he suddenly felt conscious of his body, of his bruises. Some were old and faded, as old as their days with the Torn. But there were fresh bruises too. He tried to cover the worst of them, but she stopped him. She touched his bruises. Then she stood and unlaced the back of her dress. Standing naked in front of him, she had her own bruises.

'I don't know... I've never...' he said.

'It's all right.'

She eased him back onto the stone bench. Stradling him, the curves of her body catching the last of the light, she brought them together. She led, he followed, and he'd never felt anything like it.

He woke cold against the stone. The ledge was dark, though there were the pinpricks of stars in the night sky. He heard, as much as saw, Odette dressing.

'You're going?' he said.

'We've made a mistake,' she said. 'We shouldn't have—I didn't come here for this.'

No one went to a shrine for *that* – except maybe the Neighbour's – but that wasn't what she meant.

'Odette, it was just—'

'Just what?'

'What felt right,' he said, with no other words to make himself clear.

'I didn't leave the Steppes looking for a husband.'

He stood, but she took a step away. 'No,' he said, 'you left *with* a husband.'

'That's the one story I brought with me. I came to the Union to find others.'

'What are you saying?'

'I'm sorry, Nicholas, I really am. Please, try to remember that in the days to come.'

When she was gone, he took out his pipe and played every sombre tune he knew. Then he played them all again as the sun slowly rose over the Tear.

★ ★ ★

Winter in Bordair was no winter at all. At least, not as far as Nicholas was concerned. Winter was a thing of frost crunching underfoot, of seeing your own breath and the clouds made by others, and snow in high places. But the slopes surrounding Bordair were the same bare black rock as the rest of the Tear.

It was starting to feel as if the whole Union was made up of that rock. Grass, rivers, forests – these were just stories to him now.

Nicholas stared out at the rain from the low shelter of the boardwalk bar. Rain he knew from the Steppes, but not like this. At home, the rains quickly came and went, the Painter and the Bore in a constant tussle. But in Bordair, the Bore couldn't even raise a sigh, so the rain remained like an unwelcome guest, and sheets of it fell heavy and straight down. In that way, it was predictable and easy to take shelter from, which made Nicholas's predicament all the more galling.

He had nowhere to sleep at night.

He raised his now empty glass to the woman working the bar.

'Pennies first,' she said, not even trying to hide her suspicion. He slapped them down on the wet wood and waited for his ale. At least the Caskers served it.

All his hard work since leaving the Steppes meant he had pennies for food and drink, but Bordair was full. Bordair was *full.* Every boarding house and dormitory had closed its doors, with painted signs in the windows that told a two-word story: no beds. The whorehouses were still open, but men and women spilled out of their doors and onto the street like a river that'd burst its banks. He'd tried once or twice to fight that tide, but he couldn't stand the easy caresses of the whores, the knowing looks or the leering painted faces. He had walked the streets and the boardwalks looking for sanctuary, but only found those similarly lost and alone.

If rooms were impossible to find in Bordair, looking for work was worse. No one would take a Wayward on a barge when the whole city overflowed with Casker deckhands. Many barges wintered in Bordair, waiting for the spring and the Lowlander crops that needed taking up the rivers. Those few still trading had their pick of crews. Any job that took a strong back and willing hands had Caskers lining up for it.

So, Nicholas spent his days playing his herder's pipe with a hat at his feet and his nights moving from the shelter of one balcony to another. His cloak kept him as dry as he could hope, and the winter nights in Bordair were not so cold. When he played his pipe of an afternoon, he could expect a couple of pennies from the milling crowds as they passed by. Though he may not have been desperate for the coin, he was desperate for the company and the way to pass the time. More often than not it was drunken bargemen with shouted requests for songs he didn't know. He'd learnt to assuage their anger by shouting back, 'Happy or sad?' Their need was a simple one, really, and for all their bluster, they were generous once appeased. He'd seen more than one grown man cry as he played.

He always watched the crowds for any sign of Odette.

Taking a swig of his ale, he wiped his mouth and whistled a soft tune – he'd been doing that more and more lately, a result of playing so much. Out across the water, a barge was coming in to dock. It sat low and heavy in the stillness, as if hunkering against the rain. With an idle curiosity, he watched its slow approach and then the mute comings and goings as it was unloaded.

When he and Odette parted, they had stood high on the slopes overlooking Bordair. They'd agreed to meet on the first day of spring, right at the waterside, and they would find passage upriver all the way to Perlanse. That was when the great Casker city had held some kind of hope for both of them; many hopes in fact, though he couldn't help wondering if his were so different. They hadn't spoken of the night on the Devotee's ledge, but that it wouldn't happen again was clear. That he could accept.

So much harder was how she avoided his touch, how she drew away when he was near, how cold she had become. They spoke only when necessary. He wanted to say more, to ask her what he needed to do to go back to the way they were, and he started to ask more than once, but the words stuck in his throat and he all but gagged on the taste of doubt. Even if he could find the right questions, he wasn't sure he wanted the answers. Seeing her walk away down the steep Bordair street brought a kind of lifting, a freeing he felt in his chest. But the relief was fleeting. The weight was soon replaced by a longing to see her again.

'You got more pennies in one of those pockets of yours?' the barwoman asked.

'Not today,' he lied. He drained the glass, every last drop; beer was the cleanest way to slake a thirst in Bordair. He pulled his cloak tight, raised his hood and headed out into the pelting rain.

The rain brought the smell of rotting eggs to the boardwalks, but at least it didn't burn or sting. He'd only once felt how the Painter hated the Tear, when they were at Erdan-har. He'd stood like an idiot, hand out, unbelieving of what he was feeling. The scars had since faded. Though it didn't burn here, the rain did little to help what really plagued Bordair. The reason the parts of city near the water were full to bursting.

He pressed through the throng on the boardwalk, headed towards the quieter streets away from the water. The higher he went, the fewer people he saw, until eventually, he was largely alone. That's when he started coughing. The air on the slopes of Bordair was bad – it had always been bad, the locals said, but this was something else. Now it was toxic. Worse than the floor of the Tear where a mask lined with leaves had been enough. No mask could help here. People abandoned their homes, taking what they could carry lower and lower into the city. Nicholas couldn't sleep in those empty homes for the same reason. Instead, he and others like him had developed a sense of just how much bad air he could take. It was like a shifting line that couldn't be seen, but on one side you coughed a few times in the night, and on the other you woke coughing blood. On one side it smelt of rotting eggs, on the other rotting corpses. One side your nose itched, on the other your eyes ran and wouldn't stop.

'Wave's high tonight,' a man said now, leaning out from an alleyway. That's how people like Nicholas talked of the line – like it was a wave that washed onto the shores of Bordair. 'You looking for a place?' the man asked.

Nicholas hesitated. He didn't know this man. That Nicholas didn't have anything worth stealing was a given. But people did worse than steal in Bordair. He glanced to the alley beyond but only saw shadows.

Then two skinny children appeared, as if from thin air, and stood in front of the man.

'Look, Father, that's the pipe-playing man,' the little girl said. Her cheeks were hollow and her skin had a yellowish hue.

'What's that?'

'Do you have your pipe?' the girl asked.

Nicholas reached into one of his many pockets for the instrument. The girl clapped her hands and smiled, though it wasn't a pretty smile.

'He plays for drunks down by the water,' she said to her father. He nodded, seemingly unsurprised by his daughter's sharp eye.

'There's plenty of beds through here,' the man told Nicholas. 'You'd be welcome.'

He was wary. But he was also tired of nights spent alone. He hadn't said more than five words to another person in weeks.

'Will you play for us?' the girl asked.

'I will,' he said. He crossed the street and thanked the man, who could've just let a stranger walk on by.

The man introduced himself as Lukas, then his daughter Meena and son Peter.

'You'll have to forgive Peter, he doesn't say so much. Not since... well, not since we left our home.' Lukas emptied a slop bucket into the gutter of the street.

The four of them walked deeper into the alleyway, and the night closed in around them. The children hurried ahead, keen to be the bearers of news of company. The alley turned and turned again, which created a kind of separation from the rest of the city. A way to almost forget what was happening out there. As the alley came to an end, there was a little courtyard with doors opening onto it. A fire was burning in a low dug pit, with a pot bubbling above, and a makeshift shelter to keep off the rain.

'Mother, look, it's the pipe player. The one who plays for the dr—'

'That's enough, Meena,' Lukas said gently.

The woman at the pot, Georgia, looked up, her expression blank but just as tired as anyone in Bordair. It was something they all shared. Nicholas wondered if his own exhaustion would be enough to put the woman at ease.

An older couple came out from one of the shacks and made straight for the pot.

'My mother and father,' Lukas said. 'We come here when the wave is high. So far, we haven't had any trouble. We even made a small shrine to the Stowaway.'

'I won't tell anyone,' Nicholas said.

'Somehow I know you won't.' He dropped the slop bucket a

distance away from the fire and gestured to one of the shacks. 'Make yourself comfortable, and then join us.'

The shack had a bed-frame with no mattress, and a desk with no chair. That was it. But it was dry, and the smell was marginally better inside than out. Nicholas had definitely slept in worse. He pulled the door closed behind him and joined the family at the fire.

'Look, Martha, a Wayward boy!' the old man rasped, his eyes large. 'You're about as far from home as far can be.'

'Don't stare, Rupert.'

'I'm not *staring*, I'm just looking at the boy.'

'Hello,' Nicholas said. 'Thank you for sharing your fire.'

'Would you listen to that accent? Straight from the Steppes, are you?' Rupert said. The rest of the family appeared embarrassed by the old man, but Nicholas didn't mind.

'No, I've been travelling since spring.' He held his hands out to the fire.

'Alone?'

'No, my w— Yes, alone since coming to Bordair.'

The family exchanged looks but didn't press him any further.

'You picked a rotten time to be here,' Martha said. 'That damn Wit and his sputtering mountains.'

'Volcanoes, dear.'

'Mountains, volcanoes, whatever you call them, the Wit can keep 'em all. Poisoning our air.'

'Tell the Trumpeter,' Lukas said, with a note of resignation. This was evidently an old argument. 'It's the earthquakes that are the cause of it.'

'They're causing the Tear to grow too,' Nicholas said. 'I saw it myself, from the Rusting Mountains and from Break Deep.'

A silence followed, and it wasn't just the old man staring at him wide-eyed. Martha even went so far as to make the sign of the Tear.

Eventually, Georgia passed him a bowl of stew, and the spell was broken. They ate with a kind of determination, and as he chewed, Nicholas didn't dwell on what exactly went into the pot. Swallowing the last of her food, Meena begged him to play. Her parents bought him enough time to finish his own bowl, but then there was no denying the little girl. He played soft melodies, not all sad, just the kind to match the glow of an alley fire. He played until Meena and her brother drifted off to sleep and their grandparents looked ready to join them.

'That was nice, thank you,' Georgia said. She and Lukas carried the children into one of the shacks.

In his own, he ignored the empty bed-frame and settled in the corner furthest from the door. He fell asleep thinking not once had Lukas or his family asked anything of him – excepting Meena's request and her grandfather's curiosity. He decided the pennies that tumbled into his hat tomorrow would go to this generous family.

But the wave was low the next day. He woke coughing and his eyes stinging. The alley was already deserted, the family gone. He hurried from the alley and down the sloping streets towards the waterfront.

Even as shrunken as it was due to the low wave, Bordair was still enormous. Gazing out across the water, he could just about see the far shore – a mirror of the shops, bars, docks and whorehouses that surrounded him now. When he'd first arrived, he made his way from one end to the other over the course of a few days. According to the Caskers, there was a great deal of

difference between the quarters of Bordair. He didn't see it. The
city was one huge jumble of warped wooden boards and gap-
toothed smiles and rouged faces. Huge arms and broad, inked
shoulders. Bindle-smoke and spilled beer.

And somewhere in all that mess was Odette.

When he drank, he missed her. He felt it from the pit of his
stomach up to the top of his chest, so that it was hard to swallow
sometimes. He'd had all the time under the Audience to think
on why she left him, why she needed to be alone in Bordair,
but he just couldn't see what he'd done wrong. She'd asked him
to remember she was sorry and he did. He did remember that.
But he wasn't sure he understood. As the days had flowed into
weeks, into months, he started to think maybe he hadn't done
anything wrong. Maybe it wasn't about him at all. Odette had
to be alone because of something in Odette. How could he ever
fully, truly understand such a thing? But perhaps knowing that
much was enough.

When he drank, he missed her. So he drank every day.

The wave stayed low for so long he started to wonder if he'd
ever really been up the slopes of the city. In the overcrowded
alleys and hovels where he slept each night, he still wondered
if he would meet the family that had once fed him. He also
wondered if he'd recognise them at all.

Eventually, he had his answer, finding Lukas, Georgia and
little Peter. Though he would tell the Beginner again and again
how he wished himself back into ignorance.

They were in a back street not so far from the water, near the
eastern most tip of the boardwalk. Someone had put up a few
thin boards across the back walls of the buildings, affording a little

shelter from the rain. There, lying on a bed of sodden wood and pennysheets, was Lukas and what was left of his family. Georgia and Peter clutched the man's hands as he coughed and convulsed.

The people Nicholas passed all looked strained and worried, unable to leave such a shelter but unhappy about staying. Deep down, they knew something was very wrong with the man.

'Hello, Georgia,' Nicholas said.

She looked up at her name. 'Oh, it's you.'

'Where's Meena? Her grandparents?'

Georgia shook her head. 'She liked your music. Maybe she's sitting beside the Musician now.'

'I'm sorry,' he said. The words felt small and useless. He turned to go, as if he was trespassing on their sorrow.

Lukas coughed then made a sound that Nicholas would never forget. A long, brittle sigh that spoke of more than just air leaving the man. Georgia knew. She started to weep. Peter simply stared at his father, still holding his hand tightly in his own. She gathered her son in her arms and kissed his head, sharing what strength she had left.

Nicholas was forgotten, and he knew he should leave. He wanted to leave. But something compelled him to stay. He barely knew this man or his family, but they had been kind to him when kindness was so rare as to interest any one of the Audience.

Georgia clutched her son for some time. The boy didn't say a word, didn't even cry, he just stared at the still body of his father. Perhaps it was his silence, or because she herself felt the need to do something, *anything*, but Georgia stood and said, 'He should be clean when he meets the lake.'

Those who could afford a proper burial in Bordair were set adrift on the lake, on a burning raft. Those who couldn't afford the wood or the oil were simply consigned to the water.

Georgia took her husband's shirt from him and held it under the rain. She used its once-white cloth to clean the grime and spittle from about his mouth, the dirt from his face and then his hands. More dirt fell away from his bare feet, but try as she might, they wouldn't come clean. She scrubbed and scrubbed. Whatever frail solace she'd found in the practical task shattered then. She sobbed, but still she scrubbed.

'Mother, no. It won't go away,' Peter said, his voice far too old for one so small. 'Meena's didn't.'

She dropped the shirt and looked right at Nicholas. He flinched under that gaze, assuming he'd been forgotten. 'Will you help carry him?' she asked.

'Of course.'

More men and women joined them as they left the shelter. Not even the Painter's deluge could clear the black marks from Lukas's feet or his ankles. Black marks that would come to plague those in Bordair even more than the poor air. But he met the water as beloved as anyone could hope for. Family and strangers alike carried him, told stories to the Widow as they weighed him down and then stayed at the waterside long after he'd gone.

'Widow welcome him,' Nicholas said, and others muttered the same. Slowly people drifted away, back to the shelter or wherever they'd find to sleep that night, until it was just him, Georgia and Peter.

Nicholas knelt in front of the boy. 'I'd like to hear stories about your father. And about Meena. And your grandparents. I'd like to hear them all, and I'd like to share them with anyone who will listen. Do you think you could tell me?'

Peter glanced at his mother, as if seeking permission. She smiled.

'Meena liked myrtleberries and sintas,' he said. 'She squished berries between her fingers, like this...'

'... and then she licked her sticky fingers clean. When her mother told her off for doing so, she would giggle in a wicked way – a way to make the Liar sit up and listen. That was Meena, mischief through and through.'

'Right,' one of the dockhands said. 'Fascinating.' She stood and lifted the crate she'd been sitting on. Her friend did the same.

'But I've only just started the story,' he said.

'And we've just started work,' the woman called over her shoulder. 'Come find us if you still want to book passage.'

Nicholas walked slowly back up the wharf. She would be there. She *would*. He didn't need to keep hoping so hard.

'Cockles, clams, oysters! Fresh from Break Deep,' a man shouted from beside a cart. 'Ten marks a bushel, three marks a peck, pennies for a dozen!'

Nicholas drifted over to the cart. The oysters in the buckets looked small to him and sounded expensive. But then he'd never bought oysters, only eaten them when nothing else was offered.

'Help you, sir?' the cart owner said. 'You won't find any better this side of Fenest.'

'I used to work an oyster farm,' Nicholas said.

'That so.'

'It was run by a Lowlander called Mr Samuels. He was a big man with sweaty hands and eyes that watered all the time. We'd pull oysters by the handful right out of the water—'

'You don't say.'

'—and take them up the shore in buckets – a bit bigger than these ones – to be shucked. Whole big operation it was.'

The cart owner wasn't really listening. He started picking over his wares, moving the shellfish around, hoping Nicholas would take the hint. But Nicholas didn't mind.

'Have you ever felt salt water on your hands? *Really* felt it, after hours and hours of it on your skin? Let me tell you, cracks the size of the Tear all across your knuckles. Salt, you see, it's like nothing el—'

'Hello there, madam, half a dozen oysters perhaps?' the owner said loudly.

'Hello, Nicholas.'

And there she was. Standing in front of him as plain as day. A face he'd looked for the whole winter long. A face he recognised, but also recognised how much it had changed. Gone was the roundness in her cheeks. Her skin was sallow, and there were dark rings about her eyes. She had tried, and failed, to hide a bruise near her ear. Her dress was spotted and stained in so many places it was hard to tell its true colour.

'Do I look as bad as that?' she said.

He stopped his staring. 'The season hasn't been kind to me either.'

'Then let's leave this place and never come back,' she said.

He held out his arm, but she didn't take it. So instead, he walked a little way from the cart and said, 'I've asked around for passage to Perlanse. The barge up ahead there seems sound and the price is fair.'

'Not Perlanse, Nicholas. I just want to go home.'

'Home,' he said. It was strange to hear, and strange to say. 'What happened to you, Odette?'

She wouldn't meet his eye. 'I saw... I did... I can't tell you.'

'It's all right,' he said. 'It's a long journey.'

'No. There are no words, Nicholas. None that could manage what we've both been through. I'm done with words.'

'But you came to the Union to find your stories.'

'What good are stories now?' she said. 'A story can't stop a ground-shake, or stop a stream of Wit's Blood, or stop the Tear growing.'

'You're right, it can't. But it *can* tell people of these things. I met a family, right here in Bordair, who knew nothing of the Tear expanding. A story can reach people much further away, people who need to know.'

'And you're going to tell this story?'

'If you won't, then I'll try.'

'I'm sorry,' she said. Then, more softly, 'I know I hurt you.'

'I remembered you being sorry. I remembered that.'

'Can you forgive me?' she asked.

'For what?'

She stepped closer, taking his hands in hers. Hands she'd bandaged and lathered in ointment. Hands she'd pressed up against herself. 'I saw you, playing your pipe on the boardwalks. More than once I saw you.'

'But you didn't speak to me. I looked for you, every day.'

'Can you forgive me for that?'

He glanced down at her hands. Her nails were bitten to the quick and there was a long scab just below her wrist. 'There's nothing to forgive,' he said.

She smiled. 'Then will you come back to the Steppes with me?'

One of the deckhands from the barge approached them and said, 'This your wife? You still want passage for two?'

Nicholas kissed Odette's hand. 'This is my good friend,' he said. 'And we'll sail as far up the Stave as you'll take us.'

This time, Odette did take his offered arm. 'You don't have a bag,' he said.

'Neither do you.'

'No. But I have stories, Odette. So many stories.'

'I'd like to hear them,' she said.

That was my son's story. Until it became *our* story; each and every one of us, no matter what realm we call home. It is a story of suffering, of grief and of lives irrevocably changed. You have listened here, now, but this isn't the end. Not for you, nor the person next to you.

From this moment on, we are all living this story.

Audience help us.

Thirty-Two

The final words of the Wayward story stunned everyone at Easterton Coach Station. Or that was how it felt to Cora. In the Commission box, the public gallery and in the voters' seats, there was only silence, stillness. Even the purple tunics, usually so quick to herd the Audience back into the garbing pavilion to cast their voting stones into the great wooden chest, to remove their masks and robes and become ordinary Fenestirans again, even *they* were caught in the story's spell. No one moved. No one seemed to breathe, even.

Apart from the storyteller.

Ruth, still standing on the roof of the Commission coach, dropped to her knees and covered her face. It was over. She had told the Wayward story.

That was like a signal everyone hadn't known they'd been waiting for. The public gallery erupted in a roar of noise – everyone was talking, no, *shouting* about what they'd just heard. The purple tunics hovering by the Audience and the constables stationed around the site did the same. Cora had never seen such a thing, but understood what she was witnessing: the truth was finding its audience, at last.

The Wayward's Hook, the tale Ruth told – there was no ignoring it now. The question was, what would the voters choose to do?

Cora had listened to the story from a gig parked not far from Ruth's coach, sitting on the step passengers used to climb in. The body of the gig gave some protection from the rain that had continued to fall through the story. Cora had smoked so much, the puddle at her feet was littered with bindle ends. It was the relief, relief that even now was coursing through her, making her legs weak. She felt like she'd never get up again, and really, what need *was* there to get up anyway?

Cora had done what she needed to do: keep Ruth safe so she could tell the Wayward story and share with the Union the choice they faced. Odette had asked what good were stories now, and in Nicholas's answer were the words that mattered: *a story can reach people much further away, people who need to know*. And now they did know. There was such suffering in the Wayward tale – the hardship faced by those in the Tear, in the Rusting Mountains and Bordair. How could anyone ignore that?

Ruth's suffering was there too. She had told Nicholas's story, which was actually the story *of* Nicholas. But that was Ruth's story too, and so it was also Cora's. Now, it was a story that belonged to the whole Union. The spoked wheel had turned.

Cora got to her feet and stretched her back. There'd be no more election stories for a while. A whole five years. Audience knew what would happen in the meantime, but Cora needed to make some plans. She needed a new job, that was certain, but one that gave her more time for a life of her own. Because there was Serus now, and Ruth. Cora wasn't alone anymore.

She headed for the Commission coach where Ruth had told the story. From somewhere in the gloom of the rain she caught a sharp trill, a kind of whistle – a bird. She thought of Nicholas playing his pipe and realised why Arrani had sent Ruth that token before she told her son's story. A sign of trust, good faith, something that spoke of their shared loss of Nicholas. Nicholas Ento. Cora's nephew.

He had been lost to Cora before she'd even known he existed, but Ruth was a different story. Ruth was here, now, in Fenest. She and Cora had a chance to put the missing years behind them. The election was over. They'd face the future together.

The rain was falling more heavily again, making it hard to see straight. The mud didn't help her progress, or the deep ruts left by the gigs and coaches. Cora had to keep her gaze on her feet to save falling, and only just got out of the way when a pack of constables hurtled towards her.

'Clear the way!' a familiar voice called.

It was Jenkins, leading those carrying the voting chest. Cora pressed herself against a coach to let the constables pass and heard a rhythmic clunk from inside the chest. The voting stones.

The constables were heading for the wall of the coach station, the one opposite where the rest of the election business had been sited. There must be another way in and out, one that the Commission could keep clear for this purpose. A way not even the Torn Galdensuttir or Chambers Arrani had known about. Electoral Affairs ran a tight ship. And once the voting chest left the coach station, who knew where it went? Wherever the chest was bound, the other five from the previous stories would be waiting for it, and someone in the Office of Electoral Affairs would start counting. The results would be known by morning.

Jenkins didn't see Cora. None of the constables did, and that was for the best. It was time she was going. When the chest had passed out of sight, Cora continued making her way to the Commission coach. Her thoughts were on Nullan. She trusted Electoral Affairs to take the Casker to a stitcher if that'd do any good, and to Pruett's cold room at Bernswick station if it wouldn't. The way Nullan had lolled in the constable's arms as he'd carried her away, Cora suspected the Widow had welcomed the Casker storyteller. Now it was up to Cora to tell Ruth.

But Ruth wasn't there.

The roof of the Commission coach, where Ruth had told the story, was bare against the grey sky above Easterton. That couldn't be right. Ruth would wait for Cora there, surely? Though even as Cora thought this, she realised they'd never planned for after the story. Had Ruth gone to find out about Nullan? Her sister wouldn't have just left. She wouldn't have. Not left the city. Not like before. She couldn't have gone—

The door of the Commission coach creaked open.

Cora let out a sigh of relief and stepped towards the coach. 'Ruth, thank the Audience. For a second there I thought—'

Chief Inspector Sillian climbed out of the coach.

Cora stumbled backwards, only vaguely aware of the muddy puddles splashing water up her legs. 'What are you—Where's my sister?'

'She's safe,' Sillian said. 'For now.'

Despite the rain and the mud of the coach station, the chief inspector looked as pristine as ever. Her dark uniform was spotless, and her hair was slicked into its usual harsh parting, even as Cora was clawing her own hair from her eyes in the gusty showers.

Sillian folded her arms. 'I bring you a message, Gorderheim.'

'From who?'

'From a good friend. A friend of mine and of the Union.'

Cora spat into the mud. 'Morton.'

'I see you haven't completely lost your detective faculties, despite your recent... activities.'

'Where is Ruth?' Cora shouted over the rain. The rest of the election business was a rain-blurred mess at the corner of her eye. She and Sillian might as well have been the only people in the coach station. Maybe they were. Maybe that was part of the plan. She couldn't think straight. Why was this happening now? It didn't make any sense.

'The Wayward storyteller is with my friend,' Sillian said.

'But why? Ruth's told the story. What can Morton possibly want with her now?'

'That is not for me to say.' Sillian's voice was as cold as the rain pouring down Cora's back. 'There is a coach waiting for you outside the main entrance. A Commission coach. The driver has been instructed to take you to a meeting, and *only* there. Any tricks and the guard accompanying the driver will cut your throat. Do I make myself clear?'

'But—'

'I'd get moving if I were you, Gorderheim. The Lowlander

Chambers is not the most patient of people, and you and your sister have already tried that patience sorely.'

Cora ran for the entranceway.

There was barely anyone left inside the coach station. One or two purple tunics watched her race past from the shelter of the abandoned garbing pavilion, but otherwise, she saw no one. The rain had sent everyone scurrying away. She saw the Commission coach that Sillian had said would be waiting. One of the new ones: smaller, lighter. And faster. Let the Partner hear her and let this coach be fast.

The driver appeared to recognise her, as did the woman seated beside him: Sillian hadn't lied about a guard. They said nothing when Cora yanked open the door and got in. The coach began moving before she'd even sat down. Cora kept her face close to the window but she knew where they'd be going.

The Assembly building.

It was on the other side of the city. What might Morton have had done to Ruth on her journey there? Thoughts of torture vied with questions about why Morton had snatched Ruth now. The Wayward story had been told. The election was over, bar the results. But Cora should have kept a closer eye on her sister. After all these weeks of keeping Ruth safe, of everything that had happened, all the others who had died along the way, Cora had failed.

The glass dome of the Assembly came into sight, and Cora tried to ready herself for what lay ahead, though what that could be, she had no idea. All she had with her were her old knuckledusters. If she tried to find help, what might Morton do to Ruth? Cora couldn't risk it. She had to hear what the Chambers had to say.

The security guards at the Assembly's main door looked the other way as she barrelled past them. No voice called to her as flew into the entrance hall, no one asked her business, told her she needed an appointment. There was a lad on the desk, one she recognised from previous visits, but he said nothing. There was no one else there, which made the place seem strange, as did the lamps lit to ward off the grey afternoon. No daylight found a way through the grubby glass panes of the dome. Only the masks of the Audience, hung on the walls of the Assembly's hall, watched Cora from their sightless eyes as she ran up the grand staircase.

Her breath was short and her legs ached, but she had to keep going. At the top of the stairs, she headed down the main corridor to the office where the gilded wooden doors were carved with the crossed spades of the Lowlands. The doors were half open.

For the first time since she'd started running, she stopped, but the creaking floorboards gave her away.

'No need to hang around out there, Detective,' said a cheerful voice. One Cora knew well. Though they'd only spoken a handful of times, Cora remembered every word Lowlander Chambers Morton had said to her. Every poisonous word.

Cora pushed the doors wide open so they banged back on the walls, and stepped into Morton's office.

Thirty-Three

R uth wasn't there.

But seated in the chair by the window was Lowlander Chambers Morton.

'Detective. Good to see you again.' Morton smiled.

She was talking as if this was a normal meeting, just part of Cora's work as a detective. As if nothing had changed. She was wearing her brown Chambers robes, but her gold manacles weren't visible in the low light of the grey afternoon. Here, too, lamps were lit, and the many trailing plants that filled Morton's office were dull and dead-looking.

'Won't you sit down?' Morton said, indicating the chair opposite hers.

'Where's Ruth?'

'Ah, straight to business. Just like your dear mother. An admirable trait.' Morton flicked a length of her short, grey bob out of her eyes. 'Your sister is quite safe. I'll show you.'

'What?'

Morton gestured to the window. 'Just here. You'll see.'

Cora edged closer to the window, keeping her gaze on Morton who turned to tend one of her plants.

There was a small balcony beyond the window that she hadn't noticed before.

'If you step out and look to your right,' Morton said. 'You'll find what you're looking for.'

'Don't move!' Cora said.

Morton held up her hands in mock defence.

Slowly, Cora stepped onto the balcony. There was another, part of the next office along the corridor, and on it, there was a body.

It was Ruth.

She was lying on her side, facing Cora, her mouth gagged. Her eyes were closed, and there was a bloody mark on her temple. Her hands were bound. Her feet too. Beside her on the balcony stood a Fenestiran woman. She let Cora see the knife she was holding. Short, stubby, but it would do the job.

Cora went back into the office and, in an impotent rage, threw the chair Morton had offered her across the room. Morton didn't even blink.

'You're going to do something for me, Detective.'

'I'm not a detective anymore,' Cora said, working hard to keep her voice steady, 'as you well know.'

Morton waved this away. 'Old habits. And if you do this little job for me then I'm sure I could put in a word with dear Sillian. You could be back in your office at Bernswick before the end of the week. Plus, your sister would be freed, with no further harm. This I promise you.'

'What's the job?'

'Some light... rearranging, shall we say.' Morton sat on

the arm of her chair. 'Things have not gone as they were meant to. Your sister wouldn't stand aside, and now it seems her dreamy tale has made the voters lose their judgement. The exit polls suggest the Wayward have won.'

A small flame of hope ignited inside Cora. The predictions of the pennysheets had been right. The Wayward would take control of the Assembly. Morton's walls would never be built. The Union would find a way out of the nightmare to come, and they'd do it together.

'But such things are not set in stone,' Morton said.

'What do you mean?'

'I mean, Detective, that until the Wheelhouse formally confirms the result tomorrow morning, things can still change. *You* can change them.'

A laugh escaped Cora's mouth. 'You want me to tamper with the votes? Change the result?'

'Yes,' Morton said simply. 'And if you don't, I will kill your sister.'

They stared at each other for a moment.

'That's... ridiculous,' Cora said at last.

'You and your sister have left me no choice,' Morton said. 'If Ento had stood aside, if your sister had done the same, we wouldn't be here now.'

'Why not just have the Commission announce a different result?' Cora said.

For the first time ever in Cora's presence, Morton looked shocked.

'The Commission cannot simply be ordered to do something like that, Detective! They're the Union's civil servants. They operate independently of the Assembly. They have to!'

'I don't believe you; everyone has their price. Find the right person, offer the right bribe, the results announcement can say whatever you want it to.'

'You sound so jaded, Detective. If it were that simple, do you really think I'd have gone to all this effort, bringing your sister here, bringing you?'

Cora needed a moment to take this in. Had Ruth been wrong, all this time, about the extent of corruption in Fenest? Wasn't everyone on the make, only looking out for themselves?

The woman sitting opposite her was. The most corrupt of them all.

'This is what it comes down to,' Morton said, earnest now. 'I need to win this election, and I need that win to look legitimate. When Electoral Affairs open the six voting chests tonight, they need to believe that what they see is the true result.'

'The pennysheets have already predicted a Wayward win,' Cora said. 'A landslide, some are saying.'

'Oh, come on, Detective! How often are the 'sheets wrong? No one will find another misfire notable. But the Commission – they need to believe the stones.'

'So why not just change the result yourself?' Cora said. 'Or have one of your hired hands do it.' She gestured to the window, to the woman with the knife on the next balcony. Ruth lying there with a bloodied mark on her temple. Cora needed to get her to a stitcher.

'Because I don't know where the voting chests are,' Morton said.

'You're a Chambers! How can you, of all people, not know where the voting chests are taken after each story?'

490

Morton shrugged. 'None of us do. Only the most senior people in Electoral Affairs. The constables see the chests moved from the story venues once the votes are cast, but at a certain point in their journey, the constables are relieved of their duty and only Electoral Affairs oversee the last stage, taking the chests to the place they're stored until all six stories have been told. That's when, and where, the votes are counted.'

Cora was stunned. But she had to hand it to the Office of Electoral Affairs, they ran a tight ship.

'If *you* don't know where the voting chests are,' Cora said, 'how do you expect me to find them, let alone break them open and change the election results?'

Morton smiled. 'You'll find a way, Detective. You're resourceful, tenacious – two qualities your mother had but your father lacked. And if you don't find a way, your sister dies. You've seen the others who didn't do what I asked. The ways they died.'

'And if I do find a way,' Cora said, hardly believing what she was saying, 'what then?'

'Tomorrow morning, if the Commission announce that the Lowlanders have won the election, Ruth will be on the steps of the Bernswick Division police station by noon. Unharmed. Well,' Morton smiled, 'not harmed further. I give you my word.'

'And why should I believe you?' Cora said, hearing the desperation in her voice. 'After all the things you've done in this election?'

'Your mother always trusted me,' Morton said, 'and I did well by her. It's a shame her daughters aren't so astute as to the ways of the world, but there we are. And let's be honest, Detective, if you want to see your sister alive, you have no choice but to trust me. Give me the result I need, and you and your sister will be free of all this.' Morton swept her arm around the room, and Cora knew she meant the Assembly, the Commission, all of it.

'If I do what you're asking,' Cora said, 'there will be no such thing as free, for anyone. No such thing as safe.'

'You're wrong, Cora.'

The sound of Morton saying her name made Cora flinch.

'A Lowlander-controlled Assembly, with our Perlish allies and those of the Tear who support our aims, *will* protect the north from the depredations caused by the Tear widening. We will save many people, yourself included.'

'And the rest of the Union?' Cora said. 'Those left on the wrong side of your walls?'

Morton smiled sadly. 'I cannot help everyone, Detective. But I can help some, as long as you ensure the Lowlanders win this election.'

Thirty-Four

Dusk was falling as Cora left the Assembly building, and the rain had returned. Both made for a quiet early evening in the surrounding streets. The end of the election was usually marked by noisy gatherings – folk re-told the election tales to knots of listeners across the city, in whorehouses and gaming rings, in fancy taverns, in high-ceilinged drawing rooms and in windowless basements. The six stories spilled into the alleys, the wide streets and squares, and everywhere in between. While the first story of the election, that of the Caskers, would only now be reaching the most distant parts of the Union, shared and re-shared, a chain of voices carrying it to the Steppes and to the Tear, Fenest held its breath, waiting for the results to be announced at dawn.

But there was no revelry tonight. This election had brought death and destruction to the capital, and now those tucked behind locked doors and shuttered windows would be thinking of the death and destruction to come: the Tear was widening. The world was changing. The Union needed the Wayward to control the Assembly, but all Cora could think about was Ruth lying bound and bleeding. That thought set her moving, set her planning.

She had to save Ruth, and she had an idea how.

'That dog wouldn't bite a fly! Where do you find these animals? Perlanse? Give me strength!'

Donnata Jenkins was just where Cora had hoped she'd be: high in the tiered seating overlooking the ring in the back room of the Dancing Oak. Her silvery hair was once again tied in a tight knot at the back of her neck, but half had fallen loose and hung over her flushed face. Her hands were a blur of movement, shifting from shaken fists, claws of rage and open palms of incredulity.

Cora had arrived at a break between bouts as a winning dog was patched up and her prone opponent dragged out, likely headed for the River Stave. As the sand rakers moved in to deal with the blood, Donnata checked her betting slips, and Cora chose her moment.

'Detective! What a wonderful surprise!' Donnata's eyes were bright, her tight, high cheekbones flushed. 'Do you have any tips for the next, bout? I'm a fair bit down but if I can just get—'

'No bets for me tonight,' Cora said, and Donnata's face fell.

'Your credit still bad? I'm heading that way.'

She was shuffling her slips with a desperation Cora knew only too well. Cora put her hand over Donnata's.

'I need your help.'

Donnata's feverish motions stopped. 'My help?'

'Yes, and it's a big favour. You're not going to like what

I'm about to say, but I'd ask you to listen. The life of my sister depends on it.'

Donnata folded her hands in her lap. 'You have my attention, Detective Gorderheim.'

Cora took a deep breath. 'I need to know where the election voting chests are stored, where the count takes place.'

'And why would you need to know that?'

'I... I believe there's a risk of interference.'

Donnata's eyes narrowed. 'Interference? By whom?'

'That, I can't tell you. It would put you and Jenkins – Willa – at risk.'

'I see. And what does this have to do with your sister, Detective?'

'I can't tell you that either,' Cora said, at which Donnata scoffed.

'You're asking me to give away one of the most tightly guarded Commission secrets, if not *the* most tightly guarded. We're talking top-level clearance here. Only a handful of people in Electoral Affairs ever know this information.'

'And you were one of them,' Cora said. 'You were the Director.'

Donnata's gaze strayed to the ring. The sand rakers were stepping out. It wouldn't be long until the next bout.

'I was,' Donnata said. 'But I hear *you* no longer work for the Commission at all, in any capacity.'

'That's true, but—'

'Well this is a nice surprise!' Jenkins was coming up the stairs towards them, a drink in each hand. 'I wondered if you'd be here tonight.'

'I'm nothing if not predictable,' Cora said.

Jenkins handed one of the glasses to her mother, then said to Cora, 'Can I get you something? To celebrate the election being over? It was terrible what happened to that woman at the story, the one everybody thought was the storyteller, but the *actual* 'teller, she—'

'I'm not stopping,' Cora said. 'I was just asking your mother here to help me out with some information. Something from her days in Electoral Affairs.'

Donnata folded her arms across her chest. 'Something *sizeable.*'

'Something important,' Cora said quietly.

Jenkins looked from one to the other, seemingly aware there was more to this conversation. 'Well, Mama? Can you help?'

'Willa, darling, what your friend here is asking, it's… it's quite the stretch.'

'I know,' Cora said, and looked square into Donnata's eyes. 'I appreciate the position I'm putting you in. I do. But I have to know, and it has to be now. I don't have much time.'

'Mama,' Jenkins said, sitting down beside her mother. 'You can trust the detective here. If she says she needs this information then she needs it.'

Donnata touched her daughter's cheek, and Cora looked away. Beulah was beside the ring talking to a chequers. A whore passed them with a tray of drinks. It was a normal night in the Dancing Oak, and yet in Cora's head, nothing was normal at all: Ruth was in danger. Cora had to find out where the voting chests were kept. And then?

'But what that information could be used for,' Donnata said to Jenkins. '*That* is a concern.'

Cora made to speak, but Jenkins got there first.

'Detective Gorderheim won't do anything you wouldn't do, Mama. She's a good person. Believe me.'

Cora couldn't look Jenkins in the eye but managed to nod. Donnata gave Cora one more long, appraising look then told Jenkins to go to the numbers board to find the odds on the next bout. The constable looked like she'd argue, but then to Cora's relief she headed off.

As soon as Jenkins was out of earshot, Donnata whispered to Cora, 'The Seat of the Moral Student. There's a cellar. That's where you'll find what you're looking for. Though what good that will do you, I don't know, given that there'll be people at the doors. Not many, because Electoral Affairs limit the number who know what's inside the Seat, but those who are there, they'll be armed. I can't help you with them.'

'You don't need to,' Cora said, her gaze on Beulah below. 'I don't worry over front doors. What time is the count likely to be?'

'In my day, the Director of Electoral Affairs always arrived at midnight. Late enough that the streets were quiet, but plenty of time to be sure of the numbers. No one wants to rush a recount. I can't see any reason why the midnight start would have changed.'

Jenkins was on her way back to them.

'I hope you won't betray my daughter's trust, Detective.'

Cora headed down the stairs.

When she found Serus at home, she knew this would be a story for the Latecomer, that his luck would be on her side. The Rustan was pleased to see her, a huge grin lighting up his face when he opened the door to his narrow house in Derringate. Part of her wanted to go inside, lie down with him somewhere soft and warm, out of the rain and beyond thinking about what she was going to do at the Seat of the Moral Student. But another part knew she had to keep going. Ruth. Ruth was the most important thing. So she stayed on the doorstep.

'What do you know about lock-picking?' she asked Serus.

He wrapped his woollen jacket tighter. 'I might know something. Depends what it's for.'

'Opening a lock in such a way that it could be used again.'

'You mean so someone couldn't tell it had been opened?' Serus said. 'I might know something about that.' He reached out for her. 'Cora, what's going on? Come inside, it's pouring out here.'

She stepped back, leaving the shelter of his porch and letting the cold rain fall on her.

'I'll explain on the way.'

Serus was shocked, as she had known he would be. But worse was his disappointment.

'Tell me you're not serious, Cora. That you would even consider doing what Morton wants – change the election result!'

'I... I don't know what I'm going to do. We just need to get to the Seat and then—'

'Then what?'

She had no words.

They were on one of Beulah's underground routes. As soon as Donnata had said the voting chests were in the cellar of the Seat of the Moral Student, Cora had known she could get inside without having to go through the security on the front doors.

The passage was cold, and Cora felt herself shaking. Any care for her that Serus had shown on his doorstep when she'd first arrived had slipped into its own kind of cold. But he hadn't turned back. That had to mean something. But if she went ahead and changed the result, Cora could risk losing him in the process. Life never offered her a win–win situation. For every gain, there was a loss, and the choice was hard.

She and Serus had a lantern each to light the way, but only Cora's memory of Beulah's map to guide them. There were precious few signposts in this set of passages, unlike the others Cora had used, and the lanterns seemed to make more shadows than beams of light. Cora was in the lead, and her shadow looked like some monstrous version of herself. She didn't recognise it, and she didn't want to think what that said about this whole enterprise. But if she didn't give Morton what she wanted, Ruth would be killed. *That* Cora didn't doubt, and so she kept walking, with Serus close behind.

They came to a set of low double doors on their left, set deep into the walls of the passage. The wood had a greenish tinge, and when Cora touched it, it was damp.

Serus wiped away the dirt, mildew and cobwebs to reveal a carving of a domed hat. 'Been a long time since I've worn one,' he said, 'but I know a Seminary cap when I see one.'

'Looks like we've found the Seat of the Moral Student then,' Cora said. 'Hold this.' She handed Serus her lantern. There was no handle on this side of the doors, but only one door was hanging square. After a few shoves with her shoulder, the soft wood gave way easily enough, though the cloud of dust it set free had them both coughing.

When they could breathe again, Cora motioned for Serus to be silent as she listened for any noises above – had anyone in the Seat been alerted to their presence below ground? It seemed not. She waved away the last of the dust cloud and grabbed the lantern back from Serus. Beyond the doors was a low-ceilinged room. The floor was earth, just like in the passage. Dark shapes waited in the gloom.

The voting chests.

Cora made to go inside, but Serus caught her arm.

'Cora, please – think about what you're doing, what you're putting at stake. You're choosing Ruth's life over countless others. Ruth – the person who abandoned you for thirty years!'

She shook him off. 'Are you going to help me or not?'

Serus's auburn topknot was covered in dirt and his metal cheekbones looked tarnished in the poor light. He sighed, and Cora felt a wave of sadness wash over her, so strong it felt like nausea. But stronger still was the thought of Ruth, the need to get her away from Morton.

'Let's get this over with,' he said.

Cora didn't wait for him to change his mind and stepped inside the room, Serus right behind her.

Thirty-Five

All six chests were there, set close together, as if they were animals in a field taking comfort from one another. In the corner was a staircase. Cora crept halfway up to see what was at the top: another door, this one much newer-looking and sturdier. The public area of the Seat of the Moral Student was on the other side of that door.

She could picture the Seat well – her father had brought her here as a child, hoping his daughter's stories might mean the Student would look favourably on her, help her studies. Help her be as clever as her older sister. Inside were the kind of benches and braziers found in every Seat in the capital, with an aisle running down the centre. At the front was a carved image of the Student herself. But now at the doors of this particular Seat there were armed guards who stood sentry against those passing on the street. Armed guards who never suspected the way in underground.

She told herself her father would have approved of what she was about to do. But that thought just made the nausea return. She went back down the stairs to where Serus was waiting.

'We need to open all the chests,' she told him. Even

whispering, her voice sounded loud, as if it belonged to someone else. Someone who knew what they were doing.

'Why all of them?' Serus said.

'I need to know who won. Then I need to... I just need them all open.'

Cora's fingers brushed the pattern burnt into the wood of the nearest chest. She held up her lantern. In the poor light and the jumpy shadows that she and Serus cast, it wasn't easy to see the marks in the wood. When the Director of Electoral Affairs and their minions came down here to do the count at midnight, they would need four lanterns apiece to be able to see anything. Between the light and her finger tracing the burnt lines, she thought they showed a barrel: symbol of the Casker realm.

'Realm symbols,' she whispered to Serus, 'in the wood above the locks.'

Maybe he nodded, maybe he didn't, but he seemed to have given up talking to her. Cora swallowed that hurt. At least he was focused on the job at hand. Loud in Cora's head were the words Ruth had spoken when they were on foot in West Perlanse, just before the Seeder storyteller attacked them: *When it comes down to it, to a moment of choice, which will you choose, Cora?* She told herself she still didn't know the answer to that question, and yet, to come this far, surely that was answer enough?

'You told me you could open the chests,' Cora said. 'It needs to be done in such a way that they can be re-locked without anyone knowing.'

'I will know,' he said, without looking at her, 'and so will your sister. How do you think she'll react when she finds out what you've done to save her?'

Cora said nothing.

Without warning, Serus pulled the top of his middle finger off. Where there should have been bone was a thin, ridged piece of metal.

'Is that a—?'

'A lockpick. Yes. An accident when I was younger took the end of the finger. I decided to replace it with something useful.' From a pocket of his coat Serus took another small piece of metal and set to work on the lock of the Casker chest. 'Nullan, forgive me,' he muttered, concentrating. Nothing happened.

'Are you sure you can—'

'Patience, Cora.'

'There's not enough time! The stones are counted at midnight.'

'Then stop talking and give me more light,' he said.

She did as he asked and held up the lantern. After what felt like hours, but could be measured in a few nervous breaths, there was a 'pop'. The arm of the lock released and it fell to the floor with a soft thump.

They both looked at it for a moment.

'It'll go right back on again,' Serus said.

'The others,' she murmured. 'I need them all open.'

Without a word, he turned and started on the Perlish voting chest.

When he was far enough away not to see inside, Cora opened the lid of the Casker chest. She wasn't surprised at the weight of it. Nor was she surprised by the bile threatening to rise up her throat. This was wrong. Every part of her knew that.

The chest was lined with a well-worn but plush purple

velvet. She separated the white stones from the black, making two piles – both much the same size. She counted once, then counted again. Thirty white stones. Thirty votes of "no", for the Caskers, which meant twenty black stones of "yes". Twenty Casker seats in the Assembly. Poor Nullan. It had been a hard story to hear, and it must have been a hard story to tell. Hard, but necessary.

She closed the lid of the chest and hurried in the wake of Serus and his metal finger.

The Perlish had been predictably punished as unpopular incumbents. The Torn had done fair to middling.

At the Rustan chest she stifled a gasp, for Serus's sake, glancing his way to make sure he hadn't heard; he was already working on the last chest.

She counted only nine white stones, nine votes of 'no', for the Rustans.

That meant forty-one black stones. Forty-one seats in the Assembly. They were the clear winners so far, and surely not even the Wayward story could match that?

The Seeders had managed thirty black stones. A respectable showing for the Assembly in any normal year.

And then lastly was the Wayward.

Their chest had been left at the bottom of the stairs: last story told, last chest delivered. Serus was standing there, both palms on the still closed lid, his head bowed. Cora wondered if he was telling a story to a member of the Audience, and which it might be. The Stowaway who loved secrets? Or maybe the Dissenter, who listened to tales of protest? She settled on the Keeper – justice and fairness were for that Audience member.

'Best you wait in the passage,' she said.

'What are you going to do, Cora?' His voice was strained, tight.

'I won't be long.'

'I'll leave you my lantern,' he said. 'I'd rather not see what you're about to do.'

As he passed her, he touched her shoulder, and it was all she could do not to lean into him. But she didn't, and he left her to her choice.

She opened the Wayward voting chest.

In the first flash of poor light all the stones looked black: the realm had won.

But when Cora lifted the lantern higher, the truth was revealed: there were white "no" votes among them.

Despite all the talk from the pennysheets, all the fanfare of the chequers, and all the efforts to tell Nicholas Ento's story, the voting audience hadn't been swayed.

She counted three times, so as to be certain: thirty black stones, twenty white.

The Rustans had won. Not the Wayward or the Seeders who had somehow matched each other, to the vote.

Somehow that made what she had to do even harder. In all her struggles with Morton, with all the terrible things she'd seen happening across the Union, Cora had simplified things in her own mind: the good of the Wayward, and the evil of the Seeders. Only one of those two paths could win out in the election. But here she was, stealing victory from the Rustans, whichever path she chose. And there was nothing else for it.

She turned back to the Rustan chest and reached inside. Her fingers closed on a black stone. Black for a yes vote, cast once already in judgement of a story. But there was an even greater choice that needed this stone. A choice between the Seeders or the Wayward; the wall or the welcome.

And Ruth. What about Ruth?

Cora wondered if her sister had guessed things would end this way, if she'd had an inkling at least. That day in West Perlanse, walking in the hot sun between those high white walls capped with red stones, Ruth had told her, *It doesn't matter what happens to me. Once I've said the last word of the Wayward story, my own story can end.* Cora's fingers closed round the stone. She pitched forwards and leaned her forehead against the open voting chest.

Serus had been right: it was clear what Ruth would want. She wouldn't consider a single life worth saving above so many others, not when that life had achieved its goal. And lost so much along the way. But all of that was for a reason: the Wayward were offering a new vision for the Union. Yes, the Union faced a terrible threat from the Tear widening, but the Wayward answer – to work together, move people north, find a way to live without walls – that meant more people had a chance of survival. This could be an opportunity to start again, overturn the north–south injustice that had stood for so long, and which Cora's own family had helped maintain. This was a chance for Cora to undo a wrong perpetuated by the Gorderheims. Wasn't that what Ruth would want too? Even if she wasn't alive to see it?

The years to come would be hard. Harder than anyone in the Union had ever known. No one could be sure how far the Tear would spread, what that would mean for food, water, shelter.

The black stone in Cora's hand was hot now, slippery

with her sweat. How long was left to decide? Half an hour? A lifetime?

But then, was Morton's path so bad? Some would be saved – who knew, maybe many. And those on the northern side of the wall might be best placed to shape the Union's future. After all, Fenest was where all the decisions were really made, where the Commission and the Assembly ran the Union, controlling everything, from the Northern Steppes all the way down to the Tear itself. Protecting that way of life, was that how to ensure the Union survived? It might be.

Cora didn't recognise such thoughts as her own. It was as if her parents had left the Audience to step into this dark, dank room beneath the city and were whispering in her ear. But was she really so different from them? Some days, it felt like there was no chance to escape your past, to become someone else. That was surely why Morton had chosen Cora. The Chambers assumed Cora would do as her parents had done: cheat to get what she wanted, put her personal desires above all else.

But Ruth wasn't like that, she wasn't like their parents. She'd been at odds with the Gorderheim way of thinking ever since Cora could remember. Ruth had given up Fenest for another kind of life. Given up Cora for it too. And now here was Cora with the choice to give up Ruth for the chance, just the *chance*, of a better way of life for the Union. Her fingers tightened round the stone.

This was the gamble.

Cora wasn't sure of the odds, and when that happened in the back room of the Dancing Oak, she kept her coin purse closed. But tonight, in the cellar beneath the Seat of the Moral Student, she had to put her money down.

Cora looked at the black stone in her hand, taken from the Rustan voting chest. Black for yes. She took another black stone. And another. And more until she had a whole fistful. Ten stones in total.

These she dropped into the Wayward chest.

She had made her choice.

To even out the stones she had to take ten white votes from the Wayward chest and cast them for the Rustans. She was glad Serus had been so adamant he didn't want to know the results. But it was a secret she would have to live with.

The Wayward now had the win. They would control the Assembly, for the greater good of the Union. She closed the lid on the chest and clicked the lock shut.

'You won, Ruth,' she said. 'I'm sorry.'

Epilogue

They called it Hope. In Cora's opinion, that was a little trite, but there was something to be said for the simplicity of it, for the clear message. When the Assembly had decided to build a whole new district outside the walls of Fenest, to extend the city walls, they evidently wanted everyone to know why they were doing it.

She ground out her half-smoked bindleleaf in the mud that passed as a street in Hope. She was supposed to be giving up; Serus had made her promise. Something about growing old together without the coughing and the hacking in the morning. So far she'd only half-managed it.

All along the street, buildings were going up. Wooden framed, quick as you like, crawling with carpenters like ants assaulting a picnic. People were already living in the lower floors, those who had camped on this spot not two months ago. These days, progress in Fenest wasn't so painfully slow.

Cora wandered along the street, nodding to those she recognised – waving to the many more who recognised her. Who recognised the badge.

Hope didn't just need builders. A new city district needed it all: butchers and bakers, whores and chequers, 'sheet sellers and police. The O'Shea Street station was barely more than four walls and a flat roof – no pigeons – but it needed a detective. Word was, Wayward Chambers Arrani had asked for her specifically, though Cora hadn't spoken to the man. Not since... Well, not since he became the most important man in the Union.

'Oi, watch it, you, that's my foot!'

Cora looked down to see a grubby pennysheet boy, a threadbare cap pulled low over his brow.

'Oh, sorry, Detective,' the boy said. 'Didn't realise it was you.'

'Don't give me that, Tam. Nothing happens in this mud-way without you knowing about it.'

He smiled. 'Right you are, Detective. What can I give you? *The Spoke*?'

'Damn that 'sheet to Silence,' she said. 'I'll take a *Times*.'

The boy expertly slipped a single sheet from his stack then tipped his cap to Cora. To his credit, he waited until she was a few paces away before bellowing the headline he'd just sold:

'*Hope Memorial unveiled today! Wayward make good on promise to refugees!*'

Cora winced but continued on her way, one eye on the street and the other on the 'sheet. *The Times* was full of praise for the Assembly and its swift action since the election. But more than that, *The Times* was surprised. They didn't say it outright, but it dripped from every word. No one expected so much to be done, let alone so quickly, and though there was still room for debate and the odd grumbling complaint, it was hard for most citizens to find fault in what was happening to their Union. Every decision, from the smallest tweak to the sweeping changes around them seemed to be well thought out, to the benefit of most, and delivered swiftly. No wonder that people, and the 'sheets, were surprised. In truth, they didn't quite know what to make of it.

But Cora did. She knew they had to make the best of it, while it lasted. Because nothing good ever did.

Her duties that day included the memorial ceremony. She wasn't exactly working security, but Chief Inspector Gordon wanted a full show of the newest police division in Fenest. That meant Cora had to put in an appearance, in her plain coat and all.

At the end of the street, she turned left, then right, then left again. She was still getting used to the well-ordered layout of Hope. So far it made life for the constables a lot easier, but she wondered if she'd eventually miss the winding alleys and twisting turns of her old beats. She came to the edge of the new district as she was glancing over a column – a regular feature in *The Times* – which recounted the experiences of those coming to the city from the south, first-hand. It made for grim reading. The woman recounting her story in today's 'sheet had lost both her sons on the road, to different illnesses. But *The Times* tried to end each tale on an upbeat note: her daughter had just been accepted into the Seminary.

The memorial site was a hundred yards or so distant. It was to stand on the edge of the forest where so many southerners had taken their own lives – including the one Cora had seen, all that time ago. In a decision that must certainly have pleased the Widow, with her love for death and renewal, the Assembly had ordered that Hope was to be built from wood taken from that forest. And in the same breath, to appease the grieving, they ordered full funerals – each according to their realm's traditions – for the dead, and the building of a memorial. So the city wouldn't forget.

Cora certainly wouldn't.

And neither would the woman coming towards her.

Her cowl was up, and she moved awkwardly, still recovering from her injuries. Cora had been putting off this meeting, this conversation. She knew how it would end.

'Good morning, Detective,' Nullan said.

'How are the ribs?'

'Sanga says I should rest. I tell him I'll rest when I reach Bordair.'

Cora sighed. 'You haven't changed your mind?'

'I wanted to see the memorial before I left, that's all. Ruth would've approved of what they've done here. All of it.'

The mention of her sister still brought all kinds of pains – some stabbing, some aching, all of them obvious to see.

'I'm sorry, Cora.'

She shook her head. She would have to learn to hide that pain, somehow. Time healed what the Stitcher could not, so the saying went – little good that did her now. Not long after Electoral Affairs had announced the election result, Ruth's body had been left on the steps of Bernswick station, left to be found. The case had been given to the station's newest junior detective: the one with the teeth. But somehow, the file had found its way to Cora's desk in O'Shea Street. Between them, Cora and Jenkins were building a case to bring Ruth's killer to justice. And Cora certainly knew where to find the individual responsible.

'Cora? Did you hear what I said?'

'No,' she admitted.

'I asked if you knew what the memorial looked like,' Nullan said.

'No idea. There's nothing in the 'sheets either.' Cora lit another bindleleaf, knowing she'd only smoke half of it. 'Come on then, Storyteller Nullan. Let's see how this Wayward Assembly honours the dead.'

Though Cora knew, however it was done, it would never be enough.

Acknowledgements

The end of a trilogy is a milestone we wouldn't have reached without the hard work of a brilliant team and the support of many. D.K. Fields vote black stones for:

All at Head of Zeus: our fantastic editors, Maddy O'Shea and Clare Gordon, Anna Nightingale, Jade Gwilliam, Laura Palmer and everyone involved in bringing the Tales of Fenest to readers.

Helen Crawford-White and Nina Elstad, who created the eye-catching cover designs for the trilogy, giving everything from ash beetles to wooden tillers a visual dimension that we love.

Jamie Whyte, who transformed Dave's MS Paint map of the Union into something wondrous and created the brilliant visuals for the realm symbols.

Our agent, Sam Copeland at Rogers, Coleridge and White, for, well, everything.

The booksellers, librarians and book bloggers who have supported The Tales of Fenest and helped these stories reach readers – we can't thank you enough.

All our family and friends who cheered us on from the

public gallery, keen to hear the next election story and give their exit poll predictions to the pennysheets.

From Katherine: Thanks to Belinda and Jane, again, for Tuesday Zoom calls that cheered me up when I was flagging. Thanks to Hilary Watson, a champion of Marcus who keeps an eye out for Black Jefferey's reappearance. Thanks to the Royal Literary Fund who supported my work with Fellowships between 2017 and 2020 for which I will be forever grateful.

From David: Thanks to Bev, Jamie, Jo, Jonathan, Liz, Lyndall and Tricia for all your patience, insight and much needed reassurance. The Rustan story would never have taken off if it weren't for you all (and might have risked awful puns like this). Thanks, too, to my colleagues at the University of South Wales, who continue to support my writing in more ways than is possible to mention here.

About the Author

D.K. Fields is the pseudonym for the writing
partnership of novelists David Towsey and Katherine
Stansfield. David's zombie-western The Walkin' Trilogy
is published by Quercus. Katherine's historical crime
fiction series, Cornish Mysteries, is published by Allison
& Busby. The couple are originally from the south-west
of England, and now live in Cardiff.